11/09

For Josh –

With warmest good wishes,

Best –

THE CAMPFIRE BOYS

OTHER BOOKS BY PHILIP LEE WILLIAMS

NOVELS

The Heart of a Distant Forest

All the Western Stars

The Song of Daniel

Slow Dance in Autumn

Perfect Timing

Final Heat

Blue Crystal

The True and Authentic History of Jenny Dorset

A Distant Flame

NON-FICTION

The Silent Stars Go By

Crossing Wildcat Ridge

In the Morning: Reflections from First Light

POETRY

Elegies for the Water

CHAPBOOK

A Gift from Boonie, Seymour, and Dog

THE CAMPFIRE BOYS

BY

PHILIP LEE WILLIAMS

MERCER UNIVERSITY PRESS
MACON, GEORGIA

MERCER
UNIVERSITY PRESS

Endowed by
TOM WATSON BROWN
and
THE WATSON-BROWN FOUNDATION, INC.

MUP/H788

© 2009 Mercer University Press
1400 Coleman Avenue
Macon, Georgia 31207

First Edition.

Interior design: burt&burt

Books published by Mercer University Press are printed on acid free paper
that meets the requirements of American National Standard for Information Sciences—
Permanence of Paper for Printed Library Materials.

Mercer University Press is a member of Green Press initiative (greenpressinitiative.org),
a nonprofit organization working to help publishers and printers
increase their use of recycled paper and decrease their use of fiber derived from endangered forests.
This book is printed on recycled paper.

ISBN-10: 0-88146-153-9 / / ISBN-13: 978-0-88146-153-4

Library of Congress Cataloging-in-Publication Data

Williams, Philip Lee.
The campfire boys / Philip Lee Williams. -- 1st ed.
p. cm.
Includes bibliographical references and index.
ISBN-13: 978-0-88146-153-4 (hardback : alk. paper)
ISBN-10: 0-88146-153-9 (hardback : alk. paper)
1. United States–History–Civil War, 1861-1865–Fiction.
2. Entertainers–Georgia–Fiction.
3. Confederate States of America. Army. Cobb's Legion. Infantry Battalion–Fiction.
I. Title.
PS3573.I45535C36 2009   813'.54–dc22
2009021724

For Terry Kay

Brother in art

I remain just one thing,

and one thing only,

and that is a clown.

It places me on a far higher

plane than any politician.

Charlie Chaplin

THE CAMPFIRE BOYS

NEW YORK CITY,
AUGUST 25, 1943

The United Press Teletype machine clacks away, and the windows yawn open over Fifty-Seventh Street, and the knotty traffic weaves, honking like geese aimed north or south. The newsroom of *The New York Star* grows noisy with typing reporters, shouts of editors, curses at deadline. Dense cigar clouds and cigarette smoke layer the large, open room. Ben Tayson, our editor in chief, sits there in his glass office, straw hat tilted back, radio on. It's hard to hear the tune from this window where I look out at the flow of lives. It could be any singer, entertaining half of America.

My wife called an hour ago from our home in Newark to tell me that my father did not awaken this morning. Despite his great age, and the fact that he was my father by life and not by blood, the news has grabbed me by the heart, sucked out my breath. His life and mine linked generations, and I cannot abide the idea of my home's silence, of his wild and absent laughter. He had far more influence on my son Mike than I ever did, my Mike who is on tour with Bob Hope and Frances Langford now in Europe, writing skits, singing, dancing. Hope's new movie, *Let's Face It*, with Betty Hutton, is showing at the Paramount, and Benny Goodman's band is over there tonight playing, in person, as they say. I need to get home, but maybe I'll take the late train. I could use some impersonal comfort.

The Royal Air Force has bombed Berlin, seven hundred planes giving birth to high explosives, tearing up the city's rotten heart. They've already razed Hamburg, Roosevelt is in Canada for meetings, and Ray Robinson and Henry Austin will fight at the Garden Friday night. Josh White plays tonight at the Café Society over on Sheridan Square. It's

eighty-six degrees today, and fashionable women head toward
Wanamaker's or Best and Company. The new issue of *The American
Mercury* is just out, lying there on my desk with pieces by Dorothy
Thompson and Philip Rahv, and I had been thinking of reading it on the
train. Now I will dream, no doubt, of that deep and distant past, other
battles, other wars.

I have a picture of Mike and Bob Hope on my desk, signed this
way: *For Hank, father of Mike Blackshear, a true American idiot. Love and
kisses, Bob Hope.* Sam Kratczyk, the sports editor, makes fun of the
inscription, always ragging me about being best friends with Hope, even
though he knows well enough we've never met. Mike's letters are often
hilarious, full of the troupe's misadventures in England, North Africa,
and now, Europe. I think of my son every day, and I am afraid. I cover
the theatre, film, books, the nightclubs for the newspaper, and though I
do not care that Olivia de Havilland is suing Warner's to get out of her
contract, I must report it. Mostly, though, I think of Mike, of the war,
and I feel a heavy tide of sorrow that isn't so far from an infirmity.

The old man was one hundred and four years old, or would have
been next month, one of three brothers who grew up in the antebellum
South, and the funniest man I ever met. He played virtually every
musical instrument ever made and yet spent most of his adult life lost in
the dull bank walls of a small southern Pennsylvania town. When my
own father died in Cuba during the Spanish-American war, the old man
took me for his own. I was less than a year old then, and when my father
was shot, my mother lost her reason, as they said in those days. In fact,
she went quite mad and was institutionalized until her death in 1912. I
did not know of this until I was grown, and I found her grave on the
grounds of the asylum near Poughkeepsie, a shadeless stone the size of a
breadloaf.

Hitler has named Heinrich Himmler as head of the Reich's Internal
Affairs because the war is going poorly, and Germans are unhappy. We
publish each day a new list of the war's casualties, and such sorrow often
sends me to Central Park with my pack of Old Golds, where I sit and
brood.

But now I can only think of the old man. I knew his time was at its
end, and so did he, and last Saturday evening, we sat on the back porch,

sipping cold Schlitz and looking at the deep green lawn, my much-loved rosebushes, the fragrant tea olives, the slice of cerulean sky.

~Hank, you can't imagine what it's like to just go on living and living, he said. He had been a somewhat large man even in his eighties, but he was now frail, bent and shrunken, one of the oldest men in the state. He said, Each day, waking up, I wonder what in hell God has been thinking to spare me. I feel like I should have done something worthwhile.

~Dad, you've been telling me stories all my life, I said. The Celebrated Blackshear Boys. The parrot—what was his name?

~King Lear. God, what a name for a parrot. I'd only be middle-aged in parrot years, you know. He sipped his beer with a shaking hand. His shirt and pants had terrible stains, and though Myrtice washed his clothing all the time, he never stayed clean anymore. The sounds of home: grinding roar of the washer's ringer, tinny kitchen radio, bacon frying in the black iron skillet, the church-key pivoting its sweet V in a can of cold beer.

~King Lear, I said. Right. I have all those letters, too, the ones you guys sent home from the war. You should have written a book, you know.

~A book? Christ in diapers, Hank. You're the damned journalist. I keep wondering about the Yankees. They're doing well, aren't they? When I turned a hundred I said I'd quit following baseball. Never happened.

~Dad, I'm worried about Mike. I can't help it. I know he's safe . The Army's not going to let anything happen to Bob Hope. But I wish Mikey was home. I feel all the time like I have a medicine ball in my gut.

~Maybe it's cancer.

~It's not cancer, damn it. You make everything a joke.

~Everything *is* a joke. And let me tell you something. Bob Hope's not funny. He's not nearly as funny as we were. Well, maybe he's a little funny. I've noticed he's using some of my stories. He's lucky to have Mike writing for him, and Mike was lucky to get it from the master. Me.

~You don't think much of yourself, do you? I asked. He laughed, and the sound was painful to hear.

~Me? What in hell ever gave you that idea?

What indeed. People in Salterville didn't really know the man, at least after he became respectable. He was a sober banker in a pin-striped suit, looking at the world through his finger-printed glasses, being decent, it is true, but also sober, almost dignified. When he finally left the town fifteen years ago to move in with us, not one of those he'd known there as a young man was still alive. I say people in Salterville didn't know him, but once he came through the door in the afternoons, some years after my father had died, and I had moved in with him, he underwent the most startling changes. He loosened the tie, grabbed a beer, walked around in his stocking feet. He'd grip his banjo and rip into "Turner's Reel," sing dirty songs from the Civil War era, crack jokes, and sometimes he'd even dance.

Most of all, though, he told me of his beloved brothers and their adventures. I never was sure what was true, but it didn't seem to matter much. He always swore there was a polydactylic Huron Indian named Eliot Yellowhawk who could play Beethoven sonatas like God, twelve fingers mad for motion. He laughed about the stupidity of generals, the riotous ways of soldiers not in combat. I never got tired of the stories while I was growing up. When he came to us in Newark, Mike was only ten, and his Grandpa, whom he he had rarely visited in Pennsylvania, started telling him the tales, too. Often, on a summer night, I'd hear Mike's high-pitched boy's giggle as he and the old man sat out back in the gloaming.

~My friend from church, Howard Barton, died of a stroke Sunday, I said absently. He was my age, forty-six. They said he just looked puzzled for a moment and then was dead. That was it. Confused and then gone.

~Oh hell, Hank, I've known hundreds of confused men who wouldn't ever die, the old man said. He slurped the beer. And some of the best boys I ever met died young. That goddamn war. All these goddamn wars. We'd be standing there scratching our asses, and suddenly two boys on either side of you'd be blown into red hanks by artillery. That kind of thing changes you.

~How?

~How? It makes you realize you don't own a thing in this world, not even your own ass. Just like that, you can be gone. He was trying to snap his fingers to make a point, but they were damp with beer. He tried it several times. He said, Shit.

~Howard was a good man is all, and he and Martha have three boys in the service, I said. I mean, you're over a hundred years old. Aren't you afraid of dying? He was still trying to snap his fingers, and he looked up, paused a moment, and started laughing. He whacked his knee with genuine delight.

~Judas Priest, I'm afraid of *living*, he said, barely able to get the words out for laughing. I've done everything there is to do at least a hundred times.

~Even women?

~Oh God, I hit a hundred with women before Lincoln got shot, he said. Son, Mike comes from good stock. I always hated it when my father said that. Made me feel like a steer. But he was right. Now you talk about a man with pointless enthusiasms, that was my father. And he was off again, telling the stories I'd hear dozens of times and wanted to hear again worse than almost anything in this world.

Now he's gone. And I am the vessel of his life.

THE PAPER'S THIRD EDITION HAS been put to bed. Editor Tayson has gone for drinks and dinner. He hangs out at Billy Rose's Diamond Horseshow in the Hotel Paramount over on 46th Street west of Broadway, regaling the boys with tomorrow's news. I miss the first train and the second. I call my wife and tell her I need to walk for awhile, that I'll be home by eight.

~I love you, she says. Payne's came for the body. I'll make sure he has a good suit on the for the viewing.

~It'll be the first time he's been clean in twenty years, I say. Then I almost start crying, and she knows enough to hang up. I never have understood why Myrtice loves me, but I guess falling out of love is just as hard as falling in it. I know that I loved that old man, and I know precisely what I'll have done for the funeral. But now, I want to walk.

I hike along the hot trafficky sidewalks, watching soldiers flow past, sailors, WAVES, a few Marines, cocky survivors. The war goes better each day, and some time in the next year, we will grandly invade Europe and end this madness. I tried so hard to get into the first war, but my flopping heart valve made three different doctors shake their heads: *No, you are not fit for service.* Now, I am not young enough for this one. The old man's stories were ghastly in their exquisite horror. What those brothers saw in the Civil War is beyond the valley of words.

And yet he never felt sorry for himself, never let the shadow of pity slide over his shoulders like a shawl. He was a man in all, and he never let me down.

There are so many more girls on the streets these days, and I want to kiss every one, not from the need for intimacy but just to say that I am still alive and need human contact. I see two good girlfriends, just off work, heading for a drink, laughing, bright red lipstick freshened for soldiers on leave. I am forty-seven years old, and to them I am some relic from an ancient past, bones dug up with a trowel. I wish I were young again, with the old man already old to me. God, he was funny when he drank. He was not my real father, but he was *real.* He remembered skits he and his brothers performed sixty years in the past, and he would speak all the parts. I would laugh so hard a kind of choked moroseness came over me. There was not enough mirth left in me to spit.

I'm at the Park and didn't even know I was near here. Lovers walk arm in arm. There's a black man playing a cornet for quarters. Two street mimes are trying to get out of an invisible box. And my son is in Europe's ragged heart, trying to bring the smallest part of joy to men who could die tomorrow.

Yes, I know what kind of show I'll put on for Dad's funeral. He would love it. I can hear his raspy laughter, the sound of him slapping his slack-boned knee. He may rise from the dead. God, that he would or could. And yet somehow I'm happy for him and in a way jealous that he's laid his labors down. He made sure I knew where all the documents were about the Blackshear Brothers—their letters home from the war, the words of shows written during hilarious drunks, flyers, broadsides. And oh the stories he told on his brothers.

I can't imagine my life without him, but maybe I don't have to. I think he will always be with me, but for now he's gone, off with Bob Hope and the boys in olive drab.

I find myself on a bright edge, just before the show starts, heading toward home.

BOOK ONE

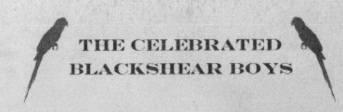

THE CELEBRATED
BLACKSHEAR BOYS

June 30, 1863
Near Chambersburg, Pn.

Dearest Mother,

 Here we are in the heart of the North, and my brother Henry was wrong: The girls do not have three legs nor do Yankees walk backwards or weep when they hear the thunder. Hah! The Celebrated Blackshear Boys continue their trek through the heart of our continent, one triumph after another. Our shows around Fredericksburg are legendary! (Even with his wound, as I have mentioned, my brother Michael made a superior lady. And Henry's pointless encounter with a minnie ball at Crampton's Gap is long forgotten.)

 Please tell Mama Blackshear that if she chooses to eat King Lear while we are gone, we would think none the less of her when this war is ended. Haw, as Michael would laugh. That a parrot should have lived since our last war against England is the kind of jest we should expect among our Present Discomfort. But ease your mind. All of the Celebrated Blackshear Boys plan to end this war alive and well.

 For nearly a week, Henry had Jim Watts convinced that a new planet made entirely of yeast bread had been discovered hiding behind the moon. Poor Jim! Tell all the Watts clan in Branton that their darling son has grown no wiser for surviving two years of war.

We are tramping toward some town called Gettysville. The boys are saying that we're bound have a big battle with the Yankees somewhere hereabouts, but if you recall my letters, this was said every night we were on the Peninsula during that first fall and winter of the war, and mostly we ate clams and lardy victuals that just escaped being hideous. Hee! Michael and I have worked up a new skit that involves Mr. Lincoln, Jeff Davis, and vastly fat woman of questionable reputation. Oh how the boys will shout! For through all these fights, through snow and rain and hail and blood and pantomimes, the Celebrated Blackshear Boys have come through shining!

More anon,

Your hilarious son
Jack

P. S. Do you have any idea what anon means?

THE CHRISTMAS SEASON, 1852

Jack Blackshear, twelve years old, blue eyes gleaming in the lantern light, stood on a chair and inspected the fuse with giddy alarm. It hung down into the cold room like a rat's tail, extending up through a punched-out knothole in the floor above where Mr. Percy Stillwell, elegant and prim, gave dancing lessons two days a week.

~That ought to do it, said Jack. The man is going to jump clean through the window when it goes off. They think he can dance now! Wait until they see the steps he does when he hears this!

~Should we alert Dr. Humprey? asked his brother Michael. He was the one who held up the lantern, which emitted a strong and familiar smell, the oily smoke of cellar trips and night hunts.

~More like Mr. Rutledge! cried Jack, referring to Branton's undertaker, a tall man who was publicly sad to be such a poor banjo player. Michael was eleven, and the youngest brother, Henry, now ten, stood guard at the stair-head, whistling and bundled to the throat in a natty crimson coat. Blackshear Mercantile occupied the town's strangest structure, a two-and-a-half-story brick building on the square, heading for the glory of three floors when Isom Blane ran out of money in 1847. *What's that you say, Blane? You can't pay me at present? Well, then you'll get what you deserve!* This was the builder, a crafty carpenter named Jenner Robidoux, lately up from New Orleans with a wife whose unnatural hair color inflamed the town ne'er-do-wells with rumors and passion. This Robidoux, whose temper was foul as a sleet storm, proceeded to add a half-story above the main floor, then threw another full story on top of that so that between two normal floors there was a squat room, five feet from floor to ceiling, that Mr. Blackshear mostly used as storage. The boys had played here when rain spat upon north Georgia since they were toddlers and their dramatic mother, Cassandra, wanted the house alone to practice her Broadwood Piano or to hone recitations, which she was prone to deliver at parties.

~I think I hear somebody! cried Henry from the stairs, and they went silent. The lantern was no problem, as they had draped nine yards of mourning muslin over the floor's single window, but every step they made gave off a sharp squeak like a long-unoiled door hinge. Henry was prone to frights, his mother's sweet baby. He did not make faces in church as his brothers did. He was not daring and a fine rider like Jack, didn't have his oldest brother's grand voice. He couldn't draw and paint as Michael could, his father's heir with oil and canvas. But he was already the most inventive writer and sat for hours on their porch during spring rainstorms, filling foolscap pages with his stories, which seem destined never to find an ending. Jack had black curly hair like the Blackshear clan, but Michael was born with the sandy hair of the Duvernets, and Henry was tow-headed. Even their parents' friends who confused the names of three boys born so closely together remembered their eyes: Jack, blue; Michael, green; and Henry, cocoa.

They stood, motionless. A breath of cold wind billowed the muslin like a sail, eased around it, wiggled the dangling fuse.

~It's just the damned wind, said Jack finally from the chair. Henry, you are the most precious thing. *So* precious.

~Shut up, Jack. Henry whispered it, still looking down the dark staircase, rubbing his under-lip pensively with the thumb and forefinger of his left hand.

~It's all set, said Michael, softly clapping his gloved hands for warmth. We're going to get caught, but it's worth it. Come on.

They came to the head of the stairs, and Michael extinguished the lantern. They clomped softly down the hollow-sounding steps, lined up like ducklings, wading through washtubs and harnesses, ladies' gingham bonnets, bolts of cloth, boxes of lye. Moonlight spread shadows across ten feet at the shop's front, and Jack stopped at the counter and removed the glass lid from a display container of thick peppermint candy.

~Here we go, boys, he said, handing each of them a chalky stick. The last supper. Michael snorted out a skein of laughter, but Henry felt a knot grip his throat. Surely God had seen everything the Blackshear boys had done, and surely He shook His head with considerable distress.

THOMAS BLACKSHEAR, FLORID AND TIPSY, ran from the canvas, which he had set on an easel before the fire, to a spot at the edge of the rich carpet, spilling blood-red Madeira from his glass in spatters down the front of his shirt. His wife, Cassandra, her red hair loose on her shoulders, reclined on the sofa in a high-collared night-cloak, arms folded over her chest.

~Is it magnificent, sweet wife? Tell me it is magnificent or I shall *perish* with regret, said Thomas Blackshear. They stared at his latest painting, twenty-four inches high and thirty-six inches broad, a well-executed landscape of a pasture near Deerskin. Ancient oaks gripped the edge of several mild acres beneath the furnace of an autumn sunset. Thomas said, Forty-seven sketches, and three months in the making!

~I may faint from the excitement, said Cassandra blandly.

~I am hungry, said Mama Blackshear, Thomas's mother, who urged her rocking chair to move on its long curves near the fireplace. Then: I want that chicken killed for dinner Sunday. She was glaring at the cage of their parrot, which Thomas's father, an ardent lover of Shakespeare, had bought in 1812 and named King Lear. The bird clung to its perch, refusing to die or even sicken, though it increasingly spoke inappropriate words learned largely from Jack. Mama Blackshear looked somewhat like a cocoon, tiny and at all times laced into black clothing. She knitted and then she did not knit, those being her two occupations.

~Mama Blackshear, that is our *parrot*, sighed Cassandra. Please try harder to think more clearly.

~I shall speak to Mrs. Cardinal about this chicken, said Mama Blackshear.

~The use of color! The way light filters into the grass of the pasture! said Thomas. He gargled down the last of his wine, walked thick-footed to the sideboard and poured another, sloshing a small strand of pearly red drops on the hardwood floor.

~Where *are* those boys? asked Cassandra. Thomas, you are too indulgent with them, and they are running to wildness. Everyone in town is saying it. It is freezing out there. Henry is always forgetting his gloves. I am awash in misery.

~Bring me a ham, said King Lear clearly.

~You *must* say it is magnificent, Cassie! Say it for me.

~I am talking about our *sons*, Thomas, and you have had entirely too much to drink.

~I'm an artist! We are prone to greater dissipations than normal men!

~You run a mercantile and sell tin cups and undergarments for old women, said Cassandra. While our sons are *not* young gentlemen. I believe Rev. Turngall's sermon Sunday was *specifically* about our family. I was so vexed I know that my face turned red.

~Really? Ah, that had not occurred to me. Perhaps I should drop by and thrash him. Or was it an honor, d'ye think? Ah, but they are giving their performance tomorrow evening! Forget the revering!

~*Reverend*, said Cassandra wearily.

~Chickens in the house, clucked Mama Blackshear. Shameful.

~It's beau-ti-fulllll, sang King Lear.

~Ah, so even the chicken knows of my talents, but my own wife dismisses them by invoking implements and garters! shouted Thomas.

A spattering of laughter on the front porch: then shoving, mild arguments, wringing the doorbell and stumbling inside. *Ladies and gentlemen*, they seemed to say: *The Celebrated Blackshear Boys!* Cassandra was out of her chair, furious, color spreading upward from her neck and across her finely shaped cheeks. Thomas made a sound like *Eh?* and watched her, dazzled as always.

~I do not know where you young men have been, but I hope you have some believable explanation this time, said Cassandra. She held the gown together at the neck for modesty's sake. Her newly sewn house slippers—made at Keltie's Tannery from multiply processed suede—seemed to Thomas like slabs of earth, as if she had risen as a myth might from the soil itself. Well?

~Mother, dearest thing, you must know where we have been! cried Jack, waving his arms. We have been preparing our performance for tomorrow night! Where else would we have been? Do you think we would be out here before Christmas in the cold of a Georgia night up to no good?

~I could not have said it with more precision, Cassandra said, almost hissing, but under complete control, dubious.

This, the boys knew, wasn't entirely a lie. They had worked up bits and pieces of dialogue and songs as they placed the firecracker, always changing things on a whim, not caring if it fell flat as long as *they* laughed, saw responsive eyes. None of their routines of the past two years, with which they had charmed church crowds and lolling barbe-cuers, seemed polished, and frequently they collapsed into self-indulgent hilarity. Cassandra had taught them all to play the piano, and Jack now strummed a guitar, sweet Michael was gaining strength on the banjo and fiddle, while Henry made women weep when he shaped a long lovely line on his flute. They told old jokes and sang, but mostly they per-formed skits, for which Henry had a remarkable talent as a writer, scenes in courtrooms, meeting houses, at political rallies. Even at ten, Henry had the keenest eye for the slack profundities of small-town politics.

~We are having chicken for supper! shouted Mama Blackshear. Get your fowling pieces before it roosts somewheres else! Her bony finger was pointing at King Lear, who seemed to shrug.

~Stop changing the subject! their mother demanded.

~Ca*saaaaaaan*dra, honey, said King Lear. The boys collapsed against each other, snorting giggles, removing their coats and stepping back to hang them on the hall tree clumsily, nearly upsetting it. They tumbled back out into the parlor, Michael staring with obvious awe at the painting.

~Papa, that is the finest yet! he said. It should be in a museum, not in our home!

~Then I forgive you whatever ill you might have committed this night! said Thomas, sloshing the Madeira again. Mama Blackshear stood and was not much taller. She walked as if her feet had not yet been broken in, coming straight for the parrot's cage. Lear clawed his way along the perch sideways as she approached, as if avoiding a Biblical leper in the street. But remember, boys, some day I shall paint the Great North! That is where the future lies! Oh what romance and joy it will be to see it!

~I want to know where you boys have been and what you have been up to! cried Cassandra. She let go the neck of her gown, and it flopped open only slightly, but Thomas sighed, tented his fingers and then wiggled them against each other, as if playing some invisible instrument with casual virtuosity. Cassandra said, And I believe I smell peppermint.

~Oh foul and cursèd peppermint! cried Jack, staggering to the sofa and falling languidly across it. He placed the back of his right hand melodramatically across his brow. That we would have sunk to *this*! Oh dearest mother, in the grip of drear peppermint! Ruined! *Ruined!*

~Forty-seven sketches, and three months in the making! cried Thomas.

Henry fell on the floor, barely able to breathe from the laughter, but Michael came closer to the landscape and admired it, pupils dilated with joy at such a fine illusion. Thomas urged his son to admire the painting more, palm up and open, as if escorting him to the fireside easel for a closer inspection. Cassandra stared at Jack, still splayed dramatically on the divan, and tried not to smile, shaking her head. What phase of moonlight had caused her to hatch such silly boys? That they were talented nearly made up for it, but they were barely under control, often beyond it, and while that held charm for children, it would be useless for a young man.

A week before, on a night when sleet cracked merrily against their bedroom window, she and Thomas had lain closely entwined in their bed, still lovers, still coveters of the other's eye color and hand-shape. She was warm and drowsy but still unwilling to let sleep drag her away. On nights such as these, all glory and freshly pressed sheets, their children had been conceived, and each time they loved, she wondered at that miracle and if it might come forth in her again.

~I worry about our sons, she said. They are infected with such high spirits. No one can expect to live with such intensity all his life. I fear they will have a terrible fall when they come in their manhood.

~Are we not artists, then, of love? whispered Thomas as he kissed the top of her head. She had laughed, understanding that mild and apt reprimand, remembering her husband's favorite invocation to her, to life as well: Do not worry so much! Joy is not so rare we should lay it in a velvet box, to be released only on holy days!

And even farther back toward her childhood: Savannah afternoons, the easy perspiration of summer and a pleasant white dress and a book to read. Her father's mild appreciation when he said it, saying, Cassie I never see you but there is a book in your hand and your eyes on a story! Or her hands on the piano keyboard as she played Chopin or the gentler parts of Beethoven. She shook her head at Jack now. Then:

~Mama Blackshear! The old woman was poking through the wooden cage bars with a pencil at King Lear, making hideous clacking sounds with the slipped plates of false teeth. The parrot evaded her with a bored slowness, understanding threat and sensing none in the old woman.

~Fetch me an axe, she said. I have a taste for *that* with a large dumpling. The parrot turned and looked at Jack and then his mother.

~Ca*saaaaaaan*dra, honey, said King Lear.

HENRY BLACKSHEAR CAME RUNNING INTO the dance studio breath-lessly, white-blond hair askew, hands working on his hat, which he held politely at chest level. Interrupted as he stepped off a stately gavotte, Mr. Percy Stillwell seemed peevish, curling his lip into a mild snarl. Five ladies of the town, who ignored the poorly braced floorboards that groaned with every dance, could not forgive such rudeness.

~Young man, mind your manners! said Forsythia Robinson, who was past forty and had been disappointed with her husband, a flour-ishing merchant and county commissioner, since their marriage two decades before. She held wan hopes that she could teach him dance steps or the ability to discuss savage Byron. Sausage-fat in her blue dress, Forsythia's jowls hung off her face as if they wished to flee her body entirely.

~Yes, ma'am, Miz Robinson, but there's this…

~Young Michael is it not? said Mr. Percy Stillwell icily.

~It is not, said Henry.

~Excuse me? Sourly, urging him to leave by stepping toward the door into the tiny dark, cold hallway and the stairs downward.

~I'm Henry, the youngest, and I came to tell you that there's a mad dog loose in town, and that if you hear a gun fire, you should all take cover immediately, for it could escape into any building it sees!

~Oh? said Mr. Percy Stillwell, tugging at his collar. The ladies gathered in a clucking flock to discuss it. Everyone in town knew and mocked Stillwell's fear of dogs. He crossed the street to avoid Myra Turnell's Toby, a pale and tiny puff of white that she bathed daily and walked on a leash made special by old Jim Trilby, leather monger to the town livery stable. Stillwell spoke sometimes, shuddering of dogs' cruel teeth and wicked intentions, over dinner at the Hotel Branton. He carried a Malacca cane with a gold ferrule and waved it wildly when a dog appeared at the other end of a block on which he strolled.

~Foaming and possessed of claws like a panther! said Henry. He held up both hands to demonstrate the peril, curling his fingers into threats. Below them: a giggly fumbling which the others, unaccountably, could not hear. Listen for the gunshot and beware! That line was Henry's own and idiotically dramatic, but he wanted to see how Mr. Percy Stillwell would receive it. The answer, immediately obvious, was with abject terror.

~Oh dear, dear, dear God! he said, his hands coming together as if one were trying to choke the other. Henry dashed out, closing the door behind him, and ran down the stairs and into the half-story storage room, where Jack stood on a chair and held a lit match one inch from the mouse-tail end of the fuse.

~Did you tell him? asked Jack.

~He's about to soil himself, said Henry, afraid and delighted in equal measure.

~Oh, oh oh! sang Michael, almost dancing with delight. The mercantile below them was full of Christmas shoppers, making a clean escape almost impossible, but they had not even discussed getting away cleanly with the crime.

~Bow-wow, said Jack, and he lit the fuse. It flashed into a fit of fizzy hissing as the spark climbed upward toward the firecracker beneath Mr. Percy Stillwell's chair. The boys tumbled out of the room and came into the stair landing, shaking with suspense. The wait lasted precisely one second, and the explosion was much sharper and louder than they'd expected, loud as a shotgun.

~Jack, be nimble! said Michael, helpless with laughter. The door on the landing above exploded open, and Mr. Percy Stillwell dashed out yelping wildly. His suit of clothes seemed to have been thrown on him, landing poorly.

~Mad dog! he shrieked. Mad dog! Oh, fierce and wild! He ran down three steps, then thinking better of it, ran back up. The cries of the women now came clear and sharp through the frigid air of the stairwell as they rushed, apparently, from one side of the room to another and back.

~Sounds like they have finally learned to dance, said Jack. Henry's nose was running, and he had erupted with hiccups that went off as rapidly as popping corn. Now, he was gasping, hiccupping, wiping his nose on the sleeve of his coat, gasping happily. The door below them opened, and their father, wearing a different face from the evening before, came dashing up the stairs and saw his sons.

~What have you...

~Mad dog! Mad dog! cried Mr. Percy Stillwell, now running wildly down the stairs and brushing the boys back. The women were shortly behind him, holding up their skirts and crying out doors from which to leave, escape routes. None of them glanced at the boys or Mr. Blackshear as they came past in a perfumed pack. Mrs. Robinson's jowls flopped over her collar, and they were the color of sunsets, the ones Thomas, and, lately, Michael, loved to paint.

CASSANDRA HAD THE SLAVES JOSHUA and Mary Faircloth and their daughter Emma Jane bring chairs from other rooms into the parlor. The show began at seven-thirty, and neighbors would gather half an hour before that for punch and cakes, for singing Christmas songs around the piano while Cassandra played.

~I intend to make a magnificent announcement this evening, said Thomas Blackshear as he dressed in a fresh white shirt, a loosely knotted bow-tie and a vest of canary yellow silk. He snugged on his evening coat and dusted threads from its lapels as if assaulting it.

~Dear Lord, not another speech about your painting, said Cassandra. She stopped dramatically before him, still wearing only her chemise, fresh from a bath and smelling of rose water.

~Much more important than that! said Thomas. He walked to the bureau of burnished oak that Papa Duvernet had given them as a marriage gift, elegantly made nearly half a century ago by a New York furniture-maker improbably named Phyfe. A mirror on top was held snugly by lyres. Jack loved the name *Phyfe* and emitted it each time he sneezed a few summers before, convulsing Henry every time. Thomas poured himself a snifter of peach brandy. He said, My God, you can all but smell the fuzz on this! He sipped it three times, accompanied by inarticulate sounds of approval.

~Please don't go and get yourself tipsy again before the guests arrive, said Cassandra. She still made no move to dress, and Thomas looked at her long, unbound red hair with yearning that she recognized and tightly controlled.

~Well, a magnificent announcement, tipsy or dull as a judge, said Thomas. Did you hear that someone fired a gun downtown this morning? I cannot say what it was about, but I had no idea Mr. Stillwell knew half so many dance steps.

~Your mother gave me a recipe this morning for Chicken Italian, said Cassandra. She sat at her vanity and picked up the flat brush with its ornately scribed silver backing. I fear she means to kill the parrot outright. Perhaps we should warn Romeo and Juliet lest their own lives be in danger. *Brush, pause, brush, pause, brush, pause.* Thomas watched, entranced.

~Juliet, perhaps, for she is mild and forgiving. Not Romeo. He would, I fear, eat her before wondering if she be proper victuals.

~That's a hideous thing to say about your own mother, Cy.

~For the love of God, please don't use that name, Cassie.

~It's what your family called you when we met. I didn't know what to call you. I did not even know the one eye was blind for nearly a year.

~Well, if you had a father who thought your half-blindness amusing enough to call *you* Cyclops, you would not be so light with names. She turned toward him and smiled beautifully, and he glogged the peach brandy to bottom of the snifter's smooth bowl.

~A rose by any other name would smell as sweet, she said. And when he came toward her, his black hair poorly combed, eyes full of lamplight, her giggling unspooled across the room like a ribbon.

~WAIT! WAIT! WAIT! JACK WAVED his arms while Michael held Henry in a firm headlock and pounded on his head with the heel of his left hand. They were upstairs in the long hallway of the Blackshear House on Academy Street, half dressed, partially prepared, and full engaged in an argument over the Mexican War. Someone passing in a fancy brougham might have seen, through the second-story windows, three boys fighting, arguing, loudly disputing the Battle of Vera Cruz.

~All I said—let me go, said Henry, was that the town must have been named after a woman!

~Idiot! cried Michael. Imbecile! There is no Vera Cruz! That would be like the battle of Jenny Lind!

~Wait! Wait! cried Jack, pulling them apart. Henry's face was flushed, and his clothing seemed to be climbing off, looking for the sanctuary of a bureau. You are both dunderheads! Stop it this minute or I will throw you both out the window. Precisely at that moment, Jack's large black dog, Romeo, appeared in the front yard and looked up toward them, barking wildly and waving his tail, which resembled a military feather. His consort, Juliet, who was smaller and tan and belonged largely to Henry, crept close to Romeo and fell over, kicking the cold December wind.

~He started it! shouted Henry, straightening his clothes. He knows as much about military history as a wart knows about a frog!

~I don't care who started it, said Jack acidly. We need to get ready for this stupid performance that we're going to do for these stupid people, or they might think you two stupider than you already are!

~That's stupid! shouted Michael. Henry started to laugh.

IF YOU BACKED AWAY FROM the hallway and came outside, you'd see two acres of pecan trees, and in their center the most magnificent house in Branton, a small town on the Georgia Railroad between Augusta and Atlanta. Now, the trees were bare and painted with the last orange light of a brief December day. The town of three thousand held its elegance and intellectual pretensions aloft like a flaming pine knot. Wealth had puddled a decade before when, for almost five years, the railroad ended here, engines turning roundabout for Augusta. Mansions went up in explosions of lumber and nail, and the town itself, a neat square of two-story brick buildings, glowed with commerce and poetry societies, hotels and the touring acts in Rutledge Hall, singers, dancers, pianists. The Amazing Negro Pianist Blind Tom came often, and the boys sat front and center when he played, awed into uncharacteristic silence. Rutledge Hall was on the north side of Main Street, while Blackshear Mercantile was on the square's western boundary, Adams Avenue.

For every white-painted palace, there were, out back somewhere, huddled slave quarters, though nothing like the clusters crumbling behind the county's plantations, which began, like their cotton fields, just past the town limits. Thomas Blackshear owned a farm three miles west of Branton, but its bounty was mostly for the family's own table, and in season he sold cantaloupes and tomatoes, peas and pears, in the store-front from metal tubs. In the northeast corner of the farm a peach orchard flourished, while on the southwest boundary thirty bearing apples trees hung heavy in the late fall with their aromatic ripeness. Thomas and his boys loved to visit the farm on Sunday afternoons, riding out in his dandy curricle, prepared finely by Joshua, Old John and Miss Bess strapped and stamping, ready to pull. Henry, small enough to sit in his father's lap in the early days, would shout *On Bon! On Jess!* as loud as he could, and the confused horses would glance back as they clopped forward, fetlock-deep in summer dust.

Branton this year had four churches downtown, and a tent meeting on the Deerskin Road where a traveling minister named Hezekiah Mount had arrived in sweltering September and never left. With cold weather, he held meetings in an old hunting lodge, whose mounted bones and antlers apparently did not shake the Spirit from those who wept there from contrition. The Blackshears were Methodists and Thomas a deacon, though he could often be seen at his post in the narthex dozing over the latest novel from Fenimore Cooper while Pastor Pearson droned from the pulpit.

A creeping liberalism had come with prosperity, a patriotism of quiet pride and international gestures. Small armies of slaves and servants groomed the yards of the wealthy, giving boxwoods weekly haircuts, yanking weeds from flagstone walkways. South of Main Street, the houses were proper but lusterless, and beyond them was a shanty town of poor whites making children faster than money.

The Branton River, heavy and sluggish during the rainy winter and spring, cut north to south through town, though in summer it dried to a tawny trace, curling around the sun-bleached boulders that grew upward from the river and through the fields north toward Athens. For decades, farmers had pulled huge gray stones from the land, and they still popped up with the plow, along with shards of ancient Indian pottery and quartz arrowheads. A few of the town's older residents still remembered the last visit from Creeks in the late 1790s, long before the site held a village, much less a town.

Three smiths hammered away at their anvils in town, making rhythmic music on pounded horseshoes, followed by the hiss of red-hot door-hinge iron dipped in buckets of water. On Tuesdays, the smell of freshly baked bread seeped from the kitchen of the Hotel Branton and spread over the downtown, around the courthouse in the center square, down Adams and Jefferson, northeast to southwest along Main. It reached the depot where drummers would step from the train, inhale, and slap their stomachs with joy. On days when an east wind tickled the tall oaks, the aroma would move like a delicious river along Academy Street and rise up the stories, awakening one dreamer then another. On those days, gentle Michael Blackshear would awaken first and call to his brothers:

~You can smell the bread, he would say with his hoarse morning voice. Oh, get a whiff of that! And his brothers would struggle from their summer sheets, ravenous and yawning, well-pleased that fate had shown them wealth, given them a place in Branton from which to view those less fortunate, those without the blessing of dreams.

And if you came back into the well-lighted hallway now, as Jack broke up the scuffle, you would see him stop and turn to his brothers.

~Barbecue, he said. And they inhaled with the deepest delight.

UNCLE LAWRENCE, BLANK TO THE point of inscrutability, licked the meat sauce from his fingers and surveyed the crowd as he sat with the boys in the front parlor, balancing a plate of barbecue on his knees. Thomas Blackshear's taciturn older brother was Branton's stationmaster, and he could go whole days without breaking into multi-syllable words.

~You boys…a skit…of some kind, he said. He was an angular man with an Adam's apple the size of a walnut. He had never married, which was amusing since the third Blackshear brother, Patrick, was a professor of history and philosophy at the Franklin College in Athens and was the father of nine. His wife, Rose Blanche, had increased their brood virtually every year with pleasure and more pounds, until now there were children from four months to nineteen years. Despite her protectiveness with her own children, four girls and five boys, Rose Blanche was, Thomas believed, an impossibly shrieky witch, and many others agreed. This branch of the Blackshears did not drive the thirty miles to Branton for the party. They expected others to come to them.

~Skits, follies, songs, card tricks! sang Jack, passing. Michael and Henry were behind, heading back upstairs to prepare after briefly descending to taste the barbecue.

~So tell me, said Martin Goodpath, whose house was nearby, do you see business improving during 1853, Thomas? He and his wife Susan were shockingly young, barely twenty, but with inherited wealth and fine training in *noblesse oblige* managed to seem older. Men could not take their eyes off Susan, with her finely boned face, chestnut hair, deep blue eyes. They had moved to Branton eighteen months before with twelve wagons and fourteen slaves, gifts from Martin's father, a prosperous importer in Charleston.

~I have a magnificent announcement to make this evening, said Thomas Blackshear. His eyes were glistening. Heads turned when Cassandra walked past, men staring at her beauty and red hair held up in a chignon, women glaring at their husbands over cups of wine punch.

~I always so much look forward to the vanities of your boys, said Susan Goodpath, who had swayed up. Such talent in ones so young must make you quite proud.

~Pride? roared Thomas. I have more pride than kings! More pride than presidents and the wise!

~The wise *guard* themselves against pride, said Cassandra, appearing from behind him and shaking her head.

~So what is Thomas's magnificent announcement? asked Martin, eyes amused. Cassandra tented her gloved fingers as if in prayer.

~Heaven only knows. A black-clothed figure with wild white hair and a laudanum haze came toward them, and there was a clearing of throats, an opening of the circle.

~Here's our fine Dr. Humprey, said Thomas. Merry Christmas to you, sir.

~Nine, seven, and four! said Dr. Israel Humprey. The others looked confused, waited. Cases of diphtheria, mumps, and measles in town, said Dr. Humprey, and winter having just started. I predict many a spade sunk in the cold ground. The group's eyes went twinkly, for Dr. Humprey spent his life in despair and rough bad temper, assuaged only by his frequent forays into his own medicine chest. His phrases were as rumpled as his clothes, and often in political meetings he would erupt into a period of red-faced shouting before his arguments lost their way, like children in the woods.

~Well, heaven help those ill, said Susan Goodpath. They shall be in our prayers.

Others ate well, forking up the rich meat that Joshua had cooked slowly for two days over the pit next to his small house out back. Cassandra glanced from the windows and saw him standing there in her husband's old blue frock coat, bathing the hog with a sack of rags, which he had tied to the end of a pole and dipped often in his sauce. Joshua was a slow man, black as a piano sharp and impossible to rile. His wife, Louisa, was the same way, but their only daughter, Emma Jane, had a hot temper and loved to whirl around and give a swift speech when put upon.

There were other houses there, too, not tumble-down shacks as many other slave quarters around town. There were Tom and Washington and Tim, lawn servants, as Cassandra called them, and Suzy and Portia and Palmyria. Toby was married to Palmyria and had five children. Portia was Tom's wife, and they had four. Washington and Suzy appeared to hate each other, but Cassandra was sure something was going on there. In fact, she had tried to promote it as a function of proper conduct. On a warm day outside last week:

~Washington, if you would be so kind as to mop the front porch, I would be grateful, said Cassandra. She was dressed plainly, in a brown cotton dress, and her hair was tied upon her head, surmounted by a blue bonnet. Mud seems to creep upon the porch from the yard like a living thing.

~He won't keep it clean, said Suzy, coming up from behind him. He don't keep nothing clean. He ain't nothing but a dirty thang hisself.

~You tongue, woman, he said, pointing at her. I done heard enough from you this fine day to last me for a spell of Sundays. I axed you not to speak in such a way before Miz Blackshear.

~I seen stray dogs cleaner than you house, she said sweetly, almost singing.

~Would you two please see fit to annoy each other some other place? said Cassandra. I awoke with a terrible headache, and surely it means the weather is changing.

~My bunion ain't ached, so, well, it ain't, said Suzy. I'll let you know when the weather changing. Cassandra stared at her, trying not to smile or laugh. She felt the heat in her face, wanted to ask more, to understand.

~I be glad to mop you porch, said Washington. Is you be kind enough to take this woman and axe her to mop the roof or something? Look for snakies in the root cellar? They probably come to her like a long-lost sister.

~Haw-haw, said Suzy. You another Ralph Walnut Emerson.

Cassandra sat on the front steps and watched them argue with fascination, and when it was over, when Washington had gone for mops and Suzy for her iron, Cassandra was still there in the warm late November sunshine, headache gone, unsure what they felt for each other. She came into the house and walked slowly through the parlor: So glad when the winter rains came, because the dust inside abated. Now there was mud.

The room was clean tonight, the ladies and their men elegant and sipping sherry and harder liquor, pleasantly convivial. And Cassandra checked the clock on the mantel and saw that the time had come, and she clapped her hands loudly three times, and the conversation mumbled to a stop, and she spoke to them, told them that soon her boys would be down with their little show.

~And at the end of the follies I shall have a magnificent announcement, said Thomas. Please do not leave until I have spoken.

~Sounds downright Biblical, said Dr. Humprey in a sour stage whisper.

UPSTAIRS, DRESSED AND RUNNING LINES, banjo sounds, a flute's fine sweetness: Jack, Michael, and Henry Blackshear awaited their mother's cue. Always, it was the same: *And now, presenting the Celebrated Blackshear Boys!* And they would tumble into the room, laughing and clapping, and people grinned without meaning to, rose slightly from their seats, prepared applause and praise.

~You knuckleheads embarrass me, and I shall thrash you both, said Jack, straightening their fine clothing like a military inspector at a dress parade. If Dr. Humprey seems put out, I'll start playing "My Kentucky Gal," and you two birds get your instruments and come in.

~What is it that Joshua puts in that barbecue sauce? asked Michael sincerely. Someone said that a main ingredient of such sauces is the blood of an ox. I cannot stand the sight of blood.

~You always were a coward, said Jack, straightening his brother's loopy black tie. The boys' clothes: black suits, frock coats, pale-blue silk vests, highly polished black riding boots, patriarchal gold watch fobs looped over their flat stomachs.

~Sir, I am not a coward, said Michael, standing at attention. Today I saved a skinny man from a mad dog. The whole town is talking about it!

~And well done! said Jack. Henry, brown eyes alight, was laughing so hard he had to remove his handkerchief and blow his nose.

Then, from the stairs, a clear, sharp woman's voice, almost clarion: And now, presenting the Celebrated Blackshear Boys!

IN A COURTROOM

(Jack is the presiding judge, sitting in a chair near the glowing fireplace, pretending to pare his nails with a huge carving knife. Giggling from the guests as they watch the prisoner, Michael, come in with his lawyer, Henry.)

JACK: We are here today in the courtroom of Branton County for the trial of Dr. Israel *Pumphrey.* Sir, you are accused of boring three patients to death. How do you plead? (*At this point, there's a howling interruption from the guests, and Dr. Humprey, though trying to appear net-tled, is clearly flattered, and the corners of his mouth twitch.*)

MICHAEL: I have to be leaving now. To be perfectly honest, I am bored beyond en*dur*ance.

HENRY: Your honor, I represent Dr. Pumphrey, and I would like to apologize for his boredom and to say to you, four, fifteen, and nine.

JACK: What's that, you say? Four, fifteen, and nine? (*Looking around the parlor at the guests, who are collapsing with laughter.*)

HENRY: That's the number of his patients, in order, still alive, now dead, and likely to succumb in the coming fortnight.

MICHAEL: I plead not guilty, your honor! These charges are a canard! I have not bored a patient to death since 1850!

JACK: Ten, fifteen, or twenty.

HENRY: Pardon, your honor?

JACK: That's how many years at labor your client shall get if he speaks before the court again without permission.

MICHAEL: This is amazingly boring.

JACK: Now, is your client guilty or not, Mr. Lawyer?

HENRY: He will admit to being tedious, sir, but not boring. (*Every Dr. Humprey by this time is shaking with laughing, clearly pleased, even delighted. The others are laughing so loud at the slack expression on Michael's face that for a long time the boys can't get to the next line. Cassandra is weeping with laughter.*)

JACK: Sir, being tedious is one thing, but do his patients fall asleep before hearing the diagnosis? There is word that a merchant, one, eh (*as if looking through papers here*) Thomas Blackfoot, became *hideously* boring after a few hours in his company! And this Blackfoot is consid-ered well, intolerably *vague* already!

IT WENT ON LIKE THIS for another eight minutes, plotless, charming them with guile. Everything seemed hilarious, but especially the boys' expressions, which they had honed for nearly two years—a slack look of confusion and offended innocence. Charmed, the guests applauded wildly, sipped sherry. The servants huddled in a semi-circle near the back, laughed along, the women covering their mirth with hands held up like fans. Finally, while all still applauded, and the muted clapping of gloved hands spilled across the room like beating wings, the boys picked up their instruments: Jack, guitar; Michael, fiddle; and Henry, flute. Without introduction, they launched into a reel called "My Darling Girl," which they played with more enthusiasm than skill. When the applause for those lively five minutes faded, they began to sing a fireside lament that Jack and Michael had written. The tune was simple, the accompaniment in the melancholy key of E minor. Henry, with his ten-year-old's sweet soprano, stood to the fore and clasped his hands together and sang.

> *We are coming home, mother, mother.*
> *You will see us then, brother, brother.*
> *And our journey shall be done*
> *Underneath the setting sun.*
> *We are coming home, mother, mother.*

The song wove through four verses, speaking in boys' words about having been on a long journey and arriving safely back home. And yet the narrator spoke of losses, of cities and small towns, battlefields and hunger. In truth, Cassandra knew, it was modeled on the Scottish songs she played and sang nearly every night, ones the boys knew warmly by heart, would come in singing, especially Michael.

Henry finished the final verse, and the song ended as he lifted his flute and played the tune a final time. The women dabbed at their eyes with scented handkerchiefs. Dr. Humprey lit a cigar and stared emptily across the room, as if bored. The applause was enthusiastic, and the Celebrated Blackshear Boys ripped off one more reel—this time with Jack on guitar, Michael playing his banjo, and small Henry banging away at the Broadwood grand piano. The guests were on their feet, hands pounding each other furiously. And the comments!

~Can you believe those boys are so talented!

~That sweet little Henry!

~Oh look at Cassandra! She is just absolutely in *love* with her boys.

And she was, and they came to her, leaning against her, sweaty and close, and her chin was up, and she said nothing, didn't need to. Then: Thomas Blackshear made his way to the front, red-faced with alcohol and Christmas tidings, holding his hands up and up and up.

~Friends, friends, friends! They began to settle down and sit once more, as Thomas smiled and held his hands up prayerfully like an orator. I have a magnificent announcement to make this night! One that I have been thinking about for some time. In the course of all things, one quality stands alone, beyond even life and the pursuit of happiness! And that is liberty! It is what we fought the British for in our grandfathers' time and what had made this country strong! Therefore, on this night, I, Thomas Blackshear, take great pride in announcing that as of this day, my slaves are forever free and may live their lives as God accords!

During the ensuing silence, a woman laughed abruptly, as if the show were still going on. Then: the scraping of chair legs and an awkward silence.

~You're *what?* said Cassandra. The boys looked confused, unsure of what had just happened. Freeing slaves was illegal in Georgia, and they all knew it.

In the back, there was the sound of a breath, a sharp intake of air, of men and women and children moving in toward each other, small sounds and the shape of anticipation. The guests seemed vaguely confused or embarrassed, but they considered themselves progressive, would never be rude to their host. A polite pattering broke out, storms of quiet gossip. Cassandra swept from the boys to her husband's side, now smiling, having understood.

~Yes, why not, she said. We can afford to hire our help, and our servants may work as free persons as well as they have worked as slaves. She took Thomas's hand, and they stood together as the others rose and came forward, taking casual congratulations. Dr. Humprey, glaring, slunk out the front door without making goodbyes, heading for his gig.

The boys whispered, punched each other, shrugged, bounced with energy. Joshua and Mary Faircloth and their daughter Emma Jane were coming forward across the room, and Henry stopped and watched, knowing some great thing had broken over them. Tears glowed like opals on Mary's face, but Emma Jane seemed nervous, held close. Mostly, Henry watched his mother's face as Jack and Michael dashed upstairs, and she seemed proud and uncertain, loving, wondering. Her eyes took note of those who swept out without saying Merry Christmas or goodbye. Henry wondered if the dancing master dined alone this night in the Hotel Branton.

THE SLAVES TOOK THEIR PAPERS and left, all of them but the Faircloths, and not long after the New Year, fireworks, and wine punch, the Blackshears found themselves with too few servants to run the house and property. Lawsuits seemed possible for the action. Other slave-owners were appalled. Thomas didn't care. He would hire servants to take the place of his lost slaves, but he would not be burdened by the steps of other men. He could make his own decisions about freedom. The Faircloths took their payment and saved it in coffee cans buried it in the yard.

~Dear, why did you do it? asked Cassandra. I mean really?

~Mmmnph?

It was after midnight now, the fire in their room banked. She lay against him, their ardor spent. A strong northwest wind rattled the windows, and moonlight left a pale lemon slice across the blankets.

~Free our slaves. Why did you do it? Was it from reading Mrs. Stowe's book?

~Mmmmnph?

~Didn't you fear it would harm your business? It was an act of great courage or foolishness, and I have not yet been able to think which. I would not have had half so much courage. Thomas turned toward her, settled very close, face to face.

~A week before, I had been sitting on the porch on Sunday, and Wiseman Robinson came past in his Brougham, and the fool did not even look at our home, but Joshua was standing by the street, and he took of his hat as the carriage passed. He took off his hat to that fool Robinson! And I felt as if something had broken in me. As if I were seeing Branton through the cracked glass of a kaleidoscope. And I became angry. That's all. I would have no person of this land bow before kings.

She kissed him.

UPSTAIRS, GOWNED AND HUDDLED BY the still-stoked fire, Michael and Jack worked on a new card game they were calling Arse. Henry watched, fascinated, unable to follow.

~No, no, no, you knucklehead! said Jack, smacking Michael on the top of his hair. Threes are kings and kings are threes, and the five of clubs is the ace of spades, and the ace of spades is the nine of diamonds!

~Then what in hell is the nine of diamonds? asked Michael. He glared suspiciously at his open hand of cards by the firelight.

~Arse! cried Jack. I win!

And they were choking, kicking, laughing, pounding away, and soon, Henry leaped upon them, and they fought, shouting *Arse! Arse!* until they were overcome with mirth and the need for sleep.

SUMMER, 1860

That bounce-gaited Pullman boy coming across the square: a lame son of the *Branton Eagle's* typesetter, and Henry Blackshear, eighteen, prying the lid from a pickle barrel.

~Good morning, younger brother, said Michael, half-dancing as he entered the front door of Blackshear Mercantile. In the back, three men discussed the merits of a pistol, and a querulous old woman poked Thomas Blackshear with a bony finger and claimed a bonnet was far too expensive.

~Closer to afternoon, said Henry. Phew. These pickles may have gone around the bend. Shall I slice one for your cultured palate?

~Complain of my tardiness, but I remind you that all week I am the town's premier schoolmaster and must help mold young minds.

~God weeps, said Henry. Look at Ned Pullman coming this way. He walks as if he had three feet and cannot decide which one to plant next. Michael turned around and looked through the plate glass window: *Coming straight here, across the dusty street and up the board sidewalk and into the shop.*

~Diddy sent me to axe is Jack sick or nothing, said Ned Pullman. He was a slack-faced urchin, perhaps ten, hair miscut, shirt reeking.

~Our brother has not reported for his assigned duties at the village scribery? asked Michael with mock horror, hand to his breast. Ack, I say. Ack.

~Ack? said Ned Pullman. What'll I tell Diddy? Them meeting out there's about to start, and Mr. Jack Blackshear meant to be writing down what they say.

They were gathering around the courthouse now, city men in elegant summer suits, straw hats, and the heat rose in waves off the three-story red-brick structure. A brass band playing badly, perhaps two songs at once, Henry thought. All week the word flowed around town like a swift rumor: Saturday, come to a meeting to discuss Our Growing Discontent.

~Where in the blazes—oh, said Henry. Oh. Hmmm.

~Go tell your father that our brother has been detained but shall be there anon, said Michael grandly.

~Huh? Ned Pullman's eyes glazed, and he blew upward to evict a stray strand of thick brown hair that drooped over his left eye. Huh?

~He'll be there directly, said Henry. Ned Pullman nodded himself and fanned his damp red face with his hat.

~Them people out there's a mite vexed, he said. How come ever-body's so vexed all the time anyway?

~Tariffs and tarts, said Michael blandly. Abolitionists and assininity. Our Southern inclination toward drawing a line and then shooting before our foes can step over it or not.

~I don't know no French, said Ned Pullman, looking down, then turning and running wildly across the street, just missing the creaking wheels of a wagon loaded with baskets of beans. Henry and Michael punched each other, laughing. One of the men speaking with Thomas Blackshear said no pistol was a sure thing, that if a man really wished to be deadly, he must have a rifled musket. Henry peered suspiciously into the pickle barrel and fished out a few that had gone black.

~That fool brother of ours is going to ruin his life, said Henry sourly.

~Oh hah, as if John Barleycorn were not *our* friend as well, said Michael. He picked out a plump pickle and crunched it, making a face as he chewed thoughtfully.

The previous autumn, all three of the Blackshear brothers had been summarily booted from Mercer University in Penfield for a performance that combined obscene songs with four bottles of very good brandy. Cassandra refused to censure her sons, instead praising their inventiveness and talent.

The University is no doubt in the wrong, she said. God have Mercer on their souls.

At this point, even Thomas, glum and ashamed, had begun to laugh as they stood in the parlor around the season's first fire. At the Branton Methodist Church in the weeks following the boys' dismissal, Cassandra and Thomas stood as if stuck in a posture of pride. The boys then took work: Michael teaching girls at Rev. Pearson's School on South Main Street and Jack as a novice journalist at the *Branton Eagle*. Henry, dreamy and sometimes ill, worked with his father at the Mercantile, which Thomas enjoyed openly.

~Let him enjoy the fruits of the morning, said Michael. These pickles are putrid. They looked at each other for a smiling moment and said at the same time:

~Raise the price! they cried.

They turned and saw, coming inside, Martin Goodpath, and Michael's eyes flared. Henry wiped his hands on the white apron and offered it. Mr. Goodpath sniffed, shook, then looked at his hand as if it were infested.

~Martin, I thought you were in Augusta on business, said Michael, gulping wildly.

~The case was settled before I had unpacked, and so I spent only last evening and was able to come back this morning on the train. I wish to surprise Susan with some small token. What would you gentlemen recommend? Do you have any new candies? Or should it be something more practical?

~Ack, said Michael. The brass band played a march with animal vigor.

JACK BLACKSHEAR ROLLED OFF SUSAN Goodpath, gasping and sweating, the bedclothes bundled and wrenched beneath his hips. The day had risen airless, the morning rich with humidity and coming heat.

~You sound as if you'd run all the way here from town, said Jack. Susan gathered her breath and giggled.

~The servants surely must know by now, she said. *Surely* they must. But they will never tell.

~I suppose I'll have to kill all of them, said Jack, thoughtfully rubbing a spot above his left eyebrow. The bedroom was huge, and the mahogany bed had stopped squeaking and bore its weight stolidly, the pineapple finials gleaming in a slant of sunlight.

~You *can't* kill them, said Susan. The Blackshears are our town's only abolitionists. Besides, if you love me, you must do as I command.

~I am yours, priestess, said Jack tenting his hands prayerfully. Whatever you wish, I shall manfully fulfill.

~You've done *that* twice already this morning, she said, kissing his ear. And you're late for work. That meeting has probably already begun.

~That idiot Robinson and the town's chaff, said Jack, sitting up. We have become a land that judges itself by how well it hates. They want someone to bleed, but they can't settle on a victim quite yet.

~I'm burning up, said Susan. She stood and walked naked to the bureau and poured water from the cream-white pitcher into its bowl and dipped her hands into it, splashed coolness on her face and neck, rubbed her damp hand languidly over her breasts as she turned, facing Jack.

~Oh Venus! said Jack with admiration.

~Is that what you call Cynthia Sims? asked Susan, suddenly darkening. She took a light robe from an overstuffed chair and put in on and walked to the window and tried fan-up a nonexistent breeze. Jack watched her with slack-mouthed desire.

~Please. I don't know what to say to you. She is a girl. She is a very sweet and kind girl, Susan. She's not a woman. I find her company reassuring.

~And I don't reassure you? asked Susan. She sounded blithe, bored.

~Vixen, said Jack, yawning. Can you ask Missy to get us some coffee? I suppose I must get dressed and arrive at the blathering before they lose steam. Can you see our house? Is anyone stirring?

Susan looked down the street through the pecan orchard toward the Blackshear mansion, which stood in its white glory as if it had grown there after a rain.

~Those twins are out doing nothing. Wait. I believe they are having some kind of argument. Is their mother ever coming home? I'm burning up. She let the robe fall off and stood back from the window, climbed into bed and curled against Jack.

~Who can say?

~When you sing "Lorena" I feel as if my soul is weeping, she said, kissing his neck. I cannot bear my life.

~We must all bear what is given to us to bear. She curled her hip upward just as a sound came, a quiet *umperg*, as if someone were moving a chair slightly and scraping its leg against the floor.

~What is that? asked Susan Goodpath.

~Frog? asked Jack. Then: the tip of a thrown pebble glancing off the upper panes of the open window.

~Someone's out there! cried Susan. She climbed madly over Jack and began to dress, while Jack craned his neck toward the steaming window light. Then:

~Psst! Psst! Jack, are you in there?

~It's Henry, said Jack.

~My God, what have you told him? Do your brothers *know*? Susan sounded fierce, ready for blood, brawly. Her face was flushed, and her eyes had narrowed with accusation.

~Hang on. Jack stepped into his trousers and walked to the window without bothering to worry or wonder. Michael stood below him just beyond a lush and aromatic boxwood hedge that encircled the Goodpath house. Lijh, a slave to the house, was some distance away warily watching Romeo and Juliet, the Blackshear dogs, which were coming toward Michael.

~Get out, get out! said Michael, waving his arms wildly. Martin's back! Henry has him cornered at the Mercantile, but he's on his way home to surprise Susan.

~I'm advising Mrs. Goodpath on her finances, said Jack blandly. He reached into one pocket and then the other and retrieved a lopsided cigar stub, which he thrust between his lips and began to chew upon thoughtfully. This presents some fiscal problems that must be considered.

~You fool, get out of there! cried Michael.

~What is the name of God is going on? asked Susan.

~Oh it's just my brother Michael saying that your husband has arrived back in town and is on his way here.

~Oh God! she said, and then she was throwing Jack's clothes out the window, pushing him toward the opening with the strength of deep fear. Jack was about to say something when he lost his balance and fell seat first, so that, for a moment, his rear hung perilously out of the window.

~What are you trying to…

But before he could say *do*, Jack Blackshear landed with a swishing thud through the boxwoods and on the warm shadowed earth, covered with scratches.

~Morning, Mrs. Goodpath, said Michael Blackshear, hat off. She realized she was standing at the window in her underclothing, hair love-wild. The curtains came together as if they were dead weight and had fallen, just as Jack staggered up through the hedges, bleeding from cuts across his cheek and chest.

~Never trust a faithful husband, said Jack, who then stepped into a gopher hole and fell headlong into the soft grass. He was still lying there, with Michael crouched into the switches, when Rev. Pearson drove his light gig around the house, bearing home, from a very short business trip, Martin Goodpath, no wiser. Romeo and Juliet joined the boys, slathering, leaping. Lijh peered into the hedge, shook his head, backed up, and walked toward the sound of the slowing wheels.

~I TELL YOU, MY FRIENDS, this coming election shall bear the weight of our futures on its broad shoulders! shouted Wiseman Robinson, thumbs in his suspenders. He stood on the courthouse steps, chins quivering with rhetoric. On all questions, President Buchanan is mute! And we have been vilified with increasing alarm by the vile villains of Boston, by Garrison (*leaving room here for boos and hisses, which cascaded through the crowd abundantly*) and his ilk.

~Ilk! Ilk! screamed Leonard Fitzpatrick, an angular clothier who dreamed of plantations and slave huts. Others in the crowd reacted with confusion. *Ilk?*

~Don't weep over spilled ilk, whispered Michael Blackshear. Jack, taking notes in a small leather-bound book, grinned, wiped off the barbed-wire row of bloodspots on his cheek with a ready handkerchief.

Branton spilled citizens and slaves in about equal abundance along Main, down Adams, and the clop of passing horses was lively. Wheels creaked for want of greasing. A jingling of mule harnesses, the dry broken backs of empty wagons. The small sons of political fathers sat in the dusty courtyard, playing jacks, scratching. Robinson had swelled the crowd, and now more than a hundred men stood eagerly before him, trolling for a glance and a nod, which could be worth cash money. Ira Manley, who owned The Sycamores, a thousand-acre plantation near Deerskin, stood near Wiseman Robinson, unruffled in a fresh white planter's suit. Pigeons in the bell tower above them cooed and flapped, gentle music. A drift of cooking from the Hotel Branton, men bent over for furtive mid-morning swigs from silver flasks. A general sense of expectation and joy trembled through the crowd.

~You tell it, Mr. Robinson! shouted Henry Brown, the town's most articulate alcoholic. Rev. Charles Merrill, pastor of the First Baptist Church, had heard enough and was wandering off, namesake son at his side.

~She's beautiful, but you're going to get shot, said Michael. Should I say anything in particular at your funeral?

~Say he was a man who loved his country, did first-rate card tricks, and played the guitar *and* women as if he had three hands.

~Hah. Listen to that ass. Mark my words, this whole thing about the colored is going to lead to a war.

~Of *course* it's going to lead to a war, said Jack, dabbing his face and looking at the blood. But the reason doesn't matter. Every fifty years, give or take a half-decade, men blow themselves up for no reason. Perhaps Mr. Darwin is on to something with the idea of selection. Idiots like Robinson stand up before others, waving their peckers like flagstaffs and scream for war. This excuse or that one. *Any* excuse.

~You're starting to sound like our addled father.

~I should hope so. Would you like for me to sing you a song about the man freeing his slaves in the year 1852?

~Nothing of *that* ilk, sir! said Michael. Robinson waved his arms, flinging sweat into the flanks of the crowd. His face was pale with rage.

~And should an abolitionist be elected…

He clawed through increasing bombast. Henry was suddenly beside his brothers in his white work apron. Jack looked at him sheepishly, raising one eyebrow into a military chevron then letting it fall.

~You look like dung, said Henry pleasantly.

~You smell like pickles, said Jack. He looked at his brothers: still so much the same, even grown now, Henry with his light blond hair and cocoa eyes, Michael sandy and sweet.

~Jack was just enlightening me on his theory of warfare, said Michael. Quite intelligent for an ass who fell out of a window to keep from being shot by the wronged husband.

~I was wondering if you had been killed, said Henry. Just so it won't come as a shock, I'm planning to blackmail you, Jack.

~Now, now, nothing of that ilk is necessary. Michael doubled over, laughing.

~What? asked Henry. What?

MICHAEL WALKED DOWN ACADEMY STREET with lovely Elizabeth Chadwick on his arm, unchaperoned but passed, like a prize, from the eyes of one nosy old maid to the next. Small and slender, blonde and religious, Elizabeth moved with tiny steps, as if seeking a place to vanish in plain sight. Now, in the deep heart of damp July, she wore a cotton dress with pale daisies she had sewn herself. She carried a small bouquet of Cherokee roses. They could see the cemetery's memorial spires not far ahead. They had been friends since childhood, sharing intimacies, learning to dance. Her father, Richmond Chadwick, had been a jolly burgher, owner of his own gristmill just south of town. The year before, he had dropped dead in his own front parlor while wondering aloud if peaches could grow in the state of Maine. Because he had invested well, Elizabeth and her two sisters, Emma and Colette, lived comfortably with their mother two doors east of the Blackshears, with only the ancient and querulous Mrs. Marcus Cardinal in between.

~I dropped in to speak with your mother yesterday, she said. Her left hand was properly hooked to Michael's crooked elbow as they slowly moved down the well-worn path beside the quiet, shady street. That parrot fluffed his wings and shouted, Alas! Poor Yorick! It nearly frightened me to death. Animals should not be able to speak. Or perhaps they should on Christmas morning early. But not a bird and not Shakespeare.

~That's the nicest thing he's said in weeks, said Michael.

~Your poor grandmother.

~Alas, poor Mama Blackshear. She's been going downhill for forty years. I didn't know the world could fashion such a gradual slope.

~Don't be unkind. She is just lost in her mind. She told me that in the spring, the parrot's tail would grow large and have great eyes with many colors.

~We once owned a peacock, said Michael. She is remembering that.

~I remember. Your mother called the peacock Fancy. For the way his tail fanned. I thought that very clever.

~Romeo ate him one spring. Such is war.

~It must be sad not to know a parrot from a peacock.

~Wiseman Robinson doesn't know his arse…

~Michael.

~Yes, yes. I'm a man now and must not speak like a wild boy. It's just that he most closely resembles something one steps in at a horse race.

~Do you like Rev. Pearson's School? When I went there, he often looked at my slate by leaning over and placing his chin very nearly on my shoulder. It made me feel weakly sick, as if I were coming down with something.

~Teaching is a calling, said Michael. I have yet to be called.

They walked past the twin mansions of the James brothers, successful merchants and farmers. Built six years before, the houses squatted splendidly behind Ionian columns, with pebbled pathways and gardens, blue-green lawns and marble statuary. Slaves snipped and manicured the grounds, slow and slower.

~Then what is it you want to do with your life? she asked. And don't say sing and play music and tell those awful jokes or do your skits. I mean adult's work.

~I'm thinking of dying in a grand and glorious charge. Or rather I would except for my infirmity.

~What infirmity?

~Cowardice, he whispered, leaning close. She laughed and hit him on the arm. Something in the air smelled lemon and it laved them. He loved the sound of her small laughter, as if something fragile had broken its moorings and fluttered upward. A large sunbonnet covered her face when she turned slightly or looked down, since Michael was nearly a foot taller.

They walked into the cemetery with its marble monuments and flat tablets. The grass had been mown, and a sweet smell of honeysuckle floated on the still air. An enormous water oak stood guard on the northern side, where the Georgia Railroad tracks stitched a neat border. Elizabeth's dress covered her small feet, and her steps were almost silent as she led Michael through the decorated stones to the family plot. That high shriek: a red-tailed hawk turning on a wing-point, held up by new thermals as he hunted. Whenever Michael thought of America or death, he could not stop considering their enormity. Vast things always had power. His father some days talked nonstop of the North. He said it often: I wish to stand upon a hill in a land without slaves and from it look upon the world, and see it as God made it and intended us to know it. One would know the secrets of the world then.

~He's in heaven looking down upon you, said Michael as Elizabeth knelt to put the flowers on her father's grave.

~I believe that, she said, standing. I have to believe that. I do not know how I could *breathe* if I did not believe that. Jesus Christ is our hope and our salvation. I do not think I could bear another day without Jesus. Such talk made Michael uncomfortable, but he knew Elizabeth had adored her father. Perhaps there were cloud-streets, gates of gold, the eternal smells of baking bread and cinnamon. The hawk passed over the fieldstone graves of the poor down the slope and disappeared into the woods, something small and limp hanging from its claws.

~LADIES AND GENTLEMEN? ARE THERE *any* gentlemen here? (*The sound of deep, brandy-oiled laughter.*) Have there *ever* been any gentlemen here? Well never mind, never mind. Have you had enough of politicians and *wise* men? Jack stood in front of a room-full of men who back-slapped and jostled for a view. Michael and Henry were behind a small blanket hung over a wire waiting for the introduction to end. Sometimes Jack could go on for five minutes or more. The room was clouded with cigar smoke and the red, alchoholed faces of men without women.

~Not wise men but *Wiseman*! cried Henry Brown from the front row. Rutledge Hall shimmered with its wall-mounted lanterns, and despite the tall windows open to the summer night, the heat was thick and stultifying. No one hid their joyous drafts from flask or flagon.

Thomas Blackshear grinned, leaning against a wall: *My boy. A piece of work.*

~Now, now, let's not criticize our local politicians! said Jack. What you hard-working men need is some entertainment!

It was his lead-in line, honed over the years at Rutledge Hall, which was upstairs in downtown Branton over Mr. Rutledge's undertaking establishment. The boys performed twice a week during most summers, with the windows thrown open to snatch any cross-breeze. Nights of blessed thundershowers were best, when gusts of wet wind blew the long white curtains, smoke-stained and limp, back into the room.

~Go to it, boys! someone cried.

~It's time…for…the…Celebrated Blackshear Boys! cried Jack. Michael and Henry, their hinges oiled with a decent wine, dashed out from beneath the blanket, and without pausing launched into "Turner's Reel," Jack with his guitar, Michael, banjo, and Henry on fiddle. They knew perhaps two dozen reels by now, honed from playing hour by hour at home—where all three still lived despite being more or less grown. Cassandra had not encouraged them to move; in fact, she was positively against it. Now, the men were on their feet, stomping, clapping, whistling. Sometimes they played for their sweethearts: Jack's Cynthia, Michael's Elizabeth, and Henry's Susannah. While Elizabeth was pliable and sweet, Cynthia and Susannah were sometimes loud, often demanding. Cynthia in particular threw dramatic fits in the street, hissingly demanded that Jack stop all this foolishness and marry her. She was furious when the boys had been cashiered from Mercer; Susannah sulked and Elizabeth told Henry (quietly) that she was sure it must be a mistake. None of the reels they played had words, and without stopping for applause, they finished one and slashed into another, even faster, and finally a third with such speed that their fingers danced along the ebony necks and elegant fretwork as if they were touching fire.

~Thataway, boys! men cried as the brothers finished, took a long courteous bow, jostled each other. The men, wreathed in smoky haloes, sat down noisily.

Henry ran behind the blanket and came out with three bonnets and handed one to each brother as they pushed forward across the splintery floor a small table and three chairs. The boys cinched on the bonnets and sat. (*Lots of giggling and pointing now, whispering.*)

HENRY: (*In a high, fey voice*) Sisters, I am just so *worried* about my husband.

MICHAEL: Why is that sister—he hasn't stopped—

HENRY: (*Leaning forward*) He has! He has stopped doing *that.*

JACK: Stopped doing what? Oh dear! You don't mean he's stopped—

(*Henry and Michael nodding here, and the men in the audience howling.*)

MICHAEL: Do you mean he's just stopped altogether or stopped with *you?*

HENRY: I can't say for certain. There *is* something quite familiar about the stable boy.

(*Looks of horror from Michael and Jack.*)

JACK: Then I believe you should do what I did with my Isaac when his eye became wandry!

HENRY: And what was that?

JACK: (*With a loud whisper*) Saltpeter in his coffee!

HENRY: (*Looking at the audience*) Saltpeter in his coffee? What effect did it have?

JACK: (*Confiding*) Well, let me put it this way, sisters. Things that had formerly pointed north now pointed south! It was a patriotic act! And where his normal gait was a march? It now becomes something of…oh…a *limp.*

MICHAEL: (*pausing for the laughter to subside*) Stout scissors would work just as well, sisters.

HENRY: I had considered just burning the stable. When I was able.

MICHAEL: But why are you not able?

HENRY: Too much work at the table. But I may burn the stable.

MICHAEL: When you are able.

JACK: Perhaps this resemblance is no more than a fable. I mean to the boy in the stable.

HENRY: No, the same bottle, just a different label.

It went on like this for five minutes, increasingly tangled, approaching the risqué and breezily veering off—of course, the stable boy's mother was named *Mabel*. When the Celebrated Blackshear Boys whipped off their bonnets for a bow, the men were punching each other, sipping draughts of lifting spirits from silvery flasks. Every time the boys had done the Three Sisters skit it had changed, a theme with variations. Sometimes it was about infidelity, at others, drunkenness. Once, out of nowhere, Michael had stood and begun to sing, in a wailing soprano, a song that began thus:

> *My husband prefers the cattle to me*
> *The cotton, the fields, and the streams.*
> *But when he sees our servant girl Rachael*
> *He's coming apart at the seams…Oh,*
> *(Refrain)*
> *I sent him away on a donkey for one,*
> *I did not allow him one pass.*
> *And when he collapses far out on the road,*
> *He always lands on his ass (on his ass).*

Jack and Henry had fallen apart, laughing with the audience— Michael had made it up, he said later, on his way to the show that night. "Donkey for One" had become a much-requested song, never sung in mixed company, of course.

~Now, if you please, something cooling after such a festive start! said Jack. The men sat, ready for a sentimental song. This one had been composed by Henry and Michael one rainy afternoon on the front porch, just when the leaves had begun to shade toward orange and gold:

> *If they laid you in the earth today*
> *My dreams would still be bright.*
> *You gave me love, and I must say*
> *That I will love you anyway*
> *When you are gone, like stars in day,*
> *You always are to me the strongest light.*

(Refrain)
Your name shall be upon my lips
On distant days in endless trips
Forever I shall seek you to confide.
Mother, you were kind to me,
You'll rest beneath the tall oak tree
And soon I will be sleeping by your side.

The boys gauged effect, adjusted words, broke it down into close, three-part harmony, with a long flute solo by Henry to end it. Grown men wept openly. (The boys privately called it "The Stupid Mother Song" and made merciless fun of it, sometimes torturing the lyrics into obscene rhymes, but they knew men *and* women loved to weep over their mothers.)

The evening wore on with courtroom shenanigans; a novelty song called "Juggling Jim" about a salesman wooing three women at the same time; and parodies of "Polly Wolly Doodle" and "Oh, Susanna!" After they men had coughed and staggered out, worn from laughing and smoking and drinking, Jack counted the money: forty-three dollars.

LARGELY DRUNK AND IN HILARIOUS high spirits, the Celebrated Blackshear Boys walked through the warm summer streets of Branton.

~What do you want us to do with your body after Mr. Martin Goodpath shoots you? Michael asked his older brother.

~I wish to be stuffed and mounted.

~Mounted where? This was Henry.

~On *Mrs.* Martin Goodpath, said Jack, erupting into a case of hiccups.

Arm over arm, they walked down West Main Street and turned toward Academy, singing, falling down, rising again. Sharp downdrafts came: an assembling storm. Soon, they knew, a pelting rain would spread across the town, but they did not hurry—detoured through the cemetery, drinking toasts to some of the dead, shouting for others to stand and be men, to come out and fight.

WINTER AND SPRING, 1861

We have no one to blame but ourselves! cried Thomas Blackshear. The country coming apart like a pair of rotten trousers and war certain! He stood behind Cassandra, who sat before the vanity, watching as Thomas brushed her long red hair. She had never enjoyed his nightly brushings, but he adored the feel and color of her hair, and she indulged him, despite the rough handling. Bah!

~Cy, what are you going to do about those twins? she asked. You are the one who freed the lot of them, and now they're amuck, up and down the street. Mrs. Cardinal has threatened to hire a man with a net.

~If we had but stood behind Breckinridge and Lane, none of this would have come to pass! said Thomas, brushing more swiftly. But there were Bell and Everett! Douglas and our own Herschel V. Johnson. Well, perhaps we should have voted for them. Now we are to kill each other over a gangly president and a Maine man idiotically named Hannibal Hamlin! I'd rather be drowned at birth than named Hannibal Hamlin! That idiot Howell Cobb. That moron Buchanan. Seizing forts and arsenals!

~You are tearing out my hair! And what will do you about those twins?

~Sorry, my dearest. But South Carolina and Mississippi and Florida and Alabama all gone from the Union! And today our own convention voting! If it comes to war, I shall instruct our boys to flee for Europe and play before the crowned heads.

~You shall do nothing of the sort, said Cassandra, wheeling and snatching the brush from her husband's hand. The room: a cold wind rattling the panes, the stoked and blazing fire, the four-poster bed with its thick weight of blankets, and over the mantel a new painting just finished by Thomas Blackshear, a portrait of his wife, loving and exact, smoothing away the slight constellation of freckles thrown across her face. Guests would arrive downstairs soon for the party, and Marianna, the new kitchen servant, had stood in the sunny yard late in the afternoon wringing her hands and asking for God's help. Not a good sign.

~Alexander Stephens does not want Georgia to...

~Stop talking about this madness for a moment, said Cassandra. What in heaven's name are you going to do about the twins?

Emma Jane Faircloth, the daughter of the Blackshear servants Joshua and Mary, had become pregnant almost nine years before, borne twin daughters in her parents' house out back, then vanished, possibly to the north with a white sailor named Bunt who had been passing through. Now the girls, Louisa and Rachel, were free like their grandparents but lively and irritable, drawing criticism from the moderate and charitable and from the slave aristocracy who thought the girls should be sold. Worse, they had three times broken into Mrs. Marcus Cardinal's house, where they apparently helped themselves to molasses candy and watched her cuckoo clock tweet the hour. Mrs. Cardinal came on to her front porch and rang a small brass bell, which in the past was a demand that her husband come quickly. Unfortunately, Mr. Cardinal had been dead now for fourteen years, though his widow seemed increasingly unaware of it.

~What *can* I do? spluttered Thomas. I have staked my reputation on being opposed to slavery, and now am I to say I was wrong?

~You weren't wrong, dear, but they have no father, and Joshua and Mary are getting old. Someone has to bring them to order, or we shall have to send them away.

~Your parents in Savannah...

~Don't even think...

The unmatched barking of two dogs erupted from outside, along with the sound of growling, like cloth being ripped.

~Romeo and Juliet, said Thomas Blackshear. The guests must be arriving. He straightened his shirt-front and dashed from the room, and Cassandra turned back to her image in the mirror and finished brushing her hair.

~There must be a reason God created men, she said to her lovely face. Though for the life of me I cannot imagine what it might have been.

FORTY GUESTS SPILLED THROUGH THE Blackshear home, sipping from crystal wineglasses, supping brandy. The men did not withdraw to smoke but instead puffed locomotive clouds of smoke from cigars and pipes and mingled with wives and lovers trained to say nothing, no matter the offense. All the conversation was about the country's collapse, much of it highly favorable, some of it in awestruck tones of horror and regret.

~The British shall be defeated! cried Mama Blackshear from her chair near the fire. And all their kind! Call the lancers! A few guests moved away.

Then: a shriek cutting through the room, a rat-tail file on the rim of a crystal goblet.

~Hello, honey! Hello, honey! Hello, honey! King Lear, the parrot, seemed to be drunk, perhaps from the alcoholic fumes. Jack, standing with Cynthia Sims, shot a glance toward Henry, who looked simultaneously smitten and horrified by Susannah Yarbrough, who was poking him in the chest with a provocative finger. She had just finished a discourse on why all Yankees should be shot. All of them, men, women, and children. If only she didn't have curly black hair and deep-set green eyes.

~Ah, the muse speaks! crowed Thomas Blackshear. Perhaps he can give auger for us what shall happen with the collapse of our America. Gather around! Everyone gather around!

~Oh dear heavens, said Cassandra. Mrs. Cardinal stood in front of Mama Blackshear, and they glared wordlessly at each other. Susan Goodpath swayed confidently on her husband's arm, smiling with open, damp lust toward Jack. Martin, without a clue, smiled at the thought of hearing wisdom from a bird. Sweet Elizabeth Chadwick came with Michael, and he could smell her faint scent, something flowery and maddening. She had spent much of Advent in prayer, feeling even quiet kisses an offense to God.

~*Advent?* Michael had cried once to his brothers. What I want is an adventure! What I want is to get out of this town for a while. Go up

North as the old man dreams. Maybe when Elizabeth sees me leaving she will come to her senses and allow me to ruin her reputation.

~I'd be glad to ruin it for you now, said Jack, in his cups.

~I'm in, said Henry. All Gaul is divided into three parts.

The swishing of hoop skirts; the displacement of smoke; wind and its ghostly bumping of the window frames; low laughter. Mary Faircloth, in the front hall, scolding the twins; Romeo and Juliet crying at the door to come inside, out of the cold, clear night. And Thomas Blackshear leading them all toward the parrot's cage, where the bird squatted on his slung swing, eyeing the procession with what appeared to be surly contempt. Uncle Lawrence, Thomas's depot-master brother, had already taken too much whiskey and was leaning perilously against a far wall, blank-faced. Jim Cedarman was there with his wife and three children, mild Jim, Thomas's business partner at the mercantile and in several other small ventures. Sober, industrious, marginally silent Jim Cedarman, with his voluble fat wife Margaret. Jim was the balance on every issue and had lately been saying secession was a kind of collective madness and would pass, like an outbreak of smallpox. Mr. Franklin Rutledge, who always seemed listing to starboard, embalmer and entertainment-hall owner, laughed at something as he came over—that laugh which sometimes erupted from the back as he drained the blood of a prosperous client. And more than two dozen others from Branton, always glad for an invitation to the Blackshear home, even those who found Thomas's sentiments on slavery an abomination. Branton's pride in moderation was almost sinful, some said, but it *was* good for business when every man felt his opinion respected.

~Now, oh great muse of the future, said Thomas, waving his hand mysteriously over King Lear's cage, can you tell us what is to become of us? Shall there be war? Shall a new country be born from the ashes? Speak to us! Thomas made a few motions he took to be Masonic, and several of the men nearby appeared offended.

Lear hopped from one end of the perch to another and then back, bowing ceremoniously.

~Watch this, whispered Jack, his eyebrows pointing downward toward his nose. Michael and Henry huddled close, giddy, ignoring Elizabeth, who did not mind, and Susannah, who stamped her foot imperiously. Romeo and Juliet were out back now, tearing frantically at the rear door, where Thomas often let them inside to commit wreckage upon the furniture. Once, he had let Romeo inside early in the morning, and the dog had run straight up the stairs and, without stopping, leapt straight on to the bed where Cassandra slept.

~Oh dear, said Thomas when he got to the scene of domestic carnage, Cassandra waving a fireplace poker at the dog and begging it to come closer for a bashing. When she came after Thomas, he fled, Romeo just behind him.

King Lear stood up regally, raising a dusty ruff on the back of his head. He coughed importantly.

~Bed the bitch! he shrieked. Appalled, the women backed away, dragging their husbands by their obedient sleeves. Bed the bitch! The Celebrated Blackshear Boys laughed uncontrollably, and Susannah was slapping Henry on the shoulder, while the upper lip of Cynthia Sims curled into a feral snarl.

~Throw the cover over that bird! cried Cassandra. Where he could have learned such filth is beyond me! She was glaring at her guilty sons, who were trying hard to avoid laughter and failing miserably.

~Give me a kiss! demanded King Lear. Put 'er there, friend! The parrot leaned down and whistled, profoundly unmusical, like a dog caught in wheel spokes. Give me a kiss!

Perhaps he means the North should kiss the South? said Thomas, hand curled in supplication beside his mouth.

~Everyone, please accept my deepest apologies for that bird, said Cassandra. Animals should not speak. It is an abomination.

~Bed the bitch! cried Lear happily.

Joshua and Mary came running into the room trying to restrain Romeo and Juliet, who had somehow broken in. The twins had begun to bang on Cassandra's Broadwood piano. Without stopping, Romeo dashed straight for Mama Blackshear, stood against her leg, and began to hump it violently.

~Tiger! cried Mama Blackshear. Ack! Tiger.

~These are signs! cried Thomas. Oh, Mama! Can you not see that this is a sign? Cassandra began to weep. The men were hunched up in their evening coats, laughing themselves into sickness, while their wives asked for traveling cloaks. Outside, lined in the side yard, the buggy horses stood in their harnesses, heads down in the cold wind, soundless.

SATURDAY NIGHT, APRIL 13, THE Blackshear brothers rode their horses two miles outside Branton to the small farm their father owned, and now were getting pleasantly drunk in a leaning cabin that squatted like an exhausted child by a narrow, tea-colored creek. The town was mad for war, with the square clogged all day, every streetcorner ripe with speechmaking and excited jostling. Still, Branton allowed Unionists their say, mannerly, considerate, except for a number of country boys who had poured into town, bearing shotguns and cursing Yankees with great violence but without much verbal variety. Cassandra had made up her mind to have King Lear suffocated and might have, except for the bird's terrified shrieking one night when Mama Blackshear, still thinking it was a chicken, had been discovered sticking a knife through the cage bars.

~Fort Sumter is now in Southern hands, said Jack. Long live something.

~You're drunk, said Henry.

~Madness, scolded Michael. Georgia secedes, then Louisiana and Texas. These blithering idiots meeting in Montgomery. That blithering idiot Jefferson Davis of Mississippi as the provisional president. That blithering idiot Mr. Alexander Stephens as vice president. And now we have President Abraham Lincoln *and* President Jefferson Davis, and the froth of partisanship, lightly whipped before, now foams like river through the South.

~Good speech, said Henry. I nominate you as president of Branton County. Long may you wave. He emitted an enormous belch and sat in a rough, sawn-lumber chair near the fire. The single room had large gaps in the chinking, and streams of cold air drained through. Parts of several constellations showed through the rotted roof shakes. Still the room, with its bleached deer skulls, crisscrossed antlers, and rows of emptied green rum bottles was cozy enough. The boys often came here to write songs and skits, to sip, to dream.

~Last night, Cynthia told me she could not *wait* for the day when I march off in my uniform to fight the country. She said it would be *so* sad and *so* romantic. I told her that if she just wanted to be sad, I'd stomp on her foot. She took it badly. Minx.

~How you can bear that woman is beyond me, said Michael.

~Easy for you to say, you escort the Virgin Mary.

~Let's go to Athens and torment Aunt Rose Blanche, said Henry. We could dress as ghosts and moan that she will soon join the Legion of the Dead.

~What has the unfaithful Mrs. Goodpath said to you about our apparent coming war? asked Michael. Jack seemed to consider it thoughtfully.

~Hmmm. Do you know what she said to me this past Saturday morning? She said men who respect their women too much do them a fatal disservice.

~How did you respond? asked Michael.

~I slapped her, said Jack, taking a long draught of brandy. Then she threw her chamber pot at me and scuffed the wall. Fortunately, it was empty. What we must remember, lads, is that all women lie just as all men do.

~Most of them lie with *you*, said Michael. I should like to lie with someone besides Minnie Penny.

~Here's to Minnie Penny, said Henry. Long may she wave! Do you remember the first time you boys took me to see her? It was the shortest assignation of my young life. She predicted that I would someday have a very unhappy wife. But then I made her eat those words.

~Among other things! shouted Jack. We should write a song about Minnie Penny. The fellows at Rutledge Hall would love it!

~I have it, said Henry, hawking and staggering to a corner to spit and then straighten out his clothes. Don't anyone say a word. Jack and Michael could seem him working over rhythm, meter, tune, words, all in near-silence. The night was cool, but they could sense that the weather was warming nicely, that soon they might come here as they had done for years, doing absolutely nothing of value and still having a very good time. Owls dueled in the woods, songs crossing, mellow and mournful. Henry pulled a crumpled sheet of foolscap from his pocket, licked a pencil stub, wrote furiously, stopping at times to read the words and snort out a drunken giggle.

He came back to the fire, cleared his throat dramatically, held up the paper.

~Gentlemen, I give you Henry Blackshear, lover of virgin *and* whore, said Jack.

~Hsst! warned Henry. Then he sang, hoarsely:

> *No one knows her last name,*
> *It could be Smith or Jones.*
> *Her game is such a fast game,*
> *She'll turn your sinews bones.*
> *She costs less than any*
> *You'll find on Adams Street.*
> *We call her Minnie Penny—*
> *Buy the sour with the sweet!*
>
> *Some men pay with pennies,*
> *Some men pay with hams.*
> *But all go in like lions*
> *And then come out like lambs.*

Michael laughed so hard it appeared for a moment he would throw up, and Jack dashed to Henry and lifted him bodily and danced him around the room, crying:

~Sing that to Elizabeth Chadwick! Oh how sweet the boy is! And how sensitive!

Then they began a favorite game they knew well enough, repeated for years.

~I want to live to be incredibly, disgustingly old, said Henry.

~And I want to be a great hero, said Michael.

~I wish to be the discover of the meaning of life, said Jack. Or at least why eggs poach. May we each be granted our wishes, or heaven be damned. Amen.

SOME TIME LONG BEFORE DAWN, the fire muttering out, the boys awoke, hungry. They discussed the situation with pounding skulls and no more brandy. Henry had lit another candle, and they sat around it, faces without apparent bodies.

~I am starved, said Jack.

~Let's ride home and rouse Mary and ask her to cook eggs and bacon, said Michael. And make three hundred gallons of coffee. We could each have a hundred gallons. Sufficient unto the day.

~It's night, said Henry.

~Come out like lambs, said Jack, grinning, wild-haired. That was good.

~At your service, said Henry, holding his head with both hands.

~Nah—let's go steal a chicken from Hoke Turnell's house. We've done it before. Now, he deserves a lesson, the secessionist trash.

Hoke was a red-faced farmer who owned one slave and beat him a considerable amount of the time. That day, Hoke had stood spluttering on the courthouse steps, saying he would soon be a soldier and would *kill every Yankee and every nigger in America to keep the South free.* He shamed even the firebrands, who might admit on the darkest nights that something was oddly wrong about slavery but utterly necessary. Wiseman Robinson had led him inside for a talking.

~I'm not afraid of Hoke, but his Petunia would scare the snakes off a Harpy, said Michael.

~Can you even imagine lying on top of *that*? asked Henry with a shudder. It would not be unlike rutting with a riverbank.

~Haw, said Jack. I'm going. Are you girls coming or not?

An oblong moon hung low through the forest, cream and pearl on the slow-moving creek. Years before, the Blackshear boys had built a trail through the swampy lowland at the edge of their father's farm, a berm extending five hundred yards and wide enough for stealthy single-file. Though successive floods had washed parts away, it was still easy to navigate by lantern-light or a strong moon. Owls moaned love songs. Henry stopped once to be sick and exclaim:

~Aye, God I hate walking. If there is a war, I'm going to be a cavalry officer. Saber and a sash. Or perhaps just a sash.

~I'm going to be a general who sits far behind the main lines and does nothing, said Jack.

~Be knuckleheads, said Michael. We will still, even in the face of mortal battle, be the Celebrated Blackshear Boys. Even Yankees will sneak through our picket lines to hear our latest creations. Jack stopped and turned to look at him.

~Elizabeth Chadwick won't wait for an idiot *performer*, said Jack. I doubt Minnie Penny would wait for that. No, we must look to our reputations. There may be an opportunity here that we are overlooking.

~Are you a rebel now? asked Henry.

~I'm a man of utter pragmatism, said Jack haughtily. Leave ideas to the philosophers like Mr. Emerson. I'm seeking the easy way out. Only a fool would seek to be ennobled by war.

~Spoken like a true coward, said Michael.

~I will always cherish those kind words, said Jack loftily.

They came from the swamp into a small, freshly plowed field, and two hundred yards beyond it was the darkened farmhouse of Hoke Turnell and his barren wife, Petunia. Hoke hated with the deep rancor of the ignorant, always felt a swindle near. The word had spread that Petunia had performed her wifely duties almost every night for the first five years of their marriage with nothing to show for it, and so Hoke had invited his own brother to take a turn, with no issue, either. Clearly, Petunia was at fault, and Hoke rarely missed an opportunity to humiliate her in public. Now, with the moon heavy and lowering, they could hear nothing but crickets and tree frogs.

~This is what it must feel like just before battle, said Henry.

~What's *that*? asked Michael. Obvious answer: the chuffing and baying of a large dog who had heard their soft talking and was now loping toward them.

~That son of a whore's gone and gotten himself another bitch, said Jack aloud. How can he expect to be robbed of chickens when there's a dog here? Jack realized that he was speaking to no one, for his brothers had vanished soundlessly the way they'd come, and soon, Jack was dashing through the swamp with them, realizing that in their first engagement with the enemy, they had retreated before a shot was fired.

Not a good sign. The dog gave up long before it reached the brothers, who were falling off the berm into the brackish water of the swamp, falling back up, laughing, hooting, and generally causing every living thing to sing, to dash about, to give way.

~YOU YOUNG MEN NOW AND giving you mother the ague, said Mary Faircloth, watching as they washed up outside her house. And with this war talk, and you all acting the fool. It ain't proper nor fitten.

~Mea maxima culpa, said Jack, raising his arms to the heavens. We just needed to clean up a bit before going inside. Just then, there was an agonized shout from the back porch: their mother in her gown and cloak, calling over and over:

~Mama Blackshear? *Mama Blackshear?* Cassandra, red hair down and shimmering in the early sun, came running into the yard and saw her sons by the yard pump. Have you boys seen your grandmother? She's not in her room! She's missing!

~Mama? cried Thomas Blackshear. He looked comic in his nightgown, which belled in the light breeze, making him appear monstrously fat. Dear, do you see her?

~ *We'll* search, said Jack, suddenly sobered. The boys, looking like utter hell, seemed a welcome sight to their father, but Cassandra was less blithe, making a face of regret, disgust. Birds sang. The boys fanned out down Academy Street with Romeo and Juliet, looking, with thrumming skulls, for their missing grandmother, but after circling the grid of short streets twice and finding nothing, they returned to the parlor where Cassandra and Thomas, dressed by now, were holding a council of war. The dogs lay idly on the front porch, tails flapping to some unheard marching song.

~Think, boys, think! cried Thomas. Cassandra looked at them: fetid, disarrayed, unshaven, and rolled her eyes, shook her head. Pretend this is war and you are being sent on a scout to find the approaching enemy!

~Bed the bitch? inquired King Lear pleasantly.

~I shall have Parrot Loaf before this day is ended! cried Cassandra. Jack began to laugh and then held his head.

~Mrs. Cardinal, said Henry presently. I would bet my last dollar that she is at Mrs. Cardinal's house. Both of them have lost their reason with age.

~Reason is neither gained nor lost with age! cried Cassandra sagely, glaring at the boys and holding a finger beneath her nose. You are grown men acting like children, and we are about to have a great war over WHAT? Men are utter idiots, all of you!

~Money, honey! shrieked King Lear, leaning over from the exertion.

~Oooh! The sound from their mother was one of defeat and wretchedness, and with her hair down, her face red, her hand balled into fists, all four of the Blackshear men paused to note how completely beautiful it made her.

~NOW, MEN, WE ARE AT war, and Mama Blackshear is the quarry, said Jack. Thomas had mounted his horse and galloped off, planning to circle one block and then another. His black gelding, Bill, walked at the same pace no matter what Thomas said, how much he kicked or whipped. Nothing mattered. The brothers were walking toward Mrs. Cardinal's house.

~I would absolutely despair if named after a bird, said Michael.

~Michael Crow, said Henry thoughtfully. Michael Mockingbird. Michael Yellow-Bellied Sapsucker.

~That's the one, said Jack. I'd be Jack Eagle. Sounds like something from Fenimore Cooper. How! He held up his hand in what he took to be Indian style. They came clumping up the broad front steps of Mrs. Cardinal's house and banged on the door, and shortly her old house servant, Lijh, came to the door, peering through the crack of an opening.

~Yes, Lijh, is Mrs. Cardinal in? asked Jack. Our grandmother, you know, old Mrs. Blackshear, is missing, and we wondered if perhaps she were with Mrs. Cardinal. Lijh's lower eyelids drooped so that he looked remarkably like a hunting dog, slack jowls, a slack expression.

~She ain't here, neither, suh, said Lijh. He was dressed in a moth-eaten red jacket that Mr. Cardinal had worn many years before when Branton County had tried for a time to institute formal foxhunts. She did leave wif you granny, though, ain't fo'ty minutes ago. I ain't axed, but Miz Cardinal says they go to get a turkey knife. Do that mean anything to you gentlemens? Turkey knife? I axed could I drive her, and she says, Marcus, don' let me stops you from going on you hunt. Then she pat me on the head and say I'm looking sick. I don' mean no disrespeck, but she losing her marble.

~*Turkey knife?* said Michael, holding his head. Henry giggled, leaning against a column.

~They walk toward the cemeltery, said Lijh, pointing. The heat gone get 'em if them ghosties don'.

~Thank you, Lijh, said Jack formally. We shall continue our expedition in the cemetery, and I congratulate you for this invaluable help.

~Um hm. He looked the boys up and down, shook his head.

The boys walked slowly, thoughtfully, down the street toward the Branton Cemetery. Henry stopped to be sick but merely leaned against the trunk of an ancient live oak for some time.

~Well, are you going to spew or not? asked Jack, taking out his pocket watch. I suppose service shall have to go on without us this morning. Imagine the Blackshear brothers missing Sunday services. God shall mourn in the streets of heaven.

~I feel as if my throat were lined with unginned cotton, said Michael, standing, perspiring freely.

~You know, we will have to volunteer for this war, or they will not let us stay here in Branton, blurted Michael. His face had grown thoughtful. Three young men singing and performing skits at Rutledge Hall while the bloom of county is off to battle for home and hearth? Papa is already considered the most eccentric man in town. It's only one step from being eccentric to being a traitor, you know.

~Are you calling Mama Blackshear a traitor? cried Jack. I challenge you to a duel!

~Very funny, said Michael. Since he's blind in one eye, people let him speak, since at least half the time someone could be coming at him with an axe, and he wouldn't know it. But we have no such advantages. Anyway, a war surely won't last until Christmas. I rather like the idea of being decked out in gold braids and marching around. We don't have professions, anyway.

~True, said Henry. You're but a schoolmarm.

~Speak for yourself, said Jack. I am an honored scribe for a fine newspaper. Henry and Michael looked at him dubiously. All right, all right. I'm a putrid excuse for a newspaperman. Bed the bitch!

~War might be a pleasure, said Henry. We shoot poorly, get lost on hunts, despise sleeping on the ground, and enjoy the greater pleasures life has to offer. I may stand for Captain when our regiment votes.

~You'll stand guard, said Jack. At your own prison cell.

~Mama Blackshear? said Michael. They began to walk toward the cemetery again, just as Thomas Blackshear, not appearing to see them, came cantering past on Bill, crying, Alert! Alert! An old woman has gone missing!

The boys found them sitting on Mr. Cardinal's flat slab in the center of the cemetery, eating cheese and bread, dressed in mourning, skirts dirty, boots folded beneath them like girls.

~Welcome to the funeral, said Mama Blackshear as the Blackshears stumbled forth. Unfortunately, Mr. Cardinal has been killed in the war.

~Lijh said you were looking for a turkey knife, said Jack, grinning at his brothers.

~No, my Marcus has been killed in the war, said Mrs. Cardinal. Who was that who shot him?

~Napoleon! cried Mama Blackshear. Then whispering, as if confidentially: Never trust the Spanish.

~Men, said Henry thoughtfully. They come in like lions but go out like lambs.

Escorting the bereaved women home, the boys sang every song they knew, and few they made up on the spot.

JULY, 1861

The town's first company, the Branton Rifles, marched off in late April amid the splendor of a brass band, speeches, and the presentation of a colorful battle flag, and with them went the sons of firebrands, the upstanding and well-educated young men of the village who spoke intensely of a state's right to secede. Now, though, the town set about gathering another company since Howell Cobb, a politician from Athens, was forming a Legion, which combined artillery, infantry, and cavalry. This second Branton company would contain older men, some ne'er-do-wells, a few weaklings, and some considered unfit for service in the spring. Cassandra measured her sons and set about making them wool uniforms, something to be warm against the Virginia winters. Henry wanted his sleeves blistered with braid, but his father spoke against it. Thomas Blackshear, in a burst of patriotism, was now painting a huge canvas he was calling *The Entry of Jefferson Davis into Jerusalem.*

~Scandalous, said Cassandra a few nights before the new company, which had been named the Branton Avengers, was to march away. At the very least, give it a new name. You of all people, the town's single abolitionist.

~Mr. Lincoln has called for troops to fight us, said Thomas. What manner of man does not fight back when challenged?

~Mr. Percy Stillwell? offered Henry. The workday had long ended, but a wet sun still hung in the sky, refusing to go down or take the suffocating heat with it. Michael sat in a chair near King Lear examining his old smooth-bore musket with grave doubt.

~That was good, said Henry. I wonder where that fool is now.

~He moved to Athens, as I recall, said Thomas, sipping from a glass of port. More tippy-toeing to be done in a college village. Ah—forgot to tell you who will be throwing his lot in with the Avengers. Quite a surprise. I would have thought him too old for battle.

~Who's that, dear? asked Cassandra, holding up a military blouse and studying its symmetries.

~Wiseman Robinson.

~That son of a…

~Jack Blackshear! said Cassandra.

~Whore, said Thomas, finishing the sentence. Cassandra closed her eyes, shook her head. King Lear leaned forward and laughed hysterically. Well, the man is certainly an idiot. *He* shall never enter into Jerusalem. In fact I have considered another canvas called *The Temptation of Alexander Stephens by Wiseman Robinson*. Very historical. Boys, I want you to listen to my advice for soldiers. Gather 'round.

~WHAT? Mama Blackshear, rocking, had suddenly grown quite deaf in May, and she periodically shouted to see if anyone might have been addressing her. WHAT?

~Nothing, Grandmother, said Henry, touching her gently on the shoulder. She smiled and continued knitting a pair of socks on which she had been working for several weeks. The first sock was the size of a child's blanket, and the second might have fit snugly on a paw of Romeo or Juliet. Everyone told her they were grand. The Blackshear Brothers came around their father, laughing and punching each other. Henry began to whistle the Minnie Penny song.

~Now, as to battle, said Thomas Blackshear, who had never been near one, the main thing is to protect one's flanks and rear.

~I'll protect *my* rear, but I'm hanged if I will protect my *brothers'* rears, said Jack. Cassandra smiled slightly and shook her head. This had, after all, been going on for many years.

~I've studied tactics of all the great wars, said Thomas. If you see an advantage, take it with all your might, with the swiftness of youth, and the strength of your weaponry!

~What if we are about to be overrun? asked Michael.

~Then I'd run away, said Thomas. Run north or south, east or west. Run low to the ground or get behind trees. Run toward a leaving train. Run behind the horse of an officer. Shed your army coat and seem addled and keep asking, Where is that pig? Will someone tell me where is that pig? Run to a large town and hide among the crowds. Pretend to be wounded and lie beneath the dead until the enemy has gone. Wait for night and crawl away on your knees and elbows.

~That is the most ridiculous advice ever given to soldiers in history, said Cassandra.

~I will live by those words! shouted Jack.

~Me, too, said Michael.

~I'm in, agreed Henry. Let us raise a toast! The Celebrated Blackshear Boys! Cowards 'til the end!

~Cowards 'till the end! cried Michael and Jack.

~I am going to be ill, said their mother.

~WHAT? shouted Mama Blackshear.

CYNTHIA SIMS CLIMBED DOWN FROM her imperious mount, Old Brevity, and stood smiling at Jack Blackshear, tapping the riding crop into her gloved left hand. She wore a crimson riding suit and perspired freely, and Jack looked at her with regret and only slightly concealed lust. The Sims plantation, Briarpath, was only one mile north of town, and they stood at the paddock where a young black groom called Samson whispered endearments to Old Brevity and led him to a cooling.

~Samson is the size of a midget, said Jack. Why the name?

~Oh, some of Daddy's *ah-rony*, said Cynthia, fanning herself with the large straw hat she'd removed. The man will have his humor. Jack, honestly, how long do you think this war is going to last, because I am sincerely vexed that it may ruin my future plans.

~Eh? Jack had never asked for her hand, but it had been understood by the families that at some point they would be wed, and Cynthia had nearly exhausted all available euphemisms for marriage. Well, they say six months. I suppose in the worst case perhaps seven months. But I think we should say our sweet good-byes.

~I have heard in town the most vile things about you, she said, petulant.

~Me? he said, me? I had rather be dead and buried in the cold winter earth than disgrace my good name.

~I wasn't worried about *your* name, she said. I was thinking of *mine*!

~Eh—well. Trust your heart, Cynthia. What does your heart say?

~That you are a man who brings great sorrow to women.

~Oh, such calumnies! Such vexations! Tell me who has said these things, and I shall thrash them near to death!

~And that I am a woman drawn to such a man! Heaven help me! She began to look faint and slumped near him, and he held her up, and saw, across the fence, that Old Brevity was prancing at the end of Samson's leash, that a man could get rich owning such animals. He whispered vague endearments, spoke couplets.

~I am quite certain I shall die in a valiant charge, anyway, said Jack loftily. You will mourn me until your dying day.

~I shall do nothing of the sort, she said, stamping away. She whirled on him. If you get yourself killed, I shall never speak with you again! Do you understand me? I shall not be made fool of!

In the hot, late-afternoon sunlight, the sun sheared through her clothes, so that Jack could see the blurred outline of her legs, and he was aroused.

ELIZABETH CHADWICK HAD BEEN WEEPING. Her face was hung with red sashes, and she dabbed her eyes with a scented handkerchief. She kept looking dreamily at Michael Blackshear's face, staring at his sandy hair, his rich eyes.

~I have prayed to know if this is part of God's purpose, but he has not answered me, she said. Oh, Michael! If only there was no war, and you were not going away!

~A man can't be a schoolmaster all his life, Elizabeth. Perhaps this will give me some new profession. Perhaps I was meant to be in the profession of soldiering.

~Oh! But Father says lewd women follow the troops. Oh please tell me you will not consort with lewd women, Michael! Please promise. In fact, Michael hadn't even considered that the burgeoning Southern army might have its own Trollop Corps, and the idea seemed suddenly enchanting. They were sitting in a swing on the Chadwick front porch, and the family dog, a wiry, snickering fox terrier named Little Bug, lay before them, snapping at gnats. Fireflies tested their wattage against the setting sunlight.

~Never shall I do a thing to disgrace you, my dearest heart. Her huge blue eyes: red with regret and worry, mouth a trembling line, hands holding her Bible, and her finger marking the third chapter of Ecclesiastes. He leaned to her, and kissed her gently on the full lips, mouth closed as hers was, and wondered at the marvels of medicine, of balms for sores, of cures for the clap.

~YOU ARE NOT GOING, AND that is the end of it, said Susannah Yarborough icily. I have spoken on the matter. It is at an end. She and Henry Blackshear walked in the grove of trees next to Henry's home. The free twins Louisa and Rachel were a hundred yards away, tormenting Romeo and Juliet with a pork bone. The sky west was purple as a bruise and tickled itself with lightning.

~I have to go, and you know it, said Henry. He could not remember how he had come to love Susannah, but the idea horrified Cassandra, who thought the eldest Yarborough daughter a loud harpy and no match for sweet Henry Blackshear. To the west, Henry could see Martin Goodpath arguing with his weeping wife. A thrill of worry ran down Henry's chest.

~You are not listening to me, said Susannah, squaring herself to him. I have spoken. I forbid it, and that's the end of it.

~Most women feel betrayed if their men do not march off to war, said Henry. Romeo was starting to growl at the girls. They didn't seem to mind, kept taunting him with the pork bone.

~Most women are not as intelligent as I am, said Susannah. Pride seemed frozen to her like frosting on a cake. I know you, Henry. You will go to the aid of some hurt soldier and get yourself shot, and I will be left alone to mourn you. I'll turn into something like Mrs. Cardinal, and I will not have it. I wish to dance. I wish to be escorted to finer parties. I wish to—isn't that your grandmother?

Henry put his hand over his eyes to cut the glare.

~My God, he said. You have to come help me. She has King Lear. And she's heading for the barn. Henry was walking quickly, disbelieving, Susannah close behind, shouting for him to stop. Romeo ran back and forth, howling and panting. The dogs stopped and turned to look at the sky: then, thunder.

THREE DAYS BEFORE THEY WERE to leave: Jack Blackshear lying in the arms of Minnie Penny, with motes hanging in a slash of hot sun that nudged through the half-cracked blinds. She was laughing raucously since they had both just farted with amazing simultaneity.

~All my business is marching off to war, she said. Jack wore only his elegant cap, dove-gray. A small black cigar drooped from his lower lip. He saluted her.

~May all your customers come home safely. You know, my brother wrote a song about you. Perhaps we shall sing it at the frolic in Rutledge Hall tomorrow night?

~A song about me? How charming! Am I naked in the song?

~My darling, you are naked to *every* man in Branton! How else could we bear a world of daily drudgery and potential wives?

All week, the Celebrated Blackshear Boys has been preparing for their final performance in town and packing for war. Jack surprised his brothers with a thick sheaf of stationery so they could write home of their adventures. Henry had practiced shooting into a bank near the railroad tracks, and for four days running he failed to pop a single spent bottle with repeated volleys. They had gone riotously swimming in the Branton River, swollen from several days of heavy rain, accompanied by their friends Lyle and Whitman Fogg, brothers eighteen months apart. Lyle had finished his studies at Mercer and was reading for the law, but Whitman, the younger, had managed through dissipation and bad luck to be no more than a blacksmith's apprentice. Lyle was certain he would be elected captain of the Avengers, while Whitman said his goal was to be cannon-fodder for the glorious cause.

~Cannon-fodder? said Michael. They lay on the sandy shore of the river in moonlight, smoking excellent cigars. Whitman had always been marked with incipient madness, the first to take a dare, the last to opt out. You mean slain, as it were, in a glorious charge?

~No. I wish to be standing in the lines, a hand casually on one hip, and then be blown into four equal parts. Then each part can chose its own country, north, south, east, or west.

~They also serve who only stand and wail, declaimed Henry.

~He's a fool, said Whitman's brother Lyle. I say we pack him full of gunpowder, stick a fuse up his ass, and roll him into the Federal lines. He'll be covered with glory.

~And the Federals will be covered, said Jack grandly, with Whitman.

~Now, Jack was dressing slowly, and Minnie Penny watched him with deep regret and pleasure.

~You'll make an excellent husband, she said, sighing. The best husbands are those who can lie as smoothly as milk poured from a jug. It must be great training for wars, this habit of lying.

~Hmmmm?

She sat up, fleshy and worn, though always willing for two dollars. She had genuinely liked Jack, however, since he'd first stumbled into her lodgings several years before. Her eyes once glowed with green fire, but now they'd gone dull, worn out from days of passionless coupling. A decade before, she'd been married in Philadelphia to a banker, it was told, but he'd been shot by another man, and Minnie, heading south by rail toward Mobile, made it as far as Branton when her money ran out. Finding a willing number of men with money, she stayed, and now the sheriff ignored the occasional rumblings from the pious.

~Men lie to get us into wars and then lie more to keep them going, she said. She stood and threw on a light gown that did little to hide her elegant body. Just as men lie to women and to each other. All life is built upon our ability to lie and then conceal it.

~Minnie Shakespeare, exit stage left.

~I'm serious, Jack. Have you considered where this all will lead? Has anyone considered it? You think there's going to be a three-month war and that in the end you will have your Confederacy. You men think that some principle is involved, a way of life or the right to be let alone. But you're all lying. Every one.

~I love you, said Jack, adjusting his trousers.

~Another lie, said Minnie Penny with a faint smile.

THE CROWD HAD BEEN RAUCOUS for half an hour already. Old Noah Bernstein, the Jewish clothing merchant, pounded the floor with the butt-end of his cane. Noah's son, David, had enrolled in the

Avengers. Henry and David had been friends since boyhood, fishing the Branton River and playing music together. David was also a hearty mimic, and his bullfrog imitation of Wiseman Robinson always left Henry howling. Most of the men puffed cigars, slouched locomotives going nowhere. The din was tremendous, and behind the broad blankets, the Celebrated Blackshear Boys were tuning their instruments and sipping whiskey.

~The Robinson shit is *out*, said Jack sagely. He could wind up being an officer.

~Hah, said Michael. I was just remembering the time we told Mr. Percy Stillwell that there was a mad dog in the street and blew up that firecracker in his dance studio. That was a good one.

~One of many, sir! said Michael. Remember the time we started playing Spat in front of Sag Doremus? Rich.

~Hee. The blithering idiot, said Jack.

Mr. Sagacity Doremus was a fop who lived well off inherited wealth, strolling around town with a dandy cane and immaculate clothing tailored just-so for his slender stride. Once he had graced the Mercantile with his presence, and the boys, who had been playing poker, shifted seamlessly into one of their invented card games, whose rules were improvised on the spot, unfolding in a series of increasingly bizarre shouts and counterclaims.

~Fig, said Henry. Nine X.

~Pock me up a trump, countered Michael.

~Spat! shouted Jack, and his brothers with great disgust threw their cards on the barrel head. Sag touched his lips three times lightly with the tips of his fingers.

~I say, what game is that you boys are playing? His manners were so refined that he carried a scented handkerchief against the possibility some unmannered horse might plop nearby.

~Oh, just an idle game of Spat, said Jack. Shall I deal you in?

~Spat? Spat? said Sag. Never heard of it, I don't believe.

~Everybody in Europe is playing it, said Michael. Their father had gone to Athens that Saturday, and the store was out of customers. May I deal you in?

~Well, I daresay so, but I do not know the rules!

~We'll show you as we go along, said Henry. Costs a dollar to play.

~Well, I can ante that much, said Sag, removing a nicely folded bill from his purse. Jack shuffled the cards to Sag and his brothers, who held their solemnity like a royal flush. He dealt them each six cards and them put the deck in the middle of the barrel.

~Haha! cried Henry. A two, a four, and a nine! He threw the cards down

~That's a pig in a poke, said Michael. Everyone has to pay Henry five dollars.

~Five dollars? cried Sag, beginning to sweat. A pig in a poke?

~Wait! I have… *this*! said Jack. He triumphantly threw down the seven of diamonds.

~Damn my eyes! cried Henry. He has the Queen of Belgium. Now we all have to pay *Jack* five dollars!

~Queen of Belgium? said Sagacity. Then what is Spat? How does one get to claim Spat? And what happens at that point?

~Let me see your cards, said Michael, reaching over to pull down Sag's hand. Umph. Sag, bad news. You have a Wilted Flagstaff.

~No question, said Jack.

~Limp as a strip of silk, said Henry.

~Spat! all three brothers shouted. Sag jumped back, scraping his chair legs and looking at them with suspicion.

~You mock me!

~Queen Victoria *herself* plays Spat, sir, said Michael, offended. Of course, everyone loses to her on purpose.

The boys finished tuning their instruments. The crowd at Rutledge Hall was getting surly, crying for Southern tunes.

~We took that idiot for eleven dollars, said Henry. Hee. Well, boys, I guess it's about time for the final performance from a truly inebriated group of young men. What?

~What? said Jack.

~What? said Michael. They dropped their smoldering cigar stubs in a bucket of water, stood and straightened themselves. Jack raised one eyebrow and pushed the blanket aside and came out to shouts and laughter.

~Sing "Dixie's Land!" screamed someone. Let us hear "The Bonnie Blue Flag," boys!

~You men seem a little anxious, said Jack, unable to stop from smiling.

~Give us the works! cried a tall, long-necked man improbably named Barney Barrister.

~And now…presenting…in their final evening of, how shall I say it—unsurpassed foolishness? Their final songs, their final skits, before going gloriously to serve their country? Gentlemen? Ladies? (*A great deal of hissing and laughter.*) For your entertainment, The Celebrated Blackshear Boys!

Michael and Henry erupted from behind the curtain, and soon they were heading downhill into "Parker's Reel," playing the verse first at a medium tempo, then faster on each pass around. The men stood and stomped, whistled, shouted, clapped along, sweating profusely, frothy with delight. The boys felt it: never this smooth, this accomplished before, never this complete solidity of rhythm and line. Jack led them faster and faster. On the fifth variation, Henry, fiddling mightily, launched himself into a limber-legged dance, and the men were wild for it. Finally, a slowing coda and an ending, rapturous turn at locomotive speed, ending with the bang of a G major chord. Deafening applause.

~Now, now, now! said Jack, holding up his arms. The men sat down, ready to be entertained. We are this evening gathered in the sight of all men for a wedding! Henry and Michael had gone behind the blanket, and they came out to laughter, Michael in an over-large black morning coat and Henry wearing a faded blue bonnet. Yes, my friends, we are here for a wedding, and they *must* be wed…for reasons that I am sure you know.

~We know, all right! shouted Lyle Fogg. Was she wonderful, Michael?

~Come forward, and let us now join in matrimony (*pretending to fumble with paper here, looking at names*) you, Abraham Lincoln to you, Miss United States of America. (*Boos and laughter.*) Am I right in assuming, Mr. Lincoln, that you have gotten Miss U. S. in trouble?

~Apparently I have, sir, said Michael.

~Miss U. S., what do you have to say about this?

~It was as if he split me half in two, said Henry coyly. By now, Rutledge Hall had fallen into a fine uproar. As if where I was one girl, now I was two.

~This is no basis for a proper marriage! cried Henry.

~Oh, that's your misunderstanding, said Michael. I'm here for a divorce.

~A divorce? (*Looking around salaciously at the audience*) From all of her?

~Well, I can't decide if I want to divorce all of her or just the south of her. Should I keep her North (*gesturing*) or her South? (*Lots of whistling and jeering, men mostly screaming* Keep her South! *A few scream* North *with impunity.*)

~It is entirely up to you which part you keep and which part you divorce, said Jack.

~Well I suppose I should keep the North, but there are days, also, when the South appeals to me, said Michael/Abe.

~But your honor, said Miss U. S., hands tented beneath her chin. He's so *ugly*. That's the main reason why we are getting a divorce.

~So there's no other man for you? asked Judge Jack sternly.

~Weellllllll…

~I knew it! cried Abe in a high-pitched voice, slapping his knee. I'm about vexed enough to split me some rails! Who is this other man?

~Do I have to say it out loud, your honor? said bonneted Henry.

~You do, Miss U. S. Who is this other man.

~Well, the problem is that part of me wants Mr. Lincoln here (*boos and laughter*) and part of me wants Mr. Jefferson Davis. At this point, the room exploded into clapping, with cheers and huzzahs lasting for nearly a minute, and Jack grinned at his brothers as if to say, I told you *that* would work. Finally, the whooping subsided, and the men shushed each other and leaned forward for the rest of the skit.

~Which part of you wants Mr. Lincoln here and which part wants this Mr. Davis? asked Jack incredulously.

~My northern part (*holding her head daintily here*) wants Mr. Lincoln but my southern part (*hands on hips and swishing seductively*) says give me Jeff Davis! The room erupted again, but this time a gunshot went off, and smoke suddenly erupted, men diving for cover, and three

men wrestled down the dull-witted Will Partain, who had been refused
by the Branton Rifles when they marched out in April. Someone kicked
Will's pistol away, but then his brother, Arnold, leaped on those grabbing
Will, and the room suddenly blossomed with fists and wrestling. Mr.
Rutledge screamed and wrung his hands, but his voice was inaudible in
the din. Sheriff Reed and five deputies appeared suddenly, warning men
outside with aimed shotguns, and the room began to drain like a tub
except for the fight between the Partains and four or five others. The
Blackshear Boys sat near the front smoking calmly, grinning and
counting their take.

~You can take the bonnet off, Henry, said Jack.

~I think he's cute with it, said Michael.

~What did you boys say? asked Sheriff Reed. He was a heavy-gutted
man with kind eyes.

~We are just poor humble entertainers, said Jack. I have no idea
why everyone is so wild at the moment. Reed sighed and looked at the
overturned chairs, the spilled bottles, the crushed-out smokes.

~It's this damn war, he said. Then he was gone, and the Blackshear
brothers gathered their instruments and headed for the buggy.

~We didn't even get to sing the Minnie Penny song, said Henry
sadly.

~We can do that one when the war is over, said Jack. If anyone is
still laughing by then.

THE BRANTON AVENGERS STOOD STIFFLY in ranks in the front
yard of the Female Academy on south Main Street, a motley lot that
drew half the crowd that the Branton Rifles had four months before.
Elizabeth Chadwick had been weeping, and stood beneath a vast oak,
eyes red-rimmed, occasionally flapping her crumpled handkerchief in
Michael's direction. Martin Goodpath stood sternly in his uniform,
glaring with pleasurable malice at Jack. The Fogg brothers argued over a
pistol, Lyle trying to snatch it from Whitman.

The sun broiled them, fanning women, old men bent up on dandy
canes, fat matrons, and a group of hatless slaves who stood in the back,
mumbling conspiracies. Pacing himself with a heavy-gutted strut was
Wiseman Robinson, self-appointed organizer, who had apparently

thought the Branton Rifles would draft him as their captain then waited helplessly as they left for Richmond three months before. Already the first battle of the war had occurred near a small town in Virginia called Manassas, and the Federal troops had fled combat, running away back toward Washington, congressmen and spectator ladies in the mob. The war would end before the Branton Avengers even got to North Carolina.

~This is the most wretched outfit I've seen in my life, whispered Michael. Half the men here are more fit for farting than firing. Jack emitted a hearty and appropriate reply.

~Sir, I congratulate you on such astuteness, he said.

~He's right, said Michael, scanning the men, who were being loosely herded into lines by Wiseman Robinson, looking ridiculous in his soft gray and braid, his cavalry hat adorned with a bull's-eye peacock feather. If we lead the Confederacy into battle, we may be defeated by Rhode Island alone.

~Why don't you suggest to General Robinson that we just go attack Rhode Island so it would be a fair fight? asked Henry. There's Cynthia Sims. She hit me with a broom last night and said that if I were not at least severely wounded she would not take me back. She would much prefer a mortal wound. I told her I would do my best to be killed, but that if I only had the trots, her name would be upon my lips. She took it poorly.

~Better than Susannah, said Jack, yawning. She made me hold my hand over my heart and promise that no drop of spirits would pass my lips as long as I am in the army, that I will neither gamble nor consort with low women. That I will not use profane language and that I will go each Sunday to whatever services are available, unless it be Presbyterian.

~What a bitch, said Michael. Did you bring the cards?

~I have three packs in my haversack along with the flasks, brim-filled. Minnie Penny has also given me a scented handkerchief for us to bear into battle as well.

~Charlotte Harlot, we hail thee, said Henry.

Now they were scattering into line, Wiseman Robinson bellowing for a formation none quite knew how to arrange, and his face grew red, jowls crimson, as he pointed at places, dragged men by their elbows. Ninety-two men in all, the Avengers finally fell in, and Miss Sincerity

Remington, daughter of the Female Academy's president, Louis, stepped lively before them and unfurled a flag, which was deep blue, with two bright yellow stars in the center next to a thickening crescent moon.

~Is that a banana? whispered Michael, squinting.

~Men of Branton, you brave Avengers! cried Sincerity, who was seventeen but looked about eleven, reed-slender, with unfortunate features squashed in the center of her face. We are here today to see you off toward battle, to defend our bold Southern Confederacy! We have chosen freedom—freedom from the vile godless creatures from the North! Freedom from those who would tell us to live our lives by their standards and not ours. And this president, this man Lincoln—no parlor in Branton would admit him! We would sooner admit an ape!

~I'd rather have Lincoln, whispered Henry. At least he wouldn't crap in the piano. Michael held on to his giggles like a man trying desperately to keep from falling from a bridge.

~Besides, said Jack with grave quiet dignity, are we not descended from apes?

~Thus Mr. Lincoln be my brother, said Henry.

~Lucky Lincoln, said Michael. Should we make him an honorary Blackshear Boy?

They realized that Sincerity had halted her presentation and was staring openly at them. Jack thrust his back to strict attention and looked at her with superior approval.

~And so, men of Branton, you brave Avengers, I give you this flag to carry into battle. Long may she wave! The Branton Brass broke into a spirited version of "Dixie's Land." Cassandra Blackshear stood with Thomas at the edge of the crowd and looked doubtfully at the men, while Susan Goodpath smiled beautifully at the words of a young man just beneath the age of service. Mama Blackshear and Mrs. Marcus Cardinal sat on a bench fanning themselves, slack and witless. Joshua and Mary Faircloth held the twins tightly, but they struggled. Slaveless country men glared at them. Jim Cedarman and his wife stood alongside Thomas. The boys' Uncle Lawrence picked his teeth and leaned against a far oak.

~I accept this flag in the name of the soon-to-be famous Branton Avengers! cried Wiseman Robinson, stentorian, chest outthrust in a patriarchal pose. Patters of applause. We shall now march forward into battle and serve as no regiment has yet before! When there is the flash of raw steel, we shall be first in the lines! When the cannon blaze, we shall charge the enemy, showing no concern for our safety but only love of country! When we face thousands of those other troops, and they are massed with muskets to shoot us down, we shall still do our duty!

One Avenger, a Waterman, fled. A few laughed and then stopped. Others in the ranks looked stricken, shuffled their feet, thinking. Jack looked at his brothers and raised one emotive eyebrow. Michael and Henry grinned. The blow came from the rear, and Henry went flying down on the parade ground, just able to break his fall, palms up.

~The hell…

~Oh damn, said Michael. Romeo! Suddenly, Juliet was with him, and the dogs licked Henry's face, wet red ribbons lapping out their love.

~O help! cried Henry Blackshear. I am slain!

No one but his brothers found it amusing, and they found it, quite possibly, the funniest thing in years.

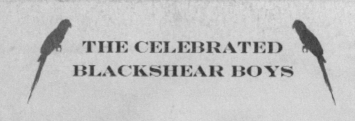

THE CELEBRATED
BLACKSHEAR BOYS

Sept. 21st, 1861
Camp Washingon, Va.

Dearest family,

We have arrived safely at this place two miles
south of Yorktown, not far from the place where
Cornwallis surrendered to Old George. In honor of
that event, your eldest son Jack has already
surrendered to various nefarious habits, but so far we
have kept him from disgracing himself in front of the
men.

To say we are vexed that Wiseman Robinson has
been elected captain is to understate matters. Mr.
Goodpath is our lieutenant, and he seems entirely
changed from the good-tempered man of yore. Most
incredibly, do you know who is Col. Cobb's adjutant?
None other than Mr. Percy Stillwell, erstwhile dance
master of Branton! He saw us during parade this
afternoon and came by to inform us that the Avengers
were the sorriest group of soldiers since Marathon
and that he planned proper training for us. Pig.

During our stop in Richmond, we managed to eat
at a fine restaurant, and Jack performed his
pickpocket act to laughter and astonishment until he
lifted the watch of an uncoated brigadier general and
was almost court-martialed. Only when we showed
him our fancy stationery did he relent, though he
gave us a dressing down. You have never in your life
seen so many soldiers milling about as we saw in
Richmond. And oh, the vice, father! You cannot
imagine the scope of gambling. I enclose five dollars.

*We are quartered here near Madison's Panola
Guards, a disciplined outfit that polishes its buckles
and boots with relish, thereby gaining advantages
already. They are in all a brave but prissy lot, and I
continue to believe that as rogues the Avengers are
better suited either to advance or retreat. Let me
describe the country. It is very hot here, and this is a
flat tidal land full of creeks and rivers. The York
River, which we glimpsed, is the width of an ocean
itself. Yorktown is fortified so much that assault upon
it must come from artillery or eagles. Federal troops
are but a few miles from us at Fort Monroe and
around it, and we have heard that there is to be a
great battle soon, but no one believes it. The air tastes
of salt and is very wet. Many of the residents of this
area have fled. There is not a tree in this
encampment, and a stiff wind blows from the River.
During battalion drill this morning, Sag Doremus
collapsed from the heat and lay where he fell for an
hour before we were permitted to aid him. He is
recovering this evening, blistered and foul-tempered.
We can see the cannon along the York River.*

*This evening we had beef, sweet potatoes, and
biscuits for supper. Many of the boys have brandy
flasks, and soon we felt convivial. We are planning a
game of Spat soon but must be careful not to get shot,
&c.*

*Mother, there is a great amount of illness here,
from measles to typhoid. David Bernstein is in our
hospital tent with the mumps, and his face looks
mule-kicked, jaw-heavy. But he is dressed very
nicely. One Irving Banks from the town of
Greensborough told Barney he was elegant as a lady's*

fan and then expired from pneumonia. (Banks, not Bernstein.) We have been well, however, and as we came to the place from Richmond by rail car, we have not had the chance yet to get footsore.

Jack says to tell Cynthia Sims that she is prettier than several of the women we saw in Richmond. Tell Mama Blackshear that the cannons hereabouts are called Parrott guns—that should give her a good laugh.

Well, Spat awaits us. More soon.

Your son,
Henry Blackshear

YORK RIVER PENINSULA, FALL-WINTER, 1861

You, sir! What in heaven's name were you thinking? Give me one good reason why I should not have you flogged!

It was September 23, and the troops awaited an inspection visit from General John Magruder, widely called The Prince for his dashing dress and love of amateur theatricals. Storm clouds huddled for an assault down the ragged Peninsula that stuck like a thumb southeast to the sea between Virginia's York and James Rivers. That day, the Blackshear brothers had been detailed to Yorktown to work on defenses, heaving cannon into gun-mounts, working until exhaustion, and now they were in no mood for such frivolities as late-day dress inspections. Through telescopes you could see the stars and stripes flying on Union ships in the river.

~Lieutenant Goodpath, what have I done now? asked Private Jack Blackshear. His eyes gleamed, and it threw Goodpath into a frenzy of rage.

~Your tunic is soiled! said the good lieutenant. And General Magruder due any moment! Do you wish him to think we are ill-fit? You look as if you have fallen from a horse.

~Fallen from a whore? asked Jack, cupping his ear. Michael dragged him back by the elbow.

~We will make sure he is presentable as we fall in, sir, said Michael.

~You'd better or I'll lash him. I swear before God that I will strip him to the waist before the men and lash him! The Avengers shall not be made fools of. Flogged, do you understand?

~Flagged, yes sire, said Jack, saluting.

~Bah! shouted Lieutenant Goodpath, turning away.

~I'll bet you five dollars you will be flogged before our first battle, said Michael.

~You don't *have* five dollars, said Jack. I stole it from your haversack. I was going to replace it when I found some fool to gamble with me. Poker?

LATE THAT AFTERNOON, SEPTEMBER 23, General John Bankhead Magruder, slightly tipsy and joyously theatrical, rode down with his cohort to Cobb's Legion, which was bedecked and standing in ranks watching the sky blacken. Magruder wore his brigadier general's stars like trophies of a fine hunt, laid out dead on his shoulders. Word had filtered from Richmond that soon he would be a major general, which suited Magruder quite well, thank you. You could always tell when General Magruder was riding past, for his aides held aloft more flags and guidons than one could find in the staging of a Shakespeare history. The fine general had supervised the South's first land-battle victory on June 10 near Big Bethel Church on the Peninsula, raising huzzahs from Richmond to New Orleans. He was a handsome man with side-whiskers, a black mustache whose tips he waxed upward, and a steady, confident gaze. He drank too much. He rarely saw his wife, Henrietta, or their children, and he did not seem, particularly, to mind. Now in charge of the Confederate defenses between the York and James rivers, he was clearly having a wonderful time.

~Best be done with this soon, sir, said a major. Look at that sky.

~Marvelous! cried Magruder. Oh blow you hurricanoes!

~Sir?

Down the ranks, the Branton Avengers tried, with the awkwardness of a new colt, to pull themselves to attention, but many of the men had just returned from a detail in Yorktown, and others were sick from bad liquor and late-night revels. Captain Robinson had gone from tent to tent that day, raging about the disorder, saying that he would not, by the holy rood of Christ, let the Avengers be the laughing stock of Cobb's Legion, but as the day passed, and messmates lay sprawled across the hot earth, some puking with amazing virtuosity, Robinson and Goodpath had taken to cleaning up certain streets of the campsite by themselves, shouting and threatening their privates with each miserable step.

The Blackshears had spent much of the day with James Peter, the Avengers' bandmaster, who had inherited seven dented brass instruments from a band in town and was now recruiting players. This Peter, who took much abuse for his name, was a soft, willowy young man with wrists like boiled leather straps and an unfortunate lazy eye that, on occasion, seemed to wander off in search of something unseen. Peter had been such a menace at rifle practice that his appointment as bandmaster had come as a relief to the all the men. He parceled out a euphonium to Jack and trumpets to Michael and Henry.

~How hard could this be? asked Jack, making a rude sound through the euphonium, turning heads, provoking merriment.

~Awful! Awful! Awful! cried Peter. Stop it, Jack! All in good time. Goodpath had come past, taken one look, and grinned maliciously.

~Did I insult Lieutenant Goodpath? asked James Peter.

~He's been a tetch bilious since Richmond, said Jack.

Magruder pulled his horse to a gallant stop in front of the Panola Guards from Madison and climbed down, bowing, tickling the ground with the feather in his hat. Thunder crawled around somewhere just west of them, but the Panolas stood like toy soldiers, downdrafts billowing their coat hems. Just past them two men from the Avengers were holding up a comrade who was still *hors de combat* from his liquor wounds.

~Men of Cobb's Legion! cried General Magruder. I salute you. And this Panola Guard from the grand town of (*turning to an aide here for a whisper into his ear*) Madison, Georgia, salutations! One of the finest grounds I have ever seen. I see you well turned out, men of pride and courage, ready to meet the enemy here in our own country! In this Virginia! (*Careful to make four clean syllables of the word.*)

~Look at that idiot, whispered Whitman Fogg, scratching his ass with a loaded derringer. He thinks he's Napoleon Bonafarte.

~Hsst! You in the ranks! cried Captain Robinson, craning to see the offender. Hsst!

~A serpent, said Henry blithely. We are slain.

~Hsst!

General Magruder paid no attention to the gathering storm, which now whipped tent flys and tumbled loose paper across the parade ground. A hat from one of the Panola Guards flipped upward, fluttered twice, then blew off east as if being pulled by an over-whipped buggy horse. He checked button lines, bowed before those with gleaming brass fittings, admired highly polished shoes with courtesy and élan. His aides eyed the sky with clear alarm among considerable throat-clearing. A flash erupted, like fire from a photographer's wand.

~Sirs, I congratulate you! Cobb's Legion certainly lives up to its glorious reputation! I say to you, well done! Well done! Magruder dipped again with his stagecraft bow, then remounted and rode the fifty yards to the Branton Avengers. He dismounted, and his face immediately went slack with clear shock, nettled.

~My God, said the general, what has happened here?

~Permission to puke? asked Private Solomon Martin.

~Damn you, said Captain Wiseman Robinson, sotto voce, through clenched teeth.

~Eh? said Magruder.

~Bleaggghhhhhhh—Private Martin vomited, then emitted a deep gurgling *earl*, and men broke ranks, moved away, swore at him.

~My God—did we not just see your fine comrades in the Branton Rifles? Magruder's aide rushed to confirm it. A few pelty raindrops pocked the dusty parade ground. A thick smell of fecund salt marshes and sea washed over them, and a few heaved from it. Jack Blackshear tuned his head to his brothers, exhibiting expertly crossed eyes. Henry fell into a giggling fit, stifled it.

~You there! cried Magruder, striding down the line angrily. Can you tell me what is so amusing? Will you share with us the cause of your inappropriate mirth?

~Sir, I apologize, said Henry, still giggling. I was still pleased from winning the largest hand of Eunuch in history last night.

~Euchre? Say what?

~No, general, *Eunuch*. It's a different game altogether. Somewhat closely allied to Spat. The loser, sir, is said to have no balls. As it were.

~My God, said Captain Robinson, rolling his eyes and wiping the sweat from his face.

~Ah ha, said General Magruder.

~Sir, the *sky*, said Magruder's aide. Rain fell much more heavily now, and Magruder's feather had begun to droop. The general looked at

Robinson with sickly confusion and then walked rapidly back to the head of the company.

~This is, quite possibly, the worst turned-out group of volunteers in the entire Confederacy, he said, almost perplexed. Then, angling away: For heaven's sake don't let the Federals see you, lest they be tempted to attack.

~When General Magruder and his cohort were gone, Captain Robinson turned violently on his men and said:

~Guard duty, everyone! And trench-works! I'll show you life with a spade!

~Permission to puke? begged, once again, the heaving Private Martin.

THE STORM BROKE VIOLENTLY AROUND them, and the Blackshear brothers huddled inside their double-tent in India rubber overcoats and leggings, listening to the crack and tremble of it all. Water puddled, swept beneath the tent wall, a small stream passing through. Jack Blackshear looked around at their messmates: the Fogg brothers, Sag Doremus, David Bernstein, and a cadaverous man named Raleigh Poole, nearing forty and certain that he would soon die in battle.

~What battle? asked David. Rain pelted the tent roof, wind lifted the flaps with rapid genuflections. It's almost October, and soon we will be in winter camps. The Yankees aren't going to attack us until spring. We will spend the next six months drilling and digging holes. May the heavens bless our new country, amen.

~I'm a dead man is all, said Raleigh. You could see his skull easily beneath the thin, taut and slightly yellowed skin of his face—a strange apparition. Henry lit a lantern against the coming darkness. I'm a dead man, dead and buried.

~No wonder you stink, said Michael.

~A song, boys, said Jack. Let's call it "The Dead Man Who Died for Me."

~Wait, said Henry. I have it: "The Corpse Who Loved Miss Aura Lee."

~"I May Be Dead, but I Can Still Hump Your Wife," said Michael. Doesn't scan very well, though.

~No, it needs to be iambic pentameter, said Jack.

~Permission to break your nose, said Lyle Fogg.

~I have an idea for an amusing joke, said Michael.

~Send all my belongings back to my Ma, said Raleigh.

~You don't have any belongings, said David.

~And your ma is dead, added Henry.

~Oh, not that! moaned Raleigh Poole.

Michael's joke, hatched during the height of the storm, had to do with Captain Robinson's toothbrush. The hefty captain could be seen most mornings shaking tooth power on his bristle brush and then vigorously scrubbing his teeth as if scraping green from a moldy fence. He would then sip water, spit and smack, run his finger along his teeth. Just after that, he'd light the first of perhaps twenty daily cigars, leaving the color of dusty moonlight on his prominent incisors. Wiseman's toothbrush was ivory handled, carved like the figurehead of a ship, expensive, and often mocked.

~Where's the captain? a private might ask.

~Over by his tent with that woman in his mouth, another would answer by rote.

~Your amusing joke being what? asked Jack.

~You know that sow that Lieutenant Goodpath is fattening? I say we get Captain Robinson's toothbrush and stick it up the pig's...

~I agree, said Henry Blackshear. But what if she squeals?

~Then she will have done more than Mrs. Robinson has done in the past decade, said Jack.

~In this rain? asked Lyle Fogg.

~As soon as the sun returns, we will be digging fortifications until our hands are bleeding, said Jack. Unless the Yankees see us and attack. They're in for a great surprise if they attack me.

~You will defeat them alone? asked David Bernstein.

~I will stage a reverse attack and reconnoiter from somewhere nearer Richmond, said Jack. Now, it seems to be that the storm is abating. In fact, the storm was at its most violent yet, blowing tents up and off their pegs, ballooning them across the campground, and lightning attacked them, a full-frontal assault.

~Hah, amusing. You idiot, said Whitman Fogg.

~A fake wound. Attack on the right flank. Come out of the tent, Captain! Oh, I am mortally injured! This was Michael.

~Agreed, said Jack.

~What in the hell are you talking about? inquired Sag Doremus.

~Perfectly clear? asked Jack.

~Perfectly, said Henry and Michael.

THE BLACKSHEAR BROTHERS CREPT ALONE through the storm, other Avengers huddled inside and holding their tents against the rough winds of late September. Rain slapped at them like soaking blankets from a clothesline. They moved from flash to flash, drenched as if river-dipped; the entire contents of the York River seemed to have risen over the Peninsula, now falling, a growling creature, fanged and feral. The brothers saw a broad bolt strike the river to their north with a viscous crack. Henry sang to raise their spirits.

> *Some men pay with pennies,*
> *Some men pay with hams.*
> *But all go in like lions*
> *And then come out like lambs.*

~Oh that Minnie Penny were here! cried Jack.

~She would be the richest lass in Virginia, said Michael. Henry, are you ready for our performance?

~Indeed I am, sir! he shouted. They reached Captain Robinson's tent, twice the size of the standard shelter, and he lived alone, luxuriating in the space, sleeping placidly on his camp cot. Jack dashed to the back while Henry and Michael came to the front flap.

~The enemy, sir! The enemy! cried Michael. I believe my brother is slain!

~Eh? Eh? cried Wiseman Robinson. He came stumbling into the rain holding aloft a lady's parasol, which dripped with rain and elegant fringe. Henry, hanging with mock wounds on his brother's shoulder, began to shake with soundless laughter.

~Ah, a fine accoutrement, as it were, said Michael, nodding at the black umbrella. As I said, I believe we are under attack, and my brother has been wounded in the fray.

~I thought it was in the shoulder, muttered Henry. Michael squeezed him hard and looked with alarm over his shoulder. The storm was more violent than ever, and a tent came wet-flapping past, five men chasing it with rococo curses. At the rear of Captain Robinson's double-tent, Jack came up from underneath like a gopher, dripping and looking for Wiseman's toiletries—there, on his field desk, arrayed with feminine precision. He dashed for the toothbrush, grabbed it. Through the open flap, Henry and Michael could see their older brother do a flailing victory dance and then disappear once more down and then out.

~Wounded where? asked Captain Robinson. Flank? On our flank? He looked into the storm with grave disgust. Have you been drinking? Aye God, I'll have you digging a trench from here to Petersburg.

~Were you *not* wounded? asked Michael. He pushed Henry away and looked him up and down. My God! It was but the thunder!

~I believe I must have been lightning-struck, but I'm less a-tingle now, shouted Henry against the thunder. God is good, sir!

~Bah, said Captain Robinson, disappearing back inside.

LIEUTENANT MARTIN GOODPATH SAT IN his tent, weeping bitter tears over his letter to Susan. He wrote:

...not believe that you would be so casual with your marriage vows, but I am told by men of considerable reputation that you have allowed into your chambers a salesman, a minister from Athens, two drummers, a traveling professor of philosophy, and our most vile neighbor Jack Blackshear. Please, dearest, tell me that this is but degraded town talk and I will believe you. I trust and believe that you have never lied to me and that—

~Perpetua? he said. Is that you?

He listened for his pig, which sat outside, staked in the rain. She had grunted at times during the thunderous crashes, but this time it sounded like a sudden squeal, as if she had been stabbed once and then left alone. Already, he had sold shares in the pig, which he aimed to slaughter at Christmas, and he'd sent home the money to his darling

Susan, but it had all been stolen in transit, somewhere in North Carolina.

~No? Then it must be the sorrow of my own heart that speaks! Oh my dear bride, please tell me that in you I see honor and restraint and modesty of manners and approach to this life. For it is this cherished ideal for which we are staking our lives and our souls in this our new Southern Confederacy!

Listening outside, watching the pig stand with an ivory-handled toothbrush protruding from its posterior, Jack Blackshear pounded his knee with laughter, sneezed, and was led away by his brothers, each of whom believed, quite honestly, that he was most intoxicated Blackshear on the field.

BLEARY, LYING IN MUD AND feeling as if mold grew along their tongues. A steaming sun rising from the Atlantic Ocean, heaving wetness across the Peninsula. Jack pushed himself up from the muck on to one elbow and felt his head, large as Georgia, swell, threaten to explode, throb.

~Has the war ended? he asked.

~Or started? asked Henry, who was sitting in a puddle and did not seem to mind.

~Oh God, come see this! cried someone from outside. Jack grinned at his brothers, and they stood, dripping, and staggered into the sun, which bled heat over them. Not a mile east, blue lines of Federals were up by their cook fires, in no hurry to do anything. Perhaps thirty Avengers were standing around Perpetua, who had broken from her stake and walked, stately, through the camp dragging her rope, war souvenir extruding proudly from her nether parts.

~Oh my God, it's Captain Robinson's *toothbrush*, said a private named Hayes. As if signaled to react, the pig seemed to realize at once that the offending bristles were pressing into tender flesh and yelped around three times, trying to salve the sting. A gangling youth named Pinson fell into the mud laughing, sounding like *gnaw, gnaw, gnaw*.

~Look out! Look out! Mad pig! cried Sag Doremus. Perhaps we should eat her to calm her pain!

~Not me, said David Bernstein, yawning. Jews don't eat pork.

~You can brush your teeth, then, said Henry. The others were tilting with mad laughter when Captain Robinson and Lieutenant Goodpath appeared before them, glowering, looking down at Perpetua with grave malice.

~Sirs, beg to report discovery of your missing pig and missing toothbrush, said Michael Blackshear, saluting. Will there be any reward attached to said discovery?

THE BLACKSHEAR BROTHERS RECEIVED SIXTEEN straight hours of guard duty in Yorktown and three days of digging works near the Warwick River as punishment, but the Captain did not report it to his superior, Col. Thomas R. R. Cobb of Athens, since the Avengers were already in bad odor with the Legion's officers. Two corporals from Branton's other unit, the Rifles, came over in the morning to offer beatings to the offending Avengers, but Lieutenant Goodpath demurred, having rescued his pig. Captain Robinson, after having removed his toothbrush, threw it in his campfire, where it blackened but would not be consumed, to his outrage.

The boys missed a much-maligned general review of the troops held near Yorktown on September 29, a Sunday. They were digging steadily, exhausted, debating whether their latest skit was worth the punishment.

~I say that it was, announced Jack, throwing a spadeful of black soil over his shoulder. From this location, they could see some of Lord Cornwallis's original dirt fortifications, cautionary and eroding. They were being guarded, musket at port arms, by one Sergeant Theo Wilkins of Athens, Georgia, a squat man who was trying, with a humorous lack of success, to grow whiskers.

~You boys getting' tired yet? asked Wilkins, sneering. Were it worth it to assault your captain's pig?

~My brother Jack there is the one who poked her, said Henry, wiping sweat from his brow. The wedding has been set for January. I hope you will be able to attend. Our brass band will be playing.

~Imagine the sorrow for Lieutenant Goodpath, said Michael blithely. Cuckolded twice by the same man.

~Back to digging with you, said Wilkins. You say this wedding will be in January?

~Oh, sorry, sir, said Michael. I completely forgot. We are eating the bride for Christmas. If you are not otherwise engaged, I am sure Lieutenant Goodpath would be honored for you to eat the bride with him.

~It wouldn't be the first bride I've partook of, said Wilkins. He took off his hat, wiped his face with a large plain handkerchief. You boys see them Yankees over there? They ain't never gone move up this land. Never. It won't never happen.

~And how do you know that? asked Jack.

~Because we have you girls to defend us, he said. I bet Jeff Davis is sleeping like a baby knowing you Avengers is down here keeping at bay Mr. Lincoln's whole rabblement. Haw.

~Sir, I challenge you to a duel with Spat cards, said Jack, removing a deck from his coat pocket.

~What in the hell is a Spat card?

~Ah, fine of you to ask me, said Jack. Now look here. . .

IN MID-OCTOBER, COBB'S LEGION, the Avengers straggling in the rear, moved down to winter quarters, one mile west of the road from Cockletown to Big Bethel on Howard's Branch at Harrod's Mill. Five miles south of Yorktown, the site was christened Camp Marion for Col. Thomas Cobb's wife. Jack left one night looking for a neighbor woman and solace, but all he found was a toothless granny who offered him crumbling cornbread and milk from a nearly dry cow.

~Did you take her anyway? asked Henry.

~Bed the bitch! cried Michael.

~Go to hell, said Jack sourly.

The brothers kept the same messmates, and they sawed trees for a one-room cabin, eight feet tall and nine feet on a side. Between days of guard duty and drills, rumors of attack, and dizzy theatricals, the boys built a fine house with a stick-and-daub chimney at one end, which drafted quite nicely on cold nights. Henry planed planks using a froe and nailed them inside the logs, while the others mixed straw and mud to chink the cracks outside. Not everyone was so industrious, and some remained tent-bound while others built walls and stretched their tents above them as roofs. The Blackshears built a shake roof, too, and their house lacked only a floor to be quite comfortable indeed. They ate well—oysters and biscuits, beef and apple butter. Illness attacked: whole companies came down with diphtheria, measles, whooping cough, dysentery, pneumonia. A boy named Tim Wencel from Deerskin, nine miles outside Branton, died in the camp hospital. On Sunday, October 27, the Avengers had potato pudding—their first desert since joining the army in July.

That night, the Blackshear Boys had announced with a printed flyer, there would be a Grand Frolic, in which they would play reels, do the Abe Lincoln playlet, even sing the Minnie Penny song. Though the boys had performed to small groups they had not yet played for all of Cobb's Legion, and this evening, clear and cool, was perfect, campfires and fine liquors arousing the men. Twice already, there had been rumors of attack and regimental mobilization, but now, the front was calm, and often the Legion could hear Yankee bands playing Northern favorites, while the southern bands played back "Dixie" and "The Bonnie Blue Flag."

Lieutenant Goodpath could see no real harm—perhaps the fools would be pathetic and turned laughingstocks. Captain Robinson lay in his new hut, drinking and missing the unquestioned power of small-town politics. By eight, nearly four hundred soldiers sat in the wide windy area on which the Legion drilled.

~You're not tuned, said Jack to Henry, who was plinking the strings of his guitar. Henry worked his pegs into fine tune, looked up in the firelight.

~I have a solo I want to do, he said. I wrote it this afternoon.

~Solo? asked Michael. About what?

~It's called "The Pig Left Behind."

~Oh ho! More digging in the Warwick River works!

~I'm game, said Michael.

~Deal me in! cried Jack.

The night was cold and windy after it had rained the evening before, but starfields swept over the Peninsula, constellations shaped to Classical stories. War—*what* war? Hundreds of campfires marked mess-mates, but they were dying before the roar of five huge bonfires around the place where the Blackshear Boys set up to play.

~Would you girls look at that crowd! said Henry with wonder. They won't be able to hear a thing we say.

~Scream, said Jack, then pass the hat. Actually the brothers' messmates were passing hats in exchange for ten percent of the profits, to be divided equally.

~I can see my breath, said Michael, who was mildly drunk.

~Just don't put a match near it, said Henry. Here we go.

And they came running forward to a pattering of applause and vigorous laughing insults, at which the Blackshears pretending to take offense and then grinned to show good humor. Henry leaped into the air with his fiddle, and when he landed, they began "Cumberland Cove," a wild reel taught them by a traveling salesman, in which they kept changing keys upward, each taking turns of sharp virtuosity. Soldiers hooted and clapped, danced with each other, threw stones in the bonfires to shoot a shower of sparks upward. They took the tempo faster and faster after each turn until their fingers flew impossibly along the ebony necks and pearled fretwork. Then: one last bang and a mad shout from the soldiers, sipping and smoking, paying no attention to the blue army a few miles to their rear.

~Thank you, thank you, men of Cobb's Legion, and I hope that you will continue to act irresponsible and intoxicated and put money in the hats that are being passed around, said Jack. We send every penny home to our old mother.

~Liar! cried a private near the front.

~For your entertainment now, ladies, here is a song written especially for this occasion and performed by my brother Henry. Be kind to the boy. This is his first war, and he doesn't know yet if he will be brave or act like an officer. (*Howling laughter.*) Henry picked up his guitar and stepped forward like a professional speaker.

~There is a sad love story that has been going around in our Legion for a few days, and I felt obliged to share it with you. So boys, take out your handkerchiefs and be prepared to dab at your eyes, as I tell this sad tale. Henry began strumming, medium tempo in a wistful F major, then sang:

Eyes like an angel and lips like a queen
The loveliest girl anyone's ever seen.
More sparkling than diamonds,
More perfect than pearls,
I loved how she dances,
Love how she whirls.

But someone malicious,
A person quite crass
Stuck a carved ivory toothbrush
Right into her—welllllllll,
Some call her fancy
With eyes sweet and kind
But to me she is always
The pig left behind.

Call me a lover and say I am blind
But I'll ne'er forget the pig left behind.

The laughter and cheering could be heard four miles away in the Yankee camp when Henry finished the song. Jack, amazed, watched as men emptied their pockets of bills and change into the passing hats. The song went through four verses, each of which Henry sang expertly. He only raised one eyebrow when he'd finished.

~How do you do that? asked Michael. Henry shrugged. Lieutenant Goodpath, furious, had rushed away from the frolic, and Captain Robinson had not even appeared, instead speaking with the Legion's senior officers this evening. Without pausing for the applause to die, the Blackshear Boys leaped forward and struck theatrical poses. Michael acted as if he was digging, then stopping periodically to wipe his face.

~Wait, wait, private, what are you digging? cried Jack, striking a haughty pose.

~Why Captain, I'm digging to Boston, sir.

~Digging to Boston? (*Looking toward the crowd as if dumbfounded.*) How in the name of all that's sacred can a man dig to Boston from Virginia?

~Well, didn't I hear you say that Yankees are devils?

~Yes, indeed!

~Well, I figure as soon as I hit hell, I'll probably be in Boston. Then we can just go down this hole and attack them from behind!

~Brilliant thinking! I hereby promote you to corporal!

~Thank you, sir! But of course it's possible that I may hit Washington first.

~Well, we *are* near Yorktown.

~No, I mean the *city*, sir. Washington City. I believe it lies near hell, if I am not mistaken. Shall I kidnap Mr. Lincoln if I see him?

~I doubt the hole is that tall! But that is also brilliant, and I promote you to sergeant.

~Thank you, sir! But of course it is possible that I may come up somewhere near Manassas.

~There's no Yankee army there anyway. (*Dozens standing and applauding now, shouting, waving hats, hoorawing.*) But since you have dug so deeply, I hereby promote you to brigadier general! Congratulations!

~And you are a captain?

~Yes, indeed! (*As if handing him the shovel.*)

~Then *you* start digging! And tell me when you reach Europe!

The show, mixing songs and skits, lasted more than an hour, and when it was finished, the Celebrated Blackshear Boys felt, with some justification, that they were now in charge of Cobb's Legion.

COLD WEATHER CAME, AND WITH it constant rumors of war, all of them false. Mornings of rime and snowy frost followed rain. The Legion marched six miles on several days running to pick corn in broad fields so the Yankees wouldn't get it. Each day, dozens of wagons-full creaked behind stolid oxen, heading back toward the miles-wide Confederate lines.

On November 10, the Avengers, along with several other companies of Cobb's Legion, had been detailed for corn pulling and were on bivouac seven miles from Camp Marion and not far from the Big Bethel battlefield of the previous June. Nearly three thousand men had been pulling corn for several days and lay exhausted in their bedrolls on the cold ground.

~I counted, and today we filled damn near two hundred wagons, said David Bernstein. This is no business for a clothier. My hands were designed for finer things. I thought we were volunteering for a war not for farm labor.

~I'm apt to run off, said Raleigh Poole. I will probably be fell on by a corn wagon and killed.

~Stop with the presentiments of death, said Jack Blackshear. I'm sick of it myself. History will refer to this as the Corn War.

~Corn War? At least we're with Colonel *Cobb*, said Henry, drawing on the ground with a stick. Michael laughed brightly, then yawned.

~That was good, he said.

~Just before dawn, a shuddering of conversation and men rising: the Yankees were moving, and officers placed Cobb's Legion into the line of battle. They began to march, and for the first time since they'd come, Henry felt a deep fear, as if a shell of disbelief had melted around him.

~You boys have your cap and cartridges boxes dry and full? asked Jack of his brothers. They quietly nodded, heads up and down in the early mist and fog. A local guide somewhere far in front led them into a swamp, mud and cold water over ankle deep, and the men cursed, kept their eyes open, but all they saw were knobbed stumps and a low forest filled with blackly angled birds' wings.

~Where are we? asked Lyle Fogg.

~Must be nearly to to Newport News, said Sag Doremus. Which is held by the Federals unless I've misunderstood the placement of troops. What's that?

A sound of hoofbeats in the water, splashing, thudding, the jangling of saddle gear, the calling of commands. *Load your guns, men!* A cavalry detachment rode up toward the troops, coats possibly blue—hard to tell in the morning mist. The detachment stood, miserable, in the water and waited for the riders to come in.

~Who are you boys? asked Lieutenant Goodpath, voice strained. He glanced for others down the line.

~We're the Cumberland Cavalry, sir. Who are you?

~Cobb's Legion, said the Lieutenant.

~Fine morning, said the cavalry officer, who wheeled on his horse and spurred it.

~They're Yankees! someone cried. Later, no one could remember a command to fire, but suddenly they were firing muskets, and a horse was falling, and men shouted, and the cavalry stopped and looked at the infantry with deep confusion. The Blackshears, after firing, ran forward with their messmates and found two writhing horses, mortally wounded. A captain lay in the muck, still.

~Goddamnit, we're CSA! cried a captain, dismounting. Cumberland Cavalry! Dear Jesus, Major Bagley! Major! But the major lay dead in the fetid water, which stank of sulfur and decayed plant matter. Another captain was shot in the hand, and a private in the leg. The horses spat bloody foam, kicked as if running, died. Henry began to gasp and staggered back away from the scene, which was lit with a single shaft of thin sunlight. Jack came after him.

~I think I shot the captain, said Henry, trembling. Dear God, our own men! Jack, what happened?

~It was an accident, said Jack softly, his arm around his youngest brother's shoulder. He looked around the swamp and said: I think we ought to shoot the guide. I'd be willing to guess we're nowhere near our placement.

~This makes me sick to death, whispered Henry, shuddering. First blood, and it's our own men. Dear God, dear God. What if they *had* been Federal troops? We could have been overrun in here and killed or taken prisoner. I thought our officers really knew their work. I really thought that. But all we're good for is picking corn and killing our own men. I want to hit someone hard, Jack.

~Hit me, then. If not in anger over this, for what I did with Susannah Yarborough. Henry lifted his head and thought of his Branton sweetheart for the first time in weeks.

~You did not, said Henry, slightly smiling.

~I did, said Jack. I'm rotten to the core. I'd like ask, however, that you hit rather than shoot me.

~Never mind it, said Henry. I did much the same with your Cynthia Sims. Jack made a face and then shrugged, and when Michael caught with them, they were moving back west out of the swamp, arms overlapped, mournful and silent.

DAYS AND DRILLING PASSED, GUARD duty and snowstorms came, edged with sleet and frigid winds from the northwest. Sometimes, artillery banged from a mile away, but the shelling was perfunctory, and no one expected a battle. This was not war: It was two armies buried in mud and ice, huddled inside cabins and tents, playing cards, writing letters home, singing, stoking the flames in stick-and-daub chimneys. Michael and the Fogg brothers built a fine floor for their cabin, and it was quite comfortable, even when snow and sleet came harder than ever on the night of December 2. Sometimes, Raleigh Poole would go to Sunday services to hear Rev. R. K. Porter of Waynesboro preach, a Presbyterian and a personal friend of Thomas R. R. Cobb. In mid-December, the artillery joined Cobb's Legion, which by now had eight infantry companies, four cavalry, and the battery with four cannon. An hour of battalion drill every evening, buying food from private sutlers, opening packages from home with salt pork, hams, even pies and pound cakes. On Christmas day, eggnog and whiskey were available for every man who wanted them, and virtually all did. The Cobb brothers made speeches on December 26, and the Legion's brass band played for the first time that day, sometimes in tune, often not, with Jack playing an especially fine solo on "The Yellow Rose of Texas."

This was not war.

On January 14, a heavy wet snow fell, and the soldiers from both sides fought snowball battles among themselves, ate oysters. The Confederates received, gratefully, a gill of whiskey each. Warm and convivial, twelve men crammed into the Blackshears' log hut, sipping shipped or pilfered liquor, smoking cigars and pipes until the air was thick. A keening wind shook up the shakes on the roof, moaned through the slats.

~Deal it boys, deal it! cried the bandmaster James Peter. He wore steel-framed eyeglasses, and each lens was smudged with a fingerprint that bulged out, whorls up. They were playing five-card draw, and Jack, with a fresh cigar stuck behind his right ear, was cutting the cards and whistling. Henry had his banjo out and was playing a run he couldn't get quite right. A nice change: The evening before, Henry had been teary, nostalgic, unsure of any cause but home.

~I'm serious, Jack. What's the point of sitting up here within earshot of the ocean and the Yankees and not doing a damned thing? I don't understand what this fight's about anyway. Do you?

~This isn't the fight, baby boy. The fight will come when the weather warms, and most of these yahoos who have said a Southern man is worth ten from the North will get to show their guts or show their tails. Some say it's about self-determination. Some say it's slavery. Some say it's about tariffs. I say it's about women.

~Huh?

~It's about women. All the women up North are pinch-faced old maids who want to ruin the man of the species. They are clawing, avaricious harpies. There is no Minnie Penny in the North.

~Is there a Cynthia Sims there?

~You had to go and ruin my comparison. Just remember, our women are hot-blooded and full of stately manipulations. Their women are cold-blooded and will slap the hand of any man who comes near, including husbands. No, be at peace. I, Jack Blackshear, will help your problem.

~By sending me home?

~By procuring a woman, he said, leaning over with a whiskey whisper.

~There are no women around here. Most every family has moved.

~*Most* is not *all*, sir.

Now, Jack shuffled and cut, shuffled and cut, as Michael showed the boys how to play a shell game with three spent tin cans and a hard brown buckeye.

~We shall now play a game of Kick Me, said Jack magisterially.

~I'm in! cried Michael. My favorite game—ninety-two dollars and nine cents. I will never forget that night! A shuffling for position and hands reaching over the upturned shipping crate that served as their table. Someone poked the fire, threw in snapped sticks, but the room was stifling already.

~What's this Kick Me? asked Sag Doremus. I don't believe I've ever heard of it.

~It's the national game of Italy, said Michael. *Molto bene.* Michael stood and bowed and shook his friend's hand.

~Huh?

~Never mind, boys, never mind. It's a dollar a hand, and if anyone hits a Purple, it's doubles from everyone.

~I don't remember hearing of this game, said James Peter, sweating, fog-lensed. What are the rules? What's a Purple?

~Just throw in, and we will show you as we go along, said Jack, glancing without expression at his brothers, who knew nothing of Kick Me, since Jack had just invented it.

~A Purple comes, oh, like once a year, said Henry. Jack was dealing to Henry, James, Sag Doremus, and Raleigh Poole, who had raised a fine black beard that grew in wild whorls, like a blackberry vine, across his thin cheeks. Much more often to get a Snarl or a Whip.

~A Whip? A Whip? What's a Whip? cried Raleigh. Henry glanced at Michael.

~Something to make a horse run. Laughter and poking. The sound, at some distance of a musket shot: trigger-happy guard on duty. No troop movements in this weather.

~All right, there's five cards each, said Jack. Ah-hum. Dit-dit-dit. Ah-hum. Dit-dit-dit. I'll go first as dealer. Jack cried sharply and threw down the five of spades and the seven of diamonds. Snarl.

~Damn! said Henry. But look at this! He slapped on the barrel-head the jack of hearts, the two of clubs, and ten of spades. A Double-Dagger!

~Damn! said Jack, lighting his cigar. I haven't seen a Double-Dagger since 1859. What do you boys have? Sag and Raleigh were scratching their heads, unwilling to admit they had no idea what was happening.

~I got a pair of fives, said Sag, throwing down.

~And I got me not a goddamn thing, said Raleigh. Shoot me, boys. He put down five cards of varied numbers and suits, none matching.

~Son of a bitch! cried Jack. Would you look what the fool drew!

~I don't see nothing worth a goddamn thing, said Raleigh quietly, staring at the cards.

~It's a Purple! shouted Henry. *In his first game!* Henry scooped up the dollars and handed them to Raleigh, shaking his head. Beginner's luck.

~I didn't even know I could play the game, said Raleigh, amazed. Luck 'uz with me tonight, boys!

~But you've got to say Kick Me to win and get the pot, said Jack.

~Kick Me, said Raleigh, and they were all over him, with eleven or twelve genial kicks in the behind, and laughter that bubbled up like over-boiled coffee.

~Michael never did get the run just right on his banjo.

BY LATE FEBRUARY, THE NEWS of a staggering Confederate defeat in the West had reached them: forts Henry and Donelson had fallen to a Union general named, of all things, U. S. Grant. Nashville was gone soon after, the first Southern capital to fall, and the men, still lined up across this bitterly cold windswept peninsula in Virginia had seen almost no combat. The rebels lost Roanoke Island to the Union—a backdoor to Richmond, the press called it. President Lincoln's twelve-year-old son Willie died, and a few firebrands in the lines exulted but most in Cobb's Legion found it troubling and poignant and a bad sign.

~Well, they finally inaugurated Jeff Davis as permanent president, said Michael Blackshear, reading a Richmond paper out loud. Listen to what he said. Ahem: Civil war there cannot be between states held together by volition only. Does anybody know what in the hell that means?

~I do, said Henry. But if I reveal it, I'd have to kill you.

~I'd rather be shot than freeze.

But the days of freezing, of card games in wind-rattled log huts, were coming to an end with March. The dreams of a six-week or six-month war had faded, and Federal troop strength grew and armies of them moved across the South, from the Mississippi River to Harper's Ferry. Drilling increased, and Cobb's Legion in early March packed and left Camp Marion, heading up the James River in steam vessels and then to Petersburg and by rail back to the town of Suffolk, which was threatened by Federal troops under General Ambrose Burnside. While the Avengers straggled along, a fierce battle between the ironclads *Monitor* and *Virginia* was taking place not far east at Hampton Roads, and depending on who told the story, the South won or lost.

At Suffolk, the men stopped near the railroad track just out of town and called the site Camp Hunter. On March 10, the weather increasingly fine: a long drumroll and the troops called out to witness the execution of a soldier from the 2nd Louisiana.

~I don't want to watch this, said Henry. I'm going to turn away. They were in a fine pine woods, but much of it had been cleared, and the condemned man sat on his own coffin, which was pulled off by one third of its length from a rickety wagon. A mule stood before it unconcerned, flapping an ear.

~I want you to take me home now, said the man. I didn't mean no harm. Boys, don't shoot me. Please don't shoot me.

~Christ, said Henry. He had always suffered a tender streak, and Jack and Michael stood at his shoulders, grim and dutiful. I don't want to watch this. But he had no choice, and the charges were read aloud by a self-important lieutenant with a feather on his pinned-up hat dancing with the wind. The squad of twelve came up. Only four or five of their muskets had been loaded at random by officers so no one would really know who fired the fatal shots. They tied the trembling soldier to a post that had been set in the soft brown soil, but the man was too frightened to stand.

~Shoot him as he sits! cried the lieutenant. He raised his sword, with its engraved blade and pearl-encrusted hilt. Gave the command. Five muskets exploded as one, and the man seemed to shudder one way and then another, then back. He took three balls in the chest. One ripped away the top of his head. No one could tell where the fifth minié ball went. Men vomited, and the lieutenant trembled with excitement and had trouble sliding the gleaming blade back into its scabbard. The mule did not flinch.

ALL THROUGH MARCH, RUMORS OF war came, and Cobb's Legion was shipped one hundred and twenty miles west to Goldsboro, but no enemy came there, either, and on April 5, they were back down the peninsula where they started, exhausted, not caring that rumors had reached them of Federal siege guns unlimbering to their front or that a major battle was underway near a small church in Tennessee called Shiloh.

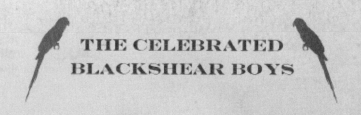

THE CELEBRATED
BLACKSHEAR BOYS

April 27, 1862
Near Yorktown, Va.

Dearest Family,

    I know that you have read from the papers that we are under siege here from the troops of General McClellan of the Union Army. They say he outnumbers us five to one, but we are holding on. This war has now been going on for a year, and all of us in the Avengers wish we were home and getting in trouble. We have been much interested in our loss at Pea Ridge in Arkansas, which appears a disaster. Nor have we gotten over the loss of so many men at Shiloh.

    Our food supplies are thin at best—parched corn is all we get some days. A far cry, I would say, from the fat days of last fall when we were just coming to the war. We have received some new volunteers, stimulated to join to avoid the ignominy of conscription, and and they seem sullen and cannot believe the shellfire, which is almost constant toward Yorktown. We are along the Warwick River, where we continue to dig trenches and fire back as we can, but I do not think we can maintain this position much longer as we are greatly outnumbered. I would not worry so much about Fort Pulaski having fallen, though I know it must concern you since it is on our own Georgia coast. It looks from the newspapers as if New Orleans will soon fall as well.

    A siege is a strange thing. All day and much of the night they are lobbing shells into our lines, and men are dying. One boy from Athens that I knew slightly, Richard Lamar, was killed by a direct hit, a shocking thing. While we are glad not to be freezing and eating boiled oysters, this war is a dramatic and terrible thing.

Jack continues as himself, performing magic tricks and doing handstands for the boys when the firing is its hottest. Michael sings much around the campfires at night, though lately he has been performing ballads that tend to make the boys weep. Then he laughs. Sometimes he is a hard man, but as you know it is to shield a tender heart. We have the same messmates, though Sag Doremus was wounded on April 3 by shellfire and was in the hospital tent for seven days before he came back. Lyle Fogg has had stomach troubles. Lt. Goodpath is proving himself the worst officer in the CSA, but the second worst officer is Capt. Robinson, so we are led by idiots and cowards. Rumor is that General Magruder may detach us and send our Avengers to Kentucky or possibly Texas, but you learn to discount such things.

It rained all last night, and none of us slept. Someone up the line decided we needed whiskey, and it was received with gratitude. Today is Sunday, and there is nothing sacred about the day—just mud and blood and firing from the Federal siege guns. Soon, I am sure, we will be moving, and I will write you again when I can.

We have tried to stay twenty yards from each other during the heaviest firing, as we do not wish you to have us all three blown apart at the same time. That will be some day—the Celebrated Blackshear Boys pulling tricks on St. Peter, flanking him, and bringing cards and music to the streets of heaven.

Your son,
Henry Blackshear

THE SEVEN DAYS

Well, I, by God, at least never stole meat from a one-legged man pushing a wheelbarrow, said Jack Blackshear, waving his arms dramatically. And somebody please tell me, sirs: If Richmond is near the southern part of this state, why in the name of holiness has our new commander christened us the Army of Northern Virginia?

~He was not one-legged, and it was a *cart*, not a wheelbarrow, said Michael with faux outrage. And I offered to pay him, and he ran off. And it was a hank of hambone that had been in his pocket. It had a picket line of fuzz and videttes of sand. It was an heroic deed.

~Oh heroes of the Branton Avengers, come forth and receive thy bounty, said Henry. Nobody stirred.

The sticky sixth day of June 1862 had come, and Cobb's Legion, having retreated up the peninsula between the James and York rivers, was within twelve miles of Richmond itself, the Southern troops harried by more than one hundred thousand Federal soldiers under the command of General George Brinton McClellan, a superb organizer but a man who needed kicking to set an army in motion. President Lincoln kicked until McClellan came down the Potomac with his troops in steamships, settled in for the siege of Yorktown. A fierce battle had erupted around Williamsburg on May 5 as the Confederates retreated northwest, but only General Magruder's rear-guard fought the Union skirmishers, and Cobb's Legion was not engaged. On May 31, the fierce but indecisive Battle of Seven Pines had taken place around the Chickahominy River, and Federals wounded the Confederate commander, General Joseph Johnston. Taking his place was fifty-five-year-old Robert Edward Lee, until now something of a functionary in Richmond and derided for his tendency to dig in—the men had been calling him the King of Spades.

It was he who had renamed the Army, hoping to stiffen its spine, give it purpose. Few knew what manner of commander he might be.

The Chickahominy River was a turgid brown thing, feral and crawling from several days of hard rain, and Cobb's Legion lay sprawled alongside it, dreaming of food and rest, having had little of either for two weeks. Now, as evening came, thousands of lightning bugs spread their bioluminescence across the river flatlands, and frogs coughed mating calls.

~I still can't believe I saw President Davis or that he came to the battlefield, said David Bernstein. He looked strange. Dyspeptic. They sat around a campfire, poking short logs, watching the brands spill upward into the still evening.

~He's blind in one eye, said Henry. A president who's half blind. Tell me there's not some omen in that.

~It's better than being half stupid, said Michael.

~Or half-assed, like Jack, said Henry.

~Hah and hah again, said Jack. At least I've never lost money in a game of Spat. I personally think President Davis was out to see if he really has an army. Some appear to think this army is, in fact, naught but a rumor.

~I heard that rumor, said Michael. In fact, our Avengers signed up for three years of the rumor, though at the moment I cannot say why.

~Because we had no decent jobs, said Jack, and our sweethearts were harridans, in the case of Henry and myself, and a weeping Sally in the case of your Elizabeth. Personally, I think Mr. Davis would have more advantage if he were *entirely* blind. Then he wouldn't have to see what's happening to his army.

~Officer riding in, said Sag Doremus. Oh heavens, it's Captain Stillwell. God, and Robinson, too.

~And you never got me that woman you promised, said Henry to Jack. I will keep you to that pledge.

Events had kept Captain Percy Stillwell of Athens away from the Blackshear brothers, but he had never forgotten them. The mad dog incident of a decade before had left him standing, humiliated, in the streets of Branton, red-faced, among a group of heaving women who

screamed at every loping mutt who wandered up. William Tappan
Thompson, in *The Southern Miscellany*, had written it thus:

> Now we find much to admire in our pleasant sister city of
> Branton, and we hear that a fashionable new dance had
> broken forth that will rival the waltz, the gallop, and the
> stately minuet. It is called, we believe, the Woof, and it was
> invented by one Mr. Percy Stillwell, who was interrupted in
> his dancing lessons by some village boys with a firecracker and
> a tall tale. Seems these boys told Mr. Stillwell that a mad dog
> was loose in town and that if he heard a gunshot he should run
> for his life. Well, sirs, the firecracker was fused off, Mr.
> Stillwell cried aloud, and into the streets he dashed, jiggling
> one leg and then another and crying for all to hear, Run! Run
> away! For a mad dog is surely in these streets! A few tried to
> emulate Mr. Stillwell's fancy steps, but found them too diffi-
> cult for amateurs. It was thought the Woof would take the
> world by storm, but alas, it has failed, though Mr. Stillwell has
> retired to Athens, where boys are perhaps better mannered and
> dancing more civilized.

Stillwell had been enraged and wrote Thompson, challenging him
to a duel, which the latter laughed off by sending a pie and an apology to
Athens. Jack didn't know it, but his application to the Franklin College
in Athens had been sabotaged personally by Stillwell, who in the past
decade had read law and set up a practice across the street from the
entrance to the college's campus. Nothing gave Percy Stillwell more
pleasure for several years.

Now, as he rode into camp, with the skittery sound of almost casual
picket musketry in the distance, Captain Wiseman Robinson joined him
on a borrowed mare, a cadaverous, sway-backed animal that walked with
the splay-footed stagger of an old man. They rode straight for the
Blackshears, who rose and stood, looking at each other with the light
smile of past victories. Behind them, the Chickahominy looked like
flowing brass in the hot sunset, melting and flowing from some vast
forge in the north.

~At your ease, said Captain Stillwell, after he had dismounted and swapped salutes with the brothers. Wiseman Robinson, too, dismounted, and his horse seemed to sigh from relief. Others from their mess moved away: Officers were never anything but bad news, though duty was duty, and a private was no more than cannon fodder. It has come to my attention that you boys are the source of considerable and ongoing discontent in the Branton Avengers and may well be personally responsible for the sorry condition of this regiment. Your conduct on the Peninsula from the time you arrived in the army until now has been reported to me

~Permission to speak? asked Jack.

~Denied, said Captain Percy Stillwell. He held a riding crop and whapped it theatrically against his gloved left palm. He was still tall and thin, but his lithe, cadaverous look had faded under ten years' added weight and maturity. His hair shaded now toward gray but was wildly long, and luxuriant and neatly trimmed mustaches curled down either side of his mouth. His lizard-cold eyes narrowed to reptilian slits.

~Permission to *dance*? said Jack. Henry turned away and made a small barking sound and then glanced sharply the other direction, as if to see its source.

~They're incorrigible, said Captain Robinson. How they came from such fine parents I cannot say. Though their father is something of the Union man still.

~Permission to *sing*? asked Henry, clearing his throat.

~Denied! cried Captain Stillwell. He smiled cruelly and began to walk around them, looking closely, as if judging a cow for sale.

~Permission to play "Turkey in the Straw" on my fiddle? asked Michael. Stillwell whipped around, and one of his gleaming spurs caught in the other, and he staggered forward and saved himself from a fall only by grasping the sleeve of Captain Robinson's coat and pulling it so hard it ripped completely off and slid down his arm like a snake shedding its skin. There was a skittering of laughter, snickering. A dead horse floated past on the river, and they all watched it, whirling in secret circles, going downstream.

~*That* is a beast who has amply served his country. The voice was familiar, alas, and the brothers turned to see that Lieutenant Martin

Goodpath had joined them. The brothers, along with their friends, had endlessly taunted Goodpath during the previous winter.

Jack's eyes narrowed. This was a perfect conjunction of incompetence or evil, and he knew nothing good would come of it. Goodpath was on foot and covered, like the others, with so much dust he seemed totemic, monstrous. A ten-pounder Parrott gun barked at perhaps a mile distant.

~Sir, I need an orderly, said Captain Percy Stillwell to Wiseman Robinson. I will take that youngest Blackshear brother, the one with the whitish hair and the malicious eye.

~It isn't malicious, sir, said Henry. It's infected. Jack worked hard not to laugh.

~Granted, said Robinson mildly. And I need an orderly myself and will take the middle brother, Michael.

~Ah, and so I need an orderly as well and will take the eldest, Jack, said Lieutenant Goodpath.

~Ahem, said Jack.

~What? What? Do you wish to say something to me, private? Goodpath was frenzied, wild-eyed, fists clenched, ready for a sucker punch.

~It's this dust, sir, said Jack, coughing and then spitting. And this Virginia reel we've been dancing all the way up the peninsula. And may I remind the Lieutenant we Blackshears are bandsmen and camp entertainers. We have always been together.

A sudden cheering broke out across the river from the Yankee lines, an odd sound, as if some long-shot had just won a foot race. An observation balloon hung, painted against the sky. All of them turned to the sound then angled back. Goodpath seemed about to explode with the frisson of his advantage.

~Well, say goodbye, he said. We need couriers. Of course, it means that you will be moving along enemy lines and could well be shot in the fracas.

~My fracas is tender from marching, said Jack emotionally. Might I request being shot in the finger?

Raleigh Poole, standing nearby, had a wheezing fit of laughter, which turned into a seizure of hacky coughing.

~Knowing your character, I'm sure it's more likely, said Lieutenant Goodpath acidly, that you will be shot in the *ass*. That is all.

THAT WAS HOW, AS RICHMOND lay threatened before the huge army of General George Brinton McClellan, the Blackshear brothers came to be separated. Their instruments and trunks were on some baggage train—wagons moving in a long trail of fine dust—and so they left each other with little more than their Enfield muskets, cartridge and cap boxes, knapsacks, haversacks, and a few crumbly morsels of cornbread.

~I'm be dead before I see you again, said Raleigh Poole. So fare you all well. I am dead, goodbye.

~Great speech, said Jack, shaking his hand. Right there with *Hamlet*.

~Thankee, said Poole. Whomever that mought be.

~Well, said Michael, preparing to leave. Well.

~I can't believe this…Henry started and then stopped.

~I'll bet you boys five dollars each that I get the first wound, said Jack. Pay me now. I'm not sure when I'll be in your vicinity again. He slapped them on the sides of their heads, walked off, following Lieutenant Goodpath.

The land around Richmond bore the open sores of trenchwork as the outnumbered Confederates awaited McClellan's pleasure. Stories of General Stonewall Jackson's victories in the Shenandoah Valley sped through the lines, gathering myth as a stone gathers torque. The heat suffocated them, and great clouds of dust accompanied troop movements. As they moved north along the Rebel lines, Captain Robinson rode his horse with elegance and a haughty glance, Michael at a double-time step to keep up.

None of them knew that for the next three weeks, McClellan would not attack, would do nothing but shift his troops, almost idly, as a chess player in a summer noon's torpor dozes off before making another move.

~YOU KNOW, I COULD JUST have you dig trenches for weeks, said Lieutenant Martin Goodpath excitedly. But it occurred to me that it would be a greater delight to pin you and watch you squirm.

~Permission to speak? It was night now, and Jack stood outside the captain's tent, which was pitched a hundred yards away from his own men toward the neater works of the Panola Guards from Madison. Frogs chorused, mad for the temperature and humidity, sang in overlapping stanzas. Thousands of campfires, Union and Confederate, lines not more than a musket-shot apart: men exhausted, sleeping on the hot earth, tentless, footsore, stomachs knotted in hunger.

~By all means.

~This war will end, and we will go home, and when we get there, people will know how we treated each other on campaigns. My brothers and I have meant to lift the spirits of the men, that's all. I do not see why we have been broken apart. As the eldest…

~My wife told me the whole story, said Lieutenant Goodpath excitedly. His face was flushed, and he took a flask from inside his wool coat and accepted a long pull from it. And do you know what? You were only one of many, Jack. One of *many*. She took lovers like a tick sips blood.

~Ack.

~At my request, she wrote out all their names. It looked like a goddamned muster roll. Melvin Tanner, for Christ's sake.

~Melvin with the big adam's apple and all those teeth? At the grist mill? Not *that* Melvin.

~And the language she uses! No one knows how foul!

~I lived with a parrot that was likely worse.

~You were nothing to her, *nothing*. She wept, made promises. I was a good man until then. I had never laid a finger on another man in anger. What she did. My God, what she did to me.

~Wait—that Tanner—he disappeared, didn't he? I seem to remember…

A wild glare spun through the Lieutenant's eyes as he inhaled sharply. His hands trembled like an old man's. He blinked, smiled as if rescued from an awkward situation.

~My compliments to Captain Jennings of the Fiftieth Alabama, said Goodpath softly, exhaling. Please tell him that we are instructed to remain in place for now.

~Yes, sir, said Jack. And how shall I find the Fiftieth Alabama?

~Find it, snapped the captain. You're good at finding wives, aren't you? At humiliating your superiors? At casual cruelties? Find it by day-break, or I'll have you brought up on charges. I will torture you. Do you understand me? I will torture you for as long as I have breath. Dismissed.

Jack saluted and walked rapidly away into the gathering darkness.

HENRY, LITHE AND DRY AS a desert in a drought, awoke the next morning at Mrs. Christian's farm and sat up. A wizened little man with a beard like a scab squatted on his haunches, rocking and chewing on a corncob pipe.

~I'm new orderly to Captain Stillwell, Henry said. His mouth felt as if he'd chewed a handful of dry crackers. Canteen?

~I know who you is, the man said. Seen you and you brothers playing down thar tward Yorktown. I'm Slap John Smith. Here, boy… handing him a dented canteen. Henry poured his throat full, sighed with gratitude, sat up and looked around. The land was hilly, pastures on which several thousand men were rising, stirring. A man nearby stood from his blanket and emitted an enormous fart.

~That's how Feeny welcomes the day, said another man. He thrust his hand out: Name's Malachi Jordan, but you can call me Grease. Everybody calls me that.

~His own pa calls him Grease, said Slap John. Now I reckon you Branton boys ain't much of a outfit. This Cobb's Legion is pretty much of a good group, though. Henry looked at Grease, who was a huge young man, no more than twenty, but possibly six-four and more than two hundred pounds. His hair was shiny and slicked back, and he was beard-less and wore an almost seraphic expression.

~I'm detached as an orderly to Colonel Stillwell, said Henry.

~You done said that, said Slap John. Now you axe me, we ain't going to no fight today. We mought not go to no fight this week. Hit's all the same to me. Are you the kind gets feared when the lead starts to flying, boy?

~I haven't been in close combat yet, admitted Henry. He took another drink from the canteen. The day would be blistering. Already, sweat poured down Henry's armpits and puddled around the waistband of his drawers. We've mostly been wandering around Virginia and North Carolina until we ran away back up here.

~I wouldn't let the Captain hear you talk that way, said Grease. He don't like to think we was retreatin'. He says it was a countermarch.

~County march my—Do you know that my Lizz took lessons from our good Captain when he was a dancy master some years past? Colonel Cobb, he's one fine one. But Stillwell, well, he ain't nothing to be leading men. He got himself elected officer on account of he's read the law. A poor man's afeard of them's read the law.

~Why are you called Slap John? asked Henry.

~My pa said I was born dead, and he was suh vexed by it all he slapped me, and I waked up screaming. I'm cousin to one of the boys in yore outfit. Name a Poole. My mother was a Poole.

~Raleigh Poole? He was my messmate.

~Good boy, mought fraidy. Slap John stood and wasn't much taller standing than he was sitting. Henry took in the sight: Michael could draw or paint this. The old man looked as if he'd been carved from a piece of dried deadfall, arms and hands knotty and leathered, and a mat of graying hair erupted from his shirt and seemed to grow into his beard, so the effect was of some ancient hairy animal. He said, You ever been separated from your brothers?

~No.

~I'm separated from *my* brother, said Grease.

~Who is he serving with? asked Henry, now standing and looking around. There was the Chickahominy not four hundred yards away, still in flood tide. Beyond it lay a blanket of blue soldiers—tens of thousands of them, it seemed.

~Satan, I'm reckoning, said Grease. Leroy, you got that fire a-going? Leroy was a boy of no more than seventeen, and he glanced warily around and might as well have been mute.

~Excuse me? said Henry.

~Grease's brother Jim was shot while pleasurin' another man's wife. Her husband come in. Jim says—what was it he says, Grease?

~He says, I'm sure glad you come in, Tom. Your wife near drowned at the Oconee River crossing, and I pulled her out and here she is. Out of them wet clothes, ain't you, Dolores?' Tom give 'em one barrel each.

~Is Tom in this outfit? asked Henry, looking warily around.

~Naw, they hung him, said Grease. He took out a hand-carved comb and ran it backward through his damp black locks. I'm thinking all three of 'ems in hell.

~Hit's all the same to me, said Slap John.

Captain Percy Stillwell burst through the fly of his nearby tent, immaculate, even in this heat wearing yellow gauntlets, a dress wool uniform, and a neatly creased hat. Men along the hillside were kindling cooking fires now, scraping up what they had, small amounts of bacon, hardtack, some infested with weevils, and some dried beef. Several of the men concocted cush, a sometimes ghastly mixture of hot bacon grease, water, bits of cut bacon, topped with crumbled cornbread or biscuits. As many swore *at* cush as swore *by* it. Henry realized he was terribly hungry. They had eaten little on the retreat, and with the lines stabilized somewhat after the Battle of Seven Pines, the men pitched in, cooking, some turning bacon with small sticks, and, unable to wait, lifting it half-fried into their mouths, from which they blew to cool the food which eating it at the same time.

~Well, Private Blackshear, said the Captain with something approaching glee, I trust you spent a good night.

~How long, sir, am I to be detached…

~I did not give you permission to speak! cried the Captain. Please carry a message to Captain Jennings of the Fiftieth Alabama. Tell him we are to stay in place for now. Report back in eight hours, or I will have you flogged.

~Captain, mayn't I go with the boy? asked Slap John. Sir? I ain't hardly fit for a fight no how. Stillwell, vastly amused, looked at the small ancient man with his beard like a scab, and his eyes watered up from unspilled laughter. He was nodding before he knew it.

~By all means. A fine team you will make. Dismissed.

~Sir, with all respect, I have no idea where the Fiftieth Alabama is, said Henry.

~You had no trouble finding a firecracker, said Stillwell with obvious and utter satisfaction. Find the Fiftieth Alabama. Henry saluted and walked off, Slap John at his side. The sun seemed to leap upward, and the oven-heat bore down on them

~What farcracker? asked Slap John.

~Did he say Jennings or Jenkins? asked Henry Blackshear.

~Mought of been either, said Slap John. He looked around. Nope, no fight today. But maybe one soon. Mought come soon. Hit's all the same to me.

~A LITTLE DEEPER, IF YOU please, said Captain Wiseman Robinson, standing at the edge of the latrine, his gut slung outward, braid brushed of dust and washed of stains. Michael Blackshear, newly minted orderly, dug deeper now, down two feet, then three, extending the line of it fifteen feet at the Colonel's direction.

~A little longer and it can be a breastwork instead of a privy, said Michael. Sir.

~Ho, funny is he? said Robinson. He had grown a bushy side beard that served to make his fat cheeks seem even broader, though he kept the sensuous upper lip and the thick under-lip clean. Very funny boy. All you Blackshears are very funny boys.

~Sir, it was for the entertainment of the men.

~Making sport of superior officers is amusing, is it?

~I've never made fun of a superior officer, said Michael, stopping to look at his work.

~Have you not often made sport of me? cried Robinson. Goddamn this heat. I wish for a battle and be done with it. I'm speaking to you, private: Have you not made sport of me?

~Pardon, Captain. I thought you meant superior men, not superior officers.

~Damn you, you little runt. If not for your father's good name I'd have you taken out and tied to a sour apple tree.

~Oh, by the way, before we left, I got a message of godspeed to you from Minnie Penny. She said you were kind to give her the money before you left. Sir.

~What? What? You insolent pup! I'll—she really said that? Damn me.

~She said you were quite ticklish.

~Always have been—damn you. The Captain made fists and shook them at the sky. At some distance: the nervous skittering of muskets—

pickets popping to stave off the tension. I have business to attend to and
have no more time to devote to you or your brothers. Now, two things,
private. First, fill in the latrine. Second, find Captain Jennings of the
Fiftieth Alabama and tell him, with my compliments, that we are
ordered to stand in our works for the nonce. That is all.

~And where might I find the Fiftieth Alabama? asked Michael.

~Ask Minnie Penny, said Colonel Wiseman Robinson. As she seems
to know everything. Dismissed.

Michael saluted as Robinson waddled off, threw down the spade
and stepped up from the works, with no intention of refilling the trench;
there was no way the corpulent Captain could punish him—if this war
ended soon, with loss or victory, he'd be headed back home looking for
votes. Michael trained his painter's eye on the rebel works and the Union
lines within sight, and he found the scene magnificent in the way
painting of dead game by Old Masters was marvelous. New leaves
greened the country, grass beaten down, and so there were washes of
green and brown. The Confederate wore gray coats, mostly, a few butternut, and the Federals new blue. Horses: brown and gray. Artillery
pieces: black and brass. Campfires: orange, yellow, yellow-orange, with
sometimes a hint of blue in the hotter flames. Past roll call, not quite to
drill: soldiers cleaning their muskets, eyes to the barrels, leaning on
elbows and reading half-ripped newspapers. Good, decent officers—and
most were—urgently talking, making hand gestures. The sky pale blue,
like heat itself, cloudless, meant to stun, leaving anything that reached
above the earth's surface in hazy relief.

Henry, like his brothers, gathered his gun, the cap and cartridge
boxes, slung the rolled blanket over his left shoulder, set his forage hat
against the sun.

IT HAD BEEN COMING TO this for months: a spring campaign of
one battle and then another. All across the country, from Texas to coastal
South Carolina, the country was convulsive with war. The day before,
Memphis fell to Union gunboats in a fight that lasted less than three
hours. Federals held most of Tennessee now. Union General Benjamin
Butler, whom his detractors called the Beast, ruled New Orleans, Today,
he would hang William Mumford for tearing down a Union flag that

had flown over the city. Stonewall Jackson, however, was brilliantly defeating the Yankee forces in the Shenandoah Valley, keeping them from joining McClellan for his push on Richmond. The rebel cavalry's Jeb Stuart planned a daring ride with his men entirely around McClellan's troops, as much for glory as actual gain. At some scale, the movements erupted like anthills, troops boiling out, prodded forward, pickets cut up, troops mauled, corps gaining espirit.

In the space between the tactics and the generals, however, soldiers ground petty axes, quarrels begun, thieves stayed busy, and stragglers wandered across the land, claiming sickness or injury or the work of couriers. Pickets skirmished along the front, sharpshooters took positions and dropped posted or wandering enemies, and General Lee planned a daring series of engagements, as if to say: *Siege be damned. We will fight our way out of this.*

Henry Blackshear and Slap John Smith fought their way out of nothing, instead walking through the lines, stopping to salute officers and ask questions, and it was soon apparent that there was no Fiftieth Alabama and that they had been sent to find a regiment invented to torment Henry.

~I think I'm just going to go back to the Legion and kill Captain Stillwell and be done with it, said Henry.

~Even talking like that 'ld get a man shot, said Slap John, stopping to take a long swallow from his canteen. You hardly know me well enough to call me friend, neither. Look at this army. It mought be splendid if it warn't wore out and starvin'.

~Grease didn't look like *he* was starving, said Michael, wiping the sweat off his neck.

~Grease is nought but baby fat and a big heart. He's still got the fat from his ma's tit. A sweet and gentle boy, and it's them who gets shot. Ah, all the kingdoms and battles on the earth is no match for it all. I'd as lief be beaten to my wife by a hog than fight this war.

~You there—who are you? A scowling lieutenant with a theatrical mustache and a glare of perpetual scorn had marched himself right up to Henry, who stood and saluted.

~Sir, Private Henry Blackshear, the Branton Avengers, Cobb's Legion, detached to Captain Percy Stillwell, Cobb's Legion command, looking for Captain Jennings of the Fiftieth Alabama. This—gesturing to Slap John—is my father.

~Do you have any papers?

~Well, no, I wasn't given any.

~Thompson? shouted the lieutenant. A sergeant came shambling over.

~Sir.

~These men are deserters. Arrest them. Sorry, boys. We have to keep order.

~Yes, sir.

~Whoa—wait a moment, sir, I am speaking with entire honesty. I have never done less than serve my country honorably. Father (*turning to Slap John*), oh how I have brought misery down upon your head! Would that mother, sick back home in Richmond had never had to see this. And now with Uncle Joe wounded, that General Lee has taken over the command. Oh, my poor family.

~Uncle *Who*? asked the lieutenant.

~Johnston, said Henry. Father, I give you my deepest apologies.

~Huh? said Slap John.

~You're saying you're General Joseph Johnston's *nephew*? asked the lieutenant.

~Un, said the sergeant, ain't you one a them Blackshot brothers— the ones does skits and plays the music for Cobb's Legion? I seen you boys down near Yorktown last winter.

~Black*shear*, said Henry proudly. Indeed. And lieutenant, I'm sure General Johnston will understand you were just doing your duty to arrest me. Of course, having been wounded, he might receive the news in somewhat ill humor. But I'm sure you will be exonerated by the court martial, possibly even decorated.

~Ah, um. Someone called the lieutenant, and he looked around in confusion. Well then, on with you. But you should have papers. Dismissed. He turned and walked rapidly away, the sergeant, a slender man of perhaps thirty, still there.

~I bet Shakespeare was never done no better, said the sergeant. Joe Johnston my ass.

When they were walking away, continuing through the lines, Slap John said, I didn't have no idea you was Joe Johnson's nephew.

~How hard, said Michael blandly, *did* your father slap you?

~Mought hard I'm told, said Slap John.

JACK BLACKSHEAR HAD NOT BEEN challenged, but after an hour of fruitless wandering, he, too realized, there was no Fiftieth Alabama, and so he began, slowly, to look for his brothers. He had an idea, but he couldn't pull it off without Michael and Henry. Things went that way for Michael, too, and in the thousands of soldiers, hundreds of positions, ponderous troop re-deployments, they became lost, asked around, camped with men they didn't know, shared what mess would take them in. Jack spent one day with some Louisiana boys who were staging louse races. Once, he saw a malcontent shot at the stake, and the condemned man stood against the long roll of the drums, cursing steadily while his orders of execution were read. The rebel cursed the South, Jefferson Davis, General Magruder, Abe Lincoln, and two women who, he shouted, were deceivers, whores, and, apparently, filers of serial lawsuits. He was still shouting when the detail fired seven musket balls into him, and he fell, groaning. He raised his head once and said *damn* in a faint voice and died.

~On the train for hell, whispered a soldier.

The privates spoke of Jeb Stuart, who on June 12 had started a wild and daring ride completely around McClellan's troops, meant to annoy and gather information, since he was outnumbered twenty to one. Michael found himself dodging roll calls, hiding from strutting officers, wondering if Captain Robinson had ordered him hunted down and arrested. No. Never happen. Once a captain with a Mississippi unit demanded to know where Michael was headed, and Michael said, looking east and then west, that he was the King of Belgium and was looking for his coach and six. The captain told an orderly to see that Michael was taken to the hospital tent and looked after for sunstroke. Once there, Michael asked for whiskey, was given a dram, and then he escaped under the back flap and wandered, merry, through a pasture of skinny, fret-faced cows.

By June 21, the Blackshear brothers had managed to crisscross the lines three times looking for each other without success, and they were dirty and hungry, almost two weeks gone from their hopeless mission and not missed—barely even remembered—by the three officers, who were busy keeping their men drilled and alert for the coming action. That Saturday, Jefferson Davis in Richmond wrote his wife: *We are preparing and taking position for the struggle which must be near at hand.*

On Sunday, June 22, Jack whistled the Minnie Penny song and idly wandering along a wash when he heard someone whistle part of a phrase back. He wheeled and saw Henry, filthy and grinning, as he sat in a redoubt, drunk and practicing card tricks before two dull-faced privates on the top of an empty hardtack crate.

~Shall I deal you in? asked Henry. We're about to start a friendly game of Kick Me.

~Brother! Where in God's name have you been? I guess you know by now there's no Fiftieth Alabama. Have you seen Michael?

~Not since we left camp. I'm drinking something that I believe may be kerosene. This is my friend Slap John Smith.

~Howdy, said Slap John. Your brother's done tolt me a right smart amount of you. How come you ain't been shot?

~I think there's a fight coming, and we need to get the hell out of here, said Jack, coming over and lifting Henry by his elbow, cards scattering into a hot wind. I've got an idea, but we need to find Michael to pull it off.

Henry told Slap John goodbye and wished him luck in not getting killed either by the Confederates or the Federals.

~His beard looks like a scab, said Jack, watching as Slap John wandered off behind the lines. Henry had trouble walking straight, and if the officers had been less busy, they might have been arrested or at least stopped, but it was clear a battle would come soon, and there was little time for anyone to notice two men walking with grave purpose and considerable chuckling along the gray lines that defended Richmond. They were still nine miles north of Cobb's Legion, which was in the southern part of the defensive arc around Richmond that extended from Mechanicsville in the north down past Savage's Station and then toward Frayser's Farm. The heat oppressed them, and the men sensed explosions of artillery and the endless crack and whiz of muskets and their .58 caliber soft-lead bullets.

~What have you been doing? asked Henry.

~I was almost arrested once as a deserter, said Jack. That wasn't an especially good day.

~Have you got any food? I feel like a wildcat's eating my insides I'm so hungry.

~Probably the bad whiskey.

~Well-diagnosed, said Henry, who then fell head-first into a trench and did not stir for several minutes.

ON JUNE 26, HENRY AND JACK still had not found Michael, but they could hear, somewhere to the north, a vicious battle unwinding itself near the end of a suffocating day. It had begun the day before: a week of decisive battles that would turn R. E. Lee into an incipient legend and wound George McClellan's reputation irreparably. The fields spilled their sick, stragglers, wounded men who flowed in bloody rags back through the lines. Darkness came.

~Do you know what happened up there today? asked Jack. They stopped near Woodbury's Bridge on the Chickahominy River, and though soldiers milled about, no major units tented there. An old man in a uniform clotted with black blood along one arm, turned around, and his hands shook as he lowered his musket to lean on.

~I'm with A. P. Hill's Division—we pushed the Yankees back from Mechanicsville 'n' there's been hell's own fighting. I had to swing wide of Yankees to walk this far. My wounds is to my side 'n' in the pit of my arm. I don't know how you boys come to be in this place, but you're about to be in the middle of a fight in the morning. I'm aimed to make Savage's Station. I'm deserted. They's boys there I know. I'm to be arrested, reckon you is, too. I *want* to be arrested's the truth. I'm ready to be arrested. Only I want to be arrested by Southern boys. Long as I get a feedin' and maybe a draught of whiskey. Then I'll be ready. I mought be too weakly to stand at the post, but by God I'll sit on a cut-down barrel. And I'll say Shoot me boys and send me home to Ma. I ain't got a family left 'n' I will not die shot by some Yankee. I will not.

The man walked unsteadily south, and sporadic fighting continued.

~I feel something bad's happened to Michael, said Henry, shivering. If one of us is gone, there can't be a Blackshear Brothers anymore.

~Buck up, boy, and don't go sob sister on me, said Jack, sighing and looking around. Come on. Let's find a sheltering place. I think the battle's going to be moving everywhere when daylight comes. I just want to get my hands on Lieutenant Goodpath.

~What would you do? They walked along the western bank of the Chickahominy now, and frogs sang. Crickets scratched without ceasing. The crackle of picket fire, still north but creeping closer.

~I would tie him to tree and tell him what a marvel his wife is in bed, the vixen.

~Vixen?

~She didn't love me, sighed Jack, tenting his fingers beneath his chin with mock solemnity.

~That bitch, said Henry. I'm surprised. She always spoke of you with fondness.

~Spoke of me? When?

~Well, once she called out your name in her sleep.

~You vile bastard. But Jack was grinning, and Henry saw his teeth in the fading light.

IN THE MORNING, HEAVY FIRING came like a closing thunderstorm, and Jack knew immediately, from what he'd heard: the divisions of A. P. Hill, James Longstreet, and D. H. Hill were pressing the Federal troops south—straight toward this place.

~Wait, said Jack. Listen.

~Shit. It's south of us. Southeast, I'd say.

~Wait. It's *west* of us, too. I'd say over near Fair Oaks. We're in a hell of a mess here. Cobb's Legion must be five, six miles south. I say we just stick to the river and make it south as fast as a hawk.

~I'm starving to death, said Henry.

~I could shoot you, if you want me to, said Jack.

~There's a dead man there—next to that oak tree. God, it's sickening. When I see a real battlefield, I may just countermarch to Georgia. Look at how he's twisted in death, Jack. Is that how we'll end up? Bloated and carrion for buzzards and wild dogs? Our poor mother. They crept closer and closer to see if the dead man were Union or Confederate, but in the hazy morning light he seemed neither—coat gone, trousers muddied.

~Could be either, said Jack.

~Waaaaaarrrrggghhhhhh! cried the corpse, leaping to it feet and waving its arms. Henry fell backwards on his ass with a thump, while Jack moved crabways, hands up for a fight.

~Jesus Christ! cried Jack.

~You girls lost? asked Michael Blackshear, grinning. Damn that was fun. Been watching you two for five minutes. More fun than trapping a skunk.

~That was a shitty thing to do, said Henry, breathing hard but starting to smile.

~But funny, said Michael. Either of you deserters got any food?

LATER, IN CAMP SHOWS UP through Virginia and Maryland and on into Pennsylvania, the Celebrated Blackshear Boys would remember how they found each other during what came to be called The Seven Days.

(*Excerpt from a skit performed near Fredericksburg in January 1863*)

JACK: Now let's decide what we're having for mess this morning, boys.

HENRY: I'd like some chicken.

MICHAEL: Bring me some hominy, your worship.

JACK: Okay, that's chicken, hominy. Warn't that a battle, men?

HENRY: Not for me. I was a chicken at Chickenhominy. I gave myself up to General McClellan.

JACK: What happened?

HENRY: Damndest thing. He surrendered to me.

JACK: Wait—you gave yourself up, and General George McClellan surrendered to *you*?

HENRY: Yep. Then I was sent to General Pope in Washington. He surrendered, too.

MICHAEL: I played in a high-stakes poker game with Abe Lincoln just last week. He ran out of money and bet Washington itself. I aim to go over there and collect it next week.

JACK: And what will you do with Washington?

MICHAEL: I aim to move it South. I was going to turn it into a city full of whores. But somebody'd already beat me to it.

The men, cold and miserable after the nightmarish battle of Fredericksburg, had laughed themselves sick, some acquiring coughing fits that took hours to stop. Now, still in the steaming early summer of 1862, the Blackshear brothers moved south toward Cobb's Legion, which was reported to be guarding an artillery battery. The Confederate troops, though wildly uncoordinated and despite the puzzling near-absence of Stonewall Jackson's troops, swept onward, and McClellan's blue-clads, though fighting hard and well, retreated due south toward the James River and along the Chickahominy. On June 29, there was a bitter battle at Savage's Station, and on June 30, the sixth day of fighting, the troops clashed in a battle that would have no less than eight names: Frayser's Farm, White Oak Swamp, Nelson's Crossroads, Glendale, Charles City Crossroads, New Market Road, Turkey Bridge, and Willis Church. Whatever its name, the battle in the mire of a desolate swamp, and poor troop coordination, weak support from Stonewall Jackson, and general chaos left no victor on the field and the Federal lines intact around a mount just north of the James River called Malvern Hill.

~God, go that way—we're taking fire, said Jack. It was true. Pickets hallooed and fired at them in the gathering darkness as the Blackshears sloshed through ankle-deep swamp water. The minié balls sounded like *siz, siz, siz* as they tumbled, deadly insects in the fetid bog. They boys moved west and found themselves under fire from Southern troops, who also hooted and shouted while firing. Not until well after midnight did they find themselves wandering, unmolested, through Confederate lines.

~So what the hell is this plan you have? asked Michael. Some South Carolina boys were sharing a plate of cush, and it was foul, greasy, and wonderful. Dawn was just yawning from the Union lines on Malvern Hill.

~Well, we each have to report back, said Jack, me to Goodpath, Henry to Stillwell, and Michael to Wiseman Robinson. Here's the plan. Firing opened along the lines, desultory at first and then increasing, with a few artillery shells from the Yankees being lobbed over the Southern lines. Michael was dubious.

~That will never work, he said. We're all going to be arrested.

~Trust me, said Jack. If there's one thing I claim to know it's human nature. Got to be today, though, when the banging starts hot. After that, they'll have no time to figure it out. Then we can deal with them later. Hah. Boys, I'm a genius. Give me ten dollars each.

~My ass, said Michael Blackshear.

THE BATTLE OF MALVERN HILL—the last fight in the Seven Days—did not start until the late afternoon. Several of General Magruder's outfits were engaged, but the Branton Avengers lay to the South ducking Union artillery fire and guarding a battery. From the sanctuary of three oak trees, the Blackshears watched as they moved:

~Dear God, we're *not* going to attack up that hill? said Henry.

Fire from the high ground was withering, and rank on rank of gray boys fell, some writhing with wounds, many deadwood, falling over, not moving. Direct hits from Parrott guns: bloody splattering, then a crimson fog. A private awaiting his turn in the charge scratched his arm nervously until blood ran like rose water into his palm.

~You boys, into line! cried a lieutenant with a sword.

~We're detached from…

~You're in line, goddamnit! The officer came toward them, threatening, and the Blackshears dropped their haversacks and loaded their muskets. Henry's mouth grew dry, and he thought of Elizabeth, of boyish pranks, fresh green onions in the summer, cold well water, his mother singing, her red hair burnished by lamplight. Michael saw the scene with his artist's eye—vast rebel battle lines on the plain below marching toward the hill, where thousands were being shot up; clouds of cannon and rifle smoke, regimental flags; gray, green, blue, burnt umber, raw sienna; brass, steel, sky, light touches of rose red. Jack considered tactics—knew at least the South had moved the enemy along a line away from Richmond, that perhaps General Lee had some plan. There were those capable, in chess, of seeing five, six moves ahead, Jack knew: a tactical prescience. Jack saw that with the clot of officers who had brought the Blackshears into this mess. Stillwell, Robinson—each had a reason, but it wasn't enough to kill for. Jack knew the divisions engaged, recognized some of Magruder's men from the days down the Peninsula, but the Avengers weren't on this field, he did not believe. Tactics, strategy, charges, retreats.

The sunset spread a smoky glow into the field before Malvern Hill, like a brass cup in a bucket of milk. Earth shook. The dying and dead up there lay in shingles like oak-tree bark. The Blackshears did not know this unit, could not see a flag, moved, step on step, toward the deafness.

~I will fear no evil, said Henry. Michael saw his younger brother's lips move. Oh what a portrait—fearful eyes, sweat, thin beard, a boy's terror, the first growth of knowledge—oh to paint that. *Thou preparest a table before me in the presence of mine enemy.*

Four hundred yards ahead, an artillery shell ripped up a company, hurling hanks of raw meat in every direction. Not quite in musket range yet. Then the peculiar whistle and hiss of Enfield rounds, the dull thump of minié balls finding flesh, the crack of a tibia, the stunned thunk of a body shot. The line buckling in front and flowing back, men crabbing so they would not be back-shot. Shouting: *Go back! Go back! We're whipped!* One man stopped and licked his lips. His left eye was on his cheek, and he reached up and tried to shove it back into the socket when a Napoleon round took off his left shoulder and half his ribs. The Blackshear boys were thrown into the earth hard, and a dying man fell across Michael and lay there. shuddering, pumping blood from five wounds. A musket shot knocked Henry's hat off, twirled it in the smoke and haze. He could not fire: Confederates came toward him. Jack fell over a wounded corporal, and the boy's bayonet, upturned, sliced through Jack's coat side to side. A beardless private with his lower jaw gone, tongue flailing wildly; a sergeant carrying a severed finger and looking around, shell-stunned; an old man with an open neck wound that spurted at each heartbeat: all horrors to be imagined, all horrors here, now.

The brothers found themselves unwounded but blood-spattered, moving back now with the retreating lines. A young soldier wept and kept saying the name *Jacob* over and over. Officers in their safety above the lines seemed puzzled, excited, seeing the deaths like knocked-over chessmen. Henry could not get his breath. Could not.

THAT NIGHT, THE SOUND FROM the wounded grew piteous, a great moan of anguish. Just before last light, Henry saw it.

~Look, he said. It looks like the whole battlefield is *crawling*. The wounded moved slowly on their stomachs, hands and knees, looking for water, hoping for morphine. Later, when the officers sifted through the casualties for the Seven Days around Richmond, the totals would be staggering. North and South together, all Americans: nearly five thousand killed and twenty-four thousand wounded.

~My God, said Michael. And for what? What? I want to get back to our messmates. Enough of this stupidity. If I'm going to die, at least let it be among friends.

Jack dictated the letter and Henry made three fair copies of it in pencil on paper he got from an Alabama private, a boy named James R. Todd.

Fiftieth Alabama
Dear (insert *Goodpath, Stillwell,* or *Robinson*)

I thank you for lending me your orderly (Jack, Michael, Henry) Blackshear during these recent days of battle. I want to assure you he did his duty as befits a man of courage and fortitude, and served well in heavy combat at Frayser's Farm. Your message was delivered, but it was impossible to send the young man back as we faced a general engagement at the time. His service to me was gallant and even noble. I have written separately to General Longstreet praising the Branton Avengers and Cobb's Legion for providing such men during this time of trial for our country.

Yours most sincerely &tc,
David M. Jennings, Col.
Fiftieth Alabama.

~I like the noble part, said Henry. But they won't believe a word of this.

~We will be arrested, said Michael.

~They can't arrest us, said Jack. We're home folk. And when they see the praise, their vanity won't let them punish us, even if they really believe there isn't a Fiftieth Alabama. Trust me, boys. Trust me.

JACK WAS RIGHT, OF COURSE. Percy Stillwell even gave the letter to General Howell Cobb and figuratively patted himself on the back. Wiseman Robinson and Martin Goodpath conferred and decided they had pulled off some coup for the Avengers, had displayed brilliance and courage *themselves*. Besides, the boys were blood-covered, bearded, bone-thin, chastised enough.

~We wasn't engaged, but I'm dead anyway, said Raleigh Poole around the fire that night. Far across the way, the Union troops moved south off Malvern Hill toward the James River and the guard of Federal gunboats. They were still not far from Richmond, but had quit the fight. McClellan, with his huge army, had failed to take the Confederate capital.

~We *were* engaged, said Henry, staring into the fire. Food was scarce, but the frightening sight of the Blackshears led the others to share cush and coffee.

~If it means anything, I want you boys to know you look like utter shit, said David Bernstein, the clothier.

~Thanks, David. It means a lot, said Jack. I just wish I knew where our instruments are.

~James Peter says you boys are needed for the band, such as it is, said Lyle Fogg. Though a stray shell bursted an euphonium. It looks like a brawler's ear.

~Well, we whipped them, anyway, said Sag Doremus. Maybe Bobby Lee wasn't the king of spades after all. Is it possible, barely, that some officer in this army knows what he is doing?

~Nah, they all said in a chorus. Henry cleared his throat and began to sing "Lorena," and it was sad and fatal, speaking of lost home, lost love, and Jack joined in, and then Michael entered, and the three-part harmony was exquisite, just as their mother taught them, and a dozen—

then three dozen—Avengers came around, and there were others, boys from Athens or Greensboro, from a South Carolina unit, brothers from Arkansas. The Blackshear boys sang "Home, Sweet Home," and some hummed, others wept.

That night, before sleep came, Henry pulled up a blanket of stars and thought of that distance in time and miles, of his father and the Mercantile, of jokes and songs, skits and satires. He remembered Malvern Hill—how could he forget it?—and wondered how long this war would press onward. At least all the Celebrated Blackshear Boys were still alive.

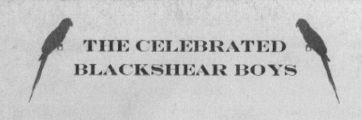

July 5, 1862
In Camp Along the New Market Road
Near Richmond

Dear Mother,
We have come through the late battles near
Richmond all in one piece and unwounded, but the
things I have seen are very nearly unspeakable.
Though the Avengers were not in combat except to be
under artillery fire while guarding a battery, Jack,
Michael, and I were detached as couriers and found
ourselves in the battle for a place called Malvern Hill.
What we saw there was beyond your ability to
comprehend. Hundreds of men fell, and the battlefield
was littered with the wounded and the dead. The cries
were pitiful—men crying out in pain with their last
breaths. I did not expect to see such things when we
marched off—I will be honest: I believe this has been
very hard on Michael, who with his painter's eye
cannot turn away but is inclined to see the
battlefields whole.
The question I have kept asking myself is this:
For what are we fighting? Death is everywhere
around us, and there seems little place now for the
kind of levity by which we have lived so long. And yet
how do we bear life, in the end, at all? So much of this
world suffers that only a very rich or very stupid
person could fail to be moved with sorrow. The
politicians and the generals sit behind us on the hills
or in Richmond and play with us as if we were no
more than checkers or chess pieces. A thousand dead

*here, five thousand dead there—to them it is tactics
and strategies, and many's the time I have wished
them ill. The Federals are no better. And yet I cannot
see the cause for it all. Is it slavery? Is it about taxes
and tariffs? Is it because they are here and won't let
us live our way of life? I've heard all those, but I will
tell you honestly that I hold no brief for slavery any
more than father has. And the way of life of which
they speak is the life of the wealthy planters and no
one else. The common man has no stake in this war
but his blood, and I've seen enough of it already—too
much. The rich and the landed did die on Malvern
Hill. Officers must lead, after all. But also dying were
poor boys with a dream, who left for adventure or
from boredom. I am philosophizing.*

*But it is a sad world here, and the heat is
oppressive, and I am very tired, and the wretchedness
of the battlefield is beyond description. Much love to
Mama Blackshear, and I hope the twins cause you no
serious vexations.*

*Love, your son,
Henry Blackshear*

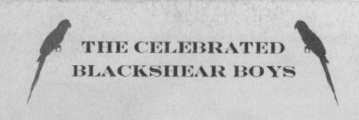

THE CELEBRATED
BLACKSHEAR BOYS

July 5, 1862

Somewhere in Virginia (?)

Hail and farewell, thou parents!

I have read glum Henry's letter, and I wanted to enclose a note along with his missive to say that what he needs is a good game of Kick Me and a smack on the head. The boy thinks too much, always has. Please cook King Lear and stuff him with giblets and send him to us. We are hungry. Romeo or Juliet would serve just as well, though you can forego the giblets with them. (Is there a passage anywhere in the Bible about killing the fatted parrot? Have a look, Mother.)

I haven't had time to write Cynthia Sims lately, but when you see her, please tell her I was brevetted a Drum Major for courage in the fights around here and now command seven hundred thousand men. I wear a uniform decorated with seven pounds of gold braid. I also possess a sword decorated with rubies, pearls, diamonds, emeralds, opals, topazes, and a tourmaline. It weighs twenty-seven pounds, but in combat my strength is that of thousands. I am known as the Spanish Cavalier, though I am not quite sure why. Perhaps it is the glorious mustache I have raised. Tell Miss Sims that when I return home I plan to build a house that will enclose nine acres, including cattle barns and hay fields. I trust she will not sneeze.

The battles hereabouts, in which the Avengers have been gloriously unengaged, were contests for the ages, and we have seen things I would not wish upon a leering drunk. Thus far, I can say that we have refused the Yankees entrance into the shoals of heaven (Richmond) and that we all now rest upon our arms or other parts of our anatomies. Both sides are so battle-thinned that further fights of any magnitude seem unlikely.

Yesterday was the old country's Independence Day, and I celebrated by inventing a new game played with cards and dominoes simultaneously. It is called Big Moose—one shouts that aloud upon winning, which occurs when the six tile and two pair turn up at the same time. I have not revealed this to anyone yet. Michael sold a drawing of the Battle of Malvern Hill to an officer of a South Carolina regiment for three dollars and eight cents. We spent the proceedings on some local cider, which had apparently turned into something far more interesting. Hiccup!

Tell Mr. and Mrs. Bernstein that their David was cited for Bravery Beneath an Artillery Caisson in Action, one of our most common honors. The Fogg brothers have each suffered minor shaving wounds. Sag Doremus is mourning the death, by cannon-fire, of a euphonium, lost in her youth.

Not much is happening now except that General McClellan has invented a new military move, the Retrograde Crab, which will soon take him into the James River, apparently. God bless him.

Please give our best to Mama Blackshear, if she happens to be in the neighborhood.

Your son,
Jack Blackshear, Esq.

CRAMPTON'S GAP

They marched across a ford in the Potomac River, stepped into Maryland, hundreds barefoot at the edge of autumn. The Army of Northern Virginia was fifty-thousand strong, and only weeks after a victory at Second Manassas, the Confederate troops snaked through the valleys of the Blue Ridge seeking to get beyond the Federals, to force their hand, find recognition from foreign governments. The land was heavy and rich this early September of 1862, with corn ripening on the stalks, orchards beginning to groan with fruit, and neat farms stitched off with fine rail fences. Small, whitewashed towns turned out, sullen watchers, as the rebel troops came through like ants. The Federals, now on their trail, did perhaps even more damage, with tens of thousands pouring across ripening fields and destroying them, messmates burning up fences, killing fowl and cattle. Robert E. Lee's first incursion into the North brought march and countermarch, cavalry scouting, skirmishes, constant probing. The men ate small rations and dust, ached for a stop, even to fight. Cobb's Legion had missed Second Manassas, had still been mired around Richmond after the Seven Days, but the new victory at the old Manassas battlefield was complete, the tattered remains of Union General John Pope's soldiers flowing back toward Washington. The slaughter had been staggering: on both sides, more than three thousand killed and sixteen thousand wounded.

Cobb's Legion, for some time now in the division of General Lafayette McLaws, had come north on a forced march in the late summer dust, and dozens had fallen out from exhaustion, some of whom died. From August 23-28, they marched across Virginia, relentlessly driven, with little time to eat. Near Rapidan Station, a soldier from Branton named Lucius Pennamon fell dead, a thin-faced young man who was only twenty. He had taken a flesh wound near Malvern Hill that festered, and after that he had never drawn a painless breath.

The Southern Army stretched up the valleys of the Blue Ridge into Maryland, and they could imagine the Federals were in motion now, flowing toward them.

~I don't think I ever want to see another thing like that Manassas battlefield, said David Bernstein. I know we won, but my *God.*

~Give me a piece of your bread, said Jack Blackshear, face taut with exhaustion. I'll trade you a song for it.

~There's no need for camp entertainers in a war, said Raleigh Poole crossly. I'm dead anyway. Fare well boys, and goodbye. This made the others laugh and lightened their mood. It was the ninth of September, and autumn barely seeped down the valleys from the north. They camped near the small town of Frederick, Maryland, and from a thousand campfires, the hunger-hollowed faces of southern boys leaned in. They drank, cooked over their fires with a dull lassitude.

~I need to talk to you, said Henry to his brother Michael. They stood and walked some distance into the edge of a cornfield, from whose stalks hundreds of ears had already been stripped. Michael lingered over the scene's magnificence: to the west, the low lovely ridge of Catoctin Mountain stretching north to south. They'd heard that the Monocacy River was on the east side of Frederick, but there was no time to go there, to swim or fish, to laze in the autumnal light. Michael had heard that a fragrant valley was just west of Catoctin, a lovely swale between it and South Mountain. There would be small, four-square towns, fine farms bordered with rail fences, sweet-faced cattle, apple trees. There had been no time on this march for pleasure of any kind, but this lingering glance brought him back. They stood next to the cornfield. Henry seemed about to cry.

~What? said Michael. Are you sick?

~I'm afraid inside, said Henry. He hugged himself and trembled a little. I don't know what's come over me. I just have this idea that something bad's about to happen, and I can't stop it.

~Something bad? Do you think you're at a Sunday school picnic? Of *course* something bad's about to happen, you ninny. We're in the army, in the middle of a war, exposed on enemy territory, with our troops spread out over fifteen miles. What did you think was going to happen? A game of high-stakes Kick Me with Abe Lincoln? Michael slapped his brother lightly on the back of the head.

~I mean, I don't know why I'm here. I feel like I'm not supposed to be here. We're all going to die in this damned army. Either our side will kill us or the other will. If this is a war to free the slaves, what does it have to do with us? All I want is to live to be old.

~Honest to God, Henry, I don't know what gets into you some-times. Once a war gets going, nobody cares who's in the right. Half the men here came because they were bored or scared not to come. A poor man can die here and be called a hero or at home and just be called a poor man. Which would you do?

~We're not poor men.

~No, we're not.

~I can't keep my spirits up. How can I keep up those of the men?

~Look, we still have these idiots Percy Stillwell, Martin Goodpath, and Wiseman Robinson as officers. We may be speaking Yankee by sunset tomorrow. Isn't that pretty funny?

~No.

~Are you thinking of fair Elizabeth?

~I might be.

~Come on, boy. I know what you need.

Henry looked at Michael as if he'd lost his mind but let him pull him by the elbow, walking in the dusk rapidly through the half-flattened cornfield toward a farmhouse not quite a mile away. Neither of them spoke. A band from somewhere tried "Dixie" but the song fell apart, and soon it was playing "Just Before the Battle, Mother," in a lugubrious way. They'd be weeping over that way. Frederick, Maryland. Who knew they would ever be here, coming across such rich farmland, keeping some-what low, and hunting for a woman?

SHE WAS AT THE THIRD house they came to, a girl of about seven-teen, standing at a windlass and pulling up a well bucket. She wore a dusty brown dress that draped poorly around her slender figure, and when she looked up, the last sun across Catoctin Mountain spread into her pale blue eyes. She startled, stepped back. Michael noted: a plain face, narrow-bridged nose, high cheeks spangled with light freckles. Her feet were bare and dirty, and she balled her toes into fists as she stared at the rebel boys in her yard. She walked to the well, removed the bucket, which seemed to slosh the evening light. Setting it down, here she came, striding with purpose toward them, wiping her hands on the flanks of her dress.

~Good evening, ma'am, I'm Michael…

Whap! She slapped Michael on the face so hard he staggered sideways, and Henry began to giggle girlishly. She turned to him rapidly, and, fast as a child catching a fly, slapped him, too. The brothers held their cheeks and stumbled back toward her, looking at each other warily. Henry couldn't stop grinning.

~I hate you damn rebels, *hate* you coming here and tromping our crops and killing our kine and ripping up the damn fences down to the ants, she said. I hate your damn uniforms. I hate your stink and your music. I hate this war, and I hate you two personally.

~Ma'am, I can't say that I blame you, said Michael.

~You can both go to hell, she said, pushing the hair out of her eyes. Now. Which one of you wants me first?

~Hnnh? said Henry Blackshear.

~My brother does, said Michael, and a fine specimen of manhood he is. Back home they call him the Giant Teapot for reasons I can't disclose on account of delicacy.

~Hnnh? said Henry.

~I *hate* you, she said slowly, dreamy now. She dropped her arms and came to Henry and stood in front of him. You want me in the barn or in the house? I don't reckon Othneil will be here any time soon.

~Who is he, and *where* is he? asked Henry. Up close, she was quite pretty, breathing hard, licking her lips.

~He's my husband. But he died last Christmas. He's still dead. You don't happen to have any chew, do you? Henry looked helplessly at Michael, who was falling apart with the need to laugh, face bright red from the slap.

~I don't chew, said Henry.

~Then I guess I'll have to open my flower for free, she said.

~Your flow—what's your name?

~Ginger McGilpin.

~That's a lot of name for such a small girl, said Michael.

~I'm guessing they don't call *you* Teapot, she said, looking him up and down with disdain. Let's get this over with. I've only got all night. She was standing closer to Henry now, but he hadn't seen her move. Strange. Come on. She took his hand, and they moved toward the house, which couldn't have, Henry thought, more than four rooms, if that.

SHE LIT AN OIL LAMP and stood in the front parlor staring at Henry with damp-lipped lust. Michael had found a whittling stick and gone to a large oak tree and sat beneath it, whistling, prepared for Henry to take his time. She seemed to wave at the buttons down the front of her dress, and it fell off. Then came the petticoat, and she was standing naked, shivering, lovely, thin, breasts outlined by lamplight, heavy, aimed at Henry, who was unbuckling his belt.

~Have you got a honey back home? Ginger asked.

~Yes.

~What's her name? A little sullen.

~I can't remember, said Henry. He was down to his drawers, which were tenting majestically. I think she's a Malone. I thought you hated rebels.

~You're pretty, she said. I don't know when I saw such a pretty boy. Othneil had naught but a nubbin. I'm pleased to see you're pecker proud.

~I ought to have some finer feelings about now, said Henry to himself but aloud. But I don't have any finer feelings.

~Are we going to rut or what?

~I could be killed in battle tomorrow, said Henry, slipping out of his drawers. Ginger made a throaty sound of approval. The sound of whistling, like a lonesome bird, seemed a little louder outside.

~I'll always mourn you dead, she said. Thinking about it later, Henry pictured them both, somehow, running toward each other at this point, emitting a smack of flesh, entwining, kissing, falling. She was biting his ear and calling him Sugar. He licked her nipples and said she was his honey girl. She dragged him toward the bedroom, and they fell into the tick. To Henry it seemed they were about to be digested by a bale of rough cotton, and he had trouble holding on to her, and at one point he could have sworn she was biting his left eyebrow. The bed hopped toward the center of the room, and she emitted small cries. Someone outside was clearly singing now.

Henry finished twice in the space of thirty minutes, but Ginger wouldn't stop, and with a crack, the bed's slats broke, and the mattress fell through on to the floor, and still she wouldn't stop. Finally, they lay in the dark room, tumbled together, soaked and gasping. A firefly had let itself inside and cast its pale glow around the room.

~You know what it means when a lightning bug comes in the house? she asked.

~Not really, said Henry.

~I don't, neither. Get up and go tell your brother I'll be *his* wife for the next hour. It doesn't mean I don't love you.

~Is your husband really dead? asked Michael, dressing, misbuttoning.

~Well, I need to come clean on that point, she said. He left me. Said he was just looking for a woman to make him biscuits and such. He went to the army, the Yankee army, and I got a letter he died a mumps in Washington City. She was laughing now. She climbed out of the collapsed bed and stood there, and a faint sliver of light from the parlor slid into the bedroom, and she blew out her cheeks, mumpy and laughing.

THEY GOT BACK TO THE Avengers some time after midnight, and Jack was smoking a corncob pipe and looking at the stars.

~You girls smell like perdition, said Jack. My congratulations. Word is no one in this army knows his ass from a hole in the ground. We're moving out at first light, so I'd suggest you get some sleep and rest whatever parts are most exercised.

~I have gotten religion, said Michael.

~I acted like an animal, said Henry, not seeming particularly sad about it.

~You *are* an animal, said Jack. You think something with the breath of God in it would slaughter each other like this? What are you boys going to name the baby?

~Alonzo, said Michael.

~Henrietta, said Henry.

~Why Alonzo? asked Jack. The Fogg boys were both snoring.

~Okay, he said, Moses Ephraim.

~Much better, said Jack. A noble moniker. Are you feeling better? Henry was almost asleep.

~Better than what?

Henry awoke several hours later, and light was barely edging up, and he glanced, yawning, at Jack's blanket and saw he was not alone. Ginger was sprawled beneath the blanket with him, snoring with her mouth open.

~Get up! Hsst! Henry shook her shoulder. Somebody sees you, they'll jail you and shoot us. Ginger sat up, smacking her lips and scratching her half-exposed left breast. Jack sat up next to her and scratched his beard. She rose, buttoned her dress and ran away, deer-fast, through the still-sleeping men, disappearing through the crippled corn stalks.

~She followed you girls, he said. Somewhat savage desires in her.

~So what are *you* going to name the baby? asked Henry, wishing for water.

~Oh I'll name him after you, said Jack. We must perpetuate the names of Cobb's Legionnaires at every cost. Wait—maybe it will be triplets. How will we know who's the father of each?

~Maybe it will be one baby with parts from the three of us. Your part will be the ass.

~I can live with that, said Jack. A noble night's work.

COBB'S BRIGADE, OF WHICH COBB'S Legion was a part, marched west out of Frederick on the next day, September 10, and sullen townsmen and women lined up to wish the Confederacy ill. Their commander Tom Cobb was on leave back in Athens to see his wife, and the Legion was in charge of Lieutenant Colonel Jeff Lamar. Howell Cobb, Tom's older brother, had been secretary of the treasury under Buchanan, and the townspeople recognized his gut, his rounded cheeks as he rode along on his horse.

~Need some more corn, Cobb? one old man cried.

~Bring on all you have! said Cobb, undaunted. We'll be back anyway when we win our independence, and we shall kick your rears and take all your corn anyway. I'll personally see you in jail, sir!

~I'll personally see you in hell! the old man cackled. Bystanders enjoyed it. Cobb looked around the town and saw a girl of perhaps twelve standing in the open upstairs window of a house, waving a Confederate flag.

~Sissy, you're the gal I'm looking for! cried Cobb. The line of march stopped for a moment, and the Blackshear brothers looked at each other doubtfully. Percy Stillwell marched right behind Cobb, and Stillwell made a cavalier gesture to the girl, which seemed fey, almost ridiculous. Cobb orated for a while, politician. Some of the crowd clapped derisively before the Legion infantry moved on through Frederick toward Catoctin Mountain.

~So, if you had to guess where we're headed, where would you think? asked David Bernstein as they marched along through the lovely countryside. A pale wash of autumn breathed along the trees near the top of Catoctin Mountain. The troops were headed toward the Burkittsville-and-Brownsville Pass, through which they would head east or South, perhaps to Harper's Ferry or a tenting ground near it.

~I'm thinking it's probably London, said Jack.

~London? cried Raleigh Poole. How'd we get here?

~Oh, I know, said Sag Doremus. There's been this drought, Raleigh, and it's been like things in the Bible, when it rained frogs or lice.

~Must of rained lice over at Frederick, said Whitman Fogg blandly, scratching. Some laughter.

~Let me finish, said Sag. This is the kind of drought that's once in a thousand years, and everything wet in the world is drying up. You can't believe it. An elephant pissing wouldn't fill up a thimble. I mean *dry*. As if the last time it rained, King George was president of the United States. The Branton River wouldn't be more than one spit. So when we thought we was coming across the Potomac into Maryland, we were really fording the Atlantic Ocean. My guess is that when we go through that mountain up there, we'll be in France.

~I be dog, said Raleigh.

~Girls, I feel a skit coming on, said Michael.

~No talking in the ranks! shouted Lieutenant Martin Goodpath. He came walking past them, out of formation, holding the front of his pants. He'd been sick for several days with what the Avengers were calling the Georgia trots. He was pale and irritated-looking, as if someone had pulled a joke on him that he didn't quite get. He said, And I'm talking about you Blackshears.

~Permission to think in the ranks? asked Henry, child-faced.

~Denied! cried Goodpath. He stumbled on past them toward the front where he could march closer to Wiseman Robinson.

~We could do that McClellan thing you've been working on, Henry, said Jack. Any of you think he's anywhere near us?

~McClellan's in England, too? asked Raleigh Poole.

THEY MARCHED THROUGH THE PASS in Catoctin Mountain into Pleasant Valley, and each man spoke with admiration and admission that it was aptly named. Before them, six miles distant, was South Mountain, a fifty-mile-long, thirteen-hundred-foot-high ridge also stretching north to south. They passed through the valley and on past South Mountain, and before them was another range called Elk Ridge. On the night of September 11, they camped near the small town of Brownsville. A soldier from Athens named Otis Hixon, who had something of a genius for foraging liquor, disappeared, dangerously, for an hour late in the day and came back with two heavy crockery jugs full of what he called Maryland Be Mighty. Hixon was a stout man with a potato nose and fingers thick as a hoe handle, and he said he'd sell the jugs to the highest bidder. Michael and Henry were startled when Jack produced twenty-three dollars and walked off with the trophies.

~You have just given away the money needed to raise our son, said Henry. I applaud your decision.

~The best audience is a drunk audience, girls, said Jack. Remember that. He let his brothers have a small glug, and they gasped whooed, smacked their lips. The night was cool but not cold, and a thousand campfires lit the land, and despite all the hard marching for the past few months, the troops sensed a fight was near and were in a fine mood from the thought.

Their messmates cooked up what they had—a little bacon, bread formed and baked on Enfield ramrods, and the rich aroma settling with the low smoke across the lovely countryside. At a distance, someone discharged a musket, and they all turned and waited, but nothing happened.

~Some fool just blowed his nose off with a dropped gun, said Lyle Fogg.

~There are many smells I'd miss, said Henry. Thanks be that I've recently smelt my favorite.

The boys' messmates got a free dram of Maryland Be Mighty, and everyone else had to pay fifty cents for a quarter-cupful. With near-empty stomachs and weak-kneed exhaustion, the liquor hit them like an artillery shell, and soon dozens of the Avengers and several from Madison's Panola Guards were giddy and giggling, telling jokes, singing and dancing. The baggage train was nowhere near the troops—nobody had seen it for three days—and so the Blackshears would have to perform without their instruments, but none of them minded. That was the infantry for you. When you lived, that was good. When you were dead, that was not so bad, either.

Just after nine, when the oil lamps of Brownsville were already going out in windows all over town, Henry leaped up and came to the front of a huge group seated in a semicircle before three bonfires of burning fence rails.

~Ladies and gentlemen! cried Henry. They clapped and laughed. And I use both terms lightly. Welcome to Maryland. Do you know what you call a person from Maryland?

~Marylander! two or three called out.

~No, you call a person from Maryland a prisoner, said Henry. (*Laughter, applause and whistling.*) Now boys, these people can't help that they're prisoners. And did you know all Maryland women have six fingers on each hand? Why, you ask? To tickle their men awake during marital duties!

Jack came stalking up, dark-faced and mugging.

~Sir, *I* am a Maryland man, and I resent your slur on my lovemaking skills! I have three fine children, and they did not arrive out of nothing.

~Ah, I know your children, said Henry. Your boy Elijah has blond hair and blue eyes, does he not?

~So?

~You and your wife both have brown hair and black eyes. And your Hannah. She is fifteen years old, and she is six and a half feet tall, and you and your wife are both dwarves.

~Are you trying to make some point?

~And your Nathan is clearly an Indian.

~And proud I am of that! cried Jack. (*The troops falling over, punching each other.*)

~So has your wife been with you all this time?

~No, she has been a victualler for the army and has traveled with fine men like these here around Brownsville. Men whose honor goes without question.

Soldiers from other companies of Cobb's Legion Infantry drifted over, and even without the benefit of liquor were having a fine time. Michael came running up, as if out of breath.

~Mr. Maryland Man, Mr. Maryland Man! cried Michael. I came from your farm just as fast as I could. Your house has been invested by outlaws! Seven of them!

~Outlaws? Outlaws? shouted Jack. Oh my dear wife! Did she manage to get a message to you?

~Yes! She said for you to come for her, but not until tomorrow afternoon at the earliest!

The skit went on like this for half an hour, half-written, half-improvised and ended with a huge round of applause that could be heard on the other side of town. The brothers came together and sang three songs, ending with a very slow, close-harmony arrangement Michael had made of "Lorena." (*Sniffy clapping, calls for something funnier.*)

HENRY: General McClellan, General McClellan!

JACK: What is it, lieutenant? Are the Rebels nearby? There must be a hundred million of them! Alarms! Alarms! Adjutant, take a letter. (*Michael rushes up, acting as if he has a pen on paper.*)

MICHAEL: Ready, sir.

JACK: Dear President Lincoln comma—wait. Dear Excellency comma—wait. I'm much more excellent than he is. Dear Abe comma I am in Maryland and surrounded by a hundred million troops headed by General Lee. My inclination is to bite my finger until it bleeds, period. Please send all the residents of New York City, Philadelphia, and Chicago, period. We would have won the latest battle of Manassas except for the fact that the rebels had eighteen million men on the field, and we had only twenty-seven effectives, period. General Pope writes from his latest posting in the Alps that he intends to take Milan, semicolon. Is that a rational objective, question mark. Yours sincerely, George B. McClellan, Emperor.

The skits lasted for nearly an hour, and when the show ended, the brothers finished off the quart of liquor that was left while Henry tried to count their take, but he kept getting to ten dollars and having to start over.

~Nothing adds up, said Henry, sleepy, happy.

~Spoken like a general, said Jack.

THE NEXT DAY, THEY PATROLLED along the base of Elk Ridge, supporting Mississippi and South Carolina troops far up the slopes, where they had been sent to beat back Federals up snooping from their garrison at Harper's Ferry. Overnight, Cobb's Legion picketed the Weaverton-Sandy Hook Road, and on Saturday, September 13, the Legion captured—the term was something of a joke—the tumble-down hamlet of Sandy Hook itself at the foot of Elk Ridge.

~More like Sandy Hookworm, said Raleigh Poole, who jumped, surprised at the laughter that greeted his joke.

That same Saturday morning, near the town of Ijamsville, south of Frederick, Company F of the 27th Indiana Volunteer Infantry in the Federal Twelfth Army Corps of the Army being led by McClellan spread out in a skirmish line. They were screening the march northward of their regiment of the Army of the Potomac, which was in wary pursuit of the Confederates. Approaching Frederick and finding the rebels gone, the skirmish line stood down, and the soldiers stacked their muskets in a field still green with summer clover. A corporal from Company F happened to see a small bundle lying in the grass, and he picked it up, delighted to see three fat cigars wrapped in a piece of paper. He congratulated himself on his luck and then saw the paper was covered with handwriting. A private from Company F happened to walk over, and together they read: *Special Orders #191*. They realized, stunned, that it was a copy of orders from General R. E. Lee himself for placement of all Confederate divisions during the invasion of Maryland. Passed through channels up to McClellan himself, the order was the key to destruction of the Southern rebellion and McClellan knew it. He would have Bob Lee now, he exulted. Though he was still slow to move, the Union general began to turn his troops toward the inevitable conflict.

That night, camping near Sandy Hook, the Branton Avengers were too exhausted from picket duty the night before to do more than eat whatever they could and spread their blankets for sleep. Henry grew pensive.

~I was thinking of mama and papa today, said Henry. I miss them. I want to go home. I think this whole war is an idiotic thing.

~Mikey, you shoot him for sedition, said Jack, lying on his blanket. I'm too tired.

~I wish I had but one paintbrush and some black, brown, and blue, said Michael. I could do this scene justice. Except for Sandy Hookworm. That's a foul little place. I wonder if there are lonely women there.

~If you find any, bring me one, said Jack. Make sure she has at least five teeth.

~I'm serious, said Henry. Remember all the good times we had back home in Branton? With Mama Blackshear and King Lear and Romeo and Juliet? Michael, don't you miss the schooroom?

~Like I miss a case of clap, said Michael, yawning.

~I do miss working for the *Eagle*, said Jack, nearly asleep. But a man who writes for a living is capable of anything.

~In the morning, between roll call and cold rations, Jack pulled out his mother's last letter and re-read it in part: *Mama Blackshear's hearing has become oddly acute for reasons we cannot fathom, and she seems to hear that parrot breathing and says she can hardly bear it. She still calls it a chicken and says we could have a delicious pie. Mrs. Cardinal came to church on Sunday wearing a huge bonnet and a petticoat. Because she was proud of the hat, it took three gentlemen, including your father, to wrestle her to a carriage and take her home so she might put on a dress. Lettie Robinson has begun to tell people all over town that her Wiseman is a Southern Hero and that he will come home covered in glory. Your father said in the mercantile that the only thing he will come home covered with is fear-sweat. The word of this got back to Lettie, and she came into the shop and cried aloud that your father was a half-blind idiot and that she would rather be ravished by Yankees than ever spend a penny there again. Your father (bless him!) said that he'd forego a thousand dollars from her just to see a Yankee chasing her down the street....*

So, a Sunday morning in Maryland, quiet, and the Legion and pieces of McLaws's Division formed, marched about, came past Sandy Hook again.

~I think I could be king of Sandy Hook, said Jack. Henry, bring unto me all the women who live thereto and strip them naked for my inspection.

~Even the fallen women? he asked, yawning.

~*Especially* the fallen women, said Jack. Why is it, boys, that we say a woman who does what nature insists is fallen? Are not we, the soldiers of the race, more fallen than a woman who gives herself for love?

~I meant to tell you, said Henry, that a couple of boys from South Carolina also spoke warmly of Ginger's favors. We may all be expecting a litter of rebels rather than a trio.

~Ack, said Jack Blackshear.

The orders did not come until late in the day: The Federal Sixth Corps poured into the valley on the other side of South Mountain and riders kept bringing reports of Blue columns everywhere. General Paul Semmes, worried about passes through South Mountain, sent a note to McLaws: *We need help.* Michael felt swept up in a magnificence, troops moving at route step, the clanking of canteens and gear, the steps of worn brogans in the dust, the blush of color at the mountains' crests. For some time the orders were unclear: Brownsville Pass or Crampton's Gap?

~They're splitting us, said David Bernstein. How come they're splitting us?

~Thus saith the Lord, amen, said Jack.

They watched as the 24th Georgia regiment and the 15th North Carolina began to march on up the valley. The idea: be in two places at once depending on whether the Yankees attempted to come through Crampton's Gap or Brownsville Pass. But before they'd gone two hundred yards, another rider came galloping in, saluted to some officer, and everyone stopped again.

~Hear that? asked Sag Doremus. They could now, clearly: massed musket fire, loud and then louder.

~Wait—I know where that's coming from, said Michael, who was better at understanding maps and terrain than most. That's over South Mountain there at Burkittsville. God, the Federals are all the way to Burkittsville.

The remainder of Cobb's Legion infantry began to ascend South Mountain itself now, walking double-quick up through the woods, finding footholds, the sounds of battle louder, then louder still. Col. Lamar was up there in front somewhere when they all crested the ridge.

~My *God*, said Raleigh Poole. Would you look at that. And they did, and the scope beggared description: Below them in the valley, pouring toward Burkittsville, were tens of thousands of Union troops, and down below at the foot of the mountain a fierce battle was engaged, though it was unclear if the Southern troops were going down the slope or the Federals were coming up.

~Girls, this is going to be interesting, said Jack.

Now, the split planned earlier happened in fact, with the 15th North Carolina pushed down to the Arnoldstown Road behind a stone wall, and the 24th Georgia sent into Whipp's Ravine, the entrance into the gap in South Mountain itself.

~Follow me, men! cried Colonel Lamar, and the Legion infantry was in motion to their right, followed soon by the 16th Georgia. And let them hear you in the valley! Suddenly, they all screamed, and the sound made Henry shiver, and he was afraid, sick with fear, hands trembling on his musket. And Michael saw the pale sky and the green valley and Catoctin Mountain farther to the east and the Union soldiers massing below, the glint of bayonet and cannon brass. The troops began positioning themselves, but Lamar kept Cobb's Legion flowing down the sharp mountainside toward the battle, moving like the Potomac, broad and split by trees as a river flows around exposed stones. Lamar rode forward, keeping his mount steady, and they came into a thinned area, where someone had been cutting wood for the coming winter, and he deployed his troops behind a stone wall in an open area and waited. His horse stumbled and fell, and Lamar rolled off but bounced up like an acrobat, smiling and waving his cap. Jack felt the cheer coming from his throat, and it surprised him. All of them were cheering, and all of them were afraid.

MY GOD, THOUGHT HENRY BLACKSHEAR, *look down there.* Whole brigades boiled upward now, and the battle was met, and it was five-thirty on an early autumn afternoon, and the white smoke from musket fire made it seem the entire valley near South Mountain was on fire. Apparently, fighting had erupted toward the north as well. From their perch, as they awaited developments, the Legion infantry could see Mountain Church Road at the foot of South Mountain and beyond it the town of Burkittsville. To the left, scenic in surrounding cornfields, was George's Whipp's farm.

~Christ God in heaven, we're outnumbered ten to one, said Hiram Bunt, a lawyer from Branton who was a seedy failure and had run for every officer's position that had opened, never garnering more than a few votes each time.

Below them, they could see the 10th Georgia just off the road, with the 8th Virginia on its right. The Union troops engaged them heavily, and suddenly, now nearly six-fifteen, the Legion fired one last round and began to fall back, and Jack realized that they would soon be the right flank of the rebel lines on South Mountain, and he knew in his stomach that they were in position to be slaughtered by a vastly larger Yankee force.

Now the shadows of the mountain folded over them as the sun was eclipsed by the crest of South Mountain, and the firing increased, now punctuated by artillery shells. Federal troops moved up the slopes now, right in front of the Legion infantry and to its right.

~Steady, men! cried Colonel Lamar.

~Jack? said Henry.

~I know. Listen. If one of us stays alive, all of us stays alive. Spread out from me and stay separate. And for God's sake, keep your heads down. If one of us falls or is captured, he will *never* be left behind. *Never!* I promise, you boys promise! They did.

The Blue troops, New Jersey units mostly, had their blood up and fought up the mountain, some of them pulling up by rocks and under-brush. The light now seemed orange as the sun began to die, but the battle rose toward them, and they knelt, Enfields loaded, caps down hard on the firing nipples, breathing hard, waiting. Smoke seemed every-where, clouds of it drifting in the light wash of wind. There were two hundred and fifty men now in the Legion Infantry. More than twelve hundred Yankees came at them in full fury. Henry saw Captain Wiseman Robinson walking back and forth, sword out, face pale as bone.

~Fire!

The Federals boiled upward now—Jack couldn't think of any other word—and worse, they came from the front *and* the right flank. The 16th Georgia was on their left, so they could not move that way; falling back to the rear would mean the entire line would fold to a Union flanking movement. Henry saw a man from Athens he'd met several times at their skits—Sergeant Benjamin Mell. He was screaming, but Henry couldn't hear a word. The Legionnaires began to be killed, first falling one-two-three and then collapsing in bloodied clumps. Henry fired and loaded, fired and loaded, looked up and down the line for his brothers, saw neither of them. Sergeant Mell moved toward Henry when two bullets plowed through him, one in the arm but the other, mortally, through his chest.

~Boys, I know I must die! he called, blood turning his words bright red. But don't leave the field! No one had even thought of leaving the field, though: They were trapped, flanked, very nearly overrun. The line fell back into a V to try and find some way to keep from being flanked, but it was no good. A bullet hit Colonel Jeff Lamar in the leg, and he collapsed to the ground. Henry was too afraid to load his gun and lay flat, watching. A few soldiers to tried to run, were cut down. Lamar said, If you fall back you will tread on my body. If you retreat, you will leave me here. Hold the line, boys! Hold it!

But it was no good, and they knew it, and a captain, also wounded, told Lamar they must fall back, and Lamar said that if the captain held him up, he'd give the order. One wounded man helped the other up. A minié ball grazed Henry's shoulder, drew blood. Not ten feet away, Lyle Fogg suddenly sat up, and three bullets hit him almost simultaneously. One blew the right side of his head away. Henry lay trembling.

~By the left flank, double quick! cried Colonel Lamar. Another bullet hit him now, and he collapsed dead on the ground. Whitman Fogg, cradling his brother, was shot through the throat and fell over, writhing for only a short time. Lieutenant Martin Goodpath waved his sword when he was hit four times in the chest, spinning him one way and then another. He fell without moving, mouth working over a blood sentence. Henry was up and running now, gun left behind, running, vaulting bodies, the *siz siz siz* of minié balls inches from his ears, arms, torso. The sound of balls thunking into bodies and trees was everywhere, and he did not look back. Cobb's Legion was being cut to pieces, and he knew it. He felt a sting in his right forearm, ignored it. He kept running upward to the crest of South Mountain, and then he was over it and going down toward the valley between it and Elk Ridge, falling tree by tree, and blood trickled down his arm and he flung it as he ran, fell, rose again, kept moving.

MICHAEL HAD BEEN LYING NEXT to Wiseman Robinson when the officer seemed to throw out all his limbs stiffly and then relax. A bullet had hit the top of his head, plowed straight through his body and come out his scrotum. Michael crawled fast away from the firing, saw them falling now, had to crawl over the dead and hideously wounded. The day was dying, too, and the smoke choked him, and there were patches of peach-colored light, bodies pumping up their last blood, great gouts of crimson creeks. A round tore through his coat sleeve, and he did not stop crawling until he was two hundred yards behind the battle, and then he rose and ran. A minié ball slammed into an oak tree, two inches from his head.

JACK BLACKSHEAR SAW, TO HIS amazement, Percy Stillwell, sitting in a puddle of sunlight, touch his chest, bring away a palmful of blood, hold it to his lips, taste it. Jack wanted to cry. Another bullet took off the top of Stillwell's head, and he reached up, put his hand into his own brain and then with an odd glance, he fell over and did not move. Jack stood and began to walk slowly away from the battle. The Union lines poured forward now, enfolding what was left of Cobb's Legion Infantry, and those still living—perhaps a third of the command—raised their hands and surrendered. The battle here was ending, though it went on to the left, even as the light began to die in the trees.

To the north, Howell Cobb desperately tried to hold Crampton's Gap itself, forming troops with the help of Colonel John Lamar, Jeff's Lamar's brother from Athens. Troops from many Confederate units spilled into the next valley, wounded, exhausted, or just afraid. He had sent back to Sandy Hook for two guns of the Legion's artillery unit, and they were now in place in the gap, aimed toward the coming Union troops. Suddenly, the New Jersey troops that had routed Cobb's Legion were coming at the right flank on the rest of Cobb's Brigade, and many of the remaining soldiers wanted to bolt toward the next valley. The soldiers lay behind a stone wall. The situation was impossible.

By now, Jack could hardly see: almost eight o'clock. He moved like a ghost through the trees down the western side of South Mountain. Firing slowed, and Jack saw below him, in the last light, thousands of whipped rebels, falling back, falling back, falling back.

ANTIETAM

The town of Sharpsburg was square as a box, and when General Layfayette McLaws's diminished and much-battered division came through two days later just after seven in the morning, the armies were already forming for a fight along a sinuous creek. Federals had decimated Cobb's Legion at Crampton's Gap, and the entire Brigade was in ruins. Back in the valley, General Howell Cobb, already being severely criticized for how he handled his troops, tried to pull his unit back together, gathering stragglers, attending to his wounded. The Blackshear brothers certainly should have been there, sitting like old comrades, dull-eyed, quarter-witted, but instead, they were back together now, marching in the right division but the wrong brigade, carrying squirrely smooth-bore muskets given to them from dead Confederates.

~My God, look at *that*, said Henry, pointing. Far ahead of them, the battle sought by McClellan, half-planned by Lee, unfolded in a massive fight, and the killing fields flowed with blood from both sides. The line of battle seemed to stretch for miles. I can't take this anymore.

~Who asked if we could take it? said Jack. Now there's not even anybody to make sport of. I can't believe all three of them are dead, and the three of us are alive.

~Wish I had a pencil at least, said Michael dreamily. If live through this, my God what a mural this will make.

McLaws's men had marched most of the night from Harper's Ferry, and now they marched, without stopping, into a battle that seemed in full blood already. From here, you could see the dead up there, past a small white church and into a cornfield, which had been cleanly harvested by musket fire. The land was hilly, leading downslope to a bucolic creek. The Blackshears let their eyes trace from left to right along a vast battlefield. Now, it seemed, Crampton's Gap would look like nothing more than a skirmish, because McClellan's Federals had caught up with Bob Lee and his troops just north of the Potomac River, past the Maryland town of Sharpsburg, and along the creek called Antietam.

THREE DAYS HAD PASSED SINCE the fighting on South Mountain, and the night of that fight, Jack Blackshear had walked from man to man, looking for his brothers, calling their names. The groaning wounded lowed like cattle. Burial details worked by lantern light, though most of Cobb's Legion dead still lay on the other side of the crest, facing Burkittsville. Several dozen had surrendered, but a number had made their way through the lines at the last moment, wounded, shot up. Jack couldn't account for his own messmates; there had been too much confusion for that. He ran across General Howell Cobb, whey-faced and trying to rally the few men left in his brigade, but they glared at him, accusing with exhausted eyes.

In the faint light, Jack could see that General McLaws, burly and bearded, had come up on horseback, with Jeb Stuart beside him. Cobb pushed back his hair, looking wildly around.

~The enemy is within fifty yards of us! Cobb shouted. What can be done? What can save us?

~My God, get control of yourself, said McLaws. More horses then, the rattle of gun carriages. Two pieces from the artillery had been brought across the valley and set up and began to fire into the pursuing Federals, who had nearly broken through Crampton's Gap. They began to fire, and ranks of Union soldiers fell, then more and even more. They fell back into the coming darkness long enough for the troops, including Jack, to move across the valley toward Elk Ridge as the Yankees slowed down and regrouped. The Southern troops lathered, stampeded, horse and man. Two regiments led by General Paul Semmes finally made it to the field, and checked the Union advance just as night flowed over the mountains of Maryland, a hushed and hushing shroud.

Next day the remnants of the Legion would fall back across the Potomac toward Charlestown, Virginia, in the face of the coming Union army, but tonight they sat in silence several miles from the enemy, and they had only handfuls of dry corn or a few green apples to eat. Jack, exhausted, could hear men weeping, inconsolable. Many could not bear the pain, begged for morphine, for someone to shoot them. Jack was certain that Henry and Michael were dead.

For his part, Henry had stanched the bleeding from his minor shoulder and forearm wounds, and had fallen down in some cool clover as soon as he was safely away from the foot of South Mountain and the firing began to fail with the light. He could not cry or feel anything but terrible exhaustion, and he slept fitfully, dreaming of Susannah Yarbrough, who was no longer loud but soft as kitten fur, gentle with him solicitous, and all night, it seemed, her lips were coming toward his, ready to touch in damp sweetness. He awoke in the darkness, some time yet from morning, and he felt a sudden and terrible fear, remembered the Legion infantry being cut to pieces on the slope of South Mountain near Crampton's Gap. He thought: *I will never forget this day. There had never been any chance at all—outnumbered at least ten to one.* At best they had been misplaced, and at worst, this was criminal negligence. The thoughts stayed with him for ten minutes before he fell asleep to moans and the jangle of cavalry horses.

Michael had fallen three times coming down the mountainside, ashamed but among hundreds like him trying to stay alive after the disastrous fight. He had come face to face with a lieutenant he did not recognize.

~Re-form, men! the lieutenant cried. He raised his arm to wave it, and he threw blood in a shower, his left hand missing but for a flapping thumb. The man fell to his seat and looked at the hand like some rare artifact or a forgotten lover.

~Wrap it, sir! said Michael, looking over his shoulder for nearing Union troops.

~That will be all, Charles. My dear boy. Daddy's darling little boy. The lieutenant had fallen over with a soft thud, motionless, and Michael had come on past him down the slope and into the valley where troops stumbled, staggered back toward Elk Ridge. He realized he had lost his rifle, and his throat was shut from dust and fear. Teams galloped with artillery pieces, coming past him, past hundreds of gray soldiers flowing south down the valley. Officers pulled up, screaming orders, waving swords. The sky purpled, heavy with striated clouds, and a coolness, blessed and fearful, settled down upon them. Michael looked back and saw the mass of beaten soldiers: Exodus. He imagined the Children of Israel, freed from a great evil, moving toward freedom, but this was a rout, a motion *from*, not *toward*. Night robbed the scene of color, all but the muzzle flashes and then the orange blast from artillery explosions.

Finally, when the pursuit slowed, Michael fell down in some trampled grass with others stopping for breath and fell asleep instantly and did not stir until he awoke with a start, fresh from a dream in which Minnie Penny was giving him a dram of liquor and laughing over some joke she'd told.

Dawn: Confederate Artillery from Maryland Heights on Elk Ridge opened up on the Union troops pouring into the valley, and Jack sat bolt upright. Officers called the men to fall in, to prepare for marching. A boy near him, beardless and thin, lay dead in the curdled half-moon of his own blood. A brief wind blew his blond hair back: blue eyes open softly and staring.

~Christ almighty, said Jack softly. He stood and looked around. From those heights, the view commanded both this valley and the town of Harper's Ferry beyond it. The troops ahead seemed to be flowing south now, and yet there was no motion where he was standing and spitting. A sergeant coughed violently nearby, and his gray whiskers flecked with blood. Back there: thousands of Federals starting to boil through Crampton's Gap, and far up the valley more and more and then more.

~Boys, there's gone be a hell of a battle somewhere soon, said a coarse private. I'd as lief not be in it.

Finally the lines began to move, and there were supply wagons, clanking soldiers, the wounded hobbling on feet that sobbed blood. Smoke wreathed Maryland Heights as the artillery kept up a steady fire across the valley and into the Federal lines. There was no order to the lines, no march, no roll call. The beaten mob gathered torque. Yes: moving to the ford they'd crossed into Maryland earlier.

Henry felt light and limber this morning, but he craned helplessly around, looking for his brothers and wishing he'd never come to this war. A man needed the safety of wife and hearth, a common job, church on Sunday, a bit of whiskey. He wondered if a soldier could simply wish himself out of war, blink back the bedroom walls of youth. Nothing was funny anymore, and there was no need for his kind.

~Move along, private! cried a sword-bearing lieutenant who still bore intimations of glory in his lips and eyes. Michael Blackshear looked to his right and gave off a weak salute like a bad smell. The lieutenant huffed and pointed his sword toward retreat, as if it were a race into the hot breath of musketry.

~Charge? asked Michael bitterly.

~That is sedition, sir! cried the lieutenant. But he was pushed ahead by the swelling rout, hundreds at his back moving away from the Yankees who now spread, ant-like, into the valley.

~That was a good one, said a private with a thick black beard. He was barefoot and crying proudly. This is some charge is right. And my brother dead up there on that mountain, aye God! The last two words: ripped out like a tree stump.

Michael double-timed along, wanting to kill someone. Maybe Blue. Maybe not.

~Well, if it's not one of the lost sisters, said Jack, suddenly beside him. Michael flung himself into his older brother's arms and hugged him while the troops moved past. Artillery fire was increasing now, Union skirmishers reaching the Confederates' rear guard. They hugged for three long seconds and fell in.

~Have you…

~I haven't seen him yet, said Jack. I don't know if he got off the mountain or not. A lot of them didn't, Mikey. I guess we must have Harper's Ferry now. You know what's the worst part?

~That wasn't the worst part?

~That wasn't even the *battle*, said Jack. That wasn't anything compared to what's coming here soon.

~Well, shit, said Michael Blackshear.

Men fell out on the march south. Some troops, unengaged at Crampton's Gap, marched onward, heading around Elk Ridge toward Harper's Ferry and then perhaps on to Sharpsburg—men in the ranks had no idea where the battle lines would set up, what might happen when they did. But the ragged remnants of Cobb's Legion moved toward the Potomac, and several could not make it, lay coughing, bleeding by the side of the column. Michael noticed: The man in front of him had a wounded foot, wrapped up in a massive bandage, and his footsteps look very much like a trail of roses.

THAT NIGHT THEY CAMPED NEAR Charlestown back across the river, and there was nothing to eat. The air felt sharp and cool, and they built fires, scrounged pockets and haversacks for grain, a stray apple. Those remaining from the Cobb's Legion infantry found each other, or at least some did, and they settled to camp nearby and await orders. Jack and Michael sat glumly by their small, sputtery fire when Henry walked up and fell to his seat with an exhausted sigh.

~Anyone for Kick me? asked Henry. They hugged. Michael thanked God.

~Bobby Lee's playing high-stakes Kick Me, said Jack. This whole army's in a mess, stretched from here up to Harper's Ferry and maybe beyond. If one man has a clue what's going on here, it would be a mystery to me.

~Our ass got kicked is what's happening here, said Henry. David!

~I'm starving to death, said David Bernstein. Starving to death isn't an old Jewish custom. They greeted their friend joyously, and suddenly Sag Doremus hobbled up, foot-shot, and even Raleigh Poole was there, dour-faced, shaking his head.

~It must have been bad, because I was worried about all you nitwits, said Jack. They talked quietly for a while about all their dead—Stillwell, Robinson, and Goodpath; the Fogg brothers, Jeff Lamar. I can't think of any other reason I'd care.

~You got hit, too, said Raleigh Poole leaning over to look at Henry's arm.

~Scratched by a bullet, said Henry with a shrug. That's like being murdered by a briar—just doesn't make any sense.

~I stink bad enough to make a mule puke, said Raleigh Poole.

~I was just about to mention that, said Michael. We could smear you with gunpowder and burn off the sweat. In fact, we could all do that. It would probably stall McClellan until Christmas. An officer had a wagonload of muskets he was passing around, old smooth-bores, shotguns, a few Springfields with shot-up stocks. The men swapped and traded cartridges until each was somewhat armed, better than nothing.

They let the fire go out and dozed on the ground, but not long afterward, they staggered up to officers' calls and formed rough ranks and marched north again, coughing, a few weeping. They could all feel it on this moonless night—a knowledge of the pending fight, a sense of carnage to come. They flowed into the rest of McLaws's Division, which was on the march from Harper's Ferry north toward Sharpsburg. Sometimes they could see only by the sparks that flew outward when the horseshoes from officers' mounts struck stone.

WHAT IS MAN THAT THOU are mindful of him? Henry was thinking it, looking without much breath at the battle, which raged ahead in heavy woods on the left, through a broad wheat field. He thought, *You fool, get ready to fight.* This is not the moment for philosophies. But something twisted him, the sense of a soured cause. Thudding pops: the ripping of fabric a thousand yards long, the puff and croup of artillery, and up ahead, down past the small white church, men falling in row after row, scythed.

~Dear God in heaven, said Jack. Y'all keep your heads down. Far to the right, at the edge of sight, hundreds more moved, and beyond that, pressed hard against Antietam Creek, more troops bulged toward each other.

The night march had been terrible. It had taken more than two hours to cross a pontoon bridge to Harper's Ferry because the flimsy structure was filled with paroled prisoners, wagon accidents, and even soldiers falling into the river, swept off crying into the darkness. No one even thought to go after them. The streets of Harper's Ferry crawled thickly with prisoners and wagons, such a disastrous mass of people that McLaws, who wanted to find provisions for his hungry men, didn't dare stop, kept pushing up toward Sharpsburg. Just before sunrise, the Confederates reached General Lee's headquarters near Sharpsburg. Cobb's Brigade—what was left of it—formed to the right of General Joseph Kershaw's.

~Forward men! an officer had cried. The Confederates came on, firing, reloading, moving the Union lines back, and the Blackshears, not wanting to be separated again, marched shoulder to shoulder into the battle. They came across a small field and through a forest, but below them were more woods and two high fences. Now the artillery fully engaged, and the field turned white with smoke, blood-crimson.

The firing was close and hot on the hilly land, and suddenly it seemed that miles of the lines erupted in firefights, and Michael gasped as he saw it: blue and butternut lines, the bronze rising sun; a glint of sunrise off cannon brass, the angled lines of rifles with their proud bayonets, the lush land, green and golden, a shawl of smoke on the shoulders of this fertile farmland. *Oh,* he thought, *how completely gorgeous! If only Father could paint this!*

~Are you going to shoot or daydream? screamed Jack, punching Michael in the shoulder. Or are you writing a new skit? Michael couldn't hear anything, but he knew, reloading and moving toward the heavy and heavier firing. Raleigh Poole suddenly sat down and pulled his coat open, and the front of his body was a blood shirt.

~I told you this would happen, he said, and Henry read his words, heard nothing. Poole slumped over, and Henry knelt by him. Raleigh's hand was dripping, and he held it to his eyes, seemed to approve, as if seing a rare and venerable flower. He coughed once, like a child down the hall at night, and was dead. Jack pulled Henry back up by his collar and pointed down the slope at the fight.

Now men were being hit all around them, arcs of blood flying up and out, and smoke from thousands of muskets eclipsed the sun, clouds from Parrott guns, thick-mouthed Napoleons. The cornfield crawled with the wounded, who went no special direction. *The whole goddamned field is crawling,* Jack thought. Another Branton man who'd survived Crampton's Gap, a blacksmith named Buck Roane, took a minié ball in the mouth, and he fell down, swatting at the pain and the wound, writhing, kicking his feet out. Then a great shudder came over him, and he spewed blood in a broad blast from his mouth, fell backward and choked to death in less than twenty seconds.

The Confederate lines were thin here, some ground having no men at all, and the fight seemed even worse to the Blackshears' left. An artillery round smashed into the small white church at a slight angle, blowing plaster off in a white shroud. Soon, the soldiers' cartridge boxes ran low, but there was no officer near, and the dead piled up everywhere, and still the Blackshear Brothers did not run or fall. Musket fire filled the air: *siz siz siz*, and also the sickening sound of bullets smacking flesh. Henry thought: *The battle seems to be ebbing here, flowing more toward the right, toward that sunken road. My God, it just goes on and on.*

THE LAND ALONG ANTIETAM CREEK held tens of thousands of troops, and flag bearers waved their banners. While the Blackshear brothers kept firing northward across an open pasture, to their right along a sunken farm road, another vast battle took place, and some distance southeast, Federal forces under General Ambrose Burnside huddled at a bridge crossing, held off by more Georgia troops under General Robert Toombs. By late morning, Burnside—who had failed even to look for places in the creek to ford—began sending his troops across the bridge, but the Georgians shot them down in ranks. It was not until late afternoon that Burnside finally secured the bridge, and his troops poured west of the creek on to the battlefield—just in time to find that southern General A. P. Hill was arriving from Harper's Ferry with his division.

When the sun began to set on this bloodiest one-day battle of the American Civil War, the losses were staggering—beyond comprehension. There had been twenty-six thousand casualties, Yankee and Rebel, and nearly five thousand shot dead. Many others would die soon of their wounds. Though Lee had been seriously outnumbered, the Federal attacks had been badly—fatally—coordinated, and worst of all, McClellan held thousands of troops in reserve because, as always, he vastly overestimated the number of Confederates on the field.

Back at the pasture, the battle had largely ended by early afternoon, and Jack and Michael had, against specific orders, dragged Raleigh Poole's body back off the battlefield and lay him beneath the shade of an oak tree in the edge of the woods. Now, as sporadic firing began to fade, Henry sat next to the body, weeping into his palms.

~I didn't even know him that well, sobbed Henry. But I can't bear it. I can't bear losing what's left of home. I'm never going to make it home. What are we doing here? In the name of God, can you tell me what we are doing here?

~We need to get you a woman, said Jack, sitting and looking over the burial parties that were already pulling the dead together into new communities as darkness slid over the Maryland earth.

~Goddamnit, I wish I'd gotten shot today, said Henry. I *want* to be shot. David Bernstein sat blank-faced in the dust next to him.

~Okay, I'll shoot you, he said. Any caliber in particular you want? It might have to be a forty-five. Or we may be out completely. In which case I'll have to bayonet you. Down the slope: a hideous scream and then a soft moaning and then nothing.

~I don't want to be bayoneted, said Henry pensively.

~There's a shotgun, said Michael, pointing to a discarded weapon. It's stock had been shot off, and it looked crippled, ancient. I might be able to find a pistol in Sharpsburg.

~Any of you boys have any idea who won the battle today? It was Sag Doremus, falling to his seat with a dusty thump. They looked at each other, then glanced at the vast battlefield before them. As far as they could see, bodies littered the landscape, some twisted into terrible angles, and smoke still floated like fog along the creek bottom. They saw light washing the Federal lines, still ample, across the way.

~No, I really don't, said Jack. From here it looks like it might have been a draw.

~A draw? said Henry. After that? *A draw?* I don't believe I could stand the thought of that battle turning out to be a draw. Look at that.

They all turned and gazed over the field, hunger clawing at their stomachs, thirst parching them all. Nearby, a corporal prayed over a friend who had just died of what seemed a minor leg wound. Except for small conversations, bored skirmishing in the distance, and the muffled moans of the wounded, the only sound was birdsong and a slight wind rustling the changing leaves on the trees about them.

~Maybe there's some kind of nobility in dying for the right thing or the wrong thing, said Jack softly.

~Say again? This was Michael. Daylight faded rapidly, and the coming night would be cool and dry.

~We never know if we're loving the right woman or the wrong one, do we? That's why we lie with the Minnie Pennies so we don't have to think about it. Cynthia, Susannah, Elizabeth—are they the right ones? Is this war over the right things? Can any war be over the right things?

~Rich man's battle, poor man's fight, said a sullen private who was barefooted. His right ankle had topography—scabs and scars.

~I'm serious, said Jack. We've had such a good time making people laugh and sing with us, such a fine time. That's always been us, the Celebrated Blackshear Boys, but maybe there's not a reason for anybody to laugh in this world. Maybe it's true what hollering preachers say, that we're sinners meant for suffering on earth and can only look for surcease of sorrow in heaven.

~I've got to fart, said Henry.

~Me, too, said Michael. I was thinking it would be impolite though. Jack sighed.

~I don't, said Jack. But I'm thinking of going back over to Frederick and marrying that gal.

~The one expecting our triplets? asked Michael. Maybe all three of us could marry her and then pass her around.

~I'm in, said Henry. I'll be married to her on Tuesdays and Thursdays.

~I'll want her at Easter, said Jack. Things are apt to rise again in that time of the year.

~Blasphemer, said Michael. What if the children look like Cobb's Legion? I mean as a whole.

~Good point. Then we each get her one day of the year. They were quiet for a time.

~I know what you girls are thinking, said Jack. You're thinking about sneaking back through enemy lines, alone and without support, across two mountain ranges into a town where there's probably forty thousand Yankees camped just to lie for a few minutes with a girl who apparently has bucked more Rebels than an unbroken horse.

~I'm in, said Henry.

~They're going to shoot you, said Sag Doremus sleepily.

~Good point, said Jack. Well, maybe we'll find another one on the way.

~I was wrong about having to fart, said Henry. Do you boys think we'll fight again in the morning?

~Too exhausted, said Jack. But I put my money on one thing. We'll be heading back across the Potomac like fleas jumping off a skunk-sprayed dog.

~I'd like to use that phrase in my next book, said Henry.

~Permission denied, said Jack. Up from the cornfield beyond, the first stench of the dead came toward them now, fetid and insistent, but they wrapped sleep over them like blankets.

Henry lay awake the longest, looking at his brothers, realizing how very much he loved them and how long this war seemed, full of great sorrows, vast distances.

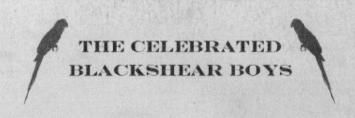

THE CELEBRATED
BLACKSHEAR BOYS

Camp Tom
October 7, 1862

Dear Mother,

    We are seven miles west of Winchester, Virginia, and I am pleased to tell you that we have come through the recent fighting with only a few scratches. But oh the terrible cost, which those back home could never understand. You see, the recent Battle of Sharpsburg was a monstrous thing, with thousands dead and wounded on the field, and following the engagement at Crampton's Gap, our Branton Avengers have been decimated, along with much of the Cobb's Legion infantry. Our army has withdrawn across the Potomac back into Virginia, and it seems the invasion of the north is at an end. Soon, winter quarters will be with us again. Oh this war will never end, Mother.

    Jack and Michael write separately. We received your letters yesterday, and though they were more than two months old, we read them with great relish. I am sorry for the damage that Romeo and Juliet caused to Mrs. Cardinal's hedges and also that Mama Blackshear has decided that she must sing in the church choir. Your description of that child weeping and calling God to strike Mama B. dead was delicious. If you see Mrs. Goodpath, please extend our condolences for her loss. Jack says that he will visit her, immediately on his return, to share memories of his knob and its fighting during the war.

Today, General Longstreet reviewed our Division, and he is a very large man, a South Carolinian as you know, with a heavy dark beard and open, honest features. General Howell Cobb's foot is so badly infected that he turned his regiment over to his brother, the other Colonel Cobb (Tom), who is back from his fortunately timed furlough in Athens. They say Howell Cobb will be leaving us and going back to Georgia, and for this he is either a hero or a coward, though no one can really tell the difference these days. General Longstreet seemed pleased with our Division, which, if it was a blanket before, is now lace.

Michael made an astonishing sketch of the fighting along Antietam Creek and sold it to a lieutenant from Augusta for four dollars, a princely sum we immediately invested. We managed to acquire a large jug of perfectly distilled spirits, which we then sold for a dollar a swallow, making nearly fifty dollars. Who says art and commerce have nothing in common?

I cannot say where we shall journey next. We still have decks of cards, and I have invented a new card game, Yankee Flush. I have won it three nights running. I intend to make up rules for the game soon.

Your fond son,
Henry Blackshear

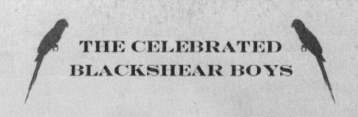

THE CELEBRATED
BLACKSHEAR BOYS

Virginia, apparently
CSA at least for now
October 8, 1862 for certain

Dear Mother,

*I am writing a sketch in which Jeff Davis is
Penelope, the Congress his suitors, and I the fearfully
virile Odysseus. Except when I reach Troy
(Richmond), I will unmask myself and demand that
we do something more useful with this army, such as
attack China.*

*Greetings comma how are you? We are alive and
starving to death. They don't say that much in the
papers, I suspect, but we are surviving on corn and
apples at the moment, half of us don't have shoes, and
we have left our dead scattered all over Maryland.
Hurrah for the Bonnie Blue Flag!*

*I have decided to change careers if the war ever
ends. I wish to become an officer because one needs no
intelligence, no judgment, no character, and no
accountability. Our recent invasion of the North was
full of sound and fury, signifying nothing. What ho,
Horatio! Never mind.*

*Tell Father that when we were most severely
tried under fire at Crampton's Gap, we did what
Blackshears have always done in battle: effected a
smart retreat. Ah well, we ran away, actually. But so
did hundreds of others, and the only reason we live to
serve another day is that we did not stand and die as
we were ordered. They would have shot us all except
we did not bring that much ordnance north of the*

Potomac. Thus, we camp, wounded and in terrible spirits, awaiting the next space on war's chessboard.

Am I not eloquent? Please give Cynthia the following message for me: If I am shot in the spot one is usually shot when running away, her name will ever be on my lips. Well, perhaps not. Please tell Uncle Lawrence that I will help him direct the trains when I return if the Yankees haven't torn up all the track from Atlanta to Augusta. Tell Joshua and Mary that the new proclamation of freedom by Mr. Lincoln for slaves came thirteen years too late for them, alas. Or rather, if we believe slavery an evil, then what in the name—never mind. This is not fruitful.

Having mentioned fruit, did I say we are starving? Please send us the following: a herd of fatted pigs, trainloads of cattle, fifteen thousand biscuits, nine hundred acres of corn, and the Atlantic Ocean full of O Be Joyful. I suppose you may have heard that instead of being commanded by Mr. Cobb of Athens, we are now being commanded by Mr. Cobb of Athens. I will cherish the distinction.

Yours truly,
Jack Blackshear (Mrs.)

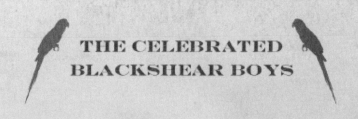

THE CELEBRATED
BLACKSHEAR BOYS

Camp Tom
Oct. 8, '62

Dear Mother and Father,

Oh that you could have seen the lines at Sharpsburg, Father. The eye could not take it all in. If one could have evicted sorrow, banished the shock, it would have been beautiful beyond description. I have been drawing it on rough paper with a pencil over and over. Flags, guns, dust, men falling, standing in their lines, the fog of warsmoke, the roar of artillery. And the humanity writhing, dead or dying, gutshot or winged—no matter to the one hurt. And all of this for miles, flags and falling, flags and falling.

Father, the cornfields were green and golden brown, and beyond the fight itself was Antietam Creek, by all stories a flat and thick-waisted stream, and beyond that low hills on which the Federals swept down into our lines. Though we were outnumbered vastly, we fought them man on man, and retired from the field hungry and ill-shod, they gained no victory. And the next morning, thousands of bodies—thousands of thousands, it seemed— stretching down the long long fields, and some twisted alive and crying piteously for water, which we did not have to give them.

Why we three have lived through this so far confounds me. There have been at least ten times when all of us should have been killed—minnie balls hissing in the air inches from our heads, the explosions of Parrott and Napoleon guns. One of our own cannon exploded at Sharpsburg and blew the entire battery apart. It is enough to give a man pause.

If I live, I wish to create a grand mural in a circle, showing a battlefield and the colors and shapes of that stunning horror.

We do not know where we go from here, but we must move soon, for being this close to Maryland and far from the larger towns of Virginia will certainly do us ill good. The most sorrowful thought is that we have not even yet begun the war and that it will go on and on and on, until all the soldiers of both sides are dead but two, and they will then either surrender to each other or kill each other.

I must close since I am hungry and tired after much drilling and the most idiotic review one can imagine (for General Longstreet—a good man). But know that we are alive and will move forth as we can and always and forever be The Celebrated Blackshear Boys.

Love to you both,
Michael

FREDERICKSBURG

From Marye's Heights, the men of Cobb's Legion, when they came up this far, could look down the hill and across a plain to the town of Fredericksburg, which lay flat and neat where the fields met the Rappahannock River. On the hills past the four-hundred-and-twenty-foot-wide river, Federal troops under the command now of General Ambrose Burnside maneuvered and waited for the arrival of pontoon bridges so they could cross into the town, then through it, advancing on the heights, where Lee had brought the Army of Northern Virginia.

Burnside might have swept through town and south toward Richmond days before, when the hills west of town were lightly defended, but the late pontoons had given Lee a chance to shift troops south, and now more than seventy-five thousand of them spread from Hamilton's Crossing in the South to somewhat north of Marye's Heights in the north. Old Man Marye live in the redbrick mansion on the heights, and below it lay Telegraph Road, which was bordered by a stone wall, the road itself cut out of the lower slope and worn down from decades of wagons and horses. Lee's headquarters was south along the same ridge, and from here, one could see the spires of Fredericksburg and beyond it the Rappahannock, which was beginning to grow ice.

Late November had come, and the sharp winds of coming winter swept down from the north, across the canal that sped water down to a holding pond, past farmhouses and woods, over Plank Road, which ran from Fredericksburg up toward Marye's Heights, whistling down Hanover Street in town. These troops camping along the heights were Longstreet's, and Cobb's Legion of McLaws's Division was back together after the disaster in Maryland.

~Huge frolic! Come to the frolic tonight! Pvt. Cass Milton cried. The Blackshears had not known him well back in Branton, an open-faced boy with no special ambitions, but in the weeks after Sharpsburg, when they were reforming their mess, Cass had grown on them. Same thing for Lowell Parker, Jim Watts, and Alpheus Carter. The only one left from their old mess was David Bernstein, but the new group was jolly enough. Weirdly, Sag Doremus had been included in a detail headed toward Richmond. Now, he, too, was gone. Cass was their favorite, though, a small, thin boy of nineteen with eyes that didn't seem to have worry in their range of expressions. He was sometimes baffled, very often eager, but never worried.

~Frolic? What are you talking about? asked a corporal from Company C. The Legion Infantry was camped west of the mansion on Marye's Heights, spread through a field where a cold wind now raked them. November back home was a cool, often wet month, when the summer work finally ended, but here it was deep winter to the Georgians, exposed, loose tent corners flapping in the wind. Smoke streamed from the chimneys of the Marye house, promising warmth the soldiers couldn't find. You couldn't dig in for winter quarters with two hundred thousand Union soldiers just across the river.

~The Celebrated Blackshear Boys have a new frolic tonight at our camp, with skits, singing, jokes. All new! All amazing! There is word some liquor may be present. I can't vouch for that myself.

~You're lying just to get me to come. Cass handed him a flyer and seemed hurt, offended.

~Lying? I swear on the career of George McClellan I'm not! McClellan had been the butt of considerable camp jokes, since Lincoln had cashiered him for a second time after he'd failed to follow up on the inconclusive fighting at Antietam Creek by driving Lee's army into the Potomac, instead letting it escape across the river. Now, Burnside was in charge.

HUGE FROLIC!

COME SEE THE

CELEBRATED

BLACKSHEAR BOYS

Tonight

AT COBB'S LEGION CAMP
NEAR THIS PLACE SOMEWHERE
SKITS, SONGS, AND OTHER IDIOCIES
TO BE ON DISPLAY.

MISS IT AT YOUR OWN RISK!

~Well then, said the corporal. Ain't nothing in this war been funny since afore we marched up north. Maybe a good laugh's the thing afore we kick them Yankees' asses back to Washington. He took the flyer and read it to himself, lips moving.

Cass Milton walked as if his bones were loosely knit, limber-limbed, dancing. His dark blond hair sprouted in all directions, thick and dirty, like a little boy. Other soldiers noticed his eyes first, luminous green globes that seemed tender, almost sentimental, worry-free. Poorly educated but well-read, he had startled Henry by reciting the first nine stanzas of Byron's *Don Juan* apropos of something Henry could not later recall. His father had died of a stroke when Cass was nine, and his mother had kept them in food by sewing and selling preserves. The soles of his brogans were loose and flappy, and he'd tied them together with some packing string he'd gotten from a sutler. Now, he came walking up to Jack Blackshear, who was throwing another stick of wood on the campfire. The tents lined up in neat rows on Marye's Heights, and the day's roll call and drill were over. Not far away, Confederate batteries sat idle, pointing toward Fredericksburg and the heights on the other side of the Rappahannock, where the Union aimed its artillery back. Soon enough, there would be a fight here, and oddly in December, it appeared, a time when the armies usually settled in for winter.

~Milton, thou shoulds't be here at this hour, said Jack grandly. Michael sat behind him tuning his fiddle. Miraculously, all their instruments had showed up two days before after having been bundled all over Maryland and northern Virginia on a vagrant supply train.

~I *am* here at this hour, said Cass Milton. Everybody thinks your broadsheets are mighty handsome, seeing as they were done in the rain on a hand-cranked printing press.

~Jack is adept at all important things, said Henry, trying out a run on the banjo. Except he's overdue in procuring us the one thing a country must have to gain its final independence.

~Freedom? asked Jim Watts.

~Women, said Henry. Jim was so bucktoothed the others joked he could eat an apple without opening his mouth. Good-hearted, he had spells of hideous headaches and was often glum. He was barefoot but didn't seem to suffer, was ashamed that he could not read, not even a single letter of the alphabet.

~I could ride me a Dutch gal from here to Florida, said Alpheus Carter. His family sharecropped near Deerskin in Branton County, his relations coming, as he said, in two classes: poor and poorer. I'm so good she'd pay me for the privilege of it all. There was a considerable amount of hooting and laughter at this, and Alpheus reacted with mock offense.

~No woman's going pay for something that only lasts thirteen seconds, said Lowell Parker. Precise, something of a dandy, Lowell was from one of the Athens companies and before the war had been studying to be a concert pianist. The Blackshears were the only men he'd found with any real musical talent, and he'd begun to hang around them in the sorry days after Antietam. Lowell had black natural ringlets, a great handlebar mustache and a neatly sculptured Van Dyke beard. Jack had raised a thick beard, but Henry and Michael still shaved themselves clean every fourth or fifth day.

~Thirteen *days* is more like it, said Alpheus. I can make a gal scream so loud she'll wake up Queen Victoria.

~Is it true General Cobb's coming tonight? asked Cass. That would be a sight.

~I'm told, said Jack indifferently. He chewed on the soaked stub of a cigar. Since Howell Cobb had gone back to Georgia, his brother, the tall, handsome Thomas Reade Rootes Cobb had been in charge of the brigade, and the men loved him far more than his stubby, politician brother. Howell's military career had fallen into pieces after Crampton's Gap, and he was back in Georgia, helping shore up the home front, as he saw it. Now, T. R. R. Cobb, clean-shaven, with longish hair and a shy smile, was their brigadier, and the men were mostly ready to die for him, though the Blackshears were dubious of his strong defense of slavery.

~General Cobb. A sight for sore eyes, said Cass. Then: We need to come up with a name for this troupe, as it ain't just you Blackshear Boys any more.

~The Celebrated Blackshear Boys and others, lower case, said Henry, musing.

~Cass Milton and the Riffraff, said Cass.

~I'd as lief hear a mule braying in a brass barn as hear you sing, said Alpheus. Though you can dance mought well. As if on cue, Cass began to dance, and they were immediately laughing at him, something ludicrous and delightful about the boy, no doubt. He jangled his bones, stepped lightly, and his eyes were so free of guile, so eager for praise, that even Jack was touched. Michael began to play a reel on the fiddle, and Jack picked up the guitar, Henry his banjo. It was "Cassandra's Reel," the one they'd written for their red-haired mother, full of delight and a hiccupping gait half-stolen from "The Bonnie Blue Flag." The others were clapping, and then buck-toothed Jim Watts joined Cass arm-in-arm, swinging him as if they were barn-dance partners, and a crowd started to gather before Jack abruptly quit.

~Hey! Don't stop, many of the boys called out, laughing, some genuinely irritated.

~Never give away free what you can sell later.

~Hah, said Alpheus. That's what that Dutch gal told me.

The others drifted off. A lazy snow flowed like a mile-wide river over them, not gathering on the ground especially. Lowell went into his part of a skit they were doing in which Lincoln and Seward were, respectively, Romeo and Juliet. He'd written much of it with Henry on the march south, and they'd been reprimanded twice in the ranks for rowdy laughing. That march might have been as terrible as the one from the Peninsula up north the summer before, but at least the weather had cooled. Soon, the roads would be muddy bogs, and fighting would become impossible. Already, they were coughing in the sick tent, and a man from Athens named Purvoy was reported near death from pneumonia.

~What are we going to do after this war? asked Henry to Michael. They stood toward the front of Marye's Heights looking down at Fredericksburg and across the Rappahannock to the Federal emplacements.

~Ride Dutch gals, said Michael.

~I'm serious. Do you think it's possible to make a living just doing this? Making up songs and such and telling jokes and the like? Doesn't seem like much of a living for a man. Everybody thinks actors are one step up from robbers or whores.

~You calling Edwin Booth a whore?

~Very funny. But with the new boys in the show, we're getting better and better. You know all the people who come through Rutledge Hall. They say Blind Tom's rich.

~Blind Tom's a genius, first of all, said Michael, and second of all, we ain't. On the other hand, people don't like geniuses. They say they do, act like they do, *pretend* they do, but in truth they like other people to be not too different from themselves. It's too hard for most people to believe there are things like geniuses.

~Sure as hell aren't any geniuses in this war.

~This war, said Michael. Let me tell you something. This war won't end until everybody is dead or enough are dead so it can't go on. Lee, Longstreet, Jackson, the fine D. H. Hill—all those generals in their fat braid aren't doing this for some country called the Confederacy. They're doing it because they love the goddamn power.

Michael was angry now, worked up as he rarely was, and Henry listened quietly.

~A man is changed by having the power to let troops live or be killed. He must feel he's only a step below God. You start to believe that there's some way to justify what happened at Sharpsburg and places like Shiloh. The way they treat troops in war no man would treat sheep in peace. If I had a good enough reason, I'd run away from this war.

~They'd shoot you, said Henry.

~They'd tie me to the post, and I'd sing "Kathleen Mavourneen," and I'd have them all crying so hard their aim would be off. Might take them half a day to hit me. But I tell you something. I have a feeling that the Federals aim to rush us right here. And I also have a feeling that this is exactly what Bobby Lee is hoping for. That canal down there is going to be flowing red in a few days. And there's not a goddamn thing on this earth can stop it.

~You think there are any women left in town?

~Probably.

~I may go buy me one before the battle. Can I bring you anything?

~Bring me one that's a tad swarthy, said Michael Blackshear. I feel the need for gypsy things.

GOOD GOD, THOUGHT JACK BLACKSHEAR, there must be four hundred soldiers sitting there in a semicircle with three huge bonfires crackling among them. They had eaten poorly for the past week, and many sat cross-legged, bare feet sticking into the cold wind. Alpheus, nothing if not versatile, had managed to get five large jugs of corn liquor, and the troupe had supped its share until giddy then given the rest away to the men, who had, against the odds, each taken a drink with polite restraint until it was all gone. Now, they cheered and clapped. Down Marye's Heights, there were farmhouses from which oil lamps glowed, and in Fredericksburg, lights smudged the windowpanes. The campfire flames of the Yankees beyond the Rappahannock and up the hills to the east also spread like firefly rubbings down the valley. New friends from the 18th Georgia were here, too. The Blackshears visited their campfires often.

~Girls, we'd better be good or we'll get attacked from either direction, said Jack.

~Kiss my ass, said Henry joyously.

~Mine, too, said Michael. Jack lit a long black cigar. He never said where he got tobacco, but he always had plenty. Neither of his brothers had taken up the habit regularly, but the slow-burning smoke smelled good now, no doubt about it.

~Here we go, said Alpheus. Y'all ready? The Blackshears had tuned up, nodded, were ready. Alpheus stepped to the front, and whistles and cheers broke over the hillslope.

~Play "Dixie!" someone cried.

~Ladies and gentlemen! cried Alpheus. Snickers and laughter, half-claps. He looked offended, turned. You mean there aren't any gentlemen here? All right then, ladies, welcome to our advertised frolic here in the lovely setting of this camp, which is about half in the middle of nowhere. Before we start, let's raise a rousing cheer for our gallant General Tom Cobb! The general, beaming down front, stood and bowed stiffly, and the men shouted, waived their hats, clapped, coughed. Cobb sat back down, face sweat-red from the nearby bonfire.

~Get on with it! shouted a white-bearded old man. I ain't got that long!

~It's my personal pleasure, said Alpheus, to welcome some damn talented boys to our frolic tonight, boys whose musical instruments have apparently been trying to run away from them all across Virginia and Maryland! And what a sorry sight is a fleeing fiddle! We're told the guitar held Crampton's Gap by itself for an hour! And that banjo? General McClellan said it was actually ten *thousand* banjos and not to advance on it without a hundred Parrott guns! But enough of my own talk. I know what you've come here to see tonight. They've been famous in Cobb's Legion since we came to the Peninsula, and now their fame will spread through the entire Army of Northern Virginia or at least through the rest of their own company. Ladies, please help me welcome to the pathe—I mean lovely town of Fredericksburg: The Celebrated Blackshear Boys!

Gleaming, smiling like seraphs, the boys ran to a spot between the fires and seemed to leap up and land playing: a new piece that Michael had put together, which combined every song dear to the Southern soldier with a homemade reel, parts of each tune rollicking in and out seamlessly. They got to a vamping point. Jack sang:

> *Your moons shine brightly up, Lorena,*
> *Smooth as cream, just like your mouth.*
> *If we keep up this way, Lorena,*
> *What's pointing north will soon be pointing south.*

The men fell apart laughing, but General Cobb, who felt there was no difference between personal morality and victory in battle, squirmed, blushed. Still, he was sanguine: Men with light hearts obeyed more readily than the truculent. Besides, *look* at them! Sitting on the snow-crusted acre, hundreds clapped, asked friends to repeat the lines, smoked poor stringy tobacco, clapped, tapped a toe. The Blackshears' faces shone, and none seemed more pleased than Jack, whose singing voice was strong, echoed down the hillslopes over toward John L. Marye's big house. The song ended, and Lowell Parker came sashaying out of a tent wearing a drapy dress he'd sewn from some discarded muslin and fanning himself, fey, flirtatious.

~Wait a minute, wait a minute! cried Jack. Miss, step forward and tell us your name, please! Lowell came up beside the crackly bonfire.

~I am Miss Petunia Fox, said Lowell.

~I see, I see! I am Judge Blackshear, and I want you to tell me, child: Are you in the family way? (*Hoots and cheers.*)

~I am, that's true, sir. I can't deny it.

~And who, my fallen woman, is the father?

~The Army of Northern Virginia, said Lowell coyly.

~Mostly me! yelled a barefoot soldier, whose red beard was spackled with spit.

~Wait, wait, ma'am! said Jack. How could an entire army be the father of your child? That's impossible.

~Well, I admit it's a trifle un*like*ly, said Lowell, even perhaps imp*rob*able, but how could I *po*ssibly single out one soldier as the most potent among such a fine group?

~I see, I see, said Jack. Now tell me the truth. Have you been with Yankees?

~Yankees! When it comes to Yankees, I consider myself to be insur*mount*able and im*preg*nable. (*The line had been Michael's, and Jack, smoking, had said, That's stupid and it won't get a laugh. Now, glancing sidelong at his brother, Jack just shrugged: The soldiers were wild for it.*)

~So why did you consent to marry, as it were, the entire Army of Northern Virginia?

~Well, aside from their manly forms and ample, ah, necessities, I promised to cook for them.

~For an entire army? Are you mad? What would you cook? (*The men leaning forward now, eyes bright, knotted stomachs, fingering harp-ribs beneath their coats.*)

~Why, I'd start with chicken fried crispy and roasted beef and some a that good Southern pork sausage, said Lowell. (*Low sounds of approval, eager eyes.*) And we'd have biscuits and cornbread like my mama used to make, golden and dripping with fresh butter or sweetened with the season's first apple butter. And there'd be peas and beans and fried okra so crisp it'd crunch in your mouth. And greens with lots of salt and pepper, cooked with the finest hank of fatback on the farm. And there'd be the richest coffee in the world, fresh roasted and ground. And apple pies and cherry pies and blackberry cobblers and oh, all the best things in the world for my boys!

General Cobb, an intelligent man, saw the shape of the skit now and smiled to himself, nodding. These Blackshear Boys knew what they were doing all right.

~You'd do all that for your husband, the Army of Northern Virginia?

~Later, honey! Later! Lowell leaped forward and dragged Cass, who was mugging and making goggle eyes, into the tent, theatrically snatching the flap down. The Blackshears were playing again, barely audible against the wild applause, the whiskey-red faces. With a brief turnaround, they launched into "The Bonnie Blue Flag," and the men were up like a shot, dancing and clapping, singing along, wildly in tune and out of it, some defiant, others half-interested.

> *We are a band of brothers, and native to the soil,*
> *Fighting for the property we gained by honest toil;*
> *And when our rights were threatened, the cry rose near and far:*
> *Hurrah for the Bonnie Blue Flag that bears a single star!*
>
> *(Chorus)*
> *Hurrah! Hurrah!*
> *For Southern rights, hurrah!*
> *Hurrah for the Bonnie Blue Flag that bears a single star.*

Without so much as a transition, while the troops still clapped and shouted, the boys retuned, launched themselves into slow, nostalgic "Aura Lee" so that the men had to settle and sit:

> *When the blackbird in the spring, on the willow tree,*
> *Sat and rocked, I heard him sing, singing Aura Lea.*
> *Aura Lea, Aura Lea, maid of golden hair,*
> *Sunshine came along with thee, and swallows in the air.*
>
> *(Chorus)*
> *Aura Lea, Aura Lea, maid of golden hair,*
> *Sunshine came along with thee, And swallows in the air.*

The applause at the end was even stronger, and many road-roughened men wiped away tears. The Blackshears put down their instruments and rearranged themselves. Henry dashed around behind a tent and came limping up and saluted Jack, who limply returned it.

~Sir, Private Blackshear, and I'd like to report to the sick tent, as I have been wounded in my foot.

~Surgeon Smith! cried Jack. Come examine this man! (*Michael comes forward, kneels, takes a look at Henry's foot and stands.*)

~I believe he can still serve, said Michael. But that foot will have to come off. (*Groans, laughter.*)

~How can I serve with only one foot? asked Henry.

~You can charge with a crutch and a pistol, said Jack.

~But my hand is also wounded! (*Michael looks at Henry's left hand.*)

~No doubt, that arm will have to come off, too, said Michael.

~Then, soldier, you will have to fire from the trenchworks.

~But my other arm is also shot! (*Michael again.*)

~Yep. That arm will have to come off, too.

~Both arms and one leg? cried Henry. Surely I will not have to serve now? Surely I have given enough to the Confederate States of America?

~Is anything else wounded, private? asked Jack, arms crossed over his chest, tapping his foot and mugging for the troops.

~Well…(*looking down at his crotch*)…not really.

~I'm not examining *that*, said Michael. But it will probably have to come off, too.

~In that case, said Henry, charge! He drew a phantom sword and ran off into the darkness to wild applause. The hats being passed around were filling with bills and change, plugs of tobacco, stub cigars, odd percussion caps, even occasional U. S. currency. Michael was playing a solo reel on the fiddle and looking at Jack, grinning.

~This feels like thievery, said Michael.

~Here's to all vices, said Jack, bowing. Long may they wave.

JUST AFTER MIDNIGHT, THE LIGHTS extinguished, fires banked, Henry, Michael, and Jack crept silently down Marye's Heights, crossed a canal on a rickety bridge, and came on across the treeless plain and into the edges of Fredericksburg. Their pockets sagging with money, they avoided CSA pickets, giggled up a froth of whiskey-fueled sentences. Turned out Jack had saved back a bottle of O Be Gladsome, and after the wild success of the performance, they'd finished it off, gulp for gulp, then decided to slip out and hunt for women.

~Are we looking for virgins or whores? asked Michael, trying without success to stop up a bad case of hiccups.

~Maybe a little of both, said Jack. Each has her own virtues. We may get shot first, though, boys. Do either of you have last words?

~I do, said Henry: Vidi, vici, veni.

~That's backwards, said Michael. Oh hah, I get the joke: *I saw, I conquered, I came.* Very amusing. I'll write that down-*eck*-for prosperity. My own last words will be Quote Madam, your breasts are large enough to nurse armies End Quote. Jack, what-*sshup*-are your last words?

~My last words: Is that thing loaded?

They giggled down an alley and came out on a cold, wind-raked street and saw a lamp light in an upstairs room. A woman was up there in her dressing gown, hair upswept in a nightcap. She smiled and motioned toward the alley from which they'd just emerged, and by the time they returned, she was there, shivering against the cold, letting them inside.

~Be as quiet as you can, she said. Do you have any food or money?

~Madam, we are traveling philanthropists, said Jack, bowing.

~What 'n' the hell's that?

~Food no, money, yes, said Henry. Will you marry me?

~Wait! said Michael. Friend or foe? Virgin or whore?

~Honey, you're in the wrong part of town for virgins, said the woman. She held a single candle, and the wind coming beneath the door was threatening to blow it out.

~Madam, your breasts are large enough to nurse armies, said Michael, bowing.

THE SOUTHERN COMMANDERS COULD NOT quite believe their good fortune: The Federal commander, Ambrose Burnside, apparently was going to cross the Rappahannock right at Fredericksburg, use the town as a shield, and make a frontal attack on the heavily entrenched rebels on Marye's Heights and down the line, which now extended seven miles, with Stonewall Jackson's men to the south and Longstreet to the north. In the middle, watching with glinting excitement, approaching exaltation, was Robert E. Lee.

A heavy fog lay along the valley on Thursday morning, December 11. Before dawn, firing broke out in town, and Southern men watched from the heights, listening, wondering.

~They come up here, aye God we gone mow em down like a scythe through wheat, said one, breath a visible mist. They ain't comin up. No way they'd be that dumb.

~Dumb's Burnside's middle name, said another, smoking what was left of a cigar. Didn't you know that?

~He musta had a mean-as-hell daddy, said the first soldier seriously. I knowed a dog named Dummy 'ut hell if I'd a named my own *kin* that.

A Mississippi brigade under the flamboyant General William Barksdale had been left in town to thwart the Federal crossing, which they were trying to effect by stretching pontoon sections across the river. Barksdale, with his long white hair and flint-eyed bloodlust, had posted his men in brick houses that faced the river. The Union troops began laying the pontoons just after midnight, but Barksdale waited languidly, and the firing hadn't been ordered until just before dawn.

There: the sound of banging in the dark, hammer-taps, bolt-turns, pontoon to pontoon, river ice cracking as they shipped out new units to nail. There: sections six-feet long, a river one hundred and thirty-five yards across at this point.

Barksdale sent a command, and the first guns had broken the silence, the others touched off as if that were a command: sharpshooters aiming at the nailing noise, and Union soldiers hit, doubled in blood, falling into the current, swept down into a dark coldness, rising once, twice, gone. Then: two guns cracked the silence for them all to keen up and fire.

It had gone on this way, right through the gray-blanket dawn, and the soldiers were slow to assemble the pontoon bridges, far from the shore. Around ten in the morning, with the fog finally burning off the river, though still skidding and curling on the ice, Burnside, frustrated, ordered his artillery to fire upon Fredericksburg itself. There on Stafford Heights beyond the river, one hundred and fifty Union cannon: *Fire!*

~Is the fight a-comin' today? asked Alpheus Carter. I need to make my peace wit' God is the fight comin' today. Even though Cobb's Legion camped a mile from Marye's Heights, they could all feel the ground tremble.

~Not today, said Jack, taking out the smoked out cigar and hurling it away. They've got to get across the river first and establish their base. Tomorrow, next day.

~It might end here, said David Bernstein. If they try to come up the slope to get us, it might just end here. And it's going to be a slaughter, Jack. Henry, pensive, said nothing.

The side of town along the river seemed to explode in shards of brick splinters, shattered boards; cobblestones flipped up and flew. The town burned.

~Should we put out all the fires here? Barksdale asked Longstreet by messenger. Old Pete, as the men called Longstreet, shrugged it off: *Keep firing*. And they did, despite the shelling, they stood in their places and kept up a hot pace against the pontoniers. Past noon, out of patience, Federal officers sent troops across on pontoon sections, and soon they were fighting Barksdale's men in the streets, and from the Heights, the soldiers watched in readiness and waited. Not until dark on December 11 had all of the Mississippi men retreated across the cold plain to the rest of Longstreet's Division.

Now, in daylight, with pontoons laid into town and also below it, the Federal troops flowed across and into the cover of Fredericksbug, and they began to take the city apart, house by house, breaking crockery, drinking whiskey, at one point using the case of a grand piano for a horse trough. Fires continued to burn themselves out, winking at the Confederate thousands.

~I want to go home now, said limber-limbed Cass Milton, trying to warm himself beside the fire. It ain't even winter here, but this cold up here's a different thing. Everything's different up here. Michael looked toward the hills and thought: charcoal black, pale orange, burnt umber. And on a plain, patches of ice, gleaming like rotted lace.

That night, Dec. 12, the Blackshear brothers, along with David Bernstein, visited friends in the 18th Georgia, who were on Marye's

Heights. They played cards, sang, drank, went to sleep. Staying out trouble seemed impossible.

UNION TROOPS POURED ACROSS, AND the next morning, soldiers knew that battle was about to erupt, something far greater than Crampton's Gap, perhaps approaching Sharpsburg in its vastness and ferocity. The 18th Georgia was up early that Saturday, December 13, and light elbowed into the crooks of the river, the crannies of Fredericksburg, but the men on Marye's Heights couldn't see it. A thick fog, the heaviest they had seen, lay below and around them, as if a vast tub had in the night been filled with milk. The Blackshears found themselves herded into formation, couldn't leave to rejoin Cobb's Legion Infantry, which this day would be guarding artillery.

~Damn if it don't sound like a beehive down there, said Oakley Jones, a tiny, elfin friend of a few weeks' standing. His nose ran into his beard, and he swiped at it, hands trembling. Henry pitied him. Sound like you'd be a-walkin' in the woods 'n' come up again' a bee tree.

~Sounds more like people talking before church, said Jack. Getting ready for something to happen. Jack was ready. In fact, he'd never felt more ready to tangle in his life, and yet he wanted to write it, too: the invisible armies, the certain fight, sounds of ten thousand brogans on the icy grass. Jackson's men cheated left a bit, tightening the lines, which extended for miles. But the 18th Georgia was here, opposite the city itself, and the Federals assembled below, bound for attack.

General Tom Cobb, up on a fine mount, galloped past them, a man who sat his horse nobly. The men came to attention as he passed, loved his ardor. Michael could not account for his own feelings. His family had never supported secession, was firmly against slavery, and yet here he was, in the thick of a coming fight, no different from the most high-blooded fire-eater. Strange. Weird. And in such a thick fog that the only navigation was by sound.

Then: Around ten that morning, the fog began to *drain*; there was no other word for it. Fredericksburg began to appear from the spires down, and within minutes, soldiers could see the fields of fire, and massing down there, forming, moving, were thousands and thousands and thousands of Union troops.

~Mother of *God*, said Henry Blackshear, fondling his rifle. They, too, were forming up now, hearing orders called, and soon they'd be placed for battle. Coming now, and rapidly as the fog slid down the steeples, over the smoldering upper stories of Fredericksburg, then finally off the plain. Cold sun painted the stunning scene in grandeur. The Georgians gasped, moved shoulder by shoulder with others in Cobb's Brigade, boys from Athens and far beyond, all the way to Carrollton. Longstreet's men, Jackson's men, the crying of orders, the sun-spark of bayonets, dull clank of canteens.

Around ten-thirty, the rebel cannon to the left of Cobb's men higher on the ridge opened up with a roar, testing ranges, while Burnside's guns on the other side of the Rappahannock did the same. Clouds of gun smoke floated across the plain. Henry thought: the flank of a dappled horse.

~Here they come, boys! cried Jack. But the Union advance, beneath the arc and explosion of hundreds of shells, was on such a scale, so wide, so deep, that two eyes could not take it in. Henry thought: As if the earth had opened and a million imps were marching from hell. Just then, the order came, and the Georgians swept down Marye's Heights.

~Stay together, brothers, said Jack. I have a feeling it won't matter today.

They came down the hill before John Marye's house to the sunken Telegraph Road, and they stood behind a well-built stone wall, put there years before to keep the field from collapsing into the road. Sappers dug deeper, throwing the dirt over the wall, and soon, the troops' emplacement was incredibly strong. The fighting was general now, the noise painful.

Henry Blackshear felt a sick fear in his stomach. How could it go from their frolic to this in such a short time? He kept thinking *how many men how many men how many men* will die today? There were other brigades now behind the stone wall, doubling in, but Cobb's men, though not the Legion Infantry, were in the front, loaded and waiting. General Cobb rallied the men, held their fire, rode along the lines. Now, in the coming violent encounter, the 18th and 24th Georgia men were the vanguard, the shield against the major thrust of troops beginning to come across the plain from Fredericksburg. Michael grabbed Jack's elbow:

~Watch your head, he said. Jack grinned and looked ahead, above the crest of the stone wall.

Though the fight has started south of them, it was clearly shifting north, and around eleven-thirty, the Yankees began to sweep from Fredericksburg across the plain. They funneled over partially dismantled bridges that spanned a six-foot-deep ditch, spillway from the canal. And suddenly there they were, heavy lines running, shouting toward the rebel lines, and officers were saying *Wait wait wait men wait men: Fire!*

The smoke took fifteen seconds to lift, but it seemed the charging Federals had simply disappeared in the volley, and the Blackshears strained to see them. The ones not killed outright—and each volley killed scores—lay writhing on the ground or running back to a small dip in the field from which they had small cover.

~Mother of God, said Henry softly. He looked around, but none of Cobb's men had been hit, and they were all reloading frantically, slipping caps up on the iron nipples, coming to full cock, taking aim. And the Federals came again now, and artillery roared against them, *for* them, but they were all shot down, too, screaming, screaming, screaming. The few survivors of the second charge retreated to the swale, reformed with reinforcements, came on again, but the same thing happened, the uniform blast, the falling men, coughing blood, some head-shot and still, others wounded in the gut and bucking, writhing, pissing in their pants. This third charge was somehow more hideous, as thousands now lay on the blood-soaked earth, heaving humps of flesh, the dead mingled with the dying, each a gravestone to the other. The fourth charge also failed, but Henry heard a smack and turned in time to see a nearby soldier fall straight backward, unmoving.

~David! Henry cried. He knelt and looked down at his friend, but the bullet had drilled a hole in the center of his forehead, and he lay in a widening pool of blood, eyes staring up at the smoky sky, sightless, pupils rapidly dilating. Henry cradled him for a moment and wept, then stood. Michael and Jack looked down, but their faces registered little emotion as they turned back to the wall and looked out into the field, where a new crop had grown and now was scythed down and awaiting harvest.

THE DAY WANED. SUNSET CAME before five on this winter day, and for the past half hour, the firing had slackened dramatically. Now, however, the Federals rose for another charge into the stone wall, and Cobb's men braced to fire.

Earlier in the day, back near a house, General Thomas R. R. Cobb had fallen, and the wound in his thigh's femoral artery flowed, and he was carried, whey-faced and dying from the field. There were a few dead Confederates up and down the lines, but it was nothing like the carnage on the plain between the stone wall and Fredericksburg. Rank on rank of Southern troops fired from the wall, stepped back to reload while another line stepped up and shot. The Union troops fell across the dead and dying in the field. They fell back, and to the utter incomprehension of all, slogged up from the dip for another rush toward the wall, and it was the same thing, the gunning, the men screaming and falling, the field crimson, the sunset deep orange-yellow, the dead grass brown. And those blue coats laid in lumps across hundreds of yards, some crawling, others convulsing. This time, the Yankees moved north, as if they might hit the stone wall on its left flank, but it was no good, as they went straight into a marsh that forced them back toward the wall where they were mowed, raked, blown apart.

~Come on, you stupid bluecoats! cried one rebel, and the others took up the taunts, but their shouts were largely into ranks of the dead and dying.

~Surely not, thought Henry, who felt he might cry. Surely not. *Surely not.* But another charge formed, and soon, in the near-dark, they came, charging, sidestepping bodies, and the Confederates waited waited waited waited: *now.* The sound left Michael's ears ringing, and when the smoke was blowing away on a cold wind, they could see the new charge had vanished like all the others, and the dead had gained comrades.

In the morning, just before the attack began, before the Union dead filled the fields, Robert E. Lee had lowered his field glasses and turned to Longstreet.

~It is well that war is so terrible, said Lee. We should grow too fond of it.

ALL NIGHT, THEN: THE CRIES of the mortally wounded, the stiffening of the dead. A Union brigade camped within easy gunshot of the stone wall, as their commanders—incredibly—planned yet another charge for the next morning. Tom Cobb was dead, and the Blackshears had taken the body of David Bernstein and laid it beneath a tree at the foot of the hill that rose sharply to John Marye's house.

~You tell me this is worth it, and I'll believe you, said Henry to his brothers. Either one of you. Just go on and tell me it's worth it. Below, the moaning, the shouts, a crawling toward or away from.

~I need to write Mr. and Mrs. Bernstein, said Jack. Shit. That makes me sick to my stomach. At least we were with him and got to bury him ourselves.

~I'm serious. Tell me this is worth it, repeated Henry.

A rib-thin dog, tongue out, appeared suddenly, loping down the lines, where the men slept on their arms. It didn't glance right or left but kept lifting its nose, scenting.

~It's smelling the blood, said Michael. How did we wind up here? This is Malvern Hill all over again.

~I think I must have shot at least twenty men out there today, said Henry. Good God, how does one ask forgiveness for such a thing? What made them keep coming and coming like that?

~Generals, said Jack bitterly. The night air was heavy and very cold, and many of the Confederates were out in the field now, stealing shoes and boots off the bodies of the dead. I bet my ass Burnside over there is telling everybody they had a great day and will finish it off in the morning. Thousands dead, thousands wounded. More dead today than live in Branton. And this wasn't battle. It was murder, it was slaughter, it was monstrous.

~Then what are we doing here? asked Henry softly. Why did we join this army anyway? I feel sick to the bottom of my soul. Listen to that! I don't think I can stand the sound of that!

Then it came across the plain between the brothers and Fredericksburg, a dull moan that seemed to grow from the land, a cow-like lowing, sharp screams, specific words: *help, water, mother, oh!,* and *God!* And the groans echoed around them—over there, no, over there, no, *there.* Not forty yards from the stone wall and then outward, and they must be suffering out there, because it is so very cold, thought Michael, bitter. Rebel soldiers, barefoot and coatless, slept huddled into each other for warmth, as if husband-to-wife, child-to-child. Some held to each other and wept, while others sat up smoking and laughing, speaking of more fights, more blood, eulogizing Tom Cobb, words toward sainthood. The troops had taken him into a house, where it was clear from the jagged wound in his thigh he could not live. Chaplain Porter prayed for him, bathed his temples with cool water. A subordinate had come in saluting and said, *The enemy is defeated, sir.* And word was that Cobb, plaster-white, had half-smiled and said *Thank God,* and died. You could hear it down the lines on the sunken Telegraph Road: *Aye God I'd not a wept for Howell Cobb but oh the loss of Tom! It is too much to bear!*

~Maybe it will be over in a few days? said Michael, wondering. He would paint this if he lived: The few lights, lanterns up the hill, death-fog beginning to swirl down the lane, licking over stone and shoulder, men in collapse and beyond the wall a field of the dead and dying, unnatural angles, headless bodies, dark stains and the across to the town.

~Do you have any idea how many men there are in the North? said Jack. Yes, we won a battle today largely because Bob Lee is just too damn smart for any commander they'd have yet. So far, the better generals have won. But they won't win forever. Don't the right ideas always win in the end? Don't they?

~I'm so tired and hungry I wouldn't mind dying myself, said Henry. A catch in his voice, easy to hear, unmuffled. A sound like sobbing but dry, cold. He shuddered as Michael slid over to him and took his younger brother in his arms, hushed him, squeezed his arms with cold, shrunken hands.

~When I think of what I saw today, I think I'm never going to get well again, said Michael, so quiet they could barely hear him. A full-bearded soldier nearby snored hideously: buzz-saw, pine-knot. I don't think I ever want to do anything again but sit in the corner like a crazy man and stare at the sun on a windowsill. I don't know where the right is anymore. I just don't know.

~We've got to stay alive first, said Jack. Do that or I swear I'll kick you boys' asses all the way home to Mama Blackshear and that foul-mouthed parrot.

The moaning on the field did not slacken, not even after midnight.

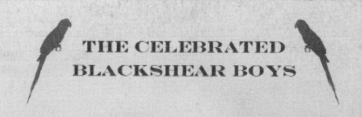

THE CELEBRATED
BLACKSHEAR BOYS

Fredericksburg, Va.
January 1, 1863

Dearest Mother,

It is late on a beautiful Thursday, New Year's Day, and from where we camp, the year 1863 does not bear witness to any coming truth. The day was bright and beautiful, but we had no breakfast, and we can still see the Union troops across the river on their own heights. Our camp today is full of talk about Lincoln's proclamation freeing the slaves. I have thought about it much and wish to speak of it now.

I have never forgotten Papa's personal example, but it goes beyond that. Slavery, as a human institution, cannot be seen as less than evil. Michael, Jack, and I have come to this conclusion during the days following the terrible battle here on December 13. You would think that Cobb's Legion Infantry would all favor slaving, as it is parcel of our fight. Quite a number of men, especially from Athens, however, find it as evil as I do, but louder, more violent voices drown us out. In truth, slavery is not much on their minds, except today, and I heard Mr. Lincoln called every oath ever inscribed on a man's heart. (Quite a few of which I have used with baroque eloquence myself.) In the pictures I have seen of Lincoln, he seems so very sad, so weighed down. And yet there is a spark of life in his eyes, as if he knew something powerful that is a secret to others. I doubt that he does. Perhaps it is merely grief, for he has had his own share. I cannot imagine—I cannot—how he must have felt about the slaughter here at Fredericksburg. I know that I am changed forever. I slew dozens, and I did it willingly; I did not do it for fear of being shot or hanged. I did it because I chose to. Just so, we have kept slaves in the South because we have chosen to do so. By which I mean, we have a choice about evil, and we embrace it at the peril it has always brought men.

This war came about because of slavery, and any other belief is a lie. If there had been no slavery, there would have been no war. It is not about states' rights or tariffs, not about tax or honor. It is simply this: The South believes the Negro is not a human, and the North believes he is. And we are to be the arbiters of who or what is human? We have not given a show or sung a song since the late battle. We claim it a great victory, but there will be thousands of men rising from the North to take the place of the slaughtered, and we cannot replace our dead. Their factories will spread and rise, and ours will soon lie as a winter field.

David Bernstein is dead, as you know. I cannot bear his absence. We have made new friends since the loss of our messmates at Crampton's Gap and Sharpsburg, but Mother we, too, are slaves here in the Army of Northern Virginia. I am not saying we are not among fine men, for we are. The boys still weep for General Tom Cobb, and all of us would die for General Lee—I would take my death on his order with no more hesitation than the order to cross a street. Longstreet may be phlegmatic, but he is the best of generals. McLaws is a good man and faithful to his troops. And yet good men may be enlisted in poor causes; history is clear on this point. Jack fears I am too gloomy to be around anymore, and perhaps he is right. We are now to prepare winter quarters here in Fredericksburg, and even now, as a sullen calm reigns here, they say a battle is underway in Tennessee. Oh Mother, what have we become?

Much love,
Henry

SNOWBOUND: WINTER, 1863

Well, son of a bitch if that snow don't aim to freeze our lovely asses until they fall off, said Jim Watts. This is the what of March, and goddamned if them clumps ain't the size of artillery shells. His beard had grown ice during his time cutting wood, and he steamed in the tent. Henry sat twiddling with a banjo tuning-peg, while Michael sketched a portrait of Elizabeth Chadwick, from whom he had lately received three letters, each of increasing ardor, the last liquid with desire.

~Well, snow will probably get you before the Yanks, even though they're now led by Frightened Joe Hooker, said Jack.

~I thought it was *Fightin'* Joe Hooker, said Alpheus, gravely concentrating on lighting a pipeful of foul-smelling tobacco.

~I be dog, said Jack. I could of swore—never mind, girls. But I'm telling you, I am sick to my soul of sitting here at Camp Jennie in these stupid streets, in the tents, even if we do have a good chimbly and some cracky sticks. I'm of a mind to seek out some trouble.

The site was named in honor of Chaplain R. K. Porter's wife, he a Waynesboro man. Cobb's Legion was in quarters along with the 16th and 24th Georgia regiments and Phillips' Legion, near the top of Howison's Hill. They been there since a week after the battle, when it became clear the Federals were through with this fight until better times. Burnside thought better times had come in mid-January, and he was determined to move his army around behind the rebels, and he'd flung the entire slogging machine north on almost impassible, then utterly impossible roads. Stuck axle-deep, wagons stopped, troops slogged to a halt, and the whole army then turned around and went back to the heights east of Fredericksburg. Lincoln had had enough, fired Burnside and replaced him with Joe Hooker, who at least had the sense to wait out the winter. It had been cold, with some warm days, but now, late in March, a howling snowstorm had descended upon the troops, and it only added to the misery. Whooping cough, dysentery, pneumonia—camp diseases spread through the tents, and all night they heard the soft painful barking of the sick. In early February, rations had nearly run out, with only biscuits to eat for several days, and men already thin grew skeletal, and the few who had bothered shaving quit. So it was now a wooly horde that lived in tents, in fields, on ridges, neat rows with streets between them, most with homemade chimneys that kept them somewhat warm. After roll call, after drill, there was little to do, and they huddled, wrote letters, read what newspapers or books they might scrounge. Boredom swept them. The Blackshear Boys had planned a show and then called it off when a cold rain raked the hills. Most of the town people who had left Fredericksburg before the fight had not returned, and hundreds of chimneys blew not a feather of smoke, day or night.

~What sorter trouble? asked green-eyed Cass Milton. He couldn't sit still, unlimbered his dancing legs from a flour barrel Michael had scrounged. The kind that gets a man beat or the kind that gets a man shot?

~Er. Ahm. Jack cracked his knuckles and pulled back the tent flap and looked out. The snow was almost two-feet deep now. Well now, gents, my personable belief is that we could move away from this place for, oh say ten full hours without being caught for naught. I'm thinking of some good tobacco, a fine meal on excellent dinnerware, and perhaps a girl of nineteen years with blue eyes and soft brown hair.

~You can leave me out of such a mad plan, said Lowell Parker with distaste.

~I'm in, said Michael.

~Me, too, said Henry. He launched into a run on the banjo, frailing away, suddenly stopping and re-tuning, something he was apt to do endlessly.

Henry had been quiet for several days. A soldier from Athens named Isaac Nimmons, who had a light tenor voice and a tendency to weep during sentimental songs, had been in the sick tent, wheezing from pneumonia, sunken, pale and paler. Henry had removed his cap when he came in to visit, a warm, head-cold kind of day, the air taut with rumors of weather. Orderlies had just covered the face of a dead boy. Isaac knew he was dying and tried to speak, but he didn't have breath for the words. Henry sat holding his hand, speaking softly of times before the war, dreams of afterward, should any of them live that long. Henry cleared his throat and sang "Lorena" softly, and Isaac shone with a trembling smile, and a massive relaxation took his parchment cheeks. Others listened, rapt. A wind made the tent canvas flap and thud, flap and thud. Henry finished.

~Not bad for somebody from a town no bigger than a hole in the road? asked Henry. But Isaac was dead, nearly beatific, and Henry put his hand across his unmoving chest, gasped an agonized cry and looked at the nurse, who shook his head, smiled grimly.

Back outside, Henry had walked for a long time, clenching and unclenching his fists, feeling like shattered iron, parasitic, dead himself. Always the most sensitive of the Blackshear brothers, he argued himself down from tears, but it was no good. He walked to a tree and leaned against it and wept. A crow clacked his beak in the scratchy branches. He wanted to damn the war aloud, to speak of it with the rage he felt. All those dead, at his side or from his own hands, *all those dead.* God had given up on the whole country, had moved His throne vast distances. Even in the cold after the battle, bodies had exploded with rot, and the stench made the burial parties gag and vomit, and they came back with snow-skin, nearly bloodless.

~Something is changing in me, said Henry that night to his brothers. They were sitting away from the stink of the tent city, trying to get a breath of fresh air. I do believe I'm flat against this war, against the South. The very idea of geography makes me ill.

~I'll make you a poultice, said Jack. One part mustard plaster, one part chicken shit, and one part brandy. I'll drink the brandy. That will be five dollars.

~Let him talk, said Michael.

~I believe I could run away, said Henry. I know I could never go home. But I don't know if I can shoot another man. That battle should never have happened. None of this should ever have happened. It was almost an epiphany. I want a real one.

Then they had been silent for a long time until Jack started throwing small pebbles at Henry, stinging his arms, hitting him on the neck, cheek. Then they were riotously fighting, having a wonderful time, mud-caked.

Now, Jack clapped his hands in anticipation.

~Well, the Celebrated Blackshear Boys will at least have an adventure, eh lads?

~I'm not writing your mother, said Lowell.

THE STORM WAS RELENTLESS, AND late in the day, snowball battles had spread, battalions across the hump of land smacking each other with icy blasts. Officers played along, allowed themselves to be captured, exchanged, paroled. Jack led them through the knee-deep snow down the western slope of the hill, past one house, then another, then a cluster of three. The day's light threatened to collapse.

~This is the kind of day one of us is going to fall down a well, said Michael.

~I'm in, said Jack.

~What kind of adventure is this, anyway? asked Henry. Back at Camp Jennie: highs spirits, screams.

~Look there, said Jack. A widow in her mourning weeds stood, snow-shouldered, beside the tombstone of an uncarved plank. A slumping house, smokeless, sagged just beyond her, and she was no more than thirty, Henry guessed, pink-cheeked, quite beautiful, thin-faced. She looked up at the Blackshears, and they could see tears frozen down her cheeks.

~Kill me, she said softly. Bury me next to my Paul. I ask that as a Christian favor.

~Ma'am, you ought to be inside, said Jack. You don't even have a fire lit. Do you have children in there? They came on close to her now, and Michael thought he'd never seen anyone quite so beautiful, sorrowful. Her eyes were dark brown, grief-ringed, and she was gloveless, hands red as cherries.

~Shoot me, she said, coming suddenly for Jack, eyes growing large. Bury me next to my Paul, for I have no reason to live no more.

They took her inside the house, which was empty and cold. A bed beside the fire was unmade, covers turned back, and a heap of soiled linen lay in the corner. Michael went to the woodpile, brought forth an armload of ice-sheeted logs, laid the fire, lit it. To his surprise, the chimney drafted well, and soon a yellow-orange blazed flared, radiated into the room. The house was quite old, two rooms downstairs, two up an angly staircase. The woman stood, helpless until Henry gently removed her coat. She did not look at any of them, seemed sightless or addled. Jack looked around for food, found some dried beef and corn meal, a cup of greasy drippings. He pulled out the iron fire-swung cooker and scooped grease into it, patted up a large bone, set it back to cook. He tore off a hank of the beef and held it to the woman.

~Here, eat this, he said.

~Jesus, look at *that*, said Henry: A foot-long rat squatted in a corner, eyeing them idly, in no hurry to move. Michael moved toward it, then a scurrying, claws on the punky flooring, gone.

~Ma'am? said Jack. There was the sound of water, and Jack looked down, and the woman was urinating in the chair, and it flowed over and down her legs, spread across the floor. Her expression was set, carved, nothing. A distant gunshot. The cabin was suddenly very dark inside, then darker, and Henry found an oil lamp, and took a taper from the fire and lit the wick, and a small light rose. Michael found a soiled towel and damped up the puddle on the floorboards, dabbed up her torn cotton stockings.

~We've got to get her out of these clothes and into bed, said Henry. *Damn* propriety. He began to work on hooks and eyes, tough buttons, and she stood like a little girl, obedient. Her undergarments were yellowed, ghastly, and Henry turned, wordlessly asking Michael what they should do.

~Let me look around, he said. He went into the other room and found a bureau and brought out some clean and folded under-drawers and a cotton nightgown. Michael said, We've got to take everything off and clean her up. Just do it.

~I'm going to see if there's help at some nearby house. You girls hold the fort.

~It's almost night, said Henry.

~So? said Jack. He opened the door, and snow exhaled into the room, was gone. Henry took her clothes off, and she stood naked and shivering beside the fire, and he wiped her off without water, saw that her body was lovely. He and Michael dressed her and put her into the bed beside the fire. She began to cry piteously and beat her temples with small fists as the windows creaked from wind.

~Ma'am, you have to help us or we can't help you, said Michael. Do you have family near? Is our brother going to run into somebody out there?

~Paul, she cried. Paul. I would have named her Susan Anne. She would have had your eyes.

JACK HIGH-STEPPED IN THE knee-deep snow, and darkness seemed to collapse upon him now, nearly a mile from Camp Jennie. He walked into a low-hanging branch, was knocked flat into a snowbank. *Not a house around here, but I'll see one soon.*

~Hell, there's nothing for a mile.

The snow continued to fall, dark and hard now, and Jack knew this was folly, and he turned back, calling help, wondering if he'd run into a house. This was how he'd imagined Indians as a boy, stealthy in a Midwest snowfall, proud, perhaps arrogant, able to survive anything. He'd never imagined war, not this kind of war, in which thousands fell dead and dying over an argument no one could settle.

He came over a hump of ground to the house, but it wasn't there, and he turned three times in the snow, wondering—no, it was here. Troops got lost all the time on marches, sent forward and then back, but not here, not now. He'd be dead in a few hours, and frozen into the shape of a statue.

~You stupid son of a bitch, he said to himself. The wind sliced him now, almost fizzy with sleety snow, stinging cheek and nose. The light was nearly gone, and soon a cold blackness would fill in the corners of the woods, sinking into cranny and crevice, painting limb and deaf leaf. He came on through to a thinner part, and a soldier sat beneath an oak tree, sleeping.

~What are you doing out here? asked Jack. You'll freeze to death. Jack knelt in the windy silence, and the man's chest seemed painted a gummy black, but it was dried blood, and he was dead, hard to the touch as polished stone. Older man, the kind who had no right to be in war. But weren't they here anyway? Grizzled men with hunched backs, beardless boys of fifteen or younger, wondering how bravery or cowardice began. The old might come for a meaningful death. How many thousands were dead of wounds, of sickness now—God the slaughters. *I've got to get me out of here.*

Jack staggered upward from the man, who must have been sitting there since being wounded in December, flailed at the snow-heavy branches, came into a clearing. Where there was nothing. A clear white-thick field, square as a garden, and across it the small cylinders of deer steps. *I'm going to die out here and be found in the spring under a tree by vultures and dogs. Don't don't don't don't let me die out here.*

THE FIRE BLAZED IN THE cabin now, and the woman sobbed but had not spoken again, responded to questions. Henry melted a potful of snow over the fire and made her drink warmed water, and she sipped for him between gasping cries. Then he boiled two nearly dried potatoes, chopped them up, fed her. Michael took soiled clothing, stuffed the wall cracks full; at least snow did not blow in anymore. Henry looked at her, and she was neither beautiful or homely, he thought, a mass of wild black curls falling into her face, huge blue eyes, frozen lakes.

~Pretty lady, please tell me who you are, said Henry, wiping her face after she had finished eating the potatoes. Her sobbing had slowed and then stopped, and she stared at Henry as one might examine a jewel, expecting it to be paste. Tell me what you were doing out there in the snowstorm. Is that your husband buried out there? Are you alone now?

~Let me die, she said.

~I won't let you die, said Henry. I won't. I'm sorry about your husband. I'm Henry Blackshear, and that's my brother Michael. Our other brother Jack is the one who went for help. We're from Georgia. She narrowed her eyes and looked over Henry's gray coat.

~Is the war over? she asked. Is the war over?

~No, he said. It will go on. She sighed.

~They wouldn't take my Paul, he had one hand, the othern caught up in a hay rake he's a boy. Oh he was a sweet and lovely boy, my Paul.

He would buy me a orange in Fredericksburg, bring me a hatful of them pecans. I'd crust 'em in a pie. He give me but one babe, and it was born dead. The fault was in me. He wanted to be in that war so bad he couldn't hardly stand it, and he went out there, and they shot him in the head. His brother seen him and brung him back, and oh his pretty face. He didn't need to be in them war. She was sobbing again now. He didn't need to be in them war and left me all alone. Let me die.

~It's dark, said Michael, rubbing his forehead. It's completely dark outside. I'm going out to look for Jack.

MICHAEL FOUND A LANTERN AND lit it, but when he stepped outside, the wind blew its flame away. He threw the lantern down in disgust and stepped knee-deep into the snow and cried, Jack! Jack! The sound of frozen wind, the fluff of falling sky. He walked twice around the house, wet-kneed, and snow sifted down the neck of his coat, pasted cold on muscle, carotid. Jack! *My voice coming back at me in a carpet satchel.* He moved straight away from the house now, and treeside drifts were waist-deep, and he navigated by the hidden presence of tree trunks, feeling them come toward him like memory. *Mother, I commit my memory into your heart: King Lear squawking, full of orotund curses, Mama Blackshear's vacancy, and oh Papa, I am walking now into the mercantile. Make good use of me.*

He wanted to paint this dark cold absence. *There must be a way to grind the color of winter storms, shadowless, lightless. The dark matted down between her legs. And yet such sorrow formed it.*

~Jack, goddamnit, answer me!

A quarter mile through the woods, stopped and holding to a beech trunk, the smooth bole, knots: a place for a boy's name, but Jack could not feel one. *Goddamn Fredericksburg of all places to die frozen to a tree instead of on the field of hah valor. A valediction. That day I was riding along the creek and the Creamer girl was naked in the middle of it, standing in a puddle of light, and there were shadows beneath her heavy breasts, and her nipples were thick, hard, and her cunt dripping water: just stood. And she did not see me, and I stilled the mare with a hand on her neck, and the Creamer girl leaned to one side to wring out her long black hair. I would have held her like this, upthrust into that valley, quaked her flesh.*

~Shit. Jack would die daydreaming in this wood, and he struggled away, splashing through the drifts, ran into the ribbed trunk of an oak tree. He cracked his head, fell back on to his seat, then a slow drip and the iron taste of blood in his mouth. He rose quickly and began to run.

~Jack! It was Michael, his brother's own voice, not forty feet away.

~Brother! Where are you? I'm freezing my ass off.

~Jack? Jesus, you scared the shit out of me. It's blackern a black cat in a closed closet. Where are you? Keep talking.

~I'll sing, said Jack:

> When the blackbird in the spring, on the willow tree,
> Sat and rocked, I heard him sing, singing Aura Lea.
> Aura Lea, Aura Lea, maid of golden hair,
> Sunshine came along with thee, and swallows in the air.

~You sound like a dog just run over by a rickety wagon, said Michael. You're getting closer.

~How's this, then? Singing raucously loud:

> When the parrot in the house, sitting on her hair,
> Shits on grandma and retreats, cageward to his lair.
> Aura Lear, Aura Lear, scabrous green and rank,
> I will ne'er forget that while still alive you stank.

~You're moving away from me, said Michael. Ho! Ho! Hoooooo!

~I'm coming that way—stay where you are. La la la la la.

~Hey—God…Jack ran flat into his brother, knocking them both into a snowbank, cocooned. That was a touching song, Jack. It almost moved me to puke.

~Thanks. They were trying to get up. You wouldn't happen to know the location of an old house around here, would you? About this high, has a runaway soldier in it, woman's lost her mind?

~Doesn't sound familiar, said Michael.

~I can smell smoke, said Jack.

~I can't believe I came out into this to save you.

~I was saving *you*, said Jack.

~Isn't there a war going on somewhere around here? I seem to forget.

They stayed side by side, creeping through the trees, palming trunks, scenting firesmoke, and in seven minutes, they saw a smudge of lantern light through a window of half-fractured bubble glass. Without speaking, they slogged on through the snow, which was still falling heavily, burst inside, trembling, heading for the fireplace.

~That was fun, said Jack. I think I'm going to do that at least once a year from now on.

~You idiots, said Henry. The woman sat up straight in bed.

~Hold on, ma'am, said Henry. Don't you...but she ran past all three of them, flung in the unstable door, which looked more like a rough parallelogram than a rectangle, ran into the night.

~Well, shit, said Jack Blackshear.

~I'll get her, said Henry. The floor swayed as he ran on frayed boot leather, and the house seemed to ache, creak. He could see almost nothing, but she had fallen just outside the door and made feral sounds, growlings, weeping insanely, sobbing. He grabbed her arm, and she fell into him, and he put his hands around and under her, lifted her to his chest, and she held on like a child, and he could smell her, and it was not unpleasant, and as he came through the door, he realized her lips were on his neck, warm, wet.

AFTER MIDNIGHT, THE SNOW STOPPED and the wind fell. There was plenty of cut firewood just outside the door, and Jack fed the fire, seemed solemn. The woman slept soundly beneath a down blanket, bed by the fire.

~We'll be arrested if we're not there for roll call in the morning, said Michael. Just thought I'd mention that. All in all, I'd rather be captured by the enemy.

~Who would that be? asked Henry. Let me ask you all something. How are we ever going to be the same again? After what we did? I don't think I can stand it. When I go to sleep at night, I see those boys coming toward the stone wall, and I am begging them not to let me kill them, but they won't stop. Why did they come? It was like Kill me next! No, kill *me* next! With hands raised like schoolboys. Her husband with one hand going out to be shot, and for what? We don't even have girls back home we love enough to fight our way back. How is it possible that all three of us wound up with sweethearts we have no intention of marrying? Our family's laid itself waste, I tell you. What are we going to do now?

~We're going to have to kick his ass, said Jack, turning to Michael.

~I'm in, said Michael.

~Can't you be serious about anything, ever? asked Henry. You realize that at least one of us is going to get killed or die of diphtheria or dysentery? And you know what? We haven't even had the great battle yet—there's going to be one that will make Fredericksburg look like a picket skirmish. God is judging us.

~Look, I hate to do this, but I'm going to point out the obvious, said Jack. His black curls were rather long now, thick beard was down to his collarbone. We're not geniuses. We're never going to cure a disease or bring world peace. We're fairly bad soldiers. If I were a worse shot, Robert E. Lee would have been knocked off Traveler a year ago. I was so scared at Crampton's Gap, I almost pissed in my pants. So we aren't particularly brave, either. But let me tell you something. We can make suffering men laugh. You *know* we can. We can make lonely heartsick men cry out their sorrows and be better for it. If we live out this war, that's what we'll be doing after the war, too. I'm as much a writer as Michael is a schoolmarm. This is who we are, girls! And we ought to embrace it and not look to higher things. Because this is what we're meant to do, whether we will have food or not. Now Henry, that's a fact.

~It is, said Michael.

~Who are you? The woman was sitting up in bed, and half her faced was buttered golden orange by the firelight. Quite beautiful now.

~Madam, we were the Celebrated Blackshear Boys, said Henry, bowing, a catch in his voice. In later years, when you are old and your grandchildren huddle around your feet, tell them that on a winter's night, you met the day's greatest performers and that they saved you from your sorrow.

~I will, she said. I don't know how come you walked out of them woods and saved me. I don't know it. I'll be all right now. My brother'll be along tomorry to check on me. You boys get on back afore there's trouble. I mean it, now. I'll ne'er think to harm myself again.

Jack and Michael could see that Henry was tearing up. They turned away, cinching their coats, ready to head back. The woman threw back the covers and came to them, and in turn she kissed each of the brothers on the cheek.

~Now we can freeze in peace, said Jack. Madam, we bid you a fond and affectionate farewell. They went outside, and the wind had died utterly, and the night was cold and still.

~I thought we were going to get drunk and find a good-time gal, said Michael.

~Never think, said Jack, heading out. You never could do that worth a shit.

MAMMOTH LUNACY!

COME SEE THE

CELEBRATED
BLACKSHEAR BOYS

Tonight
April 1, 1863

AT CAMP JENNIE

SOMEWHERE IN VIRGINIA

RIDICULOUS PLAYS, SONGS, AND

PARALYTIC DANCING FOR THE SOLDIERY.

YANKEES WELCOMED!

~AND NOW, SOLDIERS FROM THE Army of Northern Virginia—
and whoever else happens to be here tonight, including President
Lincoln—are you out there, Abe?—here is the newest sensation of Camp
Jennie, that limber-limbed dancing machine, direct from prison where
he's serving time for eating General Longstreet's horse—Private Cass
Milton!

The Celebrated Blackshear Boys broke into a fiddler's reel, and
green-eyed Cass Milton, apparently boneless, clapping, flowing up and
down with impossible motions, danced on a small stage. Hundreds
clapped and yelled under the warm, mid-April stars. Buck-toothed Jim
Watts stood not far away, moving with an utter lack of grace. Lowell
Parker kept a drumming beat with a large stick on the stage floor. When
the reel ended, the brothers launched into "The Bonnie Blue Flag," and
the men screamed and stood now, and officers watched with narrow
happy eyes. The men sat when the song ended, and Jack, with his
booming trombone voice stepped forward:

~I have an announcement to make! he shouted. We in the Yankee
army have finally run out of officers! Would anyone out there who wants
to be our commander in chief please come forward? (*Great glee and
laughter.*) Henry, affecting a rube's stupid toothy grin, came running up
to his brother.

~I'll be a general, yokeled Henry. Ahilk.

~So! You want to be the commander of the Federal forces for his
majesty King Abraham the First?

~I b'lieve I do.

~And what qualifications do you possess for this job?

~Well, first of all, I'm a idiot, said Henry, nodding and mugging for
the crowd. And I've proved over and over that I'm a coward. There's that,
un-huh, un-huh. I don't know nothing about tactics, and on a horse I
look like a dog riding a goat. (*Boundless hilarity.*) The last time I fired a
gun, I shot my captain in a delicate place. They say he'll be able to squat
in a week or so. Umm-humm. Let's see. Oh. I can't tell my left from my
right. I can't read nothing and have to make a X for my name. And I
tend to cry and roll into a ball when a battle is near.

~You sound very promising! said Jack. Could you lead two hundred
thousand men successfully into battle?

~Lord no.

~Have you ever faced virile Southern men in battle?

~I have.

~And what did you do?

~I runned off like a shot-at rabbit.

~Well, men (*turning to the crowd now*), what do *you* think? All those in favor of electing this obviously well-qualified candidate as general and new commander of the Union Army, please say aye!

A mile away, two soldiers staring glumly into a campfire sat up.

~What was that? one asked.

~Mought be the heavenly host, said the other. He chewed over the thought. Probably just thunder. Storms come this time of year. You mark my word.

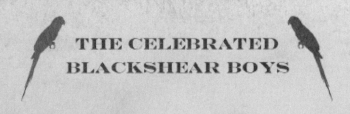

THE CELEBRATED
BLACKSHEAR BOYS

March 15, 1863
Rut in the Road, Virginia

Dear Parents,

    I am writing to let you know that the Celebrated
Blackshear Boys fare quite well, thank you, in the glorious
company of the Branton Avengers of Cobb's Legion, of
Wofford's Brigade, McLaws's Division, and some person or
another's army, period.

    I am writing this on behalf of all three sons, and we
apologize in toto for not having written more. What was left
of the pound cake arrived Tuesday last, and when it thaws,
we shall eagerly consume it. Young Henry begs to say he has
not written because he has been serving as Thinking Aide to
General R. E. Lee, whom, one would think, could think for
himself. Michael has not written because he has been on a
mission to the French Government to convince them to sell
wine to the members of Congress in Richmond even if they
won't come into the war on our side. Michael spent a pleasant
February in the French wine regions, where he wed a French
woman named Maurice, who shaved her mustache off for the
nuptials. She has borne him twelve daughters thus far, so
hopes of a son are fading. To escape the women, he has
returned to the Army without a wife or a bottle of wine.
Actually, Henry has not been a Thinking Aide to General
Lee—that was a lie. Actually, he has explored the West and
has found a new Passage to the Pacific—or at least he thought
it was such. Actually, he traveled by creek to Claypool Pond, a
local puddle apparently created by beavers not engaged in
the war. He claimed it for the Confederate States of America
and created from local hardwoods a harpoon with which to
hunt whales. Alas, he captured only a four-pound carp, which

was eaten in camp, though it be mostly bones, which makes it like most soldiers hereabouts. I myself have served as a spy for General McLaws, disguised as Mrs. James Johnson from New York City, heir to the Johnson Tinned Meat fortune. In such capacity, I had dinner with Abe and Mary Lincoln last week in the Executive Mansion. I said, Sir, we are dying to know: What are your spring plans for the armies? Where, exactly, will they be located? And he said, Mrs. Johnson, it is a secret, but I shall tell you: We intend to invade Mexico. No one is expecting it. General McClellan tells me he will be ready for attack by 1877.

How is life in Branton? Your report of Rev. Merrill's suicide was shocking, though I suppose faith is getting in shorter supply than coffee these days. Tell Papa we have grown rich from camp performances. Wait. We have spent it all. Tell Papa we are poor and to send money, preferably in U. S. currency. Our banjo is down to two strings, which makes playing it like a smile from a man with two teeth. We have j'ined the Hairy Men, though Henry's beard looks like a cotton field after harvest. I am the most manly, of course.

Thank you for including Mama Blackshear's letter. We tried to get Henry's former wife to translate it, but she had no luck. At the moment it is with a newspaper reporter from Germany who has attached himself to the Army. Once our extra guard duties are done for various camp infringements, we all expect to become generals. Speaking for myself, the honor is too much overdue to offer satisfaction.

Your loving sons,
Jack, Michael, and Henry Blackshear

Branton Georjia
Cold weather 1863

Der Boys,
　　I take pin in hand and address myswell to you
to wonder how all of you fares in the great stake of
Virginny. I'm am still alive, parse the Lard. Well,
the weathers been fowl here of late, grape storms
blowed in from the North ha ha which must mean
they were sent by Yankees the vurmin. Do you
know where a comma might go. O baffled am I.
Mrs. Cardinal and I hoisted a grate sale of baked
guds in the darky days of Janiary and we raised
nearly twelfth dollars for the Confideracy. The dog
Juliet bore nine pups benath my bedd. I leant over
with a broom to sweep thim out & throwed my back
for a twist. The suckling goes on all night & make
me sick. & that turkey which live in the parlor he
　　I take pin in hand and write you my beloathed
groundsons to say Fite on! Fite on! for the stake of
Georgia. Have you met General Washington a tall
gentlemen with a grate wigg & no smile. Question
mark. He would ware short pants & be with Mr.
Madison. Comma. Who is a tiny dwarf. the Dogg
Romeo hath brought to home a Human Legg &
where he found such a thing is beyond. Was there a
Battle of Branton I have not heard the guns.
Period.

I take pin in hand and. This itch is going to
drive me. I could dance as a girl they called me
Pransing Nancy. Ha ha ha ha ha.

Your truly,
Mama Blackshear (Mr.)

Der Boys,
    I take pin in hand and write now to let you
know that it is Devember. Oh I await your recent.
Bring me a dogg which does not expel kittns beneath
the bed oh the slurping which goes on all nite like a
storm. Have you won the war yet question mark

CHANCELLORSVILLE

On April 14, Cobb's Legion heard the news: The Union Army was crossing the Rappahannock to the north, marching south for battle. But nothing happened that day, and late in the afternoon, the rains began, and the men huddled miserably all night, hearing raindrops snap like gunfire on the leaky canvas tents. False alarms and rain: ever-present companions. They still camped on the heights west of Fredericksburg, waiting.

~A quarter pound of spoiled bacon a day, a little rice or flour when they have it, said Cass Milton, green eyes blazing. The rain was so heavy it made the fire laid in their tent fireplace spark and hiss. They're trying to starve us to death before the spring battles start.

~How come we don't do nothing all the livelong winter and then fight like hell when it warms up? asked Alpheus Carter, the sharecropper. I'm tired of sittin' in this tent and just stinking.

~I was going to talk to you about that, said Michael. He was sketching Lowell Parker, who smoked a pipe and practiced Chopin on an imaginary keyboard. I guess it's up to Frightened Joe Hooker as to what happens next.

~I have the headache powerful bad, said Jim Watts, breathing hoarsely, buck-toothed mouth hanging open. Jack tossed him a minié ball he'd been worrying in his palm for a couple of days.

~Fire one of these into your mouth and send for me tomorrow if your headache isn't better, said Jack. That will be ten dollars.

~It ain't funny, said Jim, tossing the ball back. I'd as rather just go ahead and get kilt as sit around and wait like this. Did you all hear Howard J. Turpen passed this morning? Of what mought be typhus?

~*Who*? asked Cass.

~Howard J. Turpen, from Company C, moaned Jim. He'd had the shudders for a week. To die like that before the spring battles.

~To sleep, perchance to dream, said Henry. Aye, there's the rub.

~What in hell's he talkin' about? asked Alpheus.

~We've never known, said Jack. Look, girls, the main duty of a soldier is to die for a cause. Now if somebody'd just remind me of the cause I'd be ready to die.

~Your beard's done almost up to your eyes, said Jim Watts, pressing his temples. Your orta get sheared and send that thing home. They could make some granny a sweater, haw.

~Well, said Jack, proudly, you know what they say, large beard, large manhood.

~In your case, small brain, small manhood, said Henry.

~*Yore* beard looks like a chicken's done got runned over in the road, said Jim to Henry, laughing and then grimacing from the headache. I'd give all I got for a sup of laudanum.

~All *you've* got wouldn't buy a sup from a chamber pot, said Cass.

~I know a Howard J. Turpen from Company B, said Jack blandly. Different one, I guess.

~I think there's a *General* Howard J. Turpen on Grant's staff in Mississippi, said Henry. Common enough name.

~You boys think you is so funny ha ha, said Jim Watts. But I'm tellin' you, there ain't no way we're gone win this war. And I'm just sayin' the truth of it. This war'll be going on in *1963* is the way things is moving. They told us it'd be over in sixty days, they's lying. Everbody up and down the line from Jeff Davis to me. All liars.

~It's war, you idiot, said Jack. Of course everybody's lying. Politicians turn wars into causes. Otherwise they couldn't sleep nights.

~And it ain't never gone quit raining, said Alpheus, and we gone starve to death, and I got the miseries. Oh Lord, Lord.

~Handel could have set that to music, said Lowell Parker, tired of posing. Henry cleared his throat and stood:

> And the Lord said ra————in, the Lord said ra————in,
> And give them a headache, give them a headache,
> The people of infamy shall hold their heads in pain,
> Dr-ooooooo-ooooo—wnnnn them with rain.

~That's so funny I could just wet my pants, said Alpheus sourly.

~So *that's* why you stink, said Michael.

~Fire him toward the Yankees from a siege gun, said Jack.

The rain didn't stop that night, and it fell straight down, heavy, drumming the next day, too, and there was no drill, which was the only saving grace. There was no food for the day, and the men ate what little they could find in haversacks, trade off friends and campmates.

THE SUN CAME OUT, RATIONS ARRIVED, and soon the men were in fine spirits, listening to rumors rout the lines. The Yankees moved north, moved south, planned to send a brigade in hot air balloons to drop artillery shells from a hundred feet up. They would attack just as Burnside had, through Fredericksburg and up Marye's Heights. They would swing south toward Stonewall Jackson's troops. A trial, of all things, filtered through the camp talk. When William Tatum Wofford was promoted from colonel to general after Cobb's death, one S. Z. Ruff was named colonel of the 18th Georgia. Now, Wofford was trying Ruff for cowardice under fire and lack of discipline. The men, who sided with Ruff, were already nettled with Wofford, who was trying to raise a company of sharpshooters—to give easy service for a few of his favorites, they figured. They couldn't decide if the offense came from Wofford or his commander, McLaws.

Then: Monday, April 27, the Union's Army of the Potomac began to move up the eastern side of the Rappahannock from the Fredericksburg area, with plans to ford the river to the northwest and hit the Confederates from behind. The next day, the Federal troops began to cross the river at three fords, one called Kelly's and the others Ely's and Germanna, leaving behind a strong force at Fredericksburg to screen their movement. Skirmishing started below town at Deep Run and White Oak Run. By Thursday, April 30, the Federal troops had camped around the house of the Chancellor family at a crossroads known locally as Chancellorsville, which was in the middle of an impenetrable forest called The Wilderness. A few houses scattered themselves about—the Talley and Hawkins families—and Dowdall's Tavern was just across the Turnpike from Wilderness Church.

Lee knew soon enough that more than seventy thousand Federals were in his rear, and by May 1 the South's Army of Northern Virginia was rapidly marching west, eating dust, flowing along the roads toward a certain fight somewhere near Chancellorsville.

~THIS IS BEAUTIFUL LAND, SAID MICHAEL, looking at the green woods, the brief fields. Spring was late coming this far north, but now the earth held a soft green, blurred with tender vegetation. Cobb's Legion Infantry moved west, stepping smartly along the Turnpike, heading for sure battle. The men laughed in superb humor, got limber, past-due for a bloody scrap.

~I've decided to break things off with Susannah Yarbrough if I get home, said Henry.

~Bless the Lord, the child's had his epiphany, said Jack. I've decided much the same with Cynthia Sims. Other than being a harridan, I've forgotten what her good qualities are. Why don't we trade? Wait, Susannah's a harridan, too. Maybe we could sell them, Henry. What do you think we could get?

~A man'd sell his sweetheart'd do anything, said Jim Watts, headache gone, goofy buck-toothed grin back.

~We can sell them to you, Jim, said Henry. You can have mine for a bowl of grits.

~A bowl of grits! said Jack. That's terrible, brother. I'd ask at least a ham biscuit for Cynthia, or just a biscuit if there's no ham.

~You boys is crazy, grinned Jim. An officer glared at them, hushed their idle chat.

The land was creek-rich, silty, and they could smell the earth, sense the tramp of ten thousand troops not far up the road. Something changed when battle was near, voltage on the skin, wariness in their eyes, and more: an absolute readiness to aim and fire. Even Michael lost interest in how to shift this world by paint to canvas and was thinking about Uncle Lawrence, how the man never had opinions about anything, the stationmaster in his single boarding house room, idly smoking a pipe in his off-hours, not at all amusing. The only thing Uncle Lawrence marked was time and schedules; he held no interest in women or wars. Uncle Patrick in Athens had joined Mell's Rifles in the spring of 1861 but was mustered out before they left for Virginia: recurring pneumonia, which left him weak, still willing. So much lost from Branton, though, Martin Goodpath and Wiseman Robinson both killed at Crampton's Gap. And Percy Stillwell dead and the Fogg boys, and David Bernstein, Raleigh Poole and his woes, sad Sag Doremus separated from them. They were gone to memory, mere mist on an unseen river. And replacing them, a new set of friends, Cass Milton, Lowell Parker, Jim Watts, and Alpheus Carter, boys with little in common.

Henry wondered: *What was her name?* She was standing in the snow when they came, rowdy and looking for mischief, routed by grief. And was she still alive or did she die in her bed, dreaming of dead children and her one-handed husband, no soldier, who was shot anyway? Her nakedness. The shape and color of it. The weight of her breasts as she shivered by firelight.

~I feel like I'm gettin' all limber, said Cass, shoes flapping. It reminds me of something I read in Shakespeare, but I can't recall what at the moment.

~You were born limber, said Jack. Every step you take looks like a dance.

~Dancin' toward war, said Henry. Has a nice ring to it. I feel a skit coming on, brothers.

~Take one strip of morphine and let me know if it doesn't clear up, said Jack. Nothing worse than a bad case of the skits.

~Would skits get me sent to the hospital in Richmond? asked Michael. I think I may be breaking out in skits.

~Let me see—Jack looking into his brother's eyes. Nah. You got frolics. That's something else entirely.

So, marching toward Chancellorsville, the talk went away, like sun setting, and they reached a point five miles east of Chancellorsville between the Old Fredericksburg Turnpike and the Plank Road, southeast of the Furnace Road. Up ahead the Blue army waited. Then rain began to fall, like petals at first, then saw-blades, and the Avengers marched and countermarched through the area, up slip-walled gullies, beneath sobbing trees. They moved through the dark, and pickets fired on each other, sometimes distant, often close enough to make one dance. The forces had massed now, maneuvering. Word spread that Fighting Joe

Hooker had gone frightened on his men, pulled them back into a defensive position around Chancellorsville, even though his troops outnumbered Lee's two to one.

~I bet Hooker's a pen name, said Jack. They were slogging mudward, tramping down an endless lane. His real last name's probably McClellan. His long-lost twin brother. Do they train Yankee generals to lose on purpose?

~They're just trying to teach modesty, said Michael.

~Well damn, said Alpheus, laughing. If that don't beat all.

Lightning scraped the darkness away, and they stood near a farmhouse, and another brigade elbowed up against them, heading somewhere, or not. Jack standing there like a black bear, furred. The firing seemed more like gamesmanship or wing shooting, not the vacant slaughter of Fredericksburg. That would come, though. Soon, Henry nodded. They slept in the ranks as they walked, worried about their cartridges, didn't try to wipe off the running rainwater. Ranks slammed up, accordion style, when a halt came, then the jangle of canteens and belted bayonets, tin good-luck crosses. The enemy was near, so: no speaking, an absence of marching songs, muffled coughs and long past laughter.

The rumor was right: Hooker *had* pulled back from the offensive on this Friday; shocked his own officers, flinched, concentrated in a five-mile arc around Chancellorsville. Longstreet was far to the South, guarding approaches toward Richmond, but Lee was here now, along with Stonewall Jackson. The same day, the Branton Avengers passed under heavy artillery fire through a field, and the shells plowed down deep in muddy furrows, blew the face off a Deerskin lad named Hitchings.

~In what ways, exactly, do you think hell is worse than this? asked Henry quietly when they stopped in a windy mizzle.

~Hell's when you have a fork, and there's a banquet on the other side of a big river, said Jack. That's all I have to say on the subject.

~Wrong, said Michael. Hell is accidentally starting a war and not knowing how to stop it.

~I thought that was Richmond, said Henry. Maybe they're in the same neck of the woods.

~It may be my imagination, but I think most of our fair Army has moved off and left us, said Jack. Did we miss an order to retreat or to run like hell?

~*Run like hell* is my favorite order, said Michael thoughtfully. What, exactly, would be in that banquet on the other side of the river, Jack?

~All the things a man needs to live. Beef, fowl, bread, well-cooked vegetables, ice-cold milk. And, of course, pussy.

~I'd swim over, then, said Jim Watts. A-hilk. A-hilk.

~No woman would let you near her if you laughed like that, said Henry.

~Christ! Shells suddenly blossomed around them, exploding, digging down, and Cobb's Legion Infantry hunched down in the muddy loam, didn't run, waited for orders. They came shortly, though no one heard much, and they were marching again, then coming back the same way, it seemed, placed and re-placed in the lines. Somewhere over there in the night, Old Jack and Bobby Lee. What were they talking about?

~What's that thar glow? asked Alpheus.

~Oh my God! cried Jack. Heaven save us!

~What is it? choked Alpheus.

~I think it's called sunset! wept Jack, all snotty with faux weeping.

~You a big ass, said Alpheus. Scaring me to death.

~Another shell lands nearby, it'll be an ass *hole*, said Henry idly. They burst out laughing, and the officers scurried up, threatening.

~We're back where we started, said Henry, and they were: five miles east of Chancellorsville between the Orange Turnpike and the Plank Road.

THE ENVELOPMENT OF NIGHT. THE SOLDIERS dozed on their arms, still hearing the brisk firing in the near distance. On this night around a cracker barrel, Lee and Stonewall spoke. Electrifying. Lee thought: *Divide and conquer, split my force in the face of this enemy, which already outnumbers me. I will keep up a demonstration in front of town, and you shall swing around and hit Hooker's right flank. Oh the symmetry of it, the sheer bravura!*

~Tomorrow's going to be one hell of a fight, said Cass. What was it Shakespeare said about war?

~Hooker, Hooker, wherefore art thou, Hooker? said Henry with soft theatrics.

~Now is the spring of our discontent, made glorious summer by this son of a bitch, recited Jack, orotund.

~You boys'd joke at your own funerals, said Cass. What do you say, Henry?

~I was just thinking—drowsy here and softly murmuring—how different this war would have been if it was between the East and the West instead of the North and the South.

~Whut the fuck, said Alpheus Carter, giggling.

~No, I mean it. Just picture it—the Battle of Dakota Territory. The Indians would have to fight for the West—wait we have eastern Indians, too.

~Old Hickory removed all the Cherokees to Oklahoma Territory, said Jack. They'd probably fight for the West now. But there's almost nobody *in* the West, Henry. The East would win easy. Unless the Mexicans got into it. A man who eat chili con carne can be counted on to do anything.

~Lord, a good bowl of chili right now, said Cass.

~And a fine glass of Madeira, dreamed Lowell Parker. Poured into a crystal goblet that refracts the light like the sun.

~Henry's war is sounding better and better, admitted Jack. Could we have linen tablecloths and napkins? Hurrah for the Eastern Army!

~But we'd have to walk near fifteen hundred mile for a fight, said Jim Watts, scratching his wild, uprooted hair. Anyway, I thought this here war was over the slaves. They got slaves in the West?

~Wait—the slaves are going to be siding with the West in this, said Jack. That's a complication. So we will be fighting the blacks, the Indians, and the Mexicans, not to mention the people of all the western territories. The armies will go into unmapped territories and never be heard from again.

~I feel a skit coming on, said Michael, yawning.

~Nobody would know who won, said Jack, and nobody would *care*. Modern warfare is wondrous indeed. Long live the East!

They slept for less than two hours before the officers herded them awake and set them into lines. Soon, light would come.

ON SATURDAY MORNING, MAY 2, Stonewall Jackson's troops, led by Generals Robert E. Rodes's Division, began to swing south then west on a series of obscure wagon paths through the woods. Eventually, they turned into the Brock Road, which meandered north again and joined the Orange Turnpike west of Chancellorsville not far from the Wilderness Tavern. Union scouts saw them and reported it, but none of the Federal officers thought Lee would send such a large segment of his army on some kind of hopeless flanking maneuver. He would have to be crazy to consider such a thing.

Wofford's Brigade skirmished with the Union troops in their front all day, but no one charged. No large-scale slaughters, retrievals of the dead and dying. Toward evening, the Avengers walked through an earthquake shelling, and a few were knocked down. They came across a former Yankee camp, littered with haversacks, knapsacks, blankets, and old clothes. Soggy journals, letters, raw rations. Then, as they stopped, heavy musketry far to the left.

~Would somebody please tell me which in the hell army that is? asked Jim Watts. Silence, pensiveness. Around six, deer and rabbits had come racing by the dozens out of the woods west of Chancellorsville, startling the Union soldiers. They raced before Jackson's flanking troops, who stormed out of the woods; the Federals fell back into an even tighter circle around the house. After dark, where the flank attack was over, Stonewall Jackson lay bleeding on the ground, shot by his own men as he returned from a personal reconnaisance.

Now, a sullen rest fell along the lines, and the tension must crack. They knew it to a man.

JUST AFTER DAWN ON MAY 3, the Branton Avengers, Cobb's Legion, Wofford's Brigade, all McLaws's Division, moved through the early spring fields into sight of the Blue soldiers. By now Hooker's lines collapsed backward slightly like a compressing rainbow, with Jackson coming from the West and the rest of Lee's army from the east. Jackson would lose his left arm to the surgeon's saw, and Lee would memorably say: *He has lost his left arm, and I have lost my right.* The firing here was hot and steady. The Legion crossed Furnace Road, spread over the

Turnpike, and then waded a small creek, charging an entrenched Federal line.

~We'd best spread out again! cried Jack. That's an order! This is going to be ugly today! Henry moved slightly away down the lines, and Michael slipped the other way, loading as he went. They were firing now, stopping, moving up, standing for a volley. Two hundred yards and the sound was brutal, the far edge of bearable. The fight raged, thick for several miles around Chancellorsville, but here, pressing forward, the exchanges stayed violent, red with wounds.

~Whut was that? asked Alpheus Carter. He sat down suddenly, and Jack, loading, glanced, knelt to ask, but he could hear nothing, only see the boy's mouth working, as if too timid to begin a speech. Then, the flower: a huge gushing rose in the middle of his coat, just below the sternum, pumping petals. His face changed to the color of milk. And officer prodded Jack with the point of his sword, screaming for him to stand up by God and fire. Alpheus vomited, and it was all blood, and he smiled, red and wan, fell over like a dry husk, gone.

~You poke me with that goddamn thing one more time I'll shoot you! screamed Jack.

~Consider yourself in arrest! said the officer, an Athens man named Cleveland. A minié ball tore off Cleveland's nose, then another thunked through his throat, and he fell, wrestling with his own neck, until he was dead. Jack moved forward, firing, enraged.

Henry dreamed his way through the *siz* of the hot musket fire, not believing it had come to this. He could see his red-haired mother sitting by a winter fireside, daydreaming of her youngest son, who was killed near the town of Chancellorsville. Will there be a sudden blackness? How much pain and for how long? Henry had never been so afraid before, and he trembled, dry heaved, fired. Next to him: the snap-back of Luke Adams. His father's a stationer. Other side: the splatter-spray of Tom Prestwood's brains. Young Tom, with a girl's laugh. Barely knew him. *Dear Madam, I regret to inform you.*

A musket ball ripped off one of Michael's uniform buttons, a dull brass knob at throat level, felt as if someone had grabbed him and ripped it out. He turned with the torque, found himself laughing idiotically. *Well, this makes no sense at all.* All along the lines, there was a breathless din, men dropping, Yankees in their works shot, too, slapping wounds, dropping dead. Artillery. The sky turned the color of a wound.

Far to the left, Jackson's troops seized a clearing called Hazel Grove, tightened the circle around the Federals. A Confederate shell slammed into the Chancellor House and knocked General Joseph Hooker half-senseless. Commanding but down, Hooker ordered a withdrawal toward the U. S. ford at the river, and the Federal troops, by now confused and losing ground, moved back, stumbled, fled, as the rebels poured into to Chancellorsville, occupying it by ten o'clock. The Blackshear brothers slid ranks, found each other, did not hug, stood hollow-eyed. Jack felt enraged.

~They killed Alpheus.

~Oh Lord, said Henry. My God, my God.

~Shot him dead in the chest.

~Shit, said Michael. *Memorialize nothing here: never draw any of this if I get out of it. A scene of all madness.*

Jim Watts was laughing and exulting, dancing, rebuked by an officer, calmed.

~Goddamn if that wasn't the goddamndest charge in the goddamn history of the goddamn war! he cried.

~Just shut up, said Jack.

~Why's he got bees up his ass? Jim asked Michael. Henry balled up to take a swing at Jim Watts, turned away. Firing continued, troops flowed. They were chasing the Yankees back toward the river. Not much of a stand-up fight.

The other wing of the Federal troops, as planned, came through Fredericksburg about the same time, took Marye's Heights and marched warily toward the rebel rear, but Lee sent a portion of his army back, including McLaws's Division, and they tangled at Salem Church, a few miles east of Chancellorsville, and the Federals bunched back, gave up.

A swarm of vultures rafted around Chancellorsville on the thermals, carrion-bound.

A WEEK PASSED. COBB'S LEGION infantry camped tentless on the warm earth of Virginia, awaiting another order. They had little food, but most of the men were in high spirits from another—*another!*—Yankee failure to make sense of a battlefield. Early Monday morning, May 11, and they were stirring after roll call when a soldier named Howard Mossman, a corporal from Company A, walked through camp, stopped dramatically, and said:

~I just wanted to let you boys know, if you didn't hear, that Stonewall Jackson is dead. They stood in a gasp, unfolding, pipes out. He was in a house south of Fredericksburg recovering from being shot and got the pneumonia. Passed yesterday. Mossman took his kepi off and wiped sweat from his eyes. I don't know what will become of us. I just don't.

Henry, who had always thought Jackson mad, tried to feel sadness, but nothing came. *Damned blue-eyed lunatic, but oh that was a wondrous thing at Chancellorsville. I can picture those officers clapping like it was a good chess move, but the Rappahannock is red. It's thick and filled with blood, and nobody cares. So Stonewall's dead: just another Alpheus Carter, another dead soldier on the field. So what?*

~Well, it was bound to happen, Jack said quietly to Michael. Mossman walked through the ranks, revealing the news, growing in self-importance. It's what he wanted most, and what he wants most for the whole army. To die in glorious combat. I'd kill right now for a fried chicken breast and some greasy biscuits.

~Is it going to end this year? asked Michael. They were in a flat field, and a grove of water oaks shimmered in the breeze. Sky the color of a dented tin cup. Because I'm about ready to go fight for the other side.

~We could all change side every three days, said Henry with a quiet blankness, looking at the encampment. We could probably kill each other a lot quicker. You know what, boys? I think we're all going to hell. Every man in both armies and all the politicians in Washington and Richmond. Every goddamn one of us is going to burn in the flames of hell for eternity. A whole generation dead.

~Any children you might have had would have been useless morons anyway, said Jack.

~I agree, said Michael. They wouldn't be able to count beyond three. They'd have to start over four times to add up a dozen eggs.

~Your children would be lawyers, said Henry.

~Shoot me and throw me down a well, said Jack. I'll not be the Blackshear to hatch a lawyer.

~I'd teach my children to sing and dance and carve exotic animals from a walnut limb, said Michael. Of course, they'd spend most of their time beating up Henry's children, who, let's face it, will be asking for it.

~I agree, said Jack. Henry's children will be whining, snot-nosed little cowards. I predict one will be president of the Confederacy and another King of the French.

Henry launched himself at Jack and began to wrestle him, smiled weirdly, clearly having a fine time. Michael said something like, Well, shit, and jumped in, too, and they fought ineffectually, gladly, and a crowd gathered, a few slugged each other, and then the battle was more general, dust flaming upward from the field. Officers rushed in and cried for a cease-fire, a halt. The others pulled themselves off, but by now Jack was pounding Henry on the head, saying: That's one for sense! That's one because you're an idiot! That's one from King Lear!

For thirty-six straight hours after that, the brothers, separated, walked picket duty in the woods, listening for the creep and clank of Yankees but hearing only wind and wings.

NOTHING ELSE WOULD HAPPEN, APPARENTLY. On May 18, far to the west, the army of Ulysses S. Grant began its siege of Vicksburg, the sentinel town high on a bluff above the Mississippi River, but here in Virginia, the men were restive, knowing that Marse Robert was drumming his fingers on a crackerbox somewhere, making plans. Throughout May and on into June, the army did little but drill, play cards, write letters, laugh a little. The Blackshear Boys could not raise the energy for a skit or a song. Anyway, their instruments were lost again on some supply train, which was, no doubt, headed in the opposite direction from Cobb's Legion.

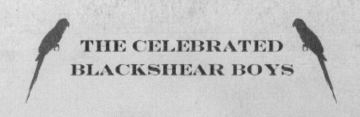

THE CELEBRATED
BLACKSHEAR BOYS

June 1, 1863
Somewhere near Chancellorsville, Va.

Dear Mother and Papa,
We have defeated the Yankees in a major battle near Chancellorsville, and the government is celebrating by starving us to death. Hail to Richmond! Erasure! I meant to say To Hell <u>with</u> Richmond. I know this will cause you grief, Mrs. Blackshear, but I regret to announce the death of your parrot, King Lear, which was beheaded and fried and mailed to your battle-weary sons yesterday. We will listen closely to see if the breasts speak when we consume them. Alas, untrue.

How fare you? Is Branton still the beautiful and lively place I remember? Wait—that was an engraving of Paradise I saw in a dream last night. The streets were lined with gems and gold, and everyone had a glass of claret and a copy of Les Miserables. Henry had just been crowned King, and he had announced that Paradise was going to attack Hell to free the spirit of Stonewall Jackson. Having heard about it, Jackson organized a Grand Army in three divisions and, last we heard, was fording the River Styx with cavalry and a cracker wagon.

Our instruments are apparently on their way to Ireland or perhaps Purgatory. Keep an eye out for them. If I know that banjo, it will head straight for a tavern and drink until it falls to the floor and breaks a string or two. The violin no doubt is in some woman's chamber, fiddling around. We have put out a reward.

I told General Wofford about Mama Blackshear, and he has promoted her to Brigadier General and assigned to her the defense of Richmond. She needs to be there by July 4, and tell her to bring firecrackers and enough broth & beef to feed two hundred thousand men for a year. She will need to pack well.

Word is that we shall be on the march soon, and we are rumored to be heading north again, perhaps to attack Canada, which in my estimation could be subdued in something under twelve hours.

Henry has had a cough for nearly two weeks. Have you ever heard the sound of someone choking a giraffe with gloves made of chain mail? Something similar. We took a vote on trading him to the Yankees for some peach cobbler and a yam. The vote was 125-123 in favor of Henry. His gratitude knows no bounds.

Well, I take pen in hand—I was supposed to say that when I started. It's how most of the boys here start letters. Seems a good way to end one as well.

Your son for the Southron Confuddleracy,
Jack Blackshear

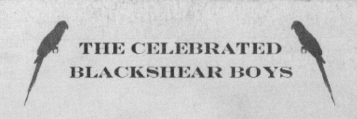

THE CELEBRATED
BLACKSHEAR BOYS

June 1, 1863
In a grove somewhere

Dearest Family,

We have seen terrible, terrible things, and I am vexed to know how I might make you know of them. I have not recovered from the shock of Fredericksburg, and yet we were thrown into battle again at Chancellorsville, about which you have no doubt read in the papers. I enclose a sketch of our attack from Michael. He says to tell Papa that he knows it is rough but that since we are hungry and lost, he has an excuse.

Most of us made it through the fight at Chancellorsville without being hurt, but our friend and messmate Alpheus Carter was shot dead. You would not know his parents, who are sharecroppers near Deerskin. It is strange how war levels us all out. A boy with whom I would not have spoken at home becomes a bosom friend in war. I did not see him dead, but Jack did & said he was shot through and expired in short order.

So many are dead, Mother. The battles around Richmond, Crampton's Gap, Sharpsburg, Fredericksburg, Chancellorsville. I feel as if I am in a tableau of death, and we are helpless to understand or stop it. What will be gained if we win? That we split the country into two poorer halves that will forever be warring if not at war? Imagine the Branton River turned to blood, as if some Mosaic plague had visited you: That is what we see all the time in this war, and we are damned, and we are cursed.

Michael's eyes, always attuned for the art of the world, are growing dulled and dim. Jack still teases up a fine joke to play on gullible men, pompous officers, but something is breaking in him, too. As for myself, I know I have always been fragile in the heart, but lately I sit shivering from the sorrow, trying (and sometimes failing) not to weep.

I have begun to feel that, down the years, men will find this an age of madness. They will ask: What was this war really about? And I have come to believe it has nothing to do with sovereignty or states' rights or taxes or tariffs or anything but slavery. We have a man in the Legion from west Georgia who said the other night that if we had, as he put it, killed all the niggers when we had the chance, then this whole war wouldn't have happened. I walked away and had to constrain myself from stripping off my uniform and joining the Federals. There is something deeply unholy about our side in this war, and I believe God will make us pay for it over and over in the years to come.

Pray for us. Pray for me.

Your loving son,
Henry Blackshear

GETTYSBURG

Cobb's Legion Infantry marched through Maryland and back into southern Pennsylvania as Robert E. Lee's second incursion into the north began that June. Late in the month, General William Wofford's Brigade invaded nearby homes on the march, liberating vast amounts of chickens, butter, bread, cherries, and brandy.

~Come back here with that medicine! You come back! A woman as ruffled as a fox-chased hen fluttered after a private who took her persimmon brandy. Jack laughed through his black wool beard. The weather was very hot and dry, and soldiers watched for a stream to ford, hoped.

~Maybe we're going to fight at Sharpsburg all over again like we did Manassas, said Henry, in a bright fine mood.

~Did we actually *win* at Sharpsburg? asked Michael.

~I take your point, said Henry. If we head to Crampton's Gap, I'm going to carry me back to ole Virginny.

~Couldn't we go some place cooler to fight? asked Henry.

~Forward to Iceland! cried Jack.

For more than a month after the victory at Chancellorsville—and the death of Stonewall Jackson—the army had marched one place and then another. Raccoon Ford on the Rapidan River, a fine camp with plenty of water and grazing land, with mountains in sight and cool enough at night for a blanket. Near Culpeper Courthouse on the Manassas Gap Railroad—a terrible march in which many dropped dead of exhaustion or thirst. (A cousin of the Foggs, one Tyler Knott, staggered out of formation, dry-heaved once, and fell dead on a jagged stone.) By now, the Blackshears just watched, solemn and glum, but they did not break ranks to help; death would find them all soon enough. Luck and time. They moved along the eastern flank of the Blue Ridge

Mountains, gorgeous country, with fields of clover and deep-green grass, but the cattle were all gone, the land turning from pasture to field. And the heat suffocated: From where would another breath come? To Martinsburg, and the fording the Potomac River again, arriving near Williamsport in Maryland on June 28 around ten in the morning.

The people of the city were gone or quiet behind closed doors in the oppressive heat. Farms lying in waste, no animals. Women had screamed at them all along the route, some baldly cursing, damning the tramping Butternuts and Grays to a fiery hell. To Southern ears, a coarseness to their voices, a twist and twang, epithets, fists raised and shaking. Camping two miles east of Chambersburg on the Harrisburg Road. Ahead, rebels destroyed four miles of railroad tracks leading into Harrisburg.

The Blackshear Boys lay on their blankets watching the stars come out over southern Pennsylvania. Dusty coughing around them, wheezy sneezing, and much talk of Vicksburg, where the siege was tightening. If Vicksburg fell, the Mississippi River would be entirely in Union hands, would split the Confederacy in half.

~I've been thinking about getting married, said Michael.

~Thanks, but you're not my sort, said Jack. Besides, I have a girl not waiting for me back home.

~You mean Susan Goodpath? asked Henry. Maybe she is waiting for you, now she's a widow and all.

~If we had half the men who have been between her legs, we could end this war in three days, said Jack, yawning.

~You mean sweet Elizabeth Chadwick? asked Henry. She's the only one of our sweethearts who isn't in some way monstrous. Why is that? Why did Jack and I choose harridans for sweethearts? It's unlike me. I'm not the sort to care for some bucolic Xantippe.

~We need to put on a show, said Jack. I'm out of potable finery. This war would be so much more amusing if both sides were drunk. If you missed the other side in a musket volley, you could puke on them.

~Vomitus bellum, said Michael, making the sign of the cross. Amen. I guess I'm talking about sweet Elizabeth. But there's something about her. She's...

~If she were any quieter, she'd be a rumor, said Jack.

~I just want to be settled in a house, said Michael. To have a huge room facing north with hundreds of yards of canvas rolled and ready. With the finest colors from all over the world. Rich crimsons, green the color of early wheat after rain. I want to spend ages painting individual blades of grass, and then when I'm finished, she would come into the study and hold my hand and say, O Michael, that is so real I think I could walk right into it. And I want to believe in something. I want to look hard at the world and know what is true, and I want to carry it on my back like a winter coat. Bearing the *true* through my painting to all the world.

~I hate it that you have no ambition, said Henry.

~Wastrel, said Jack.

~And what is wrong with ambition? Haven't we been ambitious for the Celebrated Blackshear Boys? I just want. Ah. I just want this god-damn war to be over. But I don't think it's ever going to end. If I could find a way to reach England right now, I'd probably leave.

~I'm not sure I can kill anybody else, said Henry. His voice so soft it was barely audible. Snoring men: lazy saw-bladed hardwood. I shot a man at Chancellorsville when we were making the charge, and he hunched over and then stood up and looked me straight in the eyes, not believing it, knowing the wound was mortal. I can't stop thinking: He may have been calling across the land to his wife and children, whispering goodbye in a language of blood. Brothers, remember the promise: *One of us is captured, the others find him.*

Michael and Jack said nothing now, serious and sleepy. But Jack thought: The artist who wants to control the shape of his own world, the sensitive boy with words to spare. And me, the slippery jokester, a singing fool, bound for drink and whoredom and rather enjoying the idea, guiltless. Thousands there across this field, pressed and pressing, the officers saying more more more more, we need *more.* More miles, more maneuvers, more *dead.* Dark green, and cursing women. *Who could begin to count the dead, and surely the Federal army is shadowing us, sliding up the mountain valleys, across the ridge crests, and when we spill into the open, clash, cry, pour our blood out by the five-gallon pail, enough blood to fill a Parrott gun, who then will take the victory? I, too, would get married and not for love but for peace. I would do almost anything for peace, scale*

peaks, swim seas, turn right now and walk all the way back to Georgia. The
women of Chambersburg. That harsh cry, curses. I would have cursed us
then. I curse us now.

Sleep drained the Southern soldiers, pressed them down beneath
the turning of constellations.

THE NEXT DAY THEY MARCHED onward, seven miles up the
Gettysburg Road, across some mountains by way of Fayetteville, to the
quaint village of Greenwood, where one brigade torched an ironworks
owned by Thaddeus Stevens, a member of Congress. They were coming
toward something—a sense of funneling into a vortex, and the men,
though in decent spirits, all knew it, prepared in solitary prayer, banter,
last letters. The Division's mail rider was captured by Yankees and sent by
prodding bayonet behind lines to some prison. That night, Jack wrote a
hasty letter to their parents in Branton, full of false bonhomie, the usual
lies.

They passed through Cashtown, five miles west of Gettysburg,
camped with brief, edgy fires, cleaned and re-cleaned their grip-worn
muskets, filled up with caps and cartridges.

~They're going to send us into the fight tomorrow or the next day,
said Cass Milton. His green eyes glowed in the firelight. Brands blew
upward on a slight hot wind. The air was breathless, oven-like, and they
stripped off their coats and flung them into the beat-down grass. Cass
moved his shoulders as if to unlimber them.

~I don't think I'm gone get shot or nothin', said Jim Watts. His
buck teeth looked bronze in the last light of a summer night. But O Lord
God my head is hurting me worse than anything.

~It's hurting me, too, said Jack. Stay away from mirrors or you
might have an apoplexy.

~That's cruel, said Lowell Palmer.

~Aw, Jack he don't mean nothin' by it, said Jim. I know that. I'm a
ugly boy, always have been.

~Well, at least you're a bad soldier, said Jack.

~Thankee, said Jim, grinning painfully.

~You know, I think these boys need an impromptu frolic, said Jack,
rubbing his hands together. Gather 'round boys! He was standing, and

Michael came forward, dusting off the front of his shirt, and here was Henry, eyebrows up in private's chevrons, happily ready.

~Hit's a show! someone cried. Fair firing far ahead. Someone said all the roads converged in Gettysburg. Dozens came over to the Blackshear flame, clapped up an act.

~Now gentlemen! Now gentlemen! cried Jack. We know we are on the verge of a great battle, and after tomorrow, we will all probably be lounging around heaven. (*Boos and hisses, some laughter.*) And I don't know about you, but when I get to heaven, the first thing I'm going to look for is a woman! (*Whistles and applause.*) And in that spirit, I want to sing you boys a song about the girl I left back home. Except this girl was one you—how shall I put this delicately? She was one you *paid* for love.

The men crowded up now, and the heat was thick as paste. Their stubby smokes glowed in the firefly darkness. Last tobacco in the Regiment. Some of it wasn't even tobacco but dried weeds, bitter as homesickness. The didn't even notice their own sweat-stinking smells anymore, just went on and on. They were bearded and skinny, reed-thin, raw and rough from sun and wind.

~Ah, he speaks of someone we know and dearly love! said Michael. The most famous woman in our hometown of Branton, Georgia!

~A woman who only says *no* if her honey has no money! said Henry. They were shoulder to shoulder now, silently inventing harmonies, not *saying* but *knowing*, setting the song's phantom key, working out harmony and descant.

~Ladies and soldiers, and I might say it's nice to have a few of the latter, let us introduce you to the woman who has solved all our troubles! said Jack

~Soothed the kinks out of young manhood's eternal problems! cried Henry.

~Brought joy in a joyless world! said Henry. Jack looked the brothers together, nodded for the beat, and when they began, it was in a tight three-part harmony:

> *No one knows her last name,*
> *It could be Smith or Jones.*
> *Her game is such a fast game,*

She'll turn your sinews bones.
She costs less than any
You'll find on Adams Street.
We call her Minnie Penny—
Buy the sour with the sweet!

Some men pay with pennies,
Some men pay with hams.
But all go in like lions
And then come out like lambs.

The men adored it, clapped along, and not remembering any other verses, the Blackshears repeated it three times, passing the solo around while adding baroque filigrees. The crowd, which had been exhausted and ready for sleep, came alive. Many had been around since the Peninsula days, but with the shifting of brigades and divisions, most of them had heard *of* the Blackshear Boys but had not *heard* them. Their aplomb was dazzling, as if it was one man divided into three parts. During the applause, Jack huddled with them, gave a skit's general idea.

JACK: General Hooker? General Hooker? (*Michael steps up*)

MICHAEL: What is it you want, inferior being?

JACK: I'm not an inferior being, I'm Abraham Lincoln, president of the United States. And I need to tell you something important.

MICHAEL: Then on with it! I have to seek another glorious victory like the one at Chancellorsville!

JACK: (*Baffled*) Sir, you *lost* Chancellorsville.

MICHAEL: It was a tactical reversal, sir! Look it up in any good army manual. I did it deliberately so the enemy would make another foray into the North!

JACK: At any rate, I must tell you that you are no longer in command, General Hooker. I have selected Howard Jones to be commander of all the armies. I have decided that you will be my cook.

MICHAEL: Your cook! That's a rare privilege!

JACK: Well-done!

The men clapped at the mindless nonsense, not knowing that only hours before, Lincoln had cashiered Hooker after the disaster at Chancellorsville and turned to George Meade, a man from Pennsylvania who should, at least, know the land on which the great battle seemed to be near. Henry stepped up to his brothers.

HENRY: I am General Howard Jones, new commander of the Union forces. General Hooker, you are relieved.

MICHAEL: So true! I've never been more relieved in my life! (*Howls and applause, with a few knit-browed officers wandering over, not with disdain but unsure of it anyway.*)

HENRY: And Mr. Lincoln, I would like to say that I will follow in the great tradition of all your army commanders, Scott, McDowell, McClellan, Pope, McClellan, Hooker—I'm sure I'm leaving a few out.

JACK: Ack! That's precisely what I was afraid of! How soon do you think you can lose a battle?

HENRY: Oh, almost immediately! I could lose in Virginia if you like. We could lose in Maryland, but I'm thinking it would look better if we lost in Pennsylvania. We haven't lost there before. It would make all the newspapers.

JACK: Well done!

MICHAEL: Are you ordering dinner?

JACK: Excuse me?

HENRY: General Jones, you are relieved.

MICHAEL: I sure am! But I still have to cook. So, rare or well-done?

HENRY: General have you lost your mind?

JACK: No, he's just relieved.

HENRY: Well, I am prepared to lose a battle in any state you wish, Mr. President. Have we lost a battle in Minnesota yet?

JACK: (*rubbing his forehead wanly*) Only to the Indians.

HENRY: Well, we might as well start things by losing in Pennsylvania, since it's my home state! Should we lose a skirmish first or a major engagement?

JACK: Major.

MICHAEL: I've been demoted from general to major? Well, that isn't bad for a cook, I suppose.

The Blackshears were improbably deft at this kind of banter, having done it before adoring crowds since boyhood, so they spun it out, layer by idiotic layer, as long as it held, but when it grew frayed, they sensed it, and Jack brought it to a swift close. The applause drew officers with knit brows, speaking of battle in the morning, the need for rest, the fact of moving out, the heat. Men had died ahead of them. Jack nodded. They passed a hat, and it was soon stuffed with bills and loose change, and much of the paper money was Confederate, which was now less-sought-after than Union currency.

~We'd like to close with something I know is dear to your hearts, said Jack. He raised both eyebrows, cleared his throat. That same tight harmony:

> *When the blackbird in the spring, on the willow tree,*
> *Sat and rocked, I heard him sing, singing Aura Lea*
> *Aura Lea, Aura Lea, maid of golden hair,*
> *Sunshine came along with thee, and swallows in the air.*
>
> *(Chorus)*
> *Aura Lea, Aura Lea, maid of golden hair,*
> *Sunshine came along with thee, And swallows in the air.*

They sang all the verses and then lingered, mellow and quiet, not wanting the spell to break, and then the applause was huge, but it died away under the glare of stern officers and the knowledge of what lay ahead.

In the heat of blanket beds just west of Gettysburg, the Blackshears split the money into three parts, stuffed their pockets full.

~You reckon we will get a chance to spend any of this? asked Michael.

~If I get shot, I give you boys permission to rifle my body, said Jack, lying down heavily and closing his eyes.

~Same here, said Michael.

~I'll send the money home to mother, said Henry, yawning. Or spend it on women and liquor. One of those.

~Flip a coin, said Jack, but he was already asleep.

THE BATTLE OF GETTYSBURG WOULD begin this day, July 1, 1863, but Cobb's Legion and Wofford's Brigade were not engaged, though they were aimed for it, forming from the west on the Cashtown Road toward the gentle swaying rills around Gettysburg itself. General A. P. Hill's Corps of the rebel army had been moving forward along the Chambersburg Pike earlier this morning when they ran into dismounted Federal cavalry under the command of General John Buford. By mid-morning the infantry corps of the Union's General John F. Reynolds came up, and a general engagement broke out, thousands firing, while tens of thousands moved into line for general battle on each side.

~Armadillo, said Jim Watts. A reg'lar battle of Armadillo.

~I think that's Armageddon, said Jack, jaunty in march step. How's your headache?

~Gone. Bled from the coolness of the day, said Jim. The day was already suffocating, oven heat, the kind that blistered and baked. Sunstroke and death from thirst.

~By God I feel all limber again, said Cass, who marched as if his uniform held bones with a thousand joints. It feels good to be limbered up.

Instead, they stood for hours on the Chambersburg Pike while two different divisions slogged ahead of them down the road, along with the ache and creak of the Second Corps' wagon train. They were standing, hungry in their ranks, when they turned to the sound of horses.

~Jack, would you look at that, said Michael doubtfully.

~I'm damned, said Jack. Henry and the others watched open-mouthed as General R. E. Lee and his staff came riding along the lines to the swell of a cheer, full-throated from the men behind them. Lee seemed easy, tall in the saddle, grateful for the shouts from his men. They passed along the stopped lines of sun-stunned men toward Gettysburg. Already the firing up there was heavy, the guttural thunder of artillery, the vast clap of muskets fired rank on rank.

They stood, frustrated as the battle roared toward noon and past. They leaned on one leg and then another waiting for the road to clear.

~God, it sounds like Sharpsburg or Fredericksburg all over again, said Henry with a shudder.

~It does, but I'm not God, said Jack. Close, though. God has three stripes.

~Yore gone be struck dead in battle for blasphemy, said Jim Watts.

~Something's going to happen to us here, said Henry softly. I know it. I can feel it. His brothers said nothing, just stood sweating in line as they all did until nearly four in the afternoon, when the line began to unkink, started moving down the road to a groaning cheer, from men too stiff standing to march. But there was no choice, and they headed toward the sound of battle on the hottest part of this day, tramping in a ghastly storm of gray-brown dust that choked them.

They marched until nearly midnight, getting almost to Gettysburg, where the firing had ended, collapsing near Marsh Creek on the warm ground, sleeping instantly, bellies growling. Night scraped around them on the legs of crickets, a chorus of tree frogs. They lay in clumps like the battlefield dead, snoring, speaking in sleep, jerking, sitting up, lying back down.

Henry awakened in the deep night and sat up. Not forty feet away, a rabbit sat on her haunches, nose trembling. She was still, calm as an omen, and then gone, soundless into the dark woods.

THE BATTLE STARTED AGAIN EARLY the next day, and the Branton Avengers rose and marched forward, forward now, not waylaid on the road, and soon they were on a ridge west of town that held the prominent red-brick building of a Lutheran Seminary. The Brigade stood ready for orders, with Cobb's Legion on the far left, succeeded in order by Phillips' Legion, the 16th Georgia, 24th Georgia, and 18th Georgia. The 3rd Georgia Sharpshooters moved out ahead of them, skirmishers for the line. Still, the advance was slow, turgid even.

The vast battlefield churned. Already, Kershaw's Brigade from the southern army was attacking the Union lines along the Emmitsburg Road, and Barksdale's Brigade came into line behind them. Wofford's men waited on the ridge, muskets loaded, faces intent, disbelieving.

~Good God in heaven, said Lowell Parker. It must be going on for miles and miles. I think the whole Yankee army is out there.

~And the whole Confederacy, said Michael intensely. *Oh,* he thought, *if this were but some Stereopticon picture that I could paint: sinuous lines, waving flags, great swaths of gun smoke, charge and retreat, whole lines crumpling with death or dying.*

~They ain't gone let us into this fight, said Jim Watts, and suddenly they were moving south, heading for combat, and as they marched, the sounds of battle grew deafening, then even louder. They could all see it: They would head east and try to hit the Union's left flank, a classic military move. But the Federals extended their lines, bowed out, reformed to sway with the motion of flanking. Henry thought: *Like a beast writhing.*

Ahead of them now, Barksdale's Brigade of Mississippians fought blue soldiers in a peach orchard, pushing them hard, while Kershaw's troops slogged into battle through a wheat field. To the east, two stony hills rose, one much larger than the other. Wofford's men waited, waited. They inched, the day sped. Not until four in the afternoon did things break.

They moved rapidly forward now toward the battle, into a boiling golden sun, acrid smoke, the vast bang of artillery, the faint screams of the shot, which grew louder by the step. Henry had never in his life been more afraid. Jack was wishing he'd trimmed his bib of beard; it choked him with sweat. Michael tried *not* to think.

A one-hundred-yard gap opened in the 24th Georgia, and General Wofford rode toward it at full speed, screaming for it to close up.

~Hurrah for you of the bald head! cried a battery captain. Others in the artillery took it up, saluting Wofford; soldiers always looked for a hint of valor, rewarded it, terrified, sentimental.

Cobb's Legion was into the open ground now, moving past the Emmitsburg Pike, onward toward the horror. Union artillery shells blasted through the 16th and 24th Georgia, but Cobb's Legion infantry was still whole as it moved onward. None of them believed it, but there he was: General James Longstreet, riding part way out before preparing to turn back.

~Cheer less and fight more! he shouted. Surly Dutchman, but a hell of a general, and one with perhaps vision, too.

Barksdale's men swung north toward Cemetery Ridge, but Wofford's troops moved straight forward, stretching across Wheatfield Road. The men on the left came close to the peach orchard while those on the right moved toward the wheat field and some small rocky hills. The line was four hundred yards long now, and the firing intense or insane; Henry could not imagine anything like this. Then, suddenly, the Rebel yell rose from the lines, a weird skirl that could be heard even over the firing, and they were charging now.

Charging, for Christ's sake! thought Jack Blackshear. He glanced at his brothers, looked far ahead, up at the rocky hill on which Federal troops were tightly formed. They were almost close enough for a stand-up bayonet fight now, and the lines ebbed one way, flowed another. And yet order held: colors flying as in a dress parade for a visiting officer, guns still on their right shoulders, waiting for the right distance. They were in the wheat field suddenly, and here came General William Wofford, wild on his horse, back and forth, screaming:

~Charge them, boys!

Henry thought: *By God I will. I want this. Perhaps I have always wanted this, something uncomplicated and unequivocal.* He looked down the Confederate lines: They were dirty, unkempt, uniforms filthy and ripped, and some men stopped to fire in their bare feet. Wofford's men surged into Federal batteries, capturing six Union cannon on a farm owned by a man named Weikert. Surging. Forward. Suddenly, Cobb's Legion came into the backs of fleeing Federal troops that now turned to fight, and the lines went hand to hand now, hammering with gun butts, stabbing through with bayonets, knifing through tunic and tough bone. He was screaming, could not stop, face almost crimson with it.

Henry came upon a fallen Union boy and beat him with his rifle butt.

Michael saw it, thought: *Great God.* A bayonet glanced across the knot of his left deltoid, and Michael felt nothing, pressed the barrel of his gun beneath the Yankee's chin and almost lifted him off the ground, then fired. Brains all over his face, blinding, slick bloody thing, crawling. They came in sight of Little Round Top—there it was, quite a distance ahead, but also Blue boys rushing along the ridge, forming and firing, fresh troops against the breath-starved Georgians.

Jack felt everything slow to a dream: men folding and filling, jack-knifed, spun bloody. The glint on rifle locks, just like the sun on the Branton River of a summer day, slicing through town, boys mad for jokes and frolics, joking, lying daylong, spun with summer daylight and on into night, born on the thrum of fireflies' glow. A grayback boy gargled blood, whipped the ground with both hands, thrashed. All those exposed stones on the hill! And now the Union lines extending father and farther to the right, behind stone walls, ranks firing straight down into the Butternut boys. *Oh God*—the fight was going on in long undulating lines, miles it seemed, and the hollows filled with the dead and their useless blood. Up toward Gettysburg, past the Lutheran Seminary, in the hollows, up the ridges. And good Christ the artillery! Hunting rifles fired next to each ear: land of the deaf and deafening. *I am now taking my rifle to hand and swinging—crack!—on the skull of a beardless boy, and his jaw jerked from its socket, hanging, the boy dropping his gun to put it back, hold it up, getting shot in the lungs, again in the right arm, and a buckling shot, left knee, falling like a sack tossed from the back of a wagon.*

~Fall back! We're falling back! Shouted by whom? A raging roared down the line, but the motion was rearward, hundred and hundreds, the vines of dead and dying, heads exploding.

~I'm all right, said Michael softly to nobody. Why, I'm perfectly all right. He had lost his rifle; didn't matter. He was wandering around holding his shoulder, which bled lightly down the armpit and gathered in the waistband of his pants. *If one of us is.*

~Come on! screamed Jack. We're moving back! He put his arm under Michael, turned once and saw Henry walk easily, no hurry, through the field of fire, the crop of lead, past the rocky hills and then up the slope alone, up Little Round Top, dropping his gun, arms up. Two Union soldiers rushed down the hill and grabbed Henry and pulled him up the hill. Captured.

~Fall back, goddamnit? *Fall back?* Wofford was driving his horse back and forth. *Was that him, and how could I hear anything in this din. The next one is going to split me down the back*, thought Jack. *Siz siz siz ker-BLAM!*

The men piled back into the woods. Wofford had found his Division commander, General Lafayette McLaws, was asking who in the bloody *hell* ordered them back, and McLaws was saying something about Longstreet. The men came back from the rocky hill facing it, not wanting to get shot in the back.

The firing went on up the line, down it, screams, company, regiment, brigade, corps, division, army—men in their tens of thousands swimming, stroke by stroke in a bright red lake of blood.

DARKNESS. MEN VOMITING FROM THE dust and wounds. A hot moon. Popcorn firing, pickets barking. All day Robert E. Lee's Army of Northern Virginia had hammered at the Union flanks with only modest success. *My God, how many of them were there on those heights?* Lee thought: *Tomorrow I will hit them in the center; the line must be weakest there.* Jack Blackshear leaned weeping against a tree with Michael's head in his lap.

~Press on it, it hurts worse than a thousand hornets, said Michael, gasping from the pain.

~Here's all the water I have left. It's hot and probably fetid, said Jack hoarsely. He tipped his canteen on his brother's lips, and Michael supped from the dented rim.

~Was he shot down? I'm coming and going, can't recall, said Michael.

~Captured, said Jack. He just walked straight toward them and gave up, like it was the easiest decision in the world. Cass found them, fell heavily. His stomach growled.

~Jim Watts is dead, said Cass. I tried to stop for him, but we were moving on and—shit. He got shot in the heart. Fell straight dead. Don't think he knew it at all. Just gone. And Lowell was wounded in the thigh. Might have clipped an artery. He was spouting terrible. I don't know what they did to him. Where's Henry?

~They got him, said Jack. Captured. He tore his own shirt up and bandaged Michael's shoulder, which had almost stopped bleeding. If this doesn't go septic, I think you'll be all right. Goddamn these blundering sons of bitches for this war. Goddamn them all to hell.

~Well, I reckon they plan to kill the rest of us in the morning, said Cass. I'm going to be rested when I get shot.

They slept on the open ground just west of the Emmitsburg Road, the brigades of Wofford and Kershaw. The peach orchard lay just ahead, and to their left, ready for engagement tomorrow, was the division of General George Pickett.

THE AVENGERS, AT LESS THAN half the strength they had when they left Branton, did not know it, but their part in the great Battle of Gettysburg was over. They could not imagine the carnage to come. No one could, but years later, many veterans wondered what, if anything, Lee was thinking that hot July 3. Wofford's men, shot up, beaten down, were held in reserve that blistering Friday, and when dawn came, and the Union troops were still in position, no one doubted what would happen next.

~Dear God, that old man is going to go after the center today, said Cass. There was no food, little water.

~I'm not leaving here without Henry, said Michael, wincing from his wound. It was no longer bleeding but oozed thick blood into the hard black bandage of Jack's stripped shirt. Jack wore his coat in the suffocating heat, chest bared. We have a pact.

~No way in hell we're leaving him, said Jack. Hold on. We're going to find him. Don't you worry, boy. Don't you worry.

These divisions lined up on Wofford's left: Pickett, Harry Heth— commanded by J. J. Pettigrew—and Dorsey Pender, led by Isaac Trimble. They stood in the woods at the edge of a long field that sloped for more than a mile up toward a ridge now bristling with Federal artillery around a clump of trees.

Around one o'clock on a steaming, sullen afternoon, southern Pennsylvania exploded. Southern batteries roared, pounded the ridge, while some eighty Federal cannon boomed back. Jack and Michael sat in the dirt at the woods' edge, looking at each other in utter disbelief. The barrage never let up for well more than an hour, and soon they all had a high-pitched whine in the ears, millions of mosquitoes, swamp-fed. Some shells arced over Wofford's men but most pounded up Pickett's Division, blowing holes in the huddled units, flags up and hanging limp in the edge of the forest.

Cass said something to them, wide-eyed, but either his voice was gone or their hearing had vanished; he seemed a dusty mime, eyes dilated, mouth slack with fear and exhaustion. On and on—two hours' worth of earthshaking nausea, the screaming roar, dull memories of natural sound. Jack watched as a small pebble hopskipped two feet across the hot earth and then moved back again, wild, sentient.

The Union firing began to fade, slack off, stop, and with muttering rustle the Confederate center moved from the trees into the edge of the field, formed, seemed mad for a rush.

~We're not going to be engaged, said Michael. Jack heard this: *mnt e gagd.*

Not far away, General Pickett stood in front of his commander, Longstreet, and asked if he should attack now? Old Pete, the Dutchman, who knew Lee's order was folly, could only take a gulp and nod. He never said a word. From here, Wofford's men could see it plain: The long lines of Confederates moving out in the steaming sun, walking in good order across a brilliant field of fire, heading toward the Emmitsburg Road and its rail fence. Bearers held their flags up. The sky almost cloudless, a sick flat plate of worn blue. All of Cobb's Legion—all of Wofford's men entire—stood and watched, cheering on the Virginians in the center who were heading for the entrenched Federal line, outnumbered, outgunned, outgeneraled. Michael held on to Jack's shoulder, woozy and pasty-mouthed.

~Oh dear sweet Mary mother of God sweet Jesus, said a private nearby. They aim to go to their slaughter. The cheering had slowed, stopped. Dry winds came by sometimes, raking leaves, arriving lost, mumbling away. Not until the Confederates were some distance across the field did the artillery from the North explode once more. Holes blown out in the lines: men shot, ripped up into butchered hunks of flesh. Jack thought: *Lee is back there in the woods watching what he hath wrought. Hath wrought. Biblical. Henry, where are you?*

The Legion men watched, shuddered with horror, as the southern divisions moved steadily, widely, into their deaths. Row on row of Federal soldiers stood or lay, lined behind a stone wall on that hill, and when the gray lines came close enough, they unleashed waves of rifle fire, and the rebels fell, scythed down. The heat oppressed; glinting cannon, the yellow-orange muzzle blasts, small puffs of rifle fire. Jack could imagine officers up there surging forward, urging men to come on. *Soldiers of the South! Come die for me!* And they did, hundreds, some feeling nothing, spun off into eternity with a clap and crash. Others would be writhing, gut-shot, begging already for help, for water, trying to hold in their leaking blood, clenched in ghastly pain. Wofford's men were quiet, watching, knowing.

It would not stop. The southern lines pressed upward and toward the artillery and lines of fire. Michael watched them, thinking: *The dead, the dead, the dead. Dear God in heaven, the dead.* Finally, like water beginning to leak from an ill-banked dam, they started coming back across the field. They staggered in twos and threes, some helping wounded walk and others poling across with their rifles, as if rowing a boat. Now they returned by the dozens, looking back, staggered. The Union lines kept up the heat of fire, and many rebels dropped, back-shot.

~My God, my God, what have we done? asked Michael softly.

~You, boy, hush up! said an officer from Athens. This is General R. E. Lee you are talking about, sir!

Jack wanted to say: *That old man just slaughtered five thousand, just ordered them killed as one would kill hogs in the dead of winter. He could not see past glory. Goddamn glory and goddamn all who would believe it could be found here. Longstreet didn't know what in the hell he was doing sending us into the peach orchard and to that rocky hill yesterday or perhaps he did. How could Lee have not known? You tell me that Mister Officer, how could Lee not have known? This, the man who invented Chancellorsville, the great gray genius: How could he not have known?*

It had been worse than even Cobb's Legion could see this far away. The Confederates had reached, some of them, the stone wall, where men were firing into each other from five feet, jamming bayonets into chests and throats, slicing carotid arteries in a great wide red splash. One man would write, years later: *Men going down on their hands and knees, spinning round like tops, throwing out their arms, gulping up blood, falling; legless, armless, headless. There are ghastly heaps of dead men.*

There, at the edge of the woods to the west, General Lee himself saw it, knew it finally, and was wretched in the knowledge. The men staggering back heard him say repeatedly, *This has been my fault, all this has been my fault.* The survivors cried *No! No!* But Lee, perhaps in shock, knew well enough. The new crop of dead blossomed crimson in the field. No man could ignore the evidence. The Battle of Gettysburg was over, and Lee knew it. Three horrible days, more than five thousand men dead for both sides, an appalling thirty thousand wounded in all. They would not know that on the same day Vicksburg had fallen to Grant. The Confederacy was beginning to come apart, split at the seams.

Jack expected Lee to send another wave toward the wall, but it never came. And the Federals never left the haven of their stone wall up the long slope. Night came without another fight, and Michael grew feverish now, took the shakes, and Jack held him lapward, dabbed his forehead with strip of cloth from Cass Milton's shirt.

~I can't believe it, said Cass, crying softly. I can't believe we just keep marching right up and getting killed like this. Why is this happening? What is this war about? Do you think Henry is still alive over there? My God.

~I will tell you what this war is about, said Jack. Someone had built a campfire—lots of them were doing it, though the night was not much cooler than the day. Heat lightning painted the sky to the west mauve and gold. This war is about pride, about men who make a line in the sand and say *Step over that line, and I will shoot you.* It's about stupidity and arrogance. It's about *slavery,* goddamnit. We're idiots.

~Keep it down, said Michael, sitting up. You're going to get us arrested. I feel a little better. I wish I had a ham.

~It's about officers believing they have special knowledge, about terrain, about tactics, about troops. Thinking that they have the answers because they have been promoted up the ranks. They think it's been a good day if only five hundred of their men are blown into shards of meat. Let me tell you something. Stonewall Jackson was mad. Anybody could tell it. Longstreet's one of the few sane ones, but in battles all these generals are like blind men swimming on a moonless sea at night. They grab hold to what they think is a raft, but it's the fin of a fish that 'll eat a man in one bloody goddamn gulp. Jeb Stuart, that dandy son of a bitch. That be-feathered *ass* and his goddamn gallantry. We can't win this war. They can keep pouring thousands of men into their army, and we can't replace a man.

~I'm not leaving without Henry, said Michael.

~Hell, of goddamn *course* we're not leaving with Henry, said Jack.

~What do you aim to do? asked Cass Milton.

~I'm going to bid a fond á Dieu to this army and go idiot hunting, I guess, said Jack. What in the hell was he doing walking off into the Union lines at that rocky hill, anyway, Michael?

~He was always too sensitive, said Michael. He'd been thinking about this war for a long time. I don't think he ever really got over what happened at Crampton's Gap. Cobb's Legion mostly died that day. And Henry's not the only idiot. We're all idiots. I never much believed in this war anyway.

~Fine time you picked to tell me, said Jack Blackshear.

INDEPENDENCE DAY: JULY THE FOURTH broke with a breathless heat over southern Pennsylvania, and the men awaited orders, but soon enough—late morning—it was clear that the fight was over and that Lee and his badly diminished army would be heading back toward the Potomac, limping back into Virginia. Late in the day they formed and began to march.

Jack and Michael Blackshear weren't there. Long before noon, they had crowded up on Cass. Michael's arm throbbed, but the pain was bearable.

~I'm not going to tell you anything, because I don't want you to know enough to get arrested for it, said Jack. Be a good boy, though. Eat more. You're looking thin. Clean your teeth and wash your face. You've got gunpowder all over your cheeks.

~But where…

~*Ahnt*, said Michael, waving his finger. Just remember the Celebrated Blackshear Boys. That is your only mission for now. If anyone asks, say you saw us last when we'd taken General Longstreet prisoner.

~He's on our side, said Cass, eyes glinting.

~Oh yeah, said Michael. Forgiveness, sir. I meant General Meade. Right after we captured General George Meade. And Grant.

~He's in Mississippi, said Cass.

~Let not men doubt then our reach, said Jack grandly.

They had strolled casually down the lines, farther, then farther. So easy. Clots of ambulances with acres of wounded. The hollow-eyed look of exhaustion on unhurt soldiers, the nervous stamping of ones ready to resume the killing. Some were always ready. Fists clenching, ready, almost unwilling to wait. By the time the Army of Northern Virginia began to retreat late in the day, Jack and Michael were huddled in a small cove, sipping water from a nearly dried-up spring.

Just after dark, a wild storm broke over them, rain spreading leaves, pelting down.

~What comes after a torrent? asked Jack. They sat on rocks in the middle of a nearly dry stream.

~Deluge, said Michael. Flood. End of the world.

~Build an ark. I think we have caused God great anger.

~Just great sorrow, said Michael. Only a great and enduring sorrow.

The storm roared all night, and rivulets of bloody battlefield soil flowed into all the nearby streams.

BOOK TWO

NEWARK, NEW JERSEY, AUGUST 26, 1943

After death's first shock, sometimes peace comes floating down. Not when the young perish, of course, but for the old man, I now sense a weight removed, a challenge fulfilled. I take a long walk this morning in our neighborhood, down the summer streets and their newspaper sidewalks, yards of yawning dogs. The morning is hot and still, and I imagine the morning after Gettysburg, when Lee must have known history's verdict already. Even though I loathe the South's mad support of slavery, that must have been Lee's finest moment.

They've given me a few days off from the paper, and I feel honored in a way. When the mail comes just after lunch, we don't get a letter from Mike, and Myrtice sees the twist of my face.

~You know he's bad about writing, she says. Plus he's also working for the OWI, too, don't forget that.

~I know it, I say. I was thinking about Dad, actually. I feel calmer about his death, but I can't quite imagine not having a cold beer with him in the back yard. It takes imagination longer than actuarial tables to catch up with death. I'd come to believe he wasn't ever going to die, that he'd hit a hundred and ten and then a hundred and twenty. He didn't seem like the type to die.

~We're all the type, she says, hugging me from behind. Mike had been born in the second year of our marriage, just about the time her gynecological troubles began. After that, other children were impossible, and we grieved, but not for long. She says, I'm the type, and so are you. Knowing it is what makes us great. How many people would have strength, courage, honor, or discipline if we didn't know we were going to die?

~It's funny, but the old man always tried to pretend he didn't have any of those, I say. He would veer off into a story that was hilarious along the way but never quite had a point. He did tell me about the battles, over and over, but he would come to the ghastly parts and then bounce away into some long-remembered joke. He knew. I think that's why I'll miss him most. He knew that forgetting is one of the great human achievements.

~He's laughing at you right now, she says. He always laughed when you got philosophical and in your cups. She walks around in front of me and goes into the kitchen to make coffee, and I follow her. The small room still holds the aroma of bacon and eggs, and I feel a shudder of joy.

~Do you really think we go to heaven and are reunited with our dead? I ask. With millions and millions of people there? How could we find each other? I keep wondering if he's with his brothers now.

~Maybe we're not reunited with our pasts physically, she says. Maybe heaven is being able to remember everyone and everything in our lives. The good and the bad. And not judge.

~You're pretty smart for a math professor, I say. To me, things just don't add up that neatly.

~Nothing really adds up, she says. In the calculus of the universe, even Isaac Newton was a ninny.

~I think you stole that line from Dad, I say, grinning.

~People steal their whole personalities from other people, she says. A joke is the least of it. In a way, the Celebrated Blackshear Boys are on tour in Europe right now, aren't they?

~They certainly are.

To my great surprise, we go to bed and make love, for she knows that I crave intimacy and forgetfulness, and in that sweet hour I gain both. But later, when it comes time for them to bring Dad's body home, I feel as if I need a drink, so I take one.

THE OILY MAN FROM THE funeral home has writhing hands, and he stands on the walkway as four employees wrestle the coffin up the steps and into the front parlor, on its folding bier. I'll keep him here for two days, as his will stipulates, lid closed, a spray of lilies on his roof.

~People don't bring the departed home like this as much as they used to, he says, wiping the sweat off his heavy-featured face with a handkerchief. Seems like they just want to go from the funeral home to the church to the cemetery. I did like you said, didn't mention his Civil War service in what I sent to the papers. But honest to God, I'd think that's news. There must only be a few of them left in the whole state. In the whole country! I didn't know him all that well, Hank, but he never seemed worried. Takes a strong man to be that way. I'm worried about how hot it's going to get today.

~I appreciate your thoughts, I say. Today is Thursday, and they will come get Dad for graveside services Saturday morning. I need to call the ones who will perform at the service, but they'll show up. I know it. Two old men come shuffling down the sidewalk as the workers from the funeral parlor drive away. The old men are retired first cousins, Stefano and Giovanni Cachetti, whose last name Dad always said with a loud mock sneeze. Stefano is the eldest, perhaps seventy-five, and Giovanni is somewhat younger. They immigrated with their parents from Parma when they were boys. Stefano ran the family jewelry business here in Newark for nearly half a century before his son took it over. Wives dead too young, they moved in together eight years before, and generally drink wine, smoke cigars, and live like delinquents. Dad, of course, adored them.

~Just like him to die on a Wednesday, says Stefano. A day of the week when nothing happen. Almost as bad as Tuesday.

~Nothing as bad as Tuesday, says Giovanni. Their clothes are laughably mismatched, and their hats dark and shapeless. He was only one on the street who could call us young whippersnappers. We always call him grandpa. He get a kick out of that.

~He got a kick out of everything, I say, sighing. He had in his will that we bring his coffin back here for two days. I don't see what good it does. I think he was imagining how strange it would be to me. He couldn't stand it when I was comfortable. Come on inside.

The funeral men moved the sofa to one side and placed the coffin in front of the broad window that looks over my front yard. That was in Dad's will, too. I know somehow that he is having an utterly wonderful time. The lilies are his one sentimental gesture, but he never told me why he wanted them. The Cachetti cousins take off their hats and look at the stained pine coffin. Dad had even picked it out, one so cheap that Myrtice shuddered. Now, she is back at the college, where she was the only woman professor of mathematics, indeed one of the few in the sciences at all.

~Can we view on him? asks Stefano. The lid is not entirely secured. I can see it has been left ajar if we wish to open it for inspection. I'd already seen him at the funeral parlor, and a wash of calm affection comes over me.

~Sure. I push the lilies back and open the lid, and there he lies, clean and neat, a red silk handkerchief in the breast pocket of his suit.

~Jesus, Grandpa, look at you, says Stefano. Wait, I think he going to say something. Giovanni starts giggling. The boys are clearly drunk. He talk about his death all the time.

~He did? I ask. He didn't much to me.

~You a young man, says Giovanni, his accent thicker than his cousin's. Death seem like a bad thing. Grandpa always talk about death like a woman. He couldn't wait. He say when death come, he going to drop his trouser and sing "Camptown Races." I grin.

~That was Dad, I say. That kind of genuine insensivity is what I'll miss the most.

~*Miss?* say Stefano. What is this *miss?* Hank, I still talk to my Inez, and she been gone so long. People are only dead when we forget. Is this right, Vanni?

~Dumbass, he says, then he laughs wildly, elbowing his cousin. Grandpa is saying you are a dumbass, too stupid to take your own side in an argument. Should we give him our presents now, Fano?

~Ah, the ceremony, says his cousin. Giovanni carries a small paper bag, and from it he takes a pint of Scotch and a small painted statue of the Virgin Mary.

~If you will forgive me for saying so, neither of you seems shocked that he died, I say. It's like the paper arriving, something that happens every day.

~Hank, you would go to work in the city each day, and we would sit with Grandpa in the yard and talk of many things, says Stefano, putting his white-haired hand on my shoulder. Last week he say, Boys, don't be surprised if I wake up dead soon. I keep dreaming of my brothers. They come to me, and say I am playing my banjo out of tune and that I am the worst of them. So, when we heard, we thought, well. Hank, don't be cross with us. Living each day until you die is a good thing, yes?

~Yes, I say.

~Now, let us have our ceremony, says Giovanni. He clears his throat. Then he does it again, and finally his cousin takes out a flask of something nearly poisonous and gives him a sip. That helps. We are here to grant godspeed to our not-Italian grandpa on his way to heaven or whatever. Giovanni says, He say a long time ago, When I am dead, bring me a bottle and a woman. There might be a waiting-line for heaven. So here is the bottle, some not-very-good Scotch distilled nowhere near Scotland. As for the woman, this is our little joke for Grandpa. We are sure he mean some other kind of woman. This Minnie woman he talk about?

~Minnie Penny, I say. A prostitute from the town in Georgia where he and his brothers grew up.

~But no, we bring him Our Lady, because at his age, he need comforts different from a young man's.

~At *our* age, says Stefano, laughing.

~He never understand our love for the Catholic church, says Giovanni. Once I say to him Grandpa, there is a difference between loving *women* and loving *woman*. And he says, Not if you do it right. Amen. Stefano is laughing so hard now his nose begins to run. He takes out his handkerchief and honks into it. He says, So anyway, we bring you this woman to help you on your way, and this bottle for comfort. See that you do not drink it all on your first night in the grave.

~Now I would like to sing an old Southern folk song Grandpa teach us, says Stefano. He stands straight suddenly, sings, in an oddly pleasing light baritone:

> *Your moons shine brightly up, Lorena,*
> *Smooth as cream, just like your mouth.*
> *If we keep up this way, Lorena,*
> *What's pointing north will soon be pointing south.*

He and Giovanni fall arm in arm, laughing, sipping from the silvered flask. Oh yes. I know that version of it quite well. They go on that way for another fifteen minutes, remembering, drinking, laughing, toasting the corpse. All the while, I feel as if Dad is alive again, grinning in his vast sunken old age, a cheerful ghoul.

I WAS TWELVE BEFORE I knew he wasn't my real father. He'd come home from the bank in Salterville on a Friday and play our piano for a while, mostly show songs from the Civil War, but sometimes newer tunes he'd heard at chatauquas or traveling shows that came through town. It was 1909, and the new penny with Abraham Lincoln on its face had come out. Dad loved it.

~It looks just like him, he said, taking a sip from a bottle while resting his knuckles from piano-playing.

~You actually *saw* Lincoln? I asked. I'd already hear so many fanciful stories I'd lost track of the true.

~When he gave that speech at Gettysburg, he said. With that high hat, he was at least nine feet tall. He stood up to give his remarks and hit his head on cloud and made it rain. He got the hiccups.

~You're lying, I said mildly. Our relationship was strange, in that he'd always encourged me to treat him more like an ill-mannered older brother than a father. As I said, my mother supposedly had died when I was born. It was quite common in those days. Mac Burns told me something today. I want to know the truth. The real truth.

~The *what?*

~He said you aren't my father, that you're really my grand-uncle or something. What is he talking about?

~Oh, that. He turned back to the keyboard, played a grand chromatic flourish and launched into "Polly Wolly Doodle," which he bellowed at the top of his lungs. I let him finish the chorus the last time before I grabbed his arm. His eyes darkened, and when he turned to me, there was a gentleness, a soft kindness that stunned me. He always pushed quiet feelings away, as if he'd had too many in the past and just didn't want to remember.

~A father is an older man who loves you more than anyone else, he said, in words I would never come close to forgetting. I want you to do something for me, Hank. What the boy told you is the truth, but I want you to let it lie for now. And I want you to know that I would have moved hell to Mississippi if I could change things. He paused a moment. Actually, hell is already pretty close to Mississippi. In fact, it may well be geographically within the same boundaries. He'd strayed too far into humor that wasn't working, and he knew it. It's not about the hand you're dealt. It's about the hand you play. I'll explain more soon, son. Just know that you are my only son, and I'm your only father now, and I will never let you down.

I asked him a couple of years ago if he remembered that evening, and he didn't. His memory was still sharp for a centenarian, but he seemed genuinely befuddled. It was one of the most important days of my life, however, and I recall that it snowed heavily that night, and I lay in bed, hearing the wind moan and howl, wondering how I'd come to be lost, how I fit into the fight that once tore this country apart. That night changed my life, though, and I've often gone back to it. We never know when we change someone else's life, and I've tried to live by that lesson.

I have failed, as he did. We all fail. And yet the symmetry rises over and over, that from him, through me, a new generation of American humor and entertainment is rising. I'm a few years older than Bob Hope, but even he is a kind of father to Mike, pays him well, has even promised him a small role in his next picture. I am amazed at how this life turns us. But nothing about the Celebrated Blackshear Boys is too wild for belief. And one of them lies sleeping in my front parlor now.

WE INVITE OUR FRIENDS AND his over for a reception, and they are here, drinking, eating canapés and small snacks brought by Doris Muntz, who owns the catering business two blocks over. Cars from the mid 1930s line the street—the war has made willing paupers of us all. That's Tom Hines, a haberdasher who made friends with Dad at a veteran's meeting. He was in the Spanish war, but he and Dad had a strange, irreverent love of the army, with equal amounts of laughter and profanity. He came one night eight years ago with beer and stories, and I asked if he'd known my real father who was killed in Cuba, and he hadn't. That war was as small as the Civil War was massive. Tom may be the only one in our house who seems sad. Others wander over, pat the coffin, whisper a few words. A few of the oldest here seem jealous of Dad for having leaped through the curtain, gotten it over with. My wife checks on everyone, still being the wife, even if she is a well-known mathematician. A few of my friends from the paper have come, including Ron Pletz, who covers city politics and Barney Smith, a sportswriter. Sometimes I get them free tickets to shows on Broadway. I got Barney into *Oklahoma!* and he got me into a Yankees-Red Sox game. I tell people to consider the coffin a bar, and they take me at my word, resting ash trays and drinks on Dad, toasting him, listening to a long joke in near-silence and then exploding with equal amounts of mirth and relief.

I don't make any remarks. I let them ebb and then flow, and two hours later, Myrtice and I are sitting in the cricket-quiet back yard. I've lit a cigar, and the rich sweet smoke calms me. She smokes Chesterfields, a private vice, and we both share a strong drink. Lightning flicks the eastern constellations like a snake's tongue.

~I want to talk about him, I say. Or maybe I want to talk about me. I don't feel how I thought I'd feel.

~How did you think you'd feel? She reaches over and touches my arm, and in that human moment, I am shattered like a porcelain vase, but I do not let myself cry.

~I thought it would be a relief, I admit. I've been hearing about the Celebrated Blackshear Boys my whole life, and I really thought I'd feel grateful for his life but relieved we didn't have to take care of him anymore. Now, I feel like I've been hit square by a cannonball in the heart.

~You loved him, she says.

~Myrt, it's very strange. I can't quite convince myself he's dead. You know? I don't mean that disconnection we all feel when someone dies. I mean it feels like he's still here. In fact, it feels like all three of the brothers are here. Maybe I'm losing my mind.

~They're in Europe, she whispers, with Mike. But they're here, too. Love is more real than death. And stronger. That may be the one thing all of us truly know, even when we are trying to kill ourselves in wars.

I don't say anything for awhile. I can't. I imagine two of the brothers leaving the Confederate army after the Battle of Gettysburg and looking for the third. We took Mike there when he was twelve, and I invited

Dad—he was in his eighties and still working at the bank, and he said he didn't have the time. He was lying. I tried for years to make him go back with me, but he never would.

~That long slope is where Pickett's men charged that day in July 1863, I said learnedly. I remember Myrtice wore an enormous white hat that waved in the wind. Mike shaded his eyes and nodded, looking around. Lee thought he'd softened up the flanks for two days and that the center would crumble. Worst mistake the man ever made, and he knew it immediately. He rode out, just about here, and told the returning wounded that it was all his fault. Can you imagine a politician or military leader now saying, It was all my fault?

~No, he said.

~So Lee had his finest hour and his worst at the same time. Not many people can say that, you know.

~They must have known they were going to die, Mike said. We had walked to the cemetery and stood at the monument marking where Lincoln gave the Gettysburg Address. I can't imagine just walking straight into your death like that.

~Generals lose track of human life, I said. Sometimes you have to stand up and say enough. I won't go on for you.

~Like Grandpa did.

~Yep. Mike was quiet for a minute, and I supposed he was thoughtfully considering the war, slavery, violence.

~The first man who spoke here talked for two hours, he said finally. I bet everyone in the crowd had to use the bathroom by the time Lincoln got up. I looked at Myrtice, and she was grinning beneath the huge hat. That's why the Gettysburg Address is so short. Politicians don't get re-elected by keeping people from peeing.

~Michael Blackshear! said Myrtice, trying not to giggle.

~I mean, everybody must have been dancing by then. If Lincoln had talked more than ten minutes, everybody would have exploded. It would have turned the tide of the war. Everybody would have been *in* the tide. A new lake would have formed. Boats as far as the eye could see. Of the pee, by the pee, and for the pee. Amen.

A woman standing nearby with her two small children hustled them away. I turned away, trying not to laugh, failing.

~Young man, that's enough! said Myrtice, then she, too, began to laugh hysterically. It wasn't that funny, Mike would say later, but for some reason, we were helpless, cried, leaned on the monument. We'd quit laughing, start again. It went on for more than five minutes.

After that, Mike began to write skits that he'd perform for us, stole jokes he heard at shows in the city, re-imagined American history. Dad adored it all, sometimes threw in a song as he played the banjo, shameless encouraged Mike, and, when was sixteen, began to sneak him beer and wine.

Now, the storm is getting closer, and the cannon fire of thunder rumbles and groans. The wind shifts. Dad will lie in our house all day tomorrow, Friday, then Saturday morning we will drive to Salterville for the graveside service in the afternoon. We could have buried him tomorrow, but I wanted once last day with him.

~I've been thinking of buying a parrot, I say. Myrtice blows smoke and laughs at me.

~The odds of your saying that sentence at that moment must have been about zero, she says.

~We haven't had a pet since Pigeon died, I say.

~I always thought that was a weird name for a cat, she says.

~That was between Mike and me, I say. Our secret. I don't know. Parrots can live to be more than a hundred years old. I like the idea that the Blackshear parrot might still be around in 2043. If anyone is left by then.

~People will still be around, she says. We have an amazing ability to outlast the assininity of generals and politicians.

I seriously doubt anyone in Newark had used *assininity* that whole year.

WANDERING
THROUGH THE NORTH

Huddled up, marching in mud, the rebel prisoners tramped south, looking at the dripping world of green and gray. The sun had bled back out this morning, and hayfields glistened with glass globes of rain. The line of men stretched for miles, Blue soldiers, grim and jubilant, full of joy and regret. Henry could not say where they were—Maryland, maybe. Where was Delaware? He tried to picture the map of the United States in one of his father's books in Branton. *A one-eyed man and a map. Papa and Jefferson Davis.*

~I know you boys are tired, said a guard. He was a tall man with side-whiskers and kind eyes. There ought to be food and water when we stop.

~We already eat better with you Yankees than we did with Lee, said a very small man with a look of clenched righteousness. Henry thought the Yankee's vowels sounded twisted, lemony.

~Well, said the soldier. He moved on along the lines. The tall man turned to Henry. They had not been together until the prisoners were formed for this morning's march.

~Where was you taken? he asked. I'se with Hood. Was fightin' this feller arm to arm 'n' somebody pole-axed me with a rifle butt. My head's about to ache off.

~In front of a rocky hill, said Henry. I don't recall at all well what happened to me. I remember running, and I thought everybody was right around me, and then I was being hauled up that hill. I'd lost my musket. I guess I outran my line.

~Haw, that's pret near stupid, said the tall man. I'm Bill Tilton. Mississippi man.

~Henry Blackshear, Georgia. They shook hands as they walked.

~Can you read? asked Tilton.

~Sure.

~I've had this letter for three days but ain't asked nobody to read it to me on account of the battles. He reached inside his stinking coat and shirt and brought out an opened letter, handed it to Henry. My sister Mae Ellen, she writes, but I have to find a body to read it to me. I know six, seven letters of the alphabet. She's not pretty.

~Well, being pretty isn't everything, said Henry, opening the letter.

~Actual, she's downright ugly, said Bill Tilton. And she can't cook. Her best friend's a woman thar in town 'bout in the same state. They do carry on.

~Dear Bill, read Henry. The sympathetic soldier marching them looked away. It is with great sorrow that I report the...

~Report the what? asked Bill. It is with great sorry what? Henry read on down the sheet of ill-formed letters.

~This is bad news, Bill, said Henry. You want to wait until later?

~I'll take it now, thank you.

~It is with great sorrow that I report that your brother George was killed near Vicksburg recently in the fight there. He was shot dead. When papa heard about it, he took drunk for a week and beat mama frightful so she shot him close up with his own shotgun. We are still trying to clean the parlor. Cousin Annie Elfrich is with child and has named a boy of twelve years as the father. God rot all male person but your loving self. Henry shook his head. Good God, I don't have to go on.

~Hit's all right, said Bill mildly. You go right on.

~You will remember the dog Old Buck. Now he is Dead Buck, and Mama throwed him in the same hole with papa, which was about right you ask me. Varelia and I spend our days together, and we are breaking a wild horse we caught in Crook's Bayou, and so far it is working out. We have named the horse Louisa Mae Alcott, but she has not wrote nothing yet.

~Mae Ellen has a streak of rank humors, confided Bill.

~Mama is under arrest for shooting Papa, and they are apt to hang her before it's done. I will write and tell you if that happens. I am told she is so small they will have to tie blocks on her feet to break her neck.

Well, there is life for you. Your sister, Mae Ellen. Henry handed back the letter and said, Good God, Bill, I'm sorry to have read you that.

~I wish I could of been there when she shot Pa, said Bill, grinning. My brother was a spiteful mean man. I'm not worried about them hanging Ma. She lost her mind in Fifty-Eight.

A stout, brown-bearded rebel prisoner marching alongside them said *shit* and whistled, and Bill Tilton nodded and asked him how he was doing this fine day.

HENRY HAD LIED ABOUT THE story of his capture. He *did* remember, but of the moment itself, he was mute. They had been surging toward the smaller rocky hill when he saw a stunning light ahead, halfway up the hill, the shape of a human creature, radiating a golden sheen. He had never wanted to possess a thing more in his life, was prepared to die for it. He thought: *I must be dead and this must be the City of God, and I am in the presence of the Holy One.* The air was a frame, and musket balls wove a tapestry around him, through him, whistling, humming, sentient and forgiving. He knew vaguely that he would soon be dead, that the dying might hurt, but that was a temporal matter, a passing glance. Everything fell away. He swam through the heat as if it were a cool river, through lead rainfall, into the vacuum of artillery shells. The hillside was sharp and bouldered, silent. Surely heaven must be a place of chime and soft harmonies, a field of unraised voices. The creature in the light was saturated with it, emitting gentle rays, not smiling exactly, but placid, beckoning. How long had it lasted, that transit up the slope, before he was rushed and manhandled up behind the lines, where the firing was steady and violent, toward which charges still came? Alabama boys on the Confederate's far right came on and on, but the Yankees shot them back, finally charging down the hill. Even in the woods, the heat was fantastic.

~Don't go nowhere! a sergeant cried. Several other rebel prisoners sat in a clump beneath a large hickory tree. Henry nodded. I want your word you won't go nowhere.

~You have my word, Henry had choked. The glowing shape vanished, but Henry felt like a filled canteen in a drought, watched the Union soldiers fall dead or wounded, felt his eardrums reach the point of utter satiety, shut down. He heard only a dull thrum then, not war sounds exactly, but a drumming, a great engine with a steady pulse. All day the fighting had roared, and one of the rebel captives rose and tried to creep away, got shot in the back and lay wrestling with his own death for nearly ten minutes before squeezing out his last breath. A fly lit on his eyeball, sipped the liquid from it. You couldn't breathe from the smoke. Henry was not afraid. Through the day, through that hot night of moans and entrenchment, he was never fearful. A kind Union boy, surely no more than fourteen, gave him a long drink from a canteen and a piece of bread, and Henry claimed it as Communion.

Then that terrible final day. Henry and his fellow prisoners sat in a small area behind the lines, in sight of Pickett's rush. He stood and watched the wanton slaughter. A wide-mouthed Southern soldier, eyes inflamed with disease or desire, had come within ten paces of the stone wall, was hit with cannon fire, which took his head off so quickly it was gone as he fell to the dust, a feed sack. The Federals, having repulsed the attack, screamed *Fredericksburg! Fredericksburg!* and waved their muskets in the hazy air.

The next day they were leaving, the Confederates were, and the Blue men stood in exhaustion, though many wanted to move forward on the attack. And that night: A storm came down like the Wrath of God. In the flames of lightning: One of the unsheltered captives lay dead, perhaps of an unknown wound. None minded the rain after a week of nightmare heat, or the coolness it brought, wind ripping the leaves left after three days of shelling. Henry did not even think of escape.

They ran away! We've whipped old Bobby Lee this time! The war's over! The Federals were exultant, and Henry could not quite gauge his feelings, which started to return. Surely he was the last brother; surely Michael and Jack were dead now, storied dead. He would face another march, imprisonment, but no more wars, and he felt a giddy certainty, a rightness in it. *Sooner or later, God will judge all,* he thought. *A man must know the answer to one question: For what am I willing to die?*

Not this, Henry thought. *Not slavery, an evil blot. Not taxes or tariffs. Not stains on some honor so fragile it couldn't take one moment's implied disrespect. Not any of it. Not to favor disunion. How could a man sing and laugh in the midst of that? And what was the glowing image on the small rocky hill? I just want to live to be an old man.*

They marched onward this day, and Bill Tilton acted as if he'd heard a report of the weather back home, not the collapse of his family. Henry wondered of his own. He had a sheaf of letters in the knapsack that would now be rotting on the battlefield at Gettysburg. One-eyed Papa in the calm center of the mercantile. Red-haired Cassandra Blackshear, extravagant and theatrical, the town with its loving pettiness.

He met another captive, this one a Tennessee lad named Adam Sharpe.

~You can call me Whittle, he said, shaking hands. The day was getting late now, and soon they would camp. Nothing was familiar. All Henry could say was that they were moving southeast and weren't in the mountains.

~How come Whittle? asked Bill Tilton. That's a mought strange name, no offense give.

~None took, said Whittle. A nickname give me by my grandpaw. I was a boy always out sitting on a stump whittling. I liked it right much as a name. You boys been shot yet?

~I got nicked on my ass, but I'm not apt to talk about it, said Bill. Henry shook his head.

~I was shot through the lung at Malvern Hill, he said. I was give up for dead on the battlefield, and then I woke up the next morning and got up and walked back to our lines and said, Private Adam Sharpe reporting for duty. Then I fell over on my salute. They took me to that big hospital in Richmond, and a angel name of Nurse Rose Smathers cared for me back into my life.

~*Smathers?* said Bill Tilton. That's mought like the sound of knifing soft butter on to bread. Like, Mayn't you *smather* some butter on this here heel of bread for me, Maw?

Whittle eyed him narrowly.

~You got something sideways in your craw, said Whittle. I'll carve you a cross of persimmon wood, and you can rub on it when you're apt to feel mouthy.

~Could you carve me a bear? asked the friendly Union guard. I'd sure like to have me a trinket bear for my pocket. Charms against the world.

~I had a cousin eat by a bear back home, said Bill Tilton thoughtfully.

~That's terrible, said Henry.

~Weren't naught but a baby, said Bill, shrugging. My uncle cornered hit in the yard, but my aunt won't able to let him shoot it on account of her baby's inside. She said, Don't you shoot my baby!

~But it was done eat up, said Whittle.

~You don't disobey a woman, not one with a pistol anyhows, said Bill. Anyway, when it come to children, they was seven othern. My aunt left food out for that bear for near a year, said her baby was likely hungry. They was hill folk and didn't know no better.

~You're making that up to sport me, said Whittle.

~Myself, I'm inclined to believe it, said Henry.

THEY WALKED SLOWLY THROUGH THE dripping woods, heading by the sun's position, north back toward the battlefield.

~I suppose there's a reason we're doing this, said Michael.

~I'm hoping to get us captured and shot, perhaps badly, so we can die agonizing deaths in a place a long way from home, said Jack.

~Oh, I thought it was something bad. Forgive me for doubting your motives.

~I suppose it's possible, also, that we might starve to death in this country and die rolled up in a ball screaming in hideous pain.

~Great! And I thought you were making this up as you went along. I should have known that you had this planned thoroughly. My compliments.

The land was fraught with shapely hills, and there were fields and farms. The battlefield and the town were less than half a day's walk, and many of the Federals had marched away. The shovel clatter of burial parties. They came slowly across the foot of the large hill and then down it toward a stone wall that had covered the flank of Little Round Top. Michael knew even before they reached it. Jack could be clever, after all. A man with no goals and an acid imagination, but clever.

~There's two or three over there, said Jack. And there. Gather them up and come back down here in the hollow and let's see what we have. And they went onward, bent and creeping to fetch cast-off blue coats, left in the heat, stinking, sopping from rain and sweat. They weighed thousands—millions—of tons each, thick-waisted, unraveling. The sound of soldiers on the march half a mile ahead, the crunch and easy cadence. Most of the coats were wounded, and Michael knew late what Jack knew early: These had been removed from the dead for future use and never recaptured. They squeezed the water out, arm by arm, in the breast. One had two sleeve stripes, the others one. They lay them in the sun on slabs of white rock and then crawled back down in a cove that emitted a bold spring.

~Your plan being? asked Michael. And oh that starvation thing. I believe in my own case it's started to play out.

~One day's drying for the coats, and then we pick one and wait until the last of the Federals are gone, and then we stagger wounded into a local house. They'll feed us and let us sleep in a barn. Then we'll be off to find Henry.

~We have Confederate trousers, or what's left of them. And you're crazy if you think the soldiers will be gone. A regiment will probably be left here to gloat.

~We won't move into town. We're going to move back south, because that's the direction they'll be taking the prisoners. We shadow them. I'm good at reconnoitering and shadowing.

~Since when?

~I'm working on it.

Michael didn't doubt the plan; Jack always lit trouble's fuse and then stood back, aping innocence when something exploded. He had a way of seeing around corners, of having fun until the penultimate moment of danger, then backing away, sheltered from the storms he'd ignited. Not a bad quality in a man or a boy. His odd ideas also worked out in the most unexpected ways. He was a man of true talent for idleness and craft. Perhaps he had been born for this hopeless mission.

Late in the day, they found that the coats fit quite well. Jack wore the corporal's stripes proudly, strutted in the growing shadows.

~You're a traitor, said Michael.

~I prefer whore, said Jack. It has a more lustful ring about it. A whore for the great Southern Confederacy.

~I want to say something before we go to find this friendly farmhouse, said Michael.

~Speak again, bright angel! said Jack, taking parade rest.

~I'm thinking seriously about something that has been coming around and around to me since Fredericksburg, maybe even before that. I can't say where it came from. But it won't go away.

~Maybe it's malaria.

~It's this: I'm not sure I want to go back South when the war is over. Maybe I just want to quit this war and keep going north. Some day, maybe, I'd want to go there to visit again and see if it's changed, but there was never anything there for me. Can a man be born in the wrong place, Jack? I feel more right in this blue coat after two hours than I did in a gray one after two years.

~We can talk while we walk, said Jack. But mutter and murmur. And remember this: We have the same names, and also: We're couriers from the Eleventh Corps. We were orphans from Ohio who have been with the Eleventh since the war began.

~Where'd you come up with that? Michael asked. Never mind. Go on with being a traitor.

~There comes a time when a man…

~That's enough. Good speech. We got more to worry about than not knowing which side we're on. We have to be crafty and sneaky and resourceful. We have to forget skits and songs and become bold as a dragoon.

~Slavery's the fire-breathing dragoon that will consume the South, you say?

~Haw. Ain't you the clever girl?

THEY WERE GIVEN A HANDFUL of dried beef and two biscuits each, and Henry ate greedily, washing the food down with cold water from a creek on which they camped. Night sounds: crickets, songbirds, clacking crows, and a division of tree frogs, singing *fruit fruit fruit fruit*. The friendly Union guard—whose name was Ira Moskowitz—sat with them in a sandy bottomland beneath a grove of beech trees. Henry counted: Nine prisoners in all, none inclined to escape. They didn't have the eyes for it. Ira was a gentle boy, with a reddish beard that grew in irregular whorls down his neck. Like a ginger bear.

~Do they have Jews down in the South? asked Ira. I'm Jewish is why I'm asking. You boys don't hate the Jews, do you?

~Well, the war's about the niggers, not the Jews, said Bill Tilton. We have a Jew shopkeeper back home. Fine feller, never know they killed the Lord it weren't wrote down. No disrespect to you personal.

~Live and let live is my motto, said Whittle. I have no truck, not with your Negro nor your Jew. Hating somebody's easier than fallin' offn a log.

~I hated my daddy, said Bill. More people probly hate their own kin than the colored or the Jew. I mislike your Creole, but it's in the main 'cause one stole my sweetheart to New Orleans, where she took a life of ill repute.

~What about you? asked Ira to Henry.

~One of the best friends I ever had was Jewish, said Henry. David Bernstein was his name. Died in battle like any man. His family owns a clothing store back home in Georgia. He was as fine a boy as ever walked the earth, and I will miss him until the day I die. None of this is about the Negroes or the Jews or the North or the South or anything else. It's just about baring the fangs, about being wild creatures. The *different man* is the enemy. That's what we want to convince ourselves. Because if we don't have enemies we create them. And then you choose sides, and you're a traitor or a patriot. And you fight until you're dead. My God, that slaughter at Gettysburg. Every officer on both sides should be lined up and shot.

Henry held his peace then, sat sullen in the campfire light.

~You can speak freely, said Ira.

~All the Blackshears have big mouths, said Henry, shaking his head.

~Blackshear, Black Shear, hah, said Whittle. They was three brothers famous in the army for the frolics they put on. Same name. Never seen 'em, but I heard 'em talked about. Folks said they was the funniest thing ever come down the pike. You one a them, Henry?

~No, he said. Must be somebody else.

~We believe in the same God, said Ira.

~Would you boys mind it if I's to testify? asked Bill.

~Don't do that, said Whittle. I take you on your word.

~Same God, same Old Testament, said Ira. Moses, who brought the children of Israel out of bondage. Maybe that's why Jews understand slavery. We have been there ourselves. I know you boys must want to get away something powerful. I don't reckon it matters, but they will arrest me if anybody gets away. An officer comes and counts you first thing every morning. I don't know where they aim to take you. I don't even know where in the hell we are right now. I'd guess a prison for you, but at least you won't be in the battles anymore. And some day there will be a great exodus, and you all will go free and march home, back down to your South. Maybe everything will be different then, maybe nothing will have changed. I can't say. But I don't know how a man could be in this war if he didn't think it mattered. So don't run off on me. I've tried to treat you as I'd be treated myself.

~He maketh me to lie down beside still waters, said Bill Tilton, curling up on the cool sandy soil for sleep. Yea, though I walk through the valley of the shadow of death, I will fear no evil. The end.

~It don't go like that, said Whittle.

~It do now, said Bill, soon snoring.

Henry sat for a long time looking into the campfire. Tens of thousands of soldiers were near, blue masses, strange accents, unfamiliar beliefs: a motley mix of voices and accents, names and loyalties. But the wind was not Christian, the swift creek not Jewish, the rustling beech leaves not Hindu. Henry had read Emerson and tried to place the glowing man in some transcendental context. Surely this was not religion, not a sign, no omen.

Not God.

HENRY AWOKE IN THE DARK with a dry cracked hand over his mouth and another reaching down the slack front of his pants. He tried to draw a breath, gained nothing, began to suffocate. Then he was fighting, thrashing, and the man was insanely strong.

~I'm not gone hurt you, he said, urging. You know I'm not gone hurt you.

Henry whipped, kicked, but the man held him down without apparent effort, kept reaching downward. Henry's hand landed on the man's sidearm, pulled it hard, cocked it. The night was utterly dark and otherwise silent. Crickets and frogs. The sound of water. For a moment, the man hesitated, reached oddly, as if he understood, but Henry was swift, punching the pistol into the man's soft belly and pushing upward toward the center of the rib cage. He fired. The man fell down dead on Henry, hand still in his pants. Then: a sudden sense of light and motion, lanterns, lit pine knots, bootless stampings in the dust. Henry threw the man's hand out, shuddered, sat up. He was trying to hand the pistol to a Union sergeant when the rifle butt struck him in the chin. Henry flopped over unconscious against the soldier.

~Jesus Christ, he was trying to escape, said a corporal. He's shot Sergeant Edge. They held the lantern to Edge's face, and he looked a wide rough man with oily hair and a placid, dull look. His eyes lay open, and his mouth drooped down. Blood streamed from the side of Henry's rent skull.

~He wouldn't a done that, said Bill Tilton, sitting up. He was a good boy.

~Tie that man to a tree, said the sergeant. Three men wrestled Bill to a smooth-chested beech tree, lashed him around it standing.

~Sergeant Edge is dead, said a major named Richard Garrow, who sneezed continually into a knotty silk handkerchief. Corporal, select a burial party. And Lieutenant Campbell, hogtie that reb and bring him over by my tent.

~You ain't gone arrest him, sir? asked the corporal, a thin, taut-faced man named Sam Messer. Be goddamn, if you please, sir. Man's just kilt the sergeant, and you ain't gone have him arrested *immediate*?

~I'll have *you* arrested if you question my orders again, said Major Garrow.

~No, sir, I ain't...

~Dismissed.

They tied Henry's hands behind his back, then roped them down to his looped-up feet so that he was bowed, bleeding. Two men carried him to a field tent and dropped him hard. Dust rose into the lantern light. Henry came to once or twice, and the pain in his skull was hideous, a losing argument. He could not focus; eyes shot or crossed. His back and shoulders were an organized agony. Back into a dreamless dark. Garrow sat on a campstool smoking a cigar and shaking his head, a slender man with long, harvest-colored hair held behind the ears. His neatly trimmed beard lay down along his high-pink cheeks. He had long fingers and clean nails. He rubbed a spot on his left temple for a very long time. *Stupid son of a bitch*, he thought.

Richard Garrow was from Cooperstown, New York, a small village at the end of a very large lake, a place of forests and ice. He had been a successful lawyer before the war, representing railroads and timber mills mostly, had married a sweet girl named Irene, taken her home, where he built a fine mansion, and she bore him three daughters. First thing each morning, he would take out the trifold tintype and look on those sweet daughters' faces, soft glowing girls with high collars and ringlets. He wrote Irene almost every day and spoke to his girls there, too.

Now, he sat by the campfire shaking his head over Seth Edge, a sick and prowling man, one who pawed boys and denied it, covered it up, lied smoothly. Richard somehow knew this would happen, and now he was forced to decide what to do. Henry awoke thrashing, and Richard stood off the campstool, opened his pocketknife and sliced the rope from behind Henry's back, and he flopped outward in the dust, groaning, holding his head.

~I see two of everything, said Henry, rolling. You'll only need half a firing squad. Oh shit. Richard Garrow laughed.

~You're in a bad position for wit, reb, he said.

~You wouldn't happen to have some morphine or laudanum on you, sir? asked Henry. Or a horse? Any of those would suffice. He tried to sit up, fell over with his aching head, trying it again, gained balance on his behind.

~What happened?

~I woke up and that man had one hand over my mouth and the other down my pants, said Henry. I was suffocating. So I pulled out his side arm and shot him. You could say it was to save my breath or my honor. Probably my breath. Why am I not guarded and cut loose?

~Because Edge was a monstrous aberration, said Major Garrow.

~Oh Lord, I am delivered unto a lexicographer, said Henry, tenting his fingers. Have mercy on my soul. Christ, this hurts. Garrow was very amused, laughing as he stoked the fire and then went into his tent. Henry stood and saw a dim circle of confused and glaring Union soldiers in the cricket-soft darkness. Garrow came back out with two morphine strips.

~Eat these, he said.

~Sure. Henry chewed on the drug-soaked strips, and a sea of relief flowed through him, and he sat back down. Major, can you say something to those boys. I think they are prepared to commit a monstrous aberration.

~Men, break it up, said Garrow. Edge had been pulling shit ever since First Manassas. He was a bad man, and you know it. This boy was defending himself when he woke up with Edge suffocating him and reaching down his trousers.

~That shit, said a corporal, spitting. I knowed he was one sick bastard. The Federals, ready for bed anyway, and clearly unsaddened now by the man's death, dissolved back toward their field tents.

~Are you getting surcease from your suffering? asked Garrow.

~Sir, I am greatly in your debt, said Henry. Sufficient surcease for several souls. But my head is throbbing. To whom to I have the honor of addressing?

They exchanged names and hometowns, ranks and units, pasts and passions.

~Wait, the *Celebrated Blackshear Boys*? I've heard of you. I've heard of you and your brothers, Henry. Well, maybe we'll have the chance to speak as we travel.

~Are we being taken to a prison? asked Henry.

~I have no real idea—we're in the wandering stage of General Meade's command, I believe. After Gettysburg, he wants to sit back and feel victorious for a while instead of trying to end this damned war. It *is* a damned war.

~Damned to hell, said Henry. But I never was much for it. In the main, I believe the South's positions are unworthy.

~Really. Which ones?

~All of them, said Henry, dreamy from the wound and the drug. Every damned one of them.

THE COURIERS AND ORPHANS SAYING they were from the 11th Ohio crept down woody lanes, often tree by tree, stopping to listen. A blind man at midnight could follow the troop concentrations southeast: wagon ruts, hoofprints, such soft impressions from ten thousand brogans. Soon they'd catch up in the Maryland countryside.

~When we get to the Federals, you take fifty thousand, and I'll take the other fifty, said Michael, leaning down to sip from a moss-lined stream. If you kill all yours first, fire a flare or send up a balloon. I'll be the one on the hill riding a white stallion and gesturing heroically. French Revolution kind of thing.

~Actually, I'm going to be in reserve when we attack, said Jack, whose face seemed to be disappearing in the great wool of his black beard. If you feel the battle turning against you, send a courier to me, and I'll make a command decision about which route to take as I create a retrograde movement. The Yankees will never know what hit them.

They had been walking for two days and were starving to death. Michael's hands had gone trembly, and often he would stop to lean on a tree and give in to terrible dry retching. Lee's army had faded far away, heading across the Potomac and back into Virginia. Vicksburg had fallen to the Union, and for the first time since his election, Lincoln saw hope rather than gloom. Michael and Jack only knew that their brother was in Union hands and they were commanded by blood to find him, join him, take him, or die in the trying. They could do nothing else.

Now, they were in a valley, surrounded by low and smoky blue hills, and the heat, which had blown away with the storms after Gettysburg, came back, still early in this blood-borne July. They dug bitter roots and gnawed them pulpy, ate tender shoots from a creekside. Nuts from hickory and beech: green and growing, inedible yet, and the Blackshears turned pale and thin, sickly.

Late in the day they came to a small farm snugged in a cove, scenic, with a four-square whitewashed house that bore neat green shutters. Feathers curled from the chimney of a log smokehouse, and the scent of curing ham drifted over them.

~We're about to go into the Battle of Pig Mountain, said Jack, rubbing his hands together. Are you able to fight with me, boy, for the greater good of Ohio?

~To hell with Ohio, said Michael. I'm on the side the Blackshear Nation. It is small, but it is owed much by both American principalities on this sorry continent. They crept through the trees and could see now an old man hoeing in a huge house garden: many rows of tall corn, beans staked to poles, military lines of okra. Michael drew him mentally: a thatch of gray-white hair drifting beneath a straw hat, red-burned arms and hands, sack clothing, bent, raking weeds as if timidly scratching the back of a giant. Now an old woman and a one-legged young man on a homemade crutch came toward him, sweat-stained, worn out.

~Follow my lead, said Jack. We've done this a hundred times. Don't mess up if you don't want us shot.

~Yes, mother. That last sentence would be easier to understand without two negatives.

~If you don't shut up I'm not going to get you no food.

~Haw.

They came limping out of the woods, waving, and the boy was running, poling toward the house with his crutch, no doubt for a gun. The woman moved to the old man's side and brought her stained apron up and held it, fearful, to her mouth. She wore a bonnet that might have once been blue, huddled in a widow's hump near her man, who stood brave and waiting. Michael felt touched by his honor. He was medium height and wore a white beard like a baby's bib.

~Sir, ma'am, I know you must be frightened, but you must be at your ease, said Jack in a hardscrabble Vermont accent that startled Michael. My brother and I are couriers for the 11th Ohio, and we've become lost.

~Lost and hungry, said Michael, whose accent sounded more eastern European and drew a glazed glare from Jack. The boy was poling back across the yard with an ancient flintlock rifle, which he dropped while hobbling toward them. It broke in half, dumped the powder from its pan.

~You hurt my maw and paw, and I'll cut your throats! he cried. He withdrew a knife from his waistband, and the dull blade flew off the bone handle and sailed end on end across the farmyard. Goddamnit.

~Boy, don't you blaspheme, said the old man. These here soldier boys is from Ohio. Or somewhere. They are lost and hungry, and I aim to feed 'em in Christian charity. They's no need for scuffling of any kind. Is they, gentlemen?

~Sir, scuffling is the *last* thing on our minds, said Jack.

~Lydia, set a table before us, said the old man, straightening up.

The house was neat beneath two huge elms, and the Blackshear brothers ate peas and beans, sliced salty ham, hot cornbread with butter churned the day before and kept cool in the springhouse. Rain dripped from the eves, a cool wind drifting through the open windows. Gabriel and Rachel Sisk had once farmed a hundred acres, but they'd sold it off, parcel by fenceline. Two sons were dead in the Union army, Wilbur at Antietam and John at Second Manassas. The third son, Howard, was born lame and was sullen about it, breathing hard at the Blackshears, like a nettled dog. His leg had been amputated up near his hip over five years' time.

~Say they was a big battle at Gettysburg, said Gabriel. White hair grew like a rain-starved crop along the backs of his hands. I take it our boys won the day?

~We did, sir, said Jack. Kicked the surly, beasty rebels back into their own land. Michael took small offense, made a face. Jack's glance back looked something like a shrug.

~I would kill every Southerner ever born but for the colored, said Gabriel. He made a slack fist and pounded it lightly on the table, like a judge passing sentence. For they are a species unto themselves, foul and ignorant.

~Indeed, sir, said Michael. I visited Atlanta before the war, and what I saw there frankly dumbfounded me. They acted like veritable garments. Jack made a choking noise on a forkful of peas.

~Goddamn right, said the boy. Garments all.

~Boy, don't you blaspheme, said Gabriel. Enough ill's become this house already.

~And their women—oh my word! said Michael. They lack the mammalian profundities of our northern girls. They say the most shocking things, even in their nudepapers.

Michael had to pound the choking Jack on his back; Jack: red-rimmed, weeping.

~The South is blood, said Gabriel. The South is hot and hatred. It is mean and loud and stupid and slow!

~Your words are shattering in their taut cuisine, said Michael delicately.

~I seed all this coming, said Gabriel, wild-eyed and railing. He stood like a prophet and pointed at the low smoky ceiling. I knowed from the beginning that they would not quit until this land was filled mountain by mountain with blood. And my boys' blood is part of the filling, and I ask God to smite them dead in their tracks, ever Southron man alive at this moment, and yea, them baby, too!

~Not them baby, said Rachel with quiet horror. Not them baby.

~Them baby, too! It ain't no sin to kill a rebel deadern hell!

~Don't blaspheme, said the boy Howard sourly.

~I'll break that crutch over your lame head, said Gabriel. Rachel slammed her palm on the table, and Gabriel sat down.

~Couldn't neither one of you catch a ghost in cotton basket, said Rachel. You knot my stomach, bothn you. Hush up and let these boys eat in peace. I reckon they seen terrible things.

Michael recalled it all like a mural, from Malvern Hill and Crampton's Gap, past Sharpsburg and Fredericksburg, onward to Chancellorsville and then Gettysburg. He felt his hands begin to shake, and then he was crying soundlessly, tears pattering on his plate. Jack caught his glance tenderly, hardened himself. *What has been lost in this world is lost*, Michael thought. And he recalled Henry, the bright star of their boyhood, the most gifted with words, so agile and happy, perhaps already standing in heaven, picking his teeth, checking his watch and waiting.

Rachel came around the table, her knees cracking, and she walked to Michael and stood next to him, dry-eyed, and pulled his head into the waistband of her dress, held him, ran her fingers through his hair.

Michael let go and sobbed, held on to her waist. Jack looked into his plate, holding back the tears, holding, holding.

~Let these boys be, said Rachel, and now she was crying, and none of them moved for a long time, until the rain had stopped.

HENRY AWOKE SUDDENLY AND SAT up in the first light of a hot July morning. The pain in his head was monstrous. He could smell coffee and bacon, but he took sick, stumbled away from Major Garrow's tent and vomited in some tall grass. He came back and sat, shaking, as Garrow's aide, a delicate lieutenant named Everett Greene, walked up and began to kindle a campfire.

~If it means anything, I'm glad you shot that son of a bitch, Greene said. And a good thing Major Garrow was here for it. Anybody else would have had you shot outright.

~I don't think I'd feel any different, said Henry miserably.

~Let me see to it, said Greene. He knelt beside Henry and brushed back to clots of blood and opened the wound. This is ugly and will take some cleaning. Are you bearing the pain?

~I'm alive, I think. Anything past that is nothing but a tall tale.

~You sound like an educated man, said Greene in French.

~Yes, but all the education has apparently been knocked out of me, replied Henry in unaccented French as well. Greene laughed. In English, Henry said, The major had some morphine strips. I feel bad taking them. They're for the wounded, I guess. But oh God.

Greene gave a knowing look, one of sympathy, understanding, and disapproval. He glanced toward the major's tent. Now, the entire camp was stirring, and Henry stood, blood leaking slowly down his back and saw the extent of it and thought: *Magnificent! It couldn't be Meade's entire army but surely much of it, for the tents seemed to extend for miles: company, regiment, brigade, division, corps, army.* Soldiers came out coughing, spitting, groaning, and they'd step into a clearing and piss without shame, scratching their heads and their beards, unhurried. The sun was not yet over the horizon, and there would be some time before roll call or drill.

A rider came toward them, reined in the horse just as Major Garrow came out.

~Colonel Smith's compliments, Major, he says to tell you that Lee's fled over the river and back into Virginia. And we're to follow him. Turn the men out, sir. He saluted, and Garrow returned it.

~Thank you, lieutenant. Greene, strike the tents, sound assembly. Suddenly, men were in motion all over the fields as orders spread, and men were moving, social insects, and their tents falling, horse-kicked field mounds, toppled.

~Sir, may I have permission—ahhh—to rejoin my fellow prisoners? asked Henry. And could you spare a few more of those strips? This head…

~Here, said Garrow, heading into the tent and coming out with four strips. That's all that are left. Beads of perspiration covered his upper lip. You know, I have the feeling that we could have become friends. I am at a loss to know how that could possibly be.

~We are already, said Henry. I'd be dead and buried in a shallow grave right now if it weren't for you. My side in this war has spent two years trying to kill me, and your side saved my life. I don't think I'll forget your kindness.

~I don't expect to live out the war, said Garrow, rubbing a spot on his temple. Think of me when you and your brothers are back together and singing again. Henry drew himself upright and saluted, and Garrow returned it. Lieutenant, see that Mr. Blackshear gets back to his fellow prisoners, over there in that grove. He pointed. Bugles sounded, and men spilled in what seemed concentric circles. Henry walked alongside the lieutenant, and neither said a word, not until Henry, chewing a morphine strip and starting to feel better, walked into assembly and saw Bill Tilton grinning and shaking his head.

~YOU CAN ALMOST SMELL THEM NOW, said Jack. They walked in the woods not far from a pike on which thousands of men had clearly passed a day or so before. The brothers had spent the night in the Sisks' barn, and in the morning, Rachel had fed them again. Gabriel saw them off.

~I know you boys ain't who you claim, he said. Or doing what you say. But I don't care no more. I want to be shed of all this death. I tell you, God weeps. He turned and shuffled off without saying *goodbye* or

Godspeed. Refreshed, carrying a rucksack of dried ham and biscuits, the boys made good and reflective time, watching for riders. Once, a Federal cavalry detachment came on them in a hoof-pounding gallop, and they had just made the shelter of some gnawing brambles before the soldiers rode past, surely a hundred of them. The Blackshears had to fight their way out of the briars, and came out bleeding, scratched face, torn arm.

Now, in a swinging stride, they made good time.

~General Lee, when we reach the Union army, what, exactly, is your plan of attack? asked Michael.

~I've been rethinking the plan of dividing our forces, said Jack. You have the artist's eye. I want you to look for gray and butternut. Look for anything that's *not* blue.

~Hell, general, half the troops in both armies wear the wrong colors, said Michael. A whole Union brigade at Gettysburg wore black hats. Remember? What if I mistake a regiment of Zouaves for our brother Confederate prisoners?

~I'll have to have you shot, of course, said Jack.

~I like the feel of this coat, said Michael. Don't you think I look better in blue?

~A blue dress, maybe.

~Kiss my ass, general.

~How would I know where to start?

The land was flat, then hilly, flat again, and around one bend they saw a small cabin some distance off the road, a rough place, but perhaps they might get cheese or spring water to refresh their much-lighter canteens. They stopped: cannon fire. But no, it was distant thunder, rumbling and muttering then not coming back. The path to the cabin was worn but becoming overgrown.

~Hello in there! said Jack. Anybody home?

Four scruffy Union soldiers came out of hiding around the house, pistols drawn. None of them bore stripes, and looked around as if expecting a brawl.

~Where in *hell* you boys been? he asked. Goddamnit, the whole army's moving south. Bring it here.

~We're in serious trouble, whispered Michael.

~*Now* you tell me, said Jack. Just listen close and stay with me. They walked on up the path to the cabin, and the Union soldiers came together, a crabbed and surly lot. A wind curled through the under-canopy with another throat-clearing scrape of thunder. Up close, the leader of the group wore an ugly face wound—saber slash perhaps—and his upper lip was curled into a mad glare.

~Where is it? he asked.

~It's at the hanging tree, said Jack confidently. Jenkins said it would be in a nook at them big clapping rocks at the hanging tree. They wouldn't goddamn give it to us. Dog here kilt three of 'em, ain't you, Dog?

~I eat one's liver, said Michael.

~What the fuck, said the large soldier. Who in hell is Jenkins? Did they get the money from Colonel White or not? Bastard deserved to be robbed. We join back up in Philadelphia. Our asses are hung on the damn line for this. And now you say the money's at some hanging tree?

~I wouldn't raise my voice around Dog, said Jack, glancing at Michael, whose eyes had gone demented. He opened his mouth, and a great clot of drool unwound from his mouth and looped to the ground.

~Shit fire, I ain't getting near that, said one of the other Federals, a small, frog-faced boy. He backed up a step.

~I eat their hearts, too, said Michael.

~Calm down, Dog, said Jack. Jenkins is in on it now, too. He's Colonel White's new adjutant. The Colonel is dead.

~*Dead?* cried the large soldier. We didn't plan on nobody getting kilt, goddamnit. Do you know where this hanging tree is? Are you working for this Jenkins or for Thomas?

~Thomas is dead, too, said Jack furtively. The storm was coming on them now. But Timmerman got White's money. I know that much.

~Who the *hell* is Timmerman?! cried the large soldier, who was now sweating and wiping his face.

~He's dead, too, said Michael, picking his teeth with his finger. I eat his brain with a spoon.

~Somebody shoot that *thing*! said another one of the soldiers. They were bunched and backing up.

~I wouldn't even try, said Jack, palms up. A man before Gettysburg tried to draw a pistol on him, and Dog ate his windpipe before the man could get off a shot.

~To hell with this, said one of the soldiers. The others were backing up with him, turning, going into the woods.

~Stop, you stupid fools! cried the large soldier. A flashpan of lightning blew up, very close, and the ground shook from instant thunder. The woods filled with fleeing conspirators, leaving the large soldier alone and scowling. He started to call for his men, but it was no use—they were gone, terrified.

~I'd just as lief get out a here, said Jack. Dog's stomach's been growling all morning, and when that happens, I have to get him to place where there are some people to spare.

~Grrrrr, said Michael, looking away. He was foamy now, eyes spangled with barely restrained rage. The scar-faced soldier spat and cursed, turned and ran off into the woods, over a hill. Rain began like *pot...pot...pot*, and it came then in a splatter of iambic musketry.

~I think you're ready for *Lear* now, said Jack.

~Oh let me be not mad, not mad, sweet heaven, said Michael. Keep me in temper. I would not be mad.

~A tad late, I'd wager, said Jack, heading for the tumble-down cottage.

The storm uncoiled over the hills, lashing with hail and flood, and the green snow of stripped leaves fell, skidding sidewise on the wind. One quarter of the roof had fallen in, and the tide roared in there but flowed straight down the cracked and punky flooring. Michael and Jack sat in a corner, waiting out the rain, waiting a long time.

~I've been thinking about something for a while, said Michael.

~Seems unlikely to say the least.

~I'm serious. A cannon-flash of lightning: instant wall-shaking thunder. I have just been thinking that the world has never quite seen anything like us. Do you think God could give grown men a gift for making people laugh? To get them happy by singing? What if this is a plan made of God, and we're to do this? By which I mean, that we are to remain as we have always been—the Celebrated Blackshear Boys. Jack, there is nothing else in this world that I want to do.

~I want a woman, said Jack. In the next eight minutes would be soon enough.

~It's just that I think Henry's dead. I can feel it. Do you feel that Henry's dead?

~Henry's not dead, said Jack softly. Don't you get it yet, you knucklehead?

~Get what?

~That we could not really do anything else if we wanted to. A man finds at some time, if he is lucky, the thing he's bound for. I can see it just like it was written in the scroll of God. I'll never marry. You might or might not. Henry certainly will. He is the most tender and the least certain. I would bet all the breaths left in my life that Henry is alive. But there's something else. We are no longer part of either side in this goddamned war. All those politicians thumping their chests and their Bibles, Mikey; if there's a real sin it lives among *them*. They don't think a thing of sending boys to die. They did it at the Seven Days and Crampton's Gap, by God. And those asses back in Richmond strutting after Fredericksburg and Chancellorsville. And those asses in Washington having no idea how to form an army or use it. Like grinding sausage, and those tender blasted souls all gone so early to heaven. If I were God right now, I'd be puking in a hedge.

~We can't find Henry, Jack. And we'd probably be arrested if we went back to our own lines. You do realize that we probably can't go home now.

~I know it. I knew it the minute we left the lines at Gettysburg. There's no greater crime to those fools than a man leaving his regiment to hunt a captured brother or bury a dear friend. They'd leave them to firing squads and vultures to keep the movement intact. We can go home, but it will take years. A long time after this is all over. Besides, it's not a worry to me. I'm not going to live out this war.

~Why are you saying that? The rain slackened.

~I am being stalked by the ghost of Martin Goodpath. He means to make sure I die. *Whooooooooo.*

~Well, he did have a right to be mad at you. You lay with his wife.

~And it was the best one hundred and sixty pounds of muscle and hair she'll ever have, said Jack. Actually, I was just kidding about not living out the war. I just wanted to be dramatic. Did it work?

~Not particularly.

~A failure to convince. Woe to my powers of logic.

~You don't have to worry about me eating *your* brain, said Michael, drowsy in the coming darkness. About as much sustenance as a cracker.

~You must bear with me. Pray you now, forget and forgive. I am old and foolish.

~Exeunt all, said Michael.

IF MEADE'S ARMY WAS MOVING in slow motion to harry Robert E. Lee—and they were—a detachment of thirty Federals marched the small dusty clot of Confederate prisoners southeast along an overhung road. They had stopped because an old rebel was vomiting behind a poplar tree, making a terrible sound. Corporal Ira Moskowitz yawned and scratched his left armpit.

~When I get home, I'm going to get elected to the legislature and outlaw these damned graybacks, he said. I hate lice worse than Jefferson Davis.

~Whu hell, so do we, said Whittle Davis, squatting, wheezy in his bad lung. I scratched at my crotch so hard one night when I woke up the next day my privates was as puffed up as a general.

~That's good, said Ira, grinning. A captain heading the detachment sat his horse and wiped sweat, clearly disgusted at the duty. They were marching the prisoners fourteen miles to a drop-off point before heading back to the Federal army. *Pretty sorry goddamn way to move through this land.*

~Now that you mention it, we shouldn't have birthday parties for our balls? asked Henry. What other part of us is more valuable and more fruitful?

~Damn it that's…Bill Tilton stopped and turned, as they all did: a hurried drumbeat of cavalry hoofs, faster, closer, faster, closer. The Union guards turned, muskets cocked, looking ahead down the road, while the captain steered his nervous mount back and forth across the road, pistol high, hat falling off in the dust.

~Probably ours, said Ira doubtfully, just as a rapidly moving force of Confederate cavalry came over a rise in the road, and dismounted rebels spilled from both sides of the lane. The prisoners dropped down instantly, as if executed, and the dell exploded, guards collapsing, leg- or gut-shot. A sharpshooter hit Ira Moskowitz in the turning side of his head, blowing his face off. He fell, electrically shuddering, next to Henry, died in six seconds. The rebel yell was high pitched and demonic, and the guards fought the Confederates hand to hand. The prisoners sat and watched, then rose weaponless and moved toward the thicker trees. Henry stared for a long moment of horror at Ira and then moved with them, the *siz* of a minié ball coming right past his left ear. Unlike the others, he did not stop but kept walking, then he was running and running, his head taking up the throb of his brogans. Now he was along a rock-laden creek and faster, stepping into the water and dashing up the trackless stones for a hundred feet, crossing over, climbing up a steep steep hill, reaching the top, skull oozing blood. He stepped in a foot-deep stump hole, fell hard sideways and rolled twenty yards down the hill and came to a stop, aching, before a moss-green outcropping of stone. He crawled inside the overhang, which dripped spring water from its beard. A copperhead coiled up, and Henry's hand moved apart, unwilled, grabbed the snake just beneath its hand-large head, and he hit it like a whip against the rock wall, over and over, groaning, crying. The inch-long fangs tried to dagger him, but on the fourth whack the snake went limp in his hand, and Henry threw it hard into the granite, and it bounced back, writhing for a few seconds, coming into its death with rage. Henry scrambled out of the overhang, sat gasping for breath. The firing was slowing back there: all shot down or newly dead. Listen: No footsteps, no trackers. They wouldn't come. Why would they? No horse could step down this rocky hill.

Henry saw that he was sitting ten yards from a bold stream, and he staggered to it, fell face first, washed the caked blood from his temple, drank until his belly felt distended. It was after mid-day, and they had not eaten since the noon before, and Henry trudged back up to the snake, stepped on the huge head and found a rock sharp enough to cut it off. The body must have weighted five pounds, he reckoned, and he took it and the sharp rock to the creek, where he skinned it easily, washed the flesh over and over, then ate it raw. The taste was not quite bitter or sweet, but filling. He laid the skin on a rock, and it still held unscraped lumps of snakeflesh.

He walked to a large dry white boulder in the middle of the stream, and sunlight had warmed it, and he curled up, forearm for a pillow, and slept.

The light was thin, pale as a sickling's cheek, when he awoke, very late in the afternoon. He sat up, surprised to feel relatively well. The snake had not sickened his stomach, and he drank deeply, pissed downstream for nearly thirty seconds. He looked around, threw the snakeskin into the strong current, watched it swim downstream. The cove was fraught with narratives, but he ignored them, instead, moving what he took to be north, away from the clashing rebels and Yankees. Who would know now what had become of him? He felt loose and limber, thinking of Bill and Whittle, knowing he would never see them again.

NIGHT CAME, AND GHOSTS FROM the battlefields crowded Henry in a warm crickety cove. He sat against a large dark tree and tried to sleep, but the moon rose between the canopy of oaks and beeches, chalk thumbnail. He could not sleep, kept seeing them fall slowly, fall fall fall, the ones he shot at Fredericksburg, friends blown down in the peach orchard at Gettysburg. And now he thought once more of the glowing shape that had summoned him at the small rocky hill, fire that stained the eyes but did not consume.

God did not live in the heat of battle. Indeed, He must have been in the far corner of heaven, weeping at His creatures' stupidity. But what if God had ordained the fight, made these horrors inevitable? For what reason? Not to protect the ownership of human flesh. Not to save the institution of landed aristocracy. Perhaps it was to cleanse, as John Brown had said.

~Dear God, said Henry, weeping. I don't think I am going home. I don't see how I can ever go back home.

In dreams he plucked off the stained bayonet shafts like flowers, jammed them, blade down into the loamy soil, as headstones. The dead stood and formed their lines: the Fogg brothers, mild David Bernstein, Sag Doremus, Raleigh Poole. Surely Sag was dead, too. To one side their weakling officers, Goodpath, Robinson, and Stillwell. Now, moving up front, straightening their blood-soaked tunics, poor Alpheus Carter, buck-toothed Jim Watts, precise and musical Lowell Parker. Only Cass Milton was not known dead—he was missing at Gettysburg—but some of the missing were simply unidentifiable. The heads blow off, the bodies burned black. Now the dead on the battlefield at Fredericksburg rose, blue on blue, and once again the Northern Lights swelled and arced over the heavens, not God's signal but fire in the heavens, the blaze of orb and celestial scepter.

Not to see them in this life: Cassandra Blackshear, her one-eyed artist of a husband; the lovely streets of Branton, the fragrant summer hedges, the slow clop of buggy horses on the dry autumn lanes. The mercantile where they had grown into men. He awoke.

~I think too much, said Henry out loud. I have always thought too much. An owl launched itself from a low limb and crossed the face of the moon, hunting.

THE NEXT DAY GREW COOL and rainy, and Michael sat on a rock in the edge of the forest and sighed.

~The Yankee army is moving south fast is my take on it, he said. Henry could be back in southern Virginia now. If he's even alive. And I'm starving to death. Jack scratched his beard and looked at the road below them. A farmer's plank-bed wagon creaked past, just behind a shaky, thin-ribbed mule. The farmer had no left arm and said nothing to the mule, did not lift the traces. He wore a tall-brimmed straw hat.

~So the question becomes what do we do, said Jack. If I am not mistaken, we are now traitors to both sides in the war. Which is quite a feat. I may write a song about it. "The Ballad of the Double Traitors."

~Feel free, said Michael. I'm through with this stupid Blackshear Boys crap, Jack. We're grown men.

~I am anyway. You're just wanting a sugar tit.

Michael was so thin his pants drooped, but he stood and took a swing at Jack, catching him on the side of the cheek staggering him backward.

~Bastard!

~Asshole!

Then they swung wildly, wrestling, falling, rolling on the sharp-nee-dled forest floor. Red-faced, making inarticulate sounds, cursing. Michael made a kind of hop and came up on Jack and choked him, and for a moment Jack seemed to let him, eyes wild for mirth. Then he slugged his brother on the left temple with a sharp, flat-knuckled jab, and Michael saw constellations, fell aside. Jack came up now, screaming, blood-eyed.

~Come on baby! Get up! You goddamn baby! You think I have any-thing left to be afraid of?

~Wait a minute, said Michael. I can't get my breath. He sat up and held a palm toward Jack: Hold on now. Hold on. Jack lowered his fists. Blood trickled down his left nostril across his mustache. Taste it: warm and coppery.

~Are you really hurt?

~I don't think so. I don't have the strength I did. Damn. Your nose is bleeding. Jack wiped his face, looked at the blood on his hand.

~I should go to the hospital, said Jack. Permission to leave this war.

~Permission denied. I'm still seeing everything twice.

~You can do troop estimates for General McClellan, said Jack. He always doubles the number of troops he sees coming at him anyway.

The rain came on hard now, aslant. The brothers walked south along the edge of the main road. The army had gone this way, no ques-tion. But they heard nothing, saw only occasional poor old men coming past, one astride a rickety spavined mule, another walking in a wildly unstraight line and talking to himself, laughing madly. The roads bled into mud.

HENRY AWOKE THE NEXT MORNING with needles in the back of his throat. He itched from a dozen bugbites, felt clammy, as if his skin were trying to remove itself from bone and muscle. He stood, shaky and hot, and walked to a nearby stream and sipped from the slowly sliding water. The air steamed; he could barely breathe. A headache crushed him at the temples. He walked on the road north now, scratching and wheezing, feeling himself sicken by the step, knowing. He had seen it in the army—diphtheria, measles, erysipelas, pneumonia. Men taken sick one morning and dead the next one, faces slack, eyes sinking within the topography of cheekbones. The roaming eyes of sunstroke, staggering five feet to fall and then moaning into death. All along here he saw the ruins of war—the Federal army as it had worn down the land, marching south toward the Army of Northern Virginia. *To have quit the war. The South bears its own stain and shame, will bear it for a century, Shakespearian, unable to wash it away.* Dented canteens, odd bayonets, horseshoes, cartridge boxes. Discarded coats and bloody blouses. Flapping brogans that seem poised to speak. Then: morning thunder. He walked in mud, sicker, weak to walk.

Henry sat to blow beneath an elm tree in the tassled edge of a wood. He dreamed of ironed sheets, down bed ticks, the tall windows of Branton. *All the stories I could have told.*

~Every story does not have a plot, he said out loud. Some of them just fade out like lost mirth at a party. Life gets too loud to finish.

He slept for an hour and awoke much sicker. Now he had chills and was sweating and threw away the blue coat, rose and staggered, half blind and blotched, out in the middle of the road. A few farmhouses. A small valley. *Where have I been and where am I going?* He groaned, feverish, found the sole had come off the bottom of his left brogan. Singing, keyless:

> *When the blackbird in the spring, on the willow tree,*
> *Sat and rocked, I heard him sing, singing Aura Lea*
> *Aura Lea, Aura Lea, maid of golden hair,*
> *Sunshine came along with thee, and swallows in the air.*

He kicked off the shoe and hobbled, needled flesh and soaked blouse, toward a small house backed into a piney cove, sitting prettily among a green dell. She was coming toward him with a rifle raised, aiming, hard to trigger it. He could not get his breath. He held up his hands to show he meant no harm then pressed them palm to palm in prayer beneath his chin.

~I am sick and thirsty and need help, ma'am, Henry managed. I beg of you to spare me.

~You Yankee or Confederate? she asked.

~Soldier, he rasped. Just a soldier. He could see that she was lowering the rifle, staring at him with an odd, interested glance. She was hard and plain, hair pulled straight back from her face, underlip large, plummy. The last thing he saw was her left hand, rising to her lips, as if to say, Lord, Lord, what do I do now?

~OKAY, SAID JACK, SCRATCHING AND watching for scouts and cavalry parties on the road. I'm General Lee, and I've been caught in a whorehouse in Richmond, and I'm trying to explain to Stonewall Jackson that it's a tactical move. You play Stonewall.

~He's dead, said Michael. We killed him. The South killed its maddest and wildest general.

~So what? Hamlet's dead, too.

~Did you hear that?

Rain fell hard, saturating the air. A vague drumming, then over a rise in the mud-road, saber-slapping cavalry, hats down: Federals. You could see the soaked wool weigh them down, and they rode grimly, passing south. When they were gone, Michael said:

~You can't tell where this damn thing stops or where it ends.

~That's war for you. You know, I think we may be the worst soldiers in the history of the country.

~Which country? asked Michael.

~I think I'm going to send for Susan Goodpath, said Jack. She's probably working at Minnie Penny's by now. I've never seen a woman more eager to spend all her assets in one morning.

~In a way, she was the South itself, said Michael. Proud, vain, lustful.

~Your mind's gone. That's not only trite and stupid, it's insignificant and ignorant.

~General Lee, what in heaven's name are you doing here? Sir, this is a house of ill-repute.

~General Jackson, I was, er...Sir, might I inquire what *you* are doing here?

~I have come to help mend their lost souls, sir. Women who need mending are the earth's neediest creatures. I have mended many here, sir, many! On my last visit I mended a red-haired woman named Joanne and a girl named Jeannie—you may have seen her. With the light brown hair?

~Er…actually, I have mended Jeannie on occasion myself. Now, what does all this mending have to do with our glorious war?

~I'm of the mind that some of our Northern women may need mending.

~I could take Ohio and Pennsylvania.

~Not Kentucky?

~You may have Kentucky, sir. I hear the women there are shy both of manners and teeth. Perhaps they can be mended by Mississippi men, as they are less refined than we Virginians and have roughly the same dentition.

They walked on in silence, easy and looking.

~If we had to wait out this war until its over, where would you think we should go?

~On up north. Some place we could tuck ourselves away. We both know we're not going back south.

~So it's real then.

~It's come to me, said Jack slowly, that we never fit in the South, Mikey. Strange, isn't it? We had to fight for it to lose it. I don't know that I ever could have broken away otherwise. God, I love it so much. The summer evenings, lightning bugs, ice cream and slow courtesies. But the South is rotten with the corruption of pride and slavery. I would *live* for it without those things, but goddamn if I will *die* for it. And that is that.

~We shall need to write Mother.

~You think we could find an abandoned farmhouse out here? Where is this? Maryland? We will probably have to turn first to thievery and deceit.

~I appoint you minister of thievery. I will be the ambassador of deceit.

~But first we have to find Henry. Which means we have to catch up with the whole goddamn Federal army. We're not very good at making plans, are we? I thought up staying and getting these Union coats and then following the army. It's your turn for a plan.

~Let's sit down.

They rested in the shade of a red oak. The rain blew away, and lemon light from a steaming sun colored the forest floor, right up the trunk of a squat cedar. Michael wanted a hot bath, clean clothes, a neat room, paints, brushes, a roll of canvas ready to size. He loved the color as it turned the burnt sienna soil yellow-orange. Break the world down into its shapes and colors. Drawing *en plein air*, winter smoke, the miracles of topography.

~It's about Henry, said Michael. I don't think we're going to see him again. I think we have to say that we aren't going to see him again. We are here, and he could be anywhere in the whole goddamn eastern United States by now. They could have taken him to a railhead and sent him to Chicago. He could have been stood up and shot. Maybe he was wounded and is buried back at Gettysburg. I quit when you did because I'd seen all I wanted to see. I'm ruined from Fredericksburg. There's no reason all three of us should have come out of this alive. They don't want living soldiers, Jack. They want casualty figures for the greater glory. Maybe Lee's a good man. Hell, I'm sure he is. But once it starts, they get blood in their mouths like a dog on a deer, and it can't be stopped until they run out of reasons for dying. I want to paint. That's all I've ever wanted to do. But we've got to stop thinking about Henry. And we have to stay with each other and realize that this war is going to go on, and we aren't both likely to see it end. I don't mind dying. It seems like the easiest thing in the world. I just wanted to say that.

Jack sat pensively for a moment. The faint sun crowded back into cloudbanks, and the rain came back.

~I think I prefer to mend blonde-haired women, said Jack. Now that I think about it.

THE WOMAN, WHOSE NAME WAS Euphemia Berrong, had brought Henry inside and helped him fall into her own bed. She stripped and bathed him, and he was filthy, stained the sheets. Half delirious, he grew cock-hard as she bathed his crotch, and she stared, took hold of him in her fist, let him go.

~Goddamn hell's bells, she said, walking to the window and throwing the pumped bowl of water into the tall grass. She was tall and flat-faced, with big rough hands and five rifles. A week before a straggler had crept in, found her asleep naked and leaped on her. She had tossed him halfway across the room, retrieved a Colt pistol and put it beneath his chin and led him outside.

~Ain't no need, the soldier had said. Not a boy. From New York City, red-bearded.

~Need, said Euphemia, and she blew his brains out. *Shit.* She hated getting blood on her hands. She dragged the body by its feet to a deep rocky ditch, pitched it in. Now rape a buzzard, you son of a bitch.

They came by all the time. Once she took in an Iowa man and coupled with him seven times in two days until he fled, legs shaking from exhaustion. She was unrepentant, lived away from town, gardened peas and beans, raised a hog, shot a twitching roe. Crazy Euphemia. *Be good or Crazy Euphemia will get you.* Never married, barren, blunt, wild-mouthed, hair like a crumbling hornet's nest. Crazy *Euphemia will climb in the window at night and take your children away. Or your husband. Haw.*

~Well, I reckon you're going to be dead, she said, pulling up a chair beside the bed and gazing with clucking admiration at naked and shivering Henry. Don't you worry none, acause I ain't gone let you stink. I got me a shevel, and I'll have you in the ground fifteen minutes after you breathe your last. Amen.

Sweat streamed off Henry's chest and from his temples, through his rough blond beard and onto Euphemia's clotted sheets. Each stain, she knew, was a wound, the emblem of wild grinding. She didn't care to wash them off, and the sheet was crusted, with its own mountains and valleys. Euphemia walked to a hand-made sideboard and rummaged among bags of herbs and found the right one, dumped it into a glass, tipped up a cracked porcelain pitcher, filled it with water, stirred with her finger, singing. She sniffed it, stuck in a heavy index finger and tipped it to her tongue. Very strong. She took a sip and smacked her lips, eyes open and approving. Then she knelt beside Henry and lifted him from behind the shoulders and poured off the distillate, and he tried to swallow, but some ran down his neck.

~Well goddamn, don't waste it, soldier boy, Euphemia said. I know it smells rank but you'll be mending and tipsy. And it gives some men a stout response, and should you need relief from it, whatever. I mean, I'll.

She sat back and shook her head and grinned. I honestly don't know what's wrong with me. I'd as lief have me a big old pecker as sunshine on my beans is what I'm saying.

Henry coughed and spat, fell back, slept. Euphemia went outside and hoed her beanrows and sang "Polly Wolly Doodle" and "Ring, Ring the Banjo," all on one note. She sang Camptown Races sing this song, do-dah, do-dah over and over, knowing no more of the words. A crow landed near the squashes, and she threw the hoe twenty feet at it. Missed. She said, Come back here you son of a bitch, and I'll rip out your wings with my teeth.

The soldiers were there before she could get to the house. It took three of them to hold her while two others raped. Free in the woods. Confederate colors.

~Both a you bastards together don't make one dick! she screamed. The others laughed, got ready for their turns. They were foul, with dripping beards, lost to the war, wandering. Inside the house, Henry awoke, feeling an odd hazy numbness, as if he were smoke floating in a quiet green valley. He could hear the thrashing and cursing outside, staggered to the window and saw them, dressed himself, trying not to make noise or be sick. He suffered weakness. *A widow woman who lived alone was hoeing her beans one day when a group of traveling salesman came up on her. She said, You boys can sleep here for the night, but don't none of you get near my.* No time for stories. The woman commented at each rape on the pathetic qualities of each man, spat in their faces, fought upward toward them. Henry saw their gray coats. They looked somehow familiar. He saw the stack of rifles in the corner, figured they held a load, and he dragged them softly softly softly across the floor to the window, and with a sharp breath lifted the rifle and shot the tallest man dead. They ran like mice in lantern light, and he dropped that rifle and lifted the next one, shot the squat man who had been raping her. He was standing with his cock waving and wet. Through the throat, falling to kick dirt. He shot a third one in the back, and he fell forward and ate dirt. The others were gone, woods runners. Henry stood blinking in the window. Euphemia got up, dropped her skirt, and looked at the rapists. Two were dead, but the throat-shot man writhed in pain.

~You kilt two, good shootin', she said. My pleasurables. Them herbs will give even a sick man the balls to shoot a raper. Now hang on while I finish my business. She got the hoe and came back to the one still alive and looked down at him and said, You ain't got no idear how good this is gone feel to me, you son a bitch.

She swung like a myth, unwinded, athletic, and he tried to shield himself, spitting blood, but it did no good, and it took her only one minute to cut his head off. She was laughing now, like *haw haw haw*, and she knelt and picked up the head by its lank black hair and held it up toward Henry.

~I reckon them lips ain't gone kiss no more rebel women. She threw the head to the side like a rotted melon and wiped her hands. You'll excuse me while I take this to the taking place. Go on back to bed, sweet boy. I come back I'll ride you like a racehorse.

Henry slid into his brogans and left the house and pushed back his hair and walked through the woods, moving hard and getting half a mile before stopping to sit on a rock in the rain.

~LET'S SING "BEAUTIFUL DREAMER," SAID Michael. He was crying and had been for a mile. Their stomachs had knotted with hunger, and they sang to chase fear.

~Just stop that goddamned blubbering, said Jack. I know we're in trouble. And I know I'm the one who got us into it. I'm thinking. I'm thinking.

~We can't go home, and we can't stay here, said Michael. But this is such fine country, Jack. This looks like the land God made on his day off just for the sport of it. I know what I'm going to sing.

> *We are coming home, mother, mother.*
> *You will see us then, brother, brother.*
> *And our journey shall be done*
> *Underneath the setting sun.*
> *We are coming home, mother, mother.*

Michael wept openly now, but then he was coming under control. This was near no town, but riders came up and down the pike, all

Federals, sometimes militia, often cavalry. There would be some kind of battle coming into shape down in Virginia. Maybe they were having a third go at the Manassas battlefield. Lee would be staring at land through his field glasses and directing the placement of batteries and troops. Lines on a map to him, not men breathing, with wives and children back home, not a David Bernstein, neither Jew nor Gentile, gray-bearded man or beardless boy. *Mother, mother.*

They moved off the road and into the dripping woods, and there were ancient uprooted rocks here, clear springs, at which they knelt and supped. *Take, drink. This is my blood.*

~I don't think I can go on, said Michael. He leaned against a dead hickory tree, stared at the laddered holes up the trunk, as if waiting for something to emerge. Gray-black, green light, strips of tan soil.

~I just want to say I'm sorry for this, said Jack. It didn't sound like him. I just want to say that we should have bought our way out of this war. We weren't fit for soldiers. We were too educated to be lied to. I—it seems to me I thought if we made the boys laugh, everything would be all right. I should have let Martin Goodpath shoot me. We would have been better off.

~*There's* something, said Michael. He pointed at a huge flat stone in a clearing. It's a man.

~Hey! cried Jack. No movement. You on the rock!

They came onward, and when ten feet away shouted again, moved warily, sniffing for death. They walked around the rock, and sun steamed through the canopy spread itself along the moss-smeared cracks.

~Oh my God, said Michael. Oh my God. Oh my God!

~*Henry?* said Jack. They rushed forward now, leaping ditch and stone, and came beside their brother and rolled him on to his back. He was sack-limp, eyes open in small slits, but he sat up and looked up at them, one to another, and said:

~Surrender now, or I'll show no mercy. Then he saluted and passed out in his brother Jack's arms.

BOOK THREE

TOO MANY ACRES

In later days, Jack and Michael would recall their starvation and the time they stumbled over Henry lying more dead than alive on a rock in the middle of nowhere. The youngest Blackshear lay half-limp for two days as they cared for him. Michael found a battalion of mushrooms and said they should give them a try.

~If they're poison, all of us will have gone through this for nothing, said Jack, in a faux-pensive stance. He had spent the day scouting for a house or field to rob, found nothing except one spavined wreck of a cabin that had fallen in years before.

~Starve to death or be poisoned, said Henry weakly. On the whole, I'd prefer not to pick between them.

Jack shrugged, stuffed an entire cream-colored cap in his mouth, and munched it, and a taste of earth and water and wind spread across his tongue. They waited a while and watched him.

~Woe, thou soon-to-be-dead fungal warrior, said Michael, palms uplifted toward the sky. That thou has saved us, that thou hast givest all, yea, woe unto you, mighty idiot. Selah.

~Good speech, said Jack, eating another one.

They managed to eat all the mushrooms they could find, ruined fleshy orange ears, stalky umbrellas, even a few morels, musky and pungent. Henry got better, and they sat in the darkness of a coming thunderstorm one night to decide their fate.

~I'm not going back South, said Henry. I think if we keep heading north we would be taken in by needy, loving women, fine examples of Christian sympathy and sectarian judgment, who will accept our distrust for the South with grace and kindness, who will hide us until this war is over.

~Sounds great, said Jack. I hate women like that. I want a girl who will come at me with a knife if I don't make her laugh. Who hits me in sleep because I haven't been ardent enough. Who screams at preachers and slaps horses when they don't walk right.

~Wasn't there some woman just like that in the Bible? asked Michael.

~Lady Macbeth, said Henry.

~Oh yeah, said Michael. Was she in Leviticus? Wait it was that book about liquor. Genesis.

~I don't think it's spelled that way, said Henry. If I had a drink right now, I'd sign over my birthright.

~Your birthright's not worth a boot-heel of warm spit, said Jack. Am I not grown eloquent in my latter youth. Eh?

They decided to head north, mainly because the war wasn't in that direction, and as they walked they tried to invent a story that would explain their presence—three able young men, if thin and hairy and filthy, wandering around the countryside.

~Okay, we're the three Wise Men and we're heading toward Chicago to see a baby born in a manger because there was no room in the inn, said Jack.

~Sounds good to me, said Michael, except that part about the wise men, the baby, and Chicago. Other than that, it works.

Henry suggested they be couriers carrying dispatches to the king of Canada, but Jack was pretty sure Canada didn't have a king, and Michael pointed out they didn't have any dispatches.

~We had to memorize them because they're so secret, said Henry. Jeff Davis has decided all southern troops must learn French and that we are invading Quebec. Lincoln will have to counter the move and will sign a pact with Greenland and Iceland to come in on his side in the war. Vikings land in Nova Scotia and attack John Bell Hood's Division with lances and rocks. Then things get ugly.

In the end, they moved north in the woods alongside roads, finding a few families willing to give them food and a hay loft for bed, baths, old civilian clothes. Some of the women left alone in farmhouses with children wanted to know the Blackshears' story. Many were field-hard, old at thirty, with bony children pigeon-breasted with ricketts or scaly from erysipelas. Henry shed the last weakness over fresh squash, bowls of beans cooked with slices of salt ham, thick heavy bread caked with smears of freshly churned butter. They ate cheese, unfolded from old cloth and kept in springhouses.

They moved thirty, forty miles northwest into fruitful country, whose dark soil could fertilize the sad red-dust cotton fields of Georgia. Old men wearing long whiskers but no mustaches walked stoically behind plowmules, flat hats shedding sun and rain. Sometimes, home guard units flowed by with their pennants, flintlocks, and shotguns, but they were old men and boys, stage-struck, Shakespearian. One night the Blackshears slept in a cricket-quiet glen; on others they would lie on bed-stones above the thunk and gurgle of a broad creek. The country was fragrant and bug-laden, but they loved the lack of firing, spent pleasant hours inventing ever-more-vile epithets about both sides in the war.

LATE ONE MORNING NEAR THE end of August, 1863, the Celebrated Blackshear Boys came upon a prosperous farm that lay in a sparsely settled narrow valley. The white house needed work and wasn't very large up there halfway to the summit of the western hills, but the barn was redly magnificent, huge, sprawling even, and yet somehow weak, as if having recovered from a long illness. Perhaps thirty acres of corn grew around it, and a pasture that swept up the hillside held twenty-two head of white-faced cattle.

~How do you know there are twenty-two? asked Michael. Jack was the one who had announced that precise number.

~Counted the legs and divided by four, said Jack. Old Indian trick.

~Then how many ears of corn are out there? asked Henry. Jack studied the field. The day was gorgeous, with a buttery sun, soft air, a sweet coolness.

~Seven thousand four hundred and nine. I counted the stalks and multiplied by pi. Apple pie.

~The intellectual world trembles, said Michael. An old man rode toward them on a tired brown horse with the smear of a blaze between its eyes. The Blackshears only had time to stand straight. He was carrying a shotgun across his saddle, and when he came close, they could see he had parchment skin mottled from a life's exposure to sun, hairy hands, taut thin lips, and a long caterpillar brow that went across both his eyes.

~Give me one reason I shouldn't kill you boys, the old man said. He lifted the gun but didn't exactly point it at them.

~We're carrying dispatches to the king of Canada, said Jack meekly. Jeff Davis has decided to attack Australia and is looking to strike a treaty for mutual support in the coming fight.

~That ain't funny, said the old man. He seemed more glum than angry.

~Actually, we're headed to St. Louis, said Michael. A baby has been born in a manger, and there's a star hanging over the city. It might have just been fireworks. We have to check it out.

~I thought it was Chicago, said Jack. You mean we've been following a rocket all the way from the kingdoms of the East instead of a star? Our father, the sheik, shall be most foully vexed.

~That ain't funny, neither, said the old man.

~You're a hard audience, said Henry. We're from Georgia. We were soldiers fighting with the Confederate troops, and after the fight at Gettysburg, we decided to find a better use for our talents.

~Well, just spill the beans, said Jack. Sheesh.

~Mought more likely than them other stories, said the old man. Lucky you come here first rather than walking on to Salterville.

~What's wrong with Salterville? asked Henry.

~What's awrong with Salterville? the old man almost shouted, nearly coming out of his saddle. It's where Death lives.

~I bet he gets a break on his house payments, said Jack. They probably give him free meals at the hotel, too.

~That ain't funny, neither. It's the dead asshole of the world. It's had plagues of disease, failed businesses, fires, storms, robbers, wife-beaters, and lying preachers who run off with all their congregations' money.

~Failed businesses! cried Jack. I can't bear the thought of it.

The old man's eyes crinkled at the corners, and he looked at each of the brothers in turn, shaking his head. He sighed. Henry was almost sure he smelled apples in the wind. What *was* that bright light he had followed up that stony hill? How did you know when such things were portents, illnesses, or God himself? How could you know anything?

~That was sort of funny, okay. I'm Lewis Geschnitz.

~Bless you, said Michael.

~It's German, said Lewis. I had me boys to work this land, and the damned government took them all the war, four of them, and we ain't heard a word in months now. I fret they're gone to God. Why was you boys fighting for slaves, anyway?

For once, the Blackshears said nothing, looked at each other, then away. *God*, thought Michael, *I could paint this place with such joy: the cerulean sky and its cotton clouds, the still-green pastures, the sloping acres of corn with its golden tassels. Barn the color of old apples, house with sharp eves for snow-shedding.*

~We aren't fighting for anything, said Henry. We just want to settle for a while. We would be proud to work for food.

~We would? asked Jack. Michael elbowed him in the side.

~Four fine sons, and now the damned army and the damned war have ruined me, and I'm too old to keep this going. My Mary is worn slap out, and Mama don't know which side of the bread to butter any more. He paused, but only for a moment. I ought to feel more hate for you than I seem to be feeling, fighting against my own flesh and standing here making light of it all. For all I know, one of you boys kilt one of mine. I feel a sickness of it.

~Where have your sons been engaged? asked Henry.

~We haven't heard nary a word since the fight at Fredericksburg, he said. The boys looked at each other, and Henry grew pale, beginning to break, and Jack, with his eyes, said: *Don't do that when a man with a gun's sitting over us.* The brothers stood, clearing throats, saying little. Well, we will know if they live in God's good time. God's good time. And if there's nought but hatred in this country, I'll fight that. At least there's no fight here. To the south there's a war, and to the north there's Salterville, a town being punished for its sins. Evil lives there.

~Maybe he can room with Death and free up a house, said Jack.

~This is a long shot, but you wouldn't happen to have three daughters, would you? asked Michael.

~You can work for food, but I can't pay you nothing, said Lewis. We got room in the house for you, I reckon. And no daughters. It's just me, Mary, Mama, and Eliot Yellowhawk. I wouldn't rile him.

~*Eliot Yellowhawk?* said Henry.

~He's Huron. He was walking to find his sacred burial ground or some such and stopped here and never made it any farther, said Lewis. Jack watched the man's brow suspiciously.

~A long journey is a noble thing, said Henry.

~He's from Robertson. He only walked eight mile. And that were six years ago, and we're not shed of him yet. Educated beyond need. Come on.

The Blackshears walked down the slope into the most beautiful valley they'd ever seen. Over a rill they found the apple orchard, trees heavy with still-green fruit. Soon, they would turn sunset red, and they'd be milled into apple butter or jelly. Bees hummed as they pollinated. Then, as the boys walked on, they saw the corn field more clearly, and the rows lay perfectly straight, military, and there were squares of wheat and oats, the well-tended two-story barn, and a huge house garden, still swollen with vegetables, even though frost would come in a month or so.

~This is just a thought, but do either of you suspect we were actually killed at Gettysburg and this is heaven? asked Jack.

~If so, it bumps right up against hell, said Michael. Woe to thee who stray into Salterville in search of woman or drink or other sins of the flesh.

~You girls leave the town to me, said Jack. I'll catalog all sins of the flesh and report back to you.

~Geschnitz, said Henry.

~Bless you, said Jack and Michael Blackshear.

ELIOT YELLOWHAWK WAS IN THE yard chopping stovewood, a tall muscular young man with closely cropped hair, stripped to the waist and glistening with sweat. Lewis had ridden ahead of the boys slowly as they walked, looking over the farm on its single-lane road, which is places was in need of repair from runoff. He dismounted and tied the horse to a hitching post near the front door. The house was neat and plain, with a long porch and second-story curtains blowing in on one side and out on the other. Eliot stood up and glared at the Blackshears.

~Who in the hell are you? Eliot asked. He held an axe by the end of its handle and swung it back and forth like a broadsword.

~Poor travelers down on our luck, looking for gainful employment for sustenance or lucre, said Jack. Michael backed up a step. This fool was going to get them killed some day.

~Mr. Geschnitz, should I kill them now or wait until after they've been fattened? Eliot asked. Lewis laughed bitterly and went into the house.

~Hey, that was pretty good, said Michael. Might I ask why a person of your size isn't fighting for the Union? Eliot dropped the axe and held up both hands, revealing six fingers on each of them.

~This, and being a certified savage, he said. I told them I could fire four guns at once. They laughed.

~We're poor traveling impresarios, said Jack, his tented fingers tickling each other. Have you ever considered a career as a pianist?

~Wait—you've got twelve fingers? said Henry. Really, can you play a banjo?

~Who the hell are you?

The Blackshears came on over to him, took a while to try and explain, each of them filling in chapter and verse, sometimes amusing, at others filled with a bitter sadness. Eliot crossed his arms over a huge chest and watched and listened, only nodding from time to time. The smell of cooking meat drifted from behind the house, and the Blackshears were ravenous, but they waited. They spoke of many things, ending with the desire for books.

~Are you a reader? asked Jack.

~Yep, said Eliot. You probably think my favorite book is *The Deerslayer*, don't you.

~Sure, chief, said Jack. How!

~Jesus, Jack, said Henry. Eliot began to smile and picked up the axe, and the Blackshears danced backward a step or two.

~Actually, my favorite book is *Sense and Sensibility*, said Eliot. His hands opened and closed on the well-worn axe-handle. He leaned forward and scowled fiercely. Sentimental, I guess.

The front door opened, and a handsome middle-aged woman came out, her hair pulled straight back and worn tight behind her head. She wiped her hands on a small towel, wore a plain brown dress that swished around her hook-and-eye black shoes. Her cheeks flushed from work, and her green eyes filled with light as she came into the yard and looked the boys up and down.

~I see you young men have met our over-educated help, she said. I'm Mary Geschnitz.

~Over-educated? said Eliot. If you prick me, do I not bleed?

~And we are the Brothers Blackshear, entertainers formerly of His Lesser Majesty Jefferson Davis's Army, said Jack, stepping forward, taking her right hand and kissing it gallantly. She pulled her hand back and tried not to smile. We sing, light the air with skits, and can play any and all instruments.

~Yes, well. My husband says you are willing to work for food, she said. My sons were fighting your kind, and they may all be dead. Only the fact that I'm a Christian keeps me from wishing you dead.

~I understand, but ma'am, we are absolute madmen with a hoe, said Jack. Except for Henry there. He doesn't play the hoe, though he's performed on the rake before the kings of Africa.

~I have no time for frivolity on a farm, Mary said. When we have finished all our chores, we listen to Eliot play our pianoforte, however. Perhaps he can give you boys lessons. You look hungry. The biscuits are near done. Wash up at the pump and come on inside. We can tell our stories later.

~Yes ma'am, the Blackshears said together. She turned and went up the steps, a woman who moved purposefully through her life.

~So you *do* play the piano, said Henry. Do you know any minstrel tunes.

~I'm working on a Beethoven sonata, said Eliot. Are all people in the South as stupid as you three?

~Most of them are about as stupid as Michael and somewhat as stupid as Henry, said Jack, pointing at his brothers. You see before you, however, the very incarnation of intellectual profundity.

~Do-dah, do-dah, sang Eliot with tuneful sarcasm, dusting his huge hands on his pants and walking inside.

THE HOUSE WAS STUFFED WITH middle American arcana, every-thing from cornshuck dolls, an ancient spinning wheel, and a butter churn to a Broadwood piano on which a book of music lay open. The closed windows of a homemade china hutch gleamed tightly, as if a storm were due. Inside was a set of inexpensive transfer ware, cream-colored plates and bowls feathered with rich blue edging. The drawer-pulls were roughly hammered, blacksmithed into accidental elegance. The downstairs split into two front rooms and a huge dining room and kitchen in the back, with a family-sized table covered with an oilcloth. At either end of the room were twin, rock-faced fireplaces, with a musket rack above each. Henry thought: *This is a house in which ghosts live.* The room was very hot, even though the day cooled toward dusk. The Blackshears, washed, nearly starving, looked around the room. Michael watched Jack and saw that his eyes softened, his lips parted, as if something should be said but he didn't know what.

A bizarrely tall old lady wearing widow's weeds suddenly came hustling into the room, Wringing her hands and looking wildly at the brothers. Eliot took the dipper from its handle over the sink and lowered it into a bucket of cold water the Blackshears hadn't seen. The smell of fresh biscuits prowled the room.

~Mama Geschnitz, these are our new help! screamed Mary. All three of the Blackshears jumped, and Eliot grinned and gulped. The old woman waved her arms, and it looked to Jack as if she were trying to knit air. She ran up to Michael and put her leathery face two inches from his. He could see stray hairs on her chin, a cheek wen, and eyes that looked nearly orange, catlike.

~Davy, you iss all different! she shouted. Mary, wiping her hands on a crusty apron, came fast-stepping across the room.

~Mama, that's NOT Davy! she yelled. Eliot go play the piano or something.

~Davy, by damn you have ruirnt your face, muttered Mama.

Mary had to explain it slowly, that these weren't the remnants of her sons, just three boys who had shown up, who would work, who would take no one's place. Mama glared suspiciously at the boys and tapped her foot, standing straighter, seeming taller with each moment the meal was delayed. Eliot didn't go play the piano, and Henry looked around the room and felt its broken sadness. They sat at the table, and Mary served, her small frame strong from lugging, and she brought bowls of food, plates of it, and the boys poured milk from a huge cool crock that was painted with girls who danced in joyfully flung crionolines.

~Don't none of you by damn go to Salterville, said Mama before they prayed. Hatred lives there, ja.

~And Death and Evil, reminded Jack. I hear Sickness is just renting. Michael laughed, but the Geschnitz family seemed dully dumbfounded, and while Eliot narrowed his eyes appreciatively, he didn't say anything.

~Let us pray, said Lewis. Ravenous, the boys trembled for patience. Dear Gott, maker of heaven and earth, we give you thanks for the bounty of our fields. We ask you to look after our apples and our corn and especially our wheat. The wheat worries me. Do something about that. We need a inch of rain next week, so do that. If it be your will, burn Salterville to the ground, but do not make any of them come into this valley, for I do not want to have to shoot them. Henry opened one eye, and Jack was grinning at him. Lewis had his hands folded under his chin, his eyes closed tightly. If you haven't taken our boys yet, save them through this war. The people in the South are madmen, and do with them what you will. Send them locusts. Send unto them a great flood, and washed them all into the sea. Give them the endless shits.

~Lew, for heaven's sake, hissed Mary.

~Don't interrupt me talking with Gott, he commanded. Don't let our cows go dry. Clear up Mama's mind, if that be your will.

~Davy's home! screamed Mama Geschnitz. The Blackshears went into a spasm of throat-clearing to keep from laughing aloud.

~Clear up Mama's mind, even if it make you want to scream, continued Lewis. And about these boys you have sent here, these boys who quit the war. I am not sure what to say to you about that. They may be robbers.

~This is ridiculous, said Mary.

~They MAY be robbers! he said. But I think they is not. Make them good boys who will work fifteen, seventeen hours a day without surcease or complaint. And keep Eliot from killing them with a hatchet, as his kind are wont to do. Amen.

They ate with the gusto of starving men, and Henry closed his eyes with joy and gratitude as he bit into a buttery biscuit, tasted its floury richness, the clot of freshly churned butter. And they could see in Mary's eyes, all of them, that she felt a trembling sadness and familiarity about it all. Two seats were still empty at the table, and Michael remembered the firing at Fredericksburg, how the Union soldiers that cold foggy morning did precisely as their officers commanded, stepped up, row on row to die, with no plan, no grace—witnesses to the stupidity of their own deaths.

DAYS PASSED IN THE SMALL valley, and the Blackshears grew into the rhythms of farm work, something none of them had ever done, and the days held warm, the nights cool and clotted with starfields. The barn smelled richly of hay, and there were cows and pigs and even a small slatted house with eleven layer hens and two roosters. They ate huge and abundant meals, and in the evenings, Eliot practiced Beethoven—his range and technique were astonishing—while the Blackshear Boys collapsed from fatigue, into the comfort of mattresses stuffed with goose down. The upstairs windows opened outward, and the wind that wiggled down the valley each evening made the house cool enough for light blankets and small conversations. They shared the bedroom with Eliot, who in addition to being a polydactylic pianist and Huron, was an earnest Christian and often mumbled prayers for two or three minutes before they blew out the lamps. One day they would hoe weeds in the corn, and the next they would harvest the dwindling vegetables from the house garden, milk, feed the pigs, gather eggs, inspect the apple orchard, walk happily.

~I think we should go into town this weekend, said Jack one evening. They sat on the front porch in the firefly gloaming. What's the worst they could do? Arrest and hang us?

~We could play Death and Evil in poker, and the winner gets the town, said Michael.

~You think that's funny, but Salterville is a place you wouldn't send your worst enemy, said Eliot Yellowhawk, whittling on a stick. It's like lying face down in a grease pit. No matter how much you wash, you never again feel clean.

~Jack's spent half his life lying in greasepits, said Henry. He doesn't mind not feeling clean.

~Unclean is my middle name, said Jack. What about you, Eliot? Are you too precious to soil yourself with the world? The Huron stood and leaned against one of the porch posts. The fragrant smell of burning tobacco drifted from inside, but both Lewis and his Mama smoked—it could be either.

~I moved down this way years ago, but my people live up New York, he said quietly. What is left of my people. My mother was shot while trying to beg food from a wealthy home during a snowstorm. We had nothing, my brother and I, you understand. Our father had left when my brother was born, and I was three. They didn't find my mother's body until two days later, frozen solid against a tree. She'd made it within two hundred yards of our house. So we grew up orphans. I've mostly educated myself and decided things I want to see and those I do not.

~My God, said Henry. I am so sorry, Eliot.

~Long time ago.

~If we said we were Mr. Geschnitz's nephews from Hamburg, will they believe us in town? asked Jack. Always plowing ahead, hearing nothing that would hurt. Michael sat amazed at his sparkly, calculating older brother.

~Might, said Eliot. In each town there are men who are the moral authority, who give a town its tone and rhythm. Salterville has none of those people.

~Ve iss goot Shermans, ja? asked Jack to his brothers.

~I refuse to get into character just to go to town, said Michael. Let's just wander over and see what happens. We have horses here. Just out of curiosity, does the town have any girls, Eliot?

~Ja, he said. Most are for sale, too.

~Not again, moaned Henry.

~And this is the pit of hell? asked Jack eagerly, washing his hands in the cool evening air. Are we talking about the same town?

That's how, early on a Sunday morning, the Celebrated Blackshear Boys came to be riding along a wagon trail northwest from the farm toward the town of Salterville, Pennsylvania. The day was cloudy, coolish, and the Blackshears had washed up, put on clothes left from the now-missing Geschnitz brothers. They rode abreast, not very fast, luxuriating in the gorgeous countryside, the infrequent farmsteads, enormous barns, small neat houses. Michael felt desperate for paints and linen canvas, but he was also unsettled, nervous. He missed the South only a little, his mother and father powerfully. And yet there was something arrogant and impossible about the South. *When the war ends, I'll get to New York and…to New York and draw for a newspaper and…*

~The middle Blackshear girl is sunk in thought, selah, said Jack, who'd dandied himself into a frenzy, hair oiled and parted. He alone had kept some of his facial hair, a mustache and vandyke, and he rode, proud and natty through the damp late-summer morning.

~Y'all ever think about how much where we live shapes who we are? asked Henry. About how people in the North can't be the same as people in the South, anymore than people in Salterville can be the same as people from Branton?

~Or people in war can't be the same as people in peace, said Henry, nodding.

~Or how horses in Dakota are different from horses in Virginia, said Jack. Virginia horses prance with high butts, and Dakota horses creep around behind bushes waiting to kick you in the ass. Take these Pennsylvania horses, brethren. They probably neigh in three or four languages, at least. And what about girls? The girls of Salterville can't be the same as the girls of Branton.

~God, I hope not, said Henry with a shudder.

Jack sang as they rode:

> *Oh the proud girls of Salterville*
> *All have three legs.*
> *In summer or winter they'll*
> *Bring out their kegs.*
> *And just when you're wandering,*
> *Are lost to your heading,*
> *They'll love you if you can*
> *Guess which legs they're spreading.*
>
> *Oh…ho…*
> *The ladies of Salterville*
> *Blah blah blah wedding*
> *This is getting go—od.*

~I resent your implication that the ideal of American womanhood has been lost to this much-maligned Yankee burg, said Henry.

~My God, look at the color of that field, said Michael Blackshear dreamily.

THE LAND SPREAD HILLY AND fertile, but already hints of autumn settled about. They rode for half an hour along the road, and once, to their shock, a Union cavalry detachment came over a hill, smart behind a guidon-bearer, two-by-two. The men looked at the Blackshears but didn't slow down.

~Look German, said Jack.

~Ass, said Michael.

~I really miss the army, sighed Henry. His brothers turned and stared at him.

~I say we beat him half to death until he recants, said Jack.

Houses grew more frequent now, and soon they would come to town, but already there was a crabbed, dissolute look to the place.

~You boys ever think about why we were put on this earth? asked Henry, just above their slow hoofbeats. Sun broke through the clouds, and the mist vaporized, but the houses still looked like splayed mules, about to fall from too much work.

~Absolutely, said Jack. I think about it morning, noon, and night. I think about it in the pew and in the outhouse. I think about it when I'm in a fierce fire-fight and when I'm in the arms of Minnie Penny. In fact, I may well be the most goddamn introspective man ever to live in the goddamn heartland of America. Amen.

~I was put here to paint and draw, said Michael. But I see what you're asking. If we were put here not to do something but to be something.

~That's right, said Henry. A three-legged dog, one back limb missing, ran across the road.

~How does a three-legged dog scratch an itchy ear? asked Jack. That's the kind of philosophical question that perplexes me.

~A man can do good and still have fun at it is what I'm saying, said Henry.

~A three-legged dog is being sent with a message from General Lee to President Davis, said Jack. It takes a four-legged dog an hour to make the trip, but this three-legged dog gets a stone-bruise in his right front paw and so has only two legs, really. Figure the body count of the coming battle based on that knowledge and the fact that Southern women wear larger hats than Northern women. You have five minutes. Begin.

~This goes back to the conversation about what we're going to do after the war, said Michael. It's a good question, Henry. What in the hell is *that*?

They'd reached the edge of the town square, and wildly bearded old man holding a Bible was preaching in a shrieky, tremulous voice to a fat woman in public stocks. She wriggled and cursed, pulling her hands. They rode slowly into the town square, and saw buildings that looked typhus-ridden: falling slats, paint flaking in wild strips, burned shells, and streets with deep pits filled with fly-covered water. A pig sat at the edge of the main street lazily eating a large rat.

~I thought they said the town was a wreck, said Jack. It's lovely. It's scenic. It's America's Garden Spot.

~Where is everybody? asked Michael.

~They at home since the last church was ruirnt, said a voice from behind them. They turned their horses around and saw a one-legged man leaning on crutch. He stood on the board sidewalk, which creaked, almost screamed, with his side-to-side movements. They could hear the woman in the stocks calling the man a damned bastard and a limp woman-beater.

~We are working in a small valley a piece southwest, said Jack. Man name of Geschnitz.

~Bless you, said Henry, unable to help himself.

~Right, the rebel boys who quit the war, we heard a you, said the man. I could lie and say I lost the leg in battle, but I won't lie. I'm the only man in this forsook town who don't lie for a living. My bones break like old bread. Just break. Broke all the fingers on my right hand when I fell down, just a boy. Nobody could never read my handwriting. There goes being the pianer player in a whorehouse.

~Are we going to get arrested? asked Michael, looking around. I can't believe people already know about us.

~Everbody's in everbody else's bidness here is just one reason not to live in Salterville, the man said. I break bones with joints, them without, too. Broke all my toe knuckles. Ever one a them. Yep, the last church was ruirnt. Preacher left in the middle of the night with all the collection and Mrs. Hubert R. Richter. Mr. Richter, he was our rich man, he says Damn the church, damn the preacher, damn my wife, and he burns the Methodist Church to the ground with torches and buckets of pitch turpentine. It was a good fire. We all come out to watch.

~Where does Death live? asked Jack. And Evil. We're looking to start a card game. Is there a public woman near?

~For God's sake, Jack, it's Sunday, said Henry. The pig finished the rat and stood, streched, and then fell, filled, into a mudpuddle.

~Name's Old Mac Pintzing, said the man, in case you men don't have the usual Southern pleasantries on you. Does any of you foller a profession? We could use it—undertaker, preacher, blacksmith, cooper, wagon repairman, brick-maker, baker. You asked about women. Many's the boy's gone to the war and got kilt and left wives alone to moan and thrash.

~Could you direct us to some women who are moaning and thrashing, Old Mac? asked Jack. Henry reined his horse over and kicked out at his brother.

~Jack.

~We need a chandler, mercantile man, telegraph operator, woodworker, near everthing, don't you know. We don't even have a bank robber. Then again, we don't have a bank anymore, neither.

The woman in the stocks, now released, came walking around the corner with her husband, steaming mad, waving her arms. A building across the square groaned and settled. Her neck glowed cherry. She stood red-haired and strong, while her husband seemed slump-shouldered, vacant, and she began to grapple at him with obvious lust, stopping only when she saw the Blackshears on their mounts talking down to Old Mac.

~What in the goddman *hail* do you three want? asked the husband, who briefly straightened himself and then collapsed again. The woman stood close and held his belt, rubbing it like a cat.

~These is the three retired rebels working for Geschnitz, said Old Mac. They can't do nothing.

~Says who? Jack blurted. I am a master at the pimmel lathe and bork. My brother Michael is the best copper thread machinist in the South. And Henry there is a skilled steam loom clope repairman.

~The hell's a steam loom clope? asked the man.

~I've got steam up, said the woman, too loud. She was obviously drunk, her chemise misbuttoned.

~Cranks the garongle and makes it engage the McClellan. Often, the McClellan refuses to be engaged. That's Henry's speciality. Morning, ma'am.

~Has that there pig been eating a *rat*? she asked, horrified.

~So you can see basically the whole town's turned to utter ruirn and feces, said Old Mac. You get used to it. There's a movement to burn it all, pack up, and head to Dakoty, intermarry with red Indians, and make war whoops. You boys know how to craft a war whoop?

~Most of the Indians we know play Beethoven, said Michael.

Another man erupted from an alley, carrying a black cat under one arm and a short ladder under the other. He appeared to have been run over repeatedly by some kind of farming equipment. The cat was limp, looking greenly around, bored, comfortable. A sound of pain came, apparently, from inside the town well on the public square.

~I never heard tell of no garongle, said the man with the red-haired woman. Come on, Louise, or I'll thrown you back in them head brace. Henry watched the tableau with equal mixtures of quiet delight and a shuddering disgust. The man with the ladder and the cat walked as a snail slides, his upper body seeming motionless.

~This here's Johann Beer, said Old Mac.

~I've met your family, said Jack.

~Got no family but this cat and this ladder, said Johann. Come to get my boy Johann out the well.

~He's got the same name as you? This was Michael.

~He's got two young boys and two girls not quite of marrying age, eleven and twelve, and they all named Johann.

~Your *daughters* are named Johann? asked Jack.

~No need to complicate life is what I say.

~What's the cat's name? asked Henry.

~Johann. Wife's Small Blanche. Don't get near her ma, Large Blanche. Man tried to cheat her in a card game onct years ago, and she bit off the little finger of his right hand down to the second knuckle. Then she eat it.

~Does she live with Evil? asked Michael.

~She ate a man's finger? asked Henry. Why?

~Cause she couldn't get his whole hand in her mouth, I reckon, said Johann.

The Blackshears rode around town, and a few citizens milled out and around, many shuddering off their Saturday night and smoking. The houses just off the town square were squalid, with panting dogs and scrawny strutting chickens, but two blocks north, nicer whitewashed houses began, and in their yards fairly normal people worked and took day-of-rest constitutionals. They came to a plain square house with a wide veranda, and two boys played jacks in the dust while a sweet-faced woman hung her wash on a line. She turned and looked at the Blackshears suspiciously and then something changed her, a softening, shoulders more rounded, brown eyes smiling at the corners.

~Morning, ma'am, said Jack. We're poor minstrels down on our luck, and we're searching for a venue worthy of our talents. Michael cursed, but it was too soft for anyone to know what he said.

~You've found it, she said. Her voice was a rich musical alto. The boys looked up at the riders, looked back at the jacks.

~I deserved that, said Jack. Let me introduce myself and my brothers.

~You're the ones working for Geschnitz, aren't you? The ones who left the war. Well, the war did nothing but destroy what was once a pretty town. It killed my daddy, and it killed my husband, and it killed both of my brothers, and one's missing somewhere in Tennessee. He's dead, too, I guess. We have this fine land, this rich soil, and yet if you came through town, you can see what the place has become. We're like people falling and almost but not quite hitting bottom. They drink, they lie in misery, the women sell themselves, and the buildings fall apart.

~Don't forget the preacher running off with the church money and Mrs. Hubert R. Richter, said Jack. I mean, if you want to give us the full benefit of knowing your lovely burg.

She smiled, something it appeared she had not done for some time, and her face changed into a soft and lovely shape, and Henry, instantly smitten, climbed down from his horse and walked to her, eyes to eyes, and up close, she was strong and firm, and a sweet grace played about her mouth. She invited them in, fired the cook stove out back, scrambled eggs, sliced heavy dark bread, gave them butter and blueberry jam. Her house was well-kept and had no ornament except for a picture of Abraham Lincoln cut from a magazine, framed, and hung on the plaster wall. Her name was Annie Lowell, and she was almost as tall as Henry, self-conscious of the roughness of her hands, clearly pleased to have company. The boys giggled in the rising heat of the day.

~Tell me about yourselves, she said as they lingered over coffee— real, strong coffee that tasted heavenly to Michael. He could draw her: the acquiline nose, high cheekbones, dark eyes, hair pulled behind her ears, an underlip somewhat heavier than the one above.

~Let me, said Henry, since Jack always lies, and Michael hasn't learned the entire alphabet yet.

~I got to G and then backslid to D, said Michael.

~We're from a small town in Georgia named Branton. It's everything Salterville isn't. Neat, well-mannered, prosperous, well-ordered, sort of dull. We're musicians and actors, though Jack once claimed to be a journalist, and Michael a schoolmaster. Our father runs a mercantile, and in 1852, he freed our slaves. Mother is florid and dramatic and beautiful, and our father is an artist, too, just like Michael.

~We joined the army in Sixty-One, saw combat all over the East, and in the big fight at Gettysburg, I was captured. My brothers stayed behind and found me, saved me, and then we quit the war.

~You left out the part about us rescuing the orphanage from the herd of wolves, said Jack.

~Why did you quit the war? she asked.

~I was about to say we stopped believing in it, said Henry. But the truth is we never believed in it. We had an agreement that if one of got captured, the others would come find him. I walked into the Union lines—I'm still not sure.... Anyway, I guess we're just small-town boys who want to make people happy. We sing, play instruments, put on skits. Can you sing? A glow spread across her face, and she turned and looked out the window.

~I never sing for other people, she said. She walked to the front door and looked out at her sons, saw them safe, came back.

~We've been singing for other people since we were children, said Henry. Please? If I say please?

~I sing mostly Irish songs, sing them to my boys at night. I don't know why you'd care.

~I care. Please?

She was thinking of something. Lovely girl, not pretty exactly, but intense and warm-eyed. She shrugged as if to apologize for what was about to come. Then she stood straight, closed her eyes, let herself swell into the meaning of the song, eased into it with a light soprano that cut the air with a slight edge. The song was very slow. Henry thought it the most beautiful thing he'd ever heard in his life.

> As I walked out on an evening so clear,
> A young man lamented for the loss of his dear,
> And as he lamented, full sore he did cry,
> Saying, Alas, I'm tormented, for love I must die.
>
> My dear and my jewel, my honey, said he,
> Will you let me gang wi' you a sweetheart to be?
> And my dear and my jewel, my honey, said he,
> Will you let me gang wi' you a sweetheart to be?
>
> Were I to say yes, I would say 'gainst my mind,
> And for to say no, you would think I was unkind
> For to sit and say nothing, you would say I was dumb,
> So take that for your answer and go as you come.
>
> Oh, time take you, Sally, for you are unkind,
> You pulled the lily, left the red rose behind

But the lily will yellow, and the time will come soon
When the red rose will flourish in the sweet month of June.

Oh, some court for beauty, but beauty soon fades,
Others marry for riches, get bold saucy jades,
But if I ever marry, as plain as you may see,
The wee lass that's loyal is the darling for me.

When she finished, Henry's eyes were filled with tears, and Michael stood, open-mouthed. Jack looked at his hands, cleared his throat, shook his head. They knew she had been waiting for more than two years, waiting for men who would never return. She looked at Henry and saw how deeply her singing moved him, and she began to cry, put a hand on her chest. She sobbed once audibly then held it back, and Henry was lost.

~I'd like to tell you how beautiful that was, Henry almost whispered, if you have a month or two. A single tear pearled down her cheek just as a boy's voice became audible underneath the window.

~Mama, Pigeon's back, the small voice said.

~Heavens, said Annie, shaking her head. Her face: Failing patience. There's this man who—well, you want to see what Salterville's come to. Out front. They followed her through the neat house, which Michael found almost solemn. Something about President Lincoln's eyes, infinite pain, infinite sorrow. The man needed to laugh in the worst way. Outside, clouds had come back heavy, and the dirt street looked almost bronze. A small man covered in chicken feathers and patches of tar stood before them, wearing four frying pans and a tin cup, which were tied to his shirt with strips of buckskin. One of his eyes wandered wildly around, and his beard looked like snowy moss. He held a greasy tophat, danced back and forth, and the boys, Robert and Will, grinned uncertainly. There was a string that seemed to cross his neck and come down his chest, and when he shifted again, a musical sound drifted from his back. Jack looked at Michael and raised one eyebrow.

~Pigeon, I told you not to come back, said Annie. You're crazy, and you worry me.

~I'm crazy, and I worry *me*, he nearly cackled. Henry snickered. Was talking to Izzy Blackburg downtown, and he said them southern boys that quit the war was taking the tour of our lovely town, and here they is. I could track a worm in a snowstorm.

~Doesn't take much to get famous in this town, said Jack. Who tarred and feathered you?

~Everbody! said Pigeon. Ain't much to do here. And I'm crazy.

~His real name is Clyde Fonce, and he was once a touring knife-sharpener, said Annie. He came here and lost all his money at cards, then woke up crazy one morning. He's been the town's crazy person since then. And he doesn't even drink. You wouldn't even believe the rest.

~That's true, I don't drink, said Pigeon. Water from time to time. But I have things I'm thinking you mought want to pay cash money for, not rebel money, which ain't fit for a fire or the outhouse, but American cash money.

~Pigeon, please leave, said Annie.

~Pigeon, Pigeon, of brain's there's not a smigden, sang Will and Robert, poking each other and laughing. A heavy-set woman rode past on a mule, sitting astride and glaring like a badly carved statue.

~Looky here what I have, and if what they say's true of you fellas…He reached behind his shoulder, and the pans gave off a pleasant *tink* and *tunk*, but then the man's music became thrillingly different, and he pulled from behind him a beautiful banjo, with hand-carved fretwork inlaid with nacreous playing card suits—heart, spade, club, diamond.

~Holy barn dance, girls, it's a banjer, said Jack.

~Can you play it? asked Annie. The brothers turned and looked at her. *Can we play it?* Henry shivered with memory, recalled the shows they pranced through in their parents house more than a decade past, remembered Rutledge Hall and its cavernous sound, skits on the Peninsula the first autumn of the war, frolics in Fredericksburg—the music, the blood, bone, skits. David Bernstein. *Sorrows such as this world has never.*

Jack reached out for the banjo, and the brothers looked it over. All the strings were there, but they were loose and flapping, and Jack tuned it quickly, saw that the pegs were strong, held against slipping. He began a slow introduction, and the glow from Michael's face increased in wattage by the second. Henry moved over so that they formed a semicircle, leaned close. Henry felt the edge of change, a feeling of hearth and arrival. They knew precisely when to enter, to join in honey-tight three-part harmony, and the feeling penetrated to bone and sinew:

When the blackbird in the spring, on the willow tree,
Sat and rocked, I heard him sing, singing Aura Lea
Aura Lea, Aura Lea, maid of golden hair,
Sunshine came along with thee, and swallows in the air.

Aura Lea, Aura Lea, maid of golden hair,
Sunshine came along with thee, And swallows in the air.

Windows opened. Heads craned out, querulous old women, boys with furrows between their eyes. Pigeon put his hands together as if in prayer. Annie trembled and trembled and tried not to weep, but she knew it was useless, and it broke from her, wild with joy and sorrow, and she shook her head over and over and over, meaning *yes*. Without stopping, Jack broke into a wild frailing run and then began "Turner's Reel," and the Celebrated Blackshear Boys began to clap, and Henry did a clogging stomp. They were coming now from the houses up and down the street, widows holding hand towels, grinning grannies, pretty girls almost to marrying age, the unmarried and the nearly dead, and they looked dazed, disbelieving.

~Girls, said Blackshear to his brothers, I believe I can almost hear the mercenary chink of change.

~Don't ruin it, said Henry. Please don't ruin it. He looked at Annie and thought: *If God has not abandoned all of America, I will ask him for that woman.* Forty minutes later, the boys still sang, and Annie's front yard was full, spilled into the potholed street.

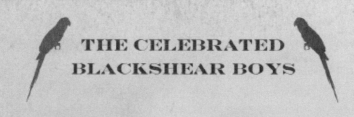

THE CELEBRATED
BLACKSHEAR BOYS

In the North
Oct. 4, 1863

Dear Mother and Father,

 *I cannot know if you will receive this, but I am
compelled to write it and to explain what has become
of us. First, all three of us are alive and well and no
longer in the army. I was captured in the battle at
Gettysburg, and my brothers stayed behind and found
me. I had escaped my captors, who were kind and fed
me. But by then something had gone out of us, and we
declared to remain in the North, perhaps forever.*

 *We are living and working on a farm, and it is
good hard labor, with a family that is rough
sometimes in manners but firm and honest. Most of
the crops have been harvested now, and we ache from
productive labor. Our apples are ready to pick, and
soon the good woman who is wife to our employer
will make apple butter and jellies, and I can almost
smell and taste them.*

 *The nearby town is a dark and bitter place, but
we have begun to make friends there and have bought
so far a banjo, fiddle, and guitar. There is a piano at
our home, and a Huron Indian, who works with us,
plays it most beautifully. We are planning a program
for some time after harvest is ended and the snows
have come in town, if we can but find a venue.*

 *I fear to ruin my luck by speaking of this, but I
have met a widow whose husband, father, and
brothers have all died for the Union cause. She is tall
and not beautiful in the normal sense, is a strong*

*mother to her two fatherless boys, and sings like
Glory. Michael has called on a girl named Iola Zoller,
and Jack is still Jack.*

*We have heard of the South's victory at
Chickamauga ten days' past, and the slaughter it
entailed. But the South can never win this war, and
the killing must end. In the end I believe mankind has
as strong a need to be entertained as it does a need to
fight. That may be the only hope we have left in this
bleak land.*

*Mother, I send all my love to you and father and
Mama Blackshear. God keep you, and if it be his will,
reunite us after this terrible time.*

Your loving son,
Henry Blackshear

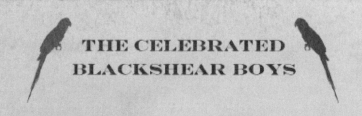

THE CELEBRATED BLACKSHEAR BOYS

Nov. ??, 186

Greetings Family and sit down,

This is enclosed with Henry's letter, which he let me read. I cried, oh I cried for days and hours and minutes, over the damp weight of his syllables comma but in the end I kicked his rear and made him write a new skit with me about a meeting in Hell a hundred years from now between Jefferson Davis and Stonewall Jackson. They both have been working as waiters in a restaurant of Fiends for seventy years, mostly washing dishes and cutting kindling for the stoves. (Hell must have a huge forest nearby, else how would the fire keep lit?) Stonewall has organized a cavalry brigade to storm heaven, but it turns out his brigade is made up mostly of lawyers and so are useless. President Davis decides to convene a meeting of his cabinet and says a decision must be made in the next thirty years.

If I were any more healthy, someone could ride me to California. Your other sons are just as fine, and Michael drinks so much milk now that he moos in his sleep. Yesterday it stormed with such violence that we were kept inside, and we tried to teach Eliot Yellowhawk, the aforementioned Indian, how to play Spat. He was not pleased and accused us of cheating and collusion, but we still took him for nearly four dollars.

This is the point in the letter for philosophy period or rather comma but in the main I choose to live with my nose in the wind. Finis.

If anyone in Branton remarks on our switch in allegiance and its possible relation to cowardice, tell them I resemble their remarks and will have satisfaction. We are told it snows so deep here that chickens can be found in the spring only by unthawing their last cluck and then following the trail. I look forward to that endeavor with great eagerness.

If the war makes it to Branton, please tell the commanding union private that your sons are proud converts and challenge him to a duel over the issue of his choosing, unless it be States Rights, slavery, tariffs, taxation, representation in Congress, and left-handedness among Asians, since we are likely to hold similar views.

Yours for Love with Strangers,
Jack Comma Blackshear Period

THE SNOW FOLLIES

Mary Geschnitz caught a catarrah in mid-October that year and nearly died, but the brothers and Eliot nursed and entertained her, and even through the hacky coughing, her laughter got her well. The first snow came blowing down in cannonball clusters early in November, and the land curled up beneath the line of woodsmoke from the house's chimneys, went to sleep for a long winter.

The war also slumped, exhausted, into its field tents, and everyone knew the following year, 1864, would be decisive. This far north in Pennsylvania, the war was only a rumor now, a far-away burrow of blood and excess, but since Lincoln's Proclamation of Emancipation, a moral weight had shifted the story. Boys and men from Salterville and nearby towns still died, a few in combat, most from disease, and the town itself grew in misery and coldness.

It snowed all night, then all the next day, heavier and then heavier, and the beasts stood, heads down, and looked up with glum familiarity. When the sun came out two days later, the snow was knee-deep, and the valley's contours had vanished into a soft sculpturing. The Blackshear brothers went back to town only once more, managing to buy a guitar from Pigeon, whose house was a tumble-down wreck of dented kettles and almost carniverous debris.

~Don't you mind them doing this to you? asked Henry. His townsmen had recently tarred and feathered Pigeon again, and the wispy tufts floated at his ears, down his arms. He scratched and shrugged.

~The heat of the tar does feel better in the cold seasons, he said. I might could get you boys a fiddle. The early snow melted and sun came back.

Apple-picking time came, and the boys spent days on ladders, plucking down the dusty red fruits, carefully setting them, cheek on cheek, in their shoulder-slung sacks, then dumping them in baskets on a wagon bed. A mule named Sissy stood stoically in harness, sometimes flapping off a bee or a flickering fly. The autumnal smell of the orchard, the hard work, the gorgeous blue sky, the gentle coolness, had left the boys ravenous and full of rakish mischief.

Now, they stood in bundles of clothes owned by Geschnitz sons, knee-deep in snow, forking hay from the barn to animals. They'd helped Lewis slaughter two hogs ten days earlier, and all three had done it without pleasure, the blood bringing memories to bear. Drifts of the new snow were five-feet deep on the sides of the barn. They could smell the rich woodsmoke from four burning fireplaces in the house, along with the kitchen stove, which was kept on a low simmer much of the winter. They'd spent three straight days the week before cutting stove wood, splitting sticks for the broad-mouthed fireplaces, feeling the knots of muscle grow.

~We've got to put on the follies in Salterville and make a lot of money, said Jack. Here endeth the lesson.

~Nine, four, twelve, said Michael. They looked at him blankly. I was thinking of Dr. Pumphrey and his cryptic way of speaking. You know what? We were damned good, even when we were just boys. You think this is something our children will inherit?

~My children will populate nations, said Jack. The three cows kept by Geschnitz gnawed placidly on hay in the dim barnlight. Every Blackshear word, every cow chaw, sent out a wispy plume of feathery body steam. Remember that woman before Crampton's Gap? She's probably whelped two or three times since then. Let's talk about our follies. Did either of you nitwits see a printing shop in Salterville? We will need posters and handbills.

~We need a place to perform, said Henry. I might be going back to town tomorrow. Or the next day.

~Swear on your honor that you will not try to corrupt the tall and lovely Miss Annie Lowell, said Jack.

~I'll swear it on *your* honor, said Henry.

~Is Jack a judge? asked Michael.

~My honor was last seen on a train heading toward France, said Jack. The Atlantic Express. With a stopover for a week in Atlantis for the sea-serpent races. Good point about my honor, and yes, I am a judge, you dunderhead. Get me my judicial wig, staff, and orb. Selah.

~We need some new skits about Salterville, said Henry. He had taken up smoking a pipe, and now the rich aroma of match and reasonably bad tobacco filled the barn.

~You could just go ahead and burn the barn down and save carelessly throwing a match in the hay, said Jack. You've just taken up pipe smoking because you think it makes you look like a thinker. We need to get you a new face to make you look like a thinker. Mikey, send to Pigeon and see if he can get a new face for our younger brother.

~New brain for you, said Michael. Lewis Geschnitz walked into the barn looking scowly and arch. Eliot Yellowhawk, wearing knee-length boots and a bright red coat, was silently stalking him, a few feet behind. He held aloft a large hatchet. Henry flinched, and Michael moved from foot to foot. Only Jack snickered, nodded. This was good.

~I'm ain't paying you jerks to stand in the barn yammering, said Lewis.

~And that was how the massacre began, said Jack. Quietly, the Indians came down like wolves, fangs dripping hot blood, and they killed the farmers, chopped them to bits before they knew their lives were to be snuffed. The end.

~Eliot, if you be behind me again with that tommyhawk, I'm gone to lose my temper, said Lewis, who didn't turn, didn't even flinch.

~Hey, thanks a lot for ruining a perfectly good attack, said Eliot, lowering the blade and walking around his boss to the Blackshears' side. How am I supposed to honor the graves of my Huron ancestors if I can't kill swiftly and precisely?

~You killed that Haydn sonata last night, said Michael.

~For pity's sake, let music at least die a natural death, added Jack.

~What in the name of God are you talking about? Lewis looked at them, but his eyes betrayed him—a softness, memory, familiar banter with sons now lost to distance and time. The Blackshears all saw it, but Michael was most moved. The light, the raw sienna color of the hay, and through the open window, miles of deep milky white. Lewis cleared his throat. We can get a deer in snow. You fools come get a gun and go to Penhill's wood and try not to kill each other.

~Henry's still tender enough to eat, said Jack. We could just shoot him here in the barn and hang him to cool from a rafter. We could have cutlets for supper.

~I'm not eating Henry, said Eliot. Some flesh is too tender, a fine meal to render.

~You just committed a couplet, said Michael. Well done.

~I prefer to eat Henry rare, said Jack. Except there's nothing rare about him.

~I have a rare talent, said Henry, for making girls love me.

~Well, we could cut out his talent and stuff it in apples for roasting, said Jack. I thought the couplet brusque and angular.

~Goddamnit, go and do something useful! cried Lewis. I could send a message to the home guard to come get you for hanging.

~I'll take the message, said Michael. When they start with the hanging, bells will be ranging.

~I prefer that my off-rhymes deal with heaving breasts and cherry-red lips, said Jack.

~It's too cold to go hunting, said Eliot. Only a savage would be out in this kind of weather.

They went hunting, wandered around Penhill's wood for three increasingly hilarious hours, fueled by flasks, jokes firing and misfiring like a handful of shotgun shells thrown in a bonfire.

HENRY AND ANNIE SAT IN her parlor sipping somewhat decent hot tea sweetened with a nip of rum. Her sons were off visiting her mother two towns over in Wentworth. The snow had melted mostly in the week since another blizzard, though it clung almost desperately to shadowed places.

~They were good strong boys, dull, with interchangeable faces and voices, she said. Most people are like most other people.

~I know it, said Henry. That's why generals can send millions to their slaughter. Henry had asked about the Geschnitz boys. Already, to Annie, they were seeming vague, lost to memory.

~But you have already said that the South is wrong, that slavery is evil, and that this war is a just one, said Annie. I believe that. Some wars must happen.

~The ones who are evil are the ones who make war inevitable, said Henry. I really don't want to talk about the war. It will be here for another year at least. Then in thirty years, there be another war, then there will be another one after that and another one after that. It will never stop. My brothers and I want to put on a show. Is there a place where we might do it that would hold three hundred or so?

~Three hundred? Everyone in this town hates each other. For fun they beat up on poor Pigeon or on each other. You could pick a church. Most have been burned. The rest are empty. Sometimes I go to the Second Methodist church and sit in one of the chairs in the sanctuary and pray for my sons. There are four empty ones, if you count the Baptist church.

The day was almost warm, since it was still six weeks until winter began, and Annie had opened her windows, but there was no wind, and a brittle silence seemed to be folded out there, almost malevolent.

~What do you pray for?

~For my boys' happiness and for a kind life, wives, children, a different town. I have been thinking of going home to live with Mother. Father died two years ago in January, and she's lonely. I'm just staying because I can't convince myself that my husband isn't coming home, though I know he isn't.

~I don't think you should move, said Henry. What if some needy stranger wandered into Salterville needing succor and you weren't here to do your Christian duty?

~That sounds like something Jack would say, she said, smiling.

They walked slowly down the street, along the edge of rough yards that glinted with junk, whose dogs growled and sulked. No one repaired the roads, and wagons crashed through knee-deep holes, though carriage drivers slowed to go around them. Downtown Salterville looked even more desolate after the storm, as if the brick had been made of unfired clay and was now crumbling, course on course. Several carriages had pulled up outside the undertaker's parlor, and smoke boiled from a metal pipe halfway up the outside wall.

~Who died? Henry asked.

~Mr. Wolff, the pickle merchant, said Annie. His wife left him many years ago and took their children. They say she told him she could never love a man who smelled like vinegar all the time.

~Isn't that in the Bible? asked Henry. Smell not of vinegar or turpentine, or yea, thy wife and thy wife's maidservant, and thy wife's maidservant's ox and thy wife's maidservant's ox's calf, shall leave thee destitute in the land of Salt.

~She remarried a rich merchant and lives in New York City.

~And Mr. Wolff is still in a pickle. Justice is cruel.

Two slack-faced young men walked down the other side of the street, and when they saw Annie, they crossed, one of them going ankle deep in a puddle, brogans sucking out the mud with a mildly hideous sound. They wore unraveling layers of threadbare clothes, and their beards were so patchy and ill-kept they might have been trimmed with a thresher. Annie: Smiling, which meant these boys were safe, perhaps ridiculous.

~I'm Norris Bickerstaff, the son of Horace and Willow Bickerstaff, who come from County Wicklow and are famous for their butter and pig's feet, the older boy said proudly. He shook hands with Henry, who then looked at the dirt that had passed between them with mild suspicion. Then my paw up and run off with the widow Schlitz, leaving Maw to raise us, but then she run off with Mr. Parsley, the watch repairman. I tried to keep the pig feet thing going, but a pig ain't got but four a them things. And the sound and the smell of pigs is a thing too much heard and smelt right in this town. So me and my brother Roane switched to goats except you can't herd a goat. Even a shepherd dog's no good to herd a goat. Miss Annie. Mister, this here's my brother.

~Howdy, said Roane.

~He ain't talkative, said Norris. He's also a mite off his beam, so if you see him wandering around town talking to hisself, don't think nothing on it. When maw run off with Mr. Parsely, Roane said, That's the last straw, and then he went nuts. He flapped like a bird for two weeks until he run out of steam and nested in the courthouse. That's what's left of the courthouse. He pointed to a charred pile of bricks on the town square. It was struck by lightning last May and everbody come out with bottles and baskets to watch it burn. Hee. The home guard kept its muskets and powder and such in it, and everybody was just screaming with dee-light. Except Mr. Pilotia, the hatter, who was kilt when a rafter blowed out and hit him in the nose, square.

~I'm crazy, nodded Roane.

They paid their respects to Annie once more and sloshed and sagged off down the street. She giggled and shook her head.

~Maybe you *should* leave, said Henry. In fact, I'm thinking of moving to some place safer, like Richmond or the Manassas battlefield.

The front doors to the Church of God had been taken off their hinges, hauled off for firewood. Inside, all the chairs were gone, too, and pigeons cooed and noodled in the rafters, flapping around, going nowhere in paticular. A banner hung behind the altar said *Jesus Saves,* and under that someone had painted *But he don't keep it in the Bank of Salterville.* Most of the windows were broken, and a few stray piles of snow lay in glistening heaps near them.

~Have you ever had an epiphany? asked Henry quietly. When you felt like God was inside you trying to get out?

~I know what you mean. She walked to the window and looked out, and in that moment Henry thought he had never seen anything quite so beautiful, so perfectly lovely. I was at a revival when I was a little girl. This was a traveling preacher in a tent. I had an uncle who had died suddenly of an apoplexy a few weeks before, and it scared me so bad I didn't think I'd ever breathe again. And I thought—there was a light, it seemed. I know I sound crazier than the Bickerstaffs. It pulsed and glowed, and I thought God was in the room. Then I had the worst headache of my whole life. Doc Abelson said the lights came from the headache I was getting. But I've always wondered.

~That's the problem, isn't it? said Henry. How can we know when something is true or not? It happened to me during the fight at Gettysburg. If I hadn't seen it, I wouldn't have let myself get captured, and my brothers wouldn't have quit the war to find me. And I wouldn't have ended up here. And I wouldn't have…

She turned, and the light seemed to shimmer around her hair. Broken glass, snow heaps, the hollow emptiness of an abandoned church. Henry stood for nearly a minute, saying nothing, looking at her.

THE BLACKSHEAR BROTHERS TUNED THEIR instruments to the piano. A cold rain blew down the valleys, and the window frames creaked in and out, in and out. They now had a guitar, a banjo, and a violin, and they practiced when they weren't working, Mr. Geschnitz pretending to find it annoying and Mary openly adoring it. When she spoke their names, it was with a gentleness almost tender. Lewis simply called all three of them *Blackshear* and let it go at that.

~I say we dress Eliot up in buckskin and let him come howling into the room in the middle of our frolic, waving his hatchet and demanding money, said Jack. Then we jump on him and beat the utter hell out of him and tell people we won't accept money for it. Then they will give us all they have. Do I understand human nature comma or what, boys?

~My grandfather killed a British soldier and ate his brains, said Eliot mildly. Then he ate the soldier's dog's brains.

~I don't think eating someone from England qualifies as cannibalism, said Michael, playing something simultaneously aimless and beautiful on the guitar. I'm not sure about British dogs. That would at least be in bad taste.

~Dog actually tastes somewhat like chicken, said Eliot. I've had feist and greyhound.

~Are you idiots making a point? asked Henry.

~I'm not, said Jack.

~Same here, said Eliot, who began one of his parlor tricks, playing "The Star-Spangled Banner" with the right hand in A-flat major and the left in C. It sounded like a tuneless small-town band, somehow hideous and yet charming. Once he played the right hand in C minor and the left hand in F-sharp major. Everyone agreed it was sublimely hideous.

~If I'm going to be in the show, I'd rather play George Washington playing Hamlet, said Eliot, stopping in mid-phrase to take a slurp of rum from a mug on the piano. To be, gentleman of the House of Burgesses, or not to be, that is the legal question to which we are apt to address today, notwithstanding precdent and local regulations and tariffs.

~I like it, said Jack. Pithy and egalitarian, yet mentally deranged. The perfect American speech.

~Better than the one give by the president at the dedication of the Gettysburg cemetery, said Lewis Geschnitz, stoking the fire. They say

Mr. Everett orated for two hours and Mr. Lincoln spoke for two minutes.

~Jack can say nothing in two hours *or* two minutes, said Henry.

~Or two days, said Michael.

~The two-day welcome-to-Salterville speech, said Jack. One of you
girls get a pencil. I feel a case of the skits coming on.

~Take kerosene on a sugar cube, said Lewis Geschnitz.

THE BEST VENUE TWO WEEKS before Christmas was the Christ
the Victor Episcopal Church, which still had a congregation of two, a
toothless old Dutchman named Siegfried Paars and a wildly religious
widow, Lotus Mingledorff. Paars was clearly an idiot and agreed with
everything the boys said. His face, Jack said, looked like an underdone
flapjack. Lotus was imperious, demanding, frugal, pinched, and perenni-
ally dressed in black.

The town's newspaper had gone of out business two years before,
and the boys of Salterville soon broke in, scattering paper, writing
obscenities on the walls in something unspeakably brown, and throwing
handfuls of type around the room.

~It was called the *Salterville Citizen*, said Pigeon, standing in the
cold room, jangling pots as he scratched his ass. Had a perscription
myself. Run a story on me, said I was colorful. I offered to sue Mr. Fears,
the editor. The next week he run a story saying I was colorless.

The Blackshears were on hands and knees looking through the
debris for type. It was mid-November, and a hideous, bone-cracking cold
had settled in, though without snow.

~I have a P, said Michael.

~Congratulations, said Jack. At least do it in the alley. Though I fear
it would compliment the materials used to write on the walls.

The sunlight shifted, and details in the debris became clearer, and
suddenly letters began to stand out, capitals, lower cases, italics—everything from seventy-two point banner fonts to agate. They set a flat
box-lid in the middle of the room and tossed type as they found it.

~I think we've got enough to set Declaration of Independence
without vowels, said Jack. That would be the Dclrtn f ndpndnc or something like that.

~That's the Welsh version, said Michael. I'm thinking of running for mayor.

~We could put out an Extra, said Jack.

~I'm the current mayor, said Pigeon. The Blackshears stopped looking for type and stared at him. Nobody else run. My slogan was Vote for Pigeon or I'll Hit You in the Head with a Pot. Never can tell where success in poly-tics comes from. I'm apt to run for president next time, but I'd need me a new slogan.

~Vote for Pigeon or He will Put a Skunk in Your Bed, said Henry.

~Don't Start Another War, said Jack loftily. Vote for the Big Chicken.

~I like that one, said Pigeon, clanking and nodding.

~Hey guys, there's a fella looking for you, and he has a shotgun and looks like the south end of a north-bound bulldog, said Eliot, crunching into the debris. Here he comes.

~Home guard? said Michael.

~Ain't really got one no more, said Pigeon. I spect it's Revering Plotts from the Epistolpalian thang. I took suit against himself myself, but our superior court's done gone inferior. The brothers laughed, and Jack made the motion of prayer, as if thanking God for good material. Everyone began to back away when the largest man the Blackshears had ever seen walked across the broken glass, his clerical collar stained with tobacco juice and God only knew what else.

~I understand you are planning a folly in my church building, said Reverend Plotts, and I am here to tell you I will burn in hell before I let it happen. The man was at least six and a half feet tall, and he wore a badly cut beard, along with a violent yet insincere scowl.

~I think there's an opening for an incineration in Hell around four, said Jack. Though I'm on good terms with Old Hop, and I'd bet if he knew it was you, he could work you in closer to three.

~That was not amusing, said the reverend, waving the shotgun to make his point.

~How, said Eliot.

~You only got that crazy German and Miss Lotus Mingledorff, said Pigeon, who then ceremonially sneezed. The German thinks he's still in

Bavaria, and if Miss Lotus was a well, she woulda been dry since fifty-nine. Henry got a case of the giggles.

~My other grandfather ate a Jesuit priest, said Eliot, yawning. Said he was stringy and tough. Can I renew your subscription to the *Citizen*, parson?

~I am not on the side of Beelzebub, said the reverend. Lo and yea.

~You *can* change sides, said Henry helpfully. We did. Besides, burning in hell might not be so bad once you get used to it. Barbecue every day. No snow. Excellent conversation.

~A cordial party atmosphere, said Michael.

~We would give you 10 percent of the proceeds, said Jack.

~Oh, okay, said Reverend Plotts, suddenly smiling and pliant. And may I ask you gentlemen to pray for the continued infertility of Miss Mingledorff? Ahem. He stepped through the shattered window and walked off down the street.

~*Ahem?* said Eliot. I thought it was amen.

~Everthing's screwed up in Salterville, said Pigeon.

~Now *that's* a slogan! said Jack. Pigeon took a step backwards and fell with a hollow crash over an upturned desk, hitting the edge of the type box and flinging it all over the room.

~Now I need another P, said Jack. Pigeon flailed, but because of the pots and pans, he couldn't get up.

~I'm stuck, he said plaintively. Would one a you boys mind scratching my ass?

MICHAEL FOUND A WRECKED BUTCHER'S shop a week later, and in the back there were dozens of sheets of heavy paper, eighteen by twenty-four inches, and he bundled them up under his arm, walked outside.

~I guess it's pointless to hope I could find some paint, he said to himself.

~You're one of those rebel boys, aren't you? a voice said. He turned and saw a woman with black curls that framed her face. She wore brown trousers and a heavy blue coat. Wind coiled her curls, and her lips parted slightly. Her eyes were green, but yellow flecks floated in the irises, and when she slightly smiled, her face changed entirely, became lovely.

Michael couldn't think of another word for her. The ones who are putting on the follies.

~Michael Blackshear, esquire, at your service, he said, bowing.

~If you're an esquire I'm the queen of England, she said. The stage comes through three times a week. You could order paint from New York, and it would be here in a week. Probably would be quicker to use the telegraph, but the Poseys cut down the poles and used the wire for fencing. It didn't work. Their cows wander all over southern Pennsylvania. I'm Portia Washington, if you can believe it. You're staying with Geschnitz.

~Bless you, said Michael. Who are the Poseys? I haven't heard of them.

~*You haven't heard of the Poseys?* she asked dramatically. Michael felt his skin grow galvanized. Her face was irregular, eyes not quite level with each other, chin just a shade too strong, cheeks very high, and nose rounded on the end. She was not tall but well shaped, and she moved like someone used to hard work. They're outlaws. They'd probably even steal your art supplies.

~Those bastards, said Michael, smacking his right fist into his left palm. Have you always lived here, Portia?

~I've got to get home, she said.

~I'll come with you.

~You haven't been invited. What if I have a large, angry husband with a rifle and a scowl?

~I've faced rifles before, but I have to admit I tremble before scowls, said Michael, shuddering. I think the scowl is underrated. If we'd had scowls at Gettysburg, General Lee might be president by now.

~I'm not married, but I had a child out of wedlock, she said defiantly. Little girl. Died of the flu a year ago next month. She was three. Better you heard it from me. You still want to be invited to my house?

Portia made coffee, and they talked for two hours running in her cozy, overheated home, and she told of her lover, a boy named Isom Weaver, who had loved her, left for war, then died of one disease or another down on the Peninsula during the war's first year. Isom had just started shaving.

~He loved me in his barn loft, she said. I knew what I was doing. He didn't seduce me. I knew the next day I was expecting. Her name was Delilah. I thought that was a happy name, but she was sickly from the start. I did all I could. My daddy is a businessman in New York, but he doesn't claim me. He sends me money, so I live all right. Not much money.

Michael told her about Branton, his half-blind artist father, their dramatic red-haried mother, about the Branton Avengers, Crampton's Gap, Fredericksburg, their shows in Virginia, about the woman in the snow. All the while, he was sketching her as she sat next to the window. She had given him a pencil, which he sharpened with his pen knife. He never asked her to pose, but she knew, and she was very still in the weak autumn light. They could smell burning leaves.

~When can I see? she asked.

~It's just a sketch, he shrugged. God it feels good to be drawing again. She stood and walked around him and looked down. The drawing was fine-lined like an Ingres, lightly rendered, deliberate, controlled, and gorgeous.

~Nobody's ever seen me like that, she said. That's not what I see in the looking glass. We get old so quick, don't we?

Suddenly, closeness came, an intimacy with loss, a need for comfort. They made love in her bed, mouth on mouth, hip to hip, and there was no sense in it, no love, not yet, just need and loneliness, a search for closeness. She smelled like flowers, and in her eyes Michael saw an illusion of depth between the flecks, as if, in falling, he could drift forever without hitting bottom.

JACK WROTE A SKIT ABOUT Salterville being named capital of the Confederacy. Henry added the national anthem, the chorus of which was:

> *Salterville, oh Salterville*
> *Thy ruins are crystal fountains*
> *Though there is no altar, will*
> *We ever reach the mountains?*
> *Freedom! Justice! in spades.*

And the ruining of the maids.
Ahem! Ahem! Ahem!

~It doesn't mean a thing, said Henry. I love it! Sounds like something Jeff Davis would write while suffering from chronic dyspepsia. I congratulate you!

~Ahem, said Michael.

Eliot composed a piece for piano he called "The Battle of Rhode Island," with snippets of Beethoven, cracked Handel, folks songs, and a triumphant version, in three keys simultaneously, of "A Mighty Fortress is Our God."

~Watching a man with twelve fingers play the piano is like being a spectator at the Armageddon of spiders, said Jack. Lewis Geschnitz snorted and rocked by the fire. Makes me itchy.

~This is so familiar, said Mary Geschnitz. She was knitting, and the needles added their clacking voice to the crackling of the fire. She looked very old suddenly, and for the first time, Henry thought of his own mother sitting at her southern fireside, wondering, worrying, and he stood and went to Mary, knelt in front of her.

~We can be your boys now, he said. Not the real ones. God knows we couldn't do that. But maybe like their happy shadows.

She lay the needlework in her lap and rubbed her cheek, as if trying to deny what she so clearly and deeply felt. Michael found himself suddenly and unexpectedly moved. Lewis oomphed his pipe, rocked, looked into the brands and flaming logs.

~I've tried to look past this war, she said quietly. I've thought of what made my sons go and what made you boys come here to me. And I mean you, too, Eliot. Maybe war has to happen sometimes. I believe in freeing the slaves. I do. That's an evil that must be defeated. But to destroy so many lives. Sometimes I just want to hit something. But before you boys came, this was a dark sad place. And now it's home again. It's come to me that you might never in your lives do a better thing.

Suddenly, sentimental, not caring much, they crowded around her, and their arms went up, holding, and Lewis almost came to join them, then he didn't.

~HAS ANYBODY SEEN THE IDIOT? Henry waved his arms, exasperated. They were in town at Christ the Victor to rehearse the show. Annie had decided to sing in public for the first time, and she stood by the stove, wringing her hands with worry, while her sons, Robert and Will, played outside in a field next to the church, throwing a ball with Mayor Pigeon, who clanked and clanged.

~He said he would be back, that he was going to see a man about a horse, said Portia. She stood near Michael, touching the sleeve of his coat. Men who say they are going to see about a horse are never seeing about a horse.

~Where's the closest place to buy a crock of O Be Joyful? asked Michael. Jack was sober once in the Fifties, but I forget the exact date.

~I could track him, said Eliot. Every Huron has the ability to track a white rabbit in a snowstorm.

~You couldn't track an elephant in a dress shop, said Henry.

~My grandfathers ate men for less that that, said Eliot, picking at a hangnail. But the truth is I'm afraid of the dark, and lo, the gloaming washes over the horizon like a baleful insistence.

~How someone with so many fingers and such a poetic sensibility wound up in this godforsaken village is beyond me, said Henry. He looked out the window, and the boys were chasing Pigeon, whose fluttering feathers made it seem he would take off shortly.

~Salterville ain't godforsaken, said Reverend Plotts, who had come in with the Bickerstaff boys, Roane and Norris. God has to have been somewhere to forsake it. He's never even been in this county.

~Iola Zoller said to tell you she hopes you burn in hell, said Norris to Michael. That you ortn't to think you're welcome no where near her again. Michael turned and looked with shame at Portia, who was grinning. She knew he had seen Iola. Everyone in Salterville knew everything about everyone.

~Maybe we should change this to the Hell Follies, said Henry. Is there anybody in this town who's *not* going to hell? They all looked at each other, but the only sound was Roane Bickerstaff scratching his crotch.

~Roane, for God's sake, grow some manners, said Annie. Can't we rehearse without Jack?

They couldn't, and so Henry and Michael went outside and began walking around the neighborhood looking for him. The day looked like a patient with consumption. Alleys snaked between tumble-down houses and shops, and puddle-water froze at the edges. Two friends, who happened to be dogs, trotted past, shoulder to shoulder, going somewhere. The Blackshears found themselves in front of a house that looked like a collapsing salt cellar or a man with his hat at a rakish angle. The front door exploded open, and a woman powdered and painted into a frenzy came dashing out just behind her grin. One shoe was unbuttoned and gapped open on her foot like a predator. She came right up to them, smelling of just-applied perfume that had the distinct after-aroma of something flammable.

~Halt, woman of the night! said Michael. We are looking for our brother Jack. He's about so high and weighs so much and looks like this. Michael hadn't moved his hands or indicated anything. He is perhaps seeking to acquire liquor.

~For two bits you can ride me to them Pacific Ocean, she said in a girlish nasal voice that sounded, to Henry, like a file on rusted metal.

~My brothers are beyond temptation, said Henry. Shame on you for hinting otherwise, harlot.

~Hey, girls, how's the show coming? It was Jack, of course, standing in her doorway, shirttail half out, a bottle of watered brandy in one hand and a tin cup in the other. Pay this young woman. I didn't introduce you. From the shape of his vowels, it was clear Jack had been drinking. Henry and Michael Blackshear, late of the CSA, this is Miss Eulalia Fonce.

~Fonce? Are you related to…

~She's Pigeon's younger sister, and secretary to the town council, hiccuped Jack. Mighty progressive town to have a woman as an official, eh? Henry, donate a shilling to the woman's good graces.

Henry flipped her a quarter, and they dragged Jack back toward the church, and along the way he sang the Minnie Penny song, howled once, then asked Henry for a cigar. The two friends who were dogs, having apparently completed their visit, came loping back past them and disappeared into the gloom.

WHEN THE BLACKSHEARS CAME BACK to the church, several more had wandered up to watch the rehearsal. The Bickerstaffs, Reverend Plotts, the Lowell boys, and Pigeon sat near the stove. Siegfried Paas, the near-mute Dutchman and church member, sat quietly reading the Book of Common Prayer upside down. Two miscellaneous and blank-faced women sat in chairs near the back, while an obviously drunken young man wearing a bright yellow duster walked in a circle, his boots squeaking like some small mammal being eaten by a tiger.

~Excuse, me, but who are you? asked Henry. They had cleared the altar and set out chairs to rehearse some skits.

~That's Timmie Posey! said Portia in an excited stage whisper. One of our outlaws!

~Give me all your money! cried Timmie, whose features were crammed into a small space in the center of his face. Just funning with you. Folks says me and my brothers is outlaws, but we have only robbed four or six stagecoaches, two trains, and that brush salesman from Pittsburgh who kept coming through here. But he had it coming.

~He did, said Reverend Plotts.

~You also robbed the Bank of Salterville, reminded Annie, apparently without acrimony. Quite a scene. Waving guns in the air, riding in circles on your horses, screaming like banshees.

~We did rob it, and there weren't but worthless railroad bonds and old lady McGuane's bottle of pennies, said Timmie. We burned the bonds and took the pennies over to Miss McGuane. She'd forgot about them. There's ain't no future in being a outlaw in America. So I've decided to go into acting.

They all looked at him blankly. The Blackshears took up their instruments, tuned, and Jack started with a wild chromatic run before sending them, like a shiver, into "Turner's Reel," which they played wildly, each taking a turn at the melody while the others improvised in harmony. The few people in the church began to move toward the front, entranced, and even Siegfried Paas tapped his foot, though utterly out of rhythm. Timmie Posey struck a succession of postures, as if trying out for the part of a statue in a drama. Michael watched him with amusement, a boy of maybe twenty, who looked as much like an outlaw as Pigeon did like Abe Lincoln. They finished the reel, and then they accompanied

Annie in "The Little Irish Lad," and at first her voice trembled, then it became utterly incandescent. When she finished, Portia hugged her, and they stood by the stove, since the room was getting colder and colder. The Blackshears and Eliot ran through their Salterville sketch, and Robert and Will howled with laughter, and even Pigeon banged and clanked around happily. Mr. Paas's expression never changed, and Timmie Posey practiced his quick draw at his own reflection in a window.

They rehearsed for an hour, then announced it was time to leave, began to blow out the dozen kerosene lamps.

~I'll see Annie home, said Henry.

~I'll do the same with Portia, nodded Michael.

~I'll visit with Eulalia and meet you girls at the burned down courthouse in an hour for our legendary ride home in the dark, said Jack, words somewhat muffled by the cigar in his mouth.

~That's my sister, said Pigeon. She's the town clerk and a Happy Woman. Too bad her bidness dried up before she did.

~What am *I* supposed to do? asked Eliot Yellowhawk.

~See if you can find that white rabbit in the snowstorm, said Michael. If that doesn't work, find a priest or a city official to barbecue.

~We had us a cannibal in 1856, said Pigeon. But we run him out a town. Some things is too tasteless, even for Salterville.

THROUGH THE COLD BRITTLE DARKNESS: Henry and Annie, arm in arm, bundled, close. A gunshot cracked half a town over, followed by a firecracker-string of laughter. The wind made their eyes tear.

~This is the first time I've been happy in so long, said Annie. Robert and Will trailed, came past, went sideways, returned. I don't think this town's ever seen anything like you boys. I wake up, and I think you won't be with me anymore. And I smile because I've had you at least this long.

~You smell like vanilla, said Henry, stopping and turning to her. I want to kiss you. My God, you're lovely.

~Yes, she said, and she stood tiptoe and kissed him, and the boys crowded close and cried *Woo-woo-woo!* in girlish voices, then popped away, giggling. Henry and Annie stood breath to breath.

~You taste like heaven, said Henry, then he kissed her again. For a town mired in hell, you're its one angel.

~Flap flap, she laughed. He walked her home slowly, avoiding the moon, which lay in mudpuddles like a cream dollar.

~Less elegant, without restraint, Michael and Portia all but ran to her house, shed the winter skin of their clothing, and made rambunctious, slat-cracking love. They used resolve and restraint to make it last three minutes.

~I'd like to wear you like a dress, Portia whispered into his ear. Or like pantalettes. I can't get close enough.

~I'll be your dress, but I draw the line at being ladies undergarments, said Michael, gasping and wishing he had a ladle of cold well water.

~We make a fine couple, said Portia.

~I know, said Michael, remounting, to her obvious delight, but a couple of *what*?

Jack dashed back to Eulalia Fonce's house, but she was pleasuring Norris Bickerstaff, while Roane sat in her parlor waiting his turn. Jack found her stash of liquor, took a pleasant burning gulp, tottered back outside. Their horses were in the Salterville stable next to the burned down courthouse, and he walked there to find Timmie Posey sitting glumly on a saddle tree, spinning the cylinder of his six-shooter in the moonbright shadows.

~I just want to be good at something, said Timmie. I am a bad outlaw. Boo. I couldn't scare a hen off a nest.

~How is it you and your brothers managed to avoid Mr. Lincoln's draft? asked Jack. Forgive the gibbous slant of my consonants, for I have indulged in noxious potables.

~Huh?

~I'm drunk, said Jack.

~Oh, me, too. Look, I want to be a actor. All's I think to do now is to be a actor. Couldn't you give me something to do, put me in the show?

~Can you sing?

~I know two songs, said Timmie, erping back a belch. One is "Dixie" and the other one ain't.

~Can you dance? Tell jokes? How's your memory?

~Oh I remember everthing I ever heard or read in my whole life.

~Okay, we will write something for you. All you have to do is say the words at the right time.

~I can do that, said Timmie. Give me all your money.

~Are you robbing me? Forget it. Wait. You give *me* all your money for putting you in the show.

~Aw, said Timmie. He flipped a silver dollar through the yeasty barn, and it caught the moonlight, head, tails, heads, tails.

Michael and Henry got back to the stables, and they rode into the deep cold and sat their horses in the cream-yellow middle of Salterville, side by side. They looked around at the town's ruins, the broken-back buildings, cracked sheet glass, burned hulls. Jack inhaled drunkenly and patted his chest with both hands.

~This is the kind of place where a man could put down roots, he said. A place where order is a tradition, and clean living is a habit. Pigeon staggered past, drunk and giddy, singing "Buffalo Gals" on one note and dancing and clanging, at first noisily and then into silence.

~I'm going to Louisiana for to see my Susie-Anna, said Michael. He kicked his horse, and the other horses, Eliot in the lead, ambled forward, and beneath a heavy cheese moon the Blackshears sang their way on to the road south.

America lay before them, huge and wild, broad-shouldered, worth saving. Dogs crossed and recrossed the road; a fen of coyotes bayed away some threat. The boys had left their instruments in Christ the Victor, but they didn't need them to sing, and the Celebrated Blackshear Boys did "Down in the Valley," starting in unison on the chorus then breaking into three-part harmony on the verses. Jack lit a cigar and began "Old Dan Tucker," but Michael wasn't having it and started to sing "The Yellow Rose of Texas," and Henry, in the same spirit came in five bars later with "Listen to the Mockingbird." The quodlibet grew dazzling, harmonies so tight a sunbeam couldn't glow between them. Even the horses seemed to clop out the right rhythm.

~You know, these are the good old days, said Henry, when they finished. My God, we're good.

~I need to fart, but I'm too tired, said Jack. Michael obliged him.

SNOW FOLLIES!

THURSDAY NEXT

AT WHAT'S LEFT OF THE EPISCOPAL CHURCH

THE CELEBRATED
BLACKSHEAR BOYS

(WHOEVER THEY ARE.)

Price Fifty Cents

MUSIC! SKITS! INSANITY!

DOORS OPEN AT 7.
THE TROUBLE BEGINS AT 8.

THE CHURCH WAS FULL BY seven-fifteen, and it was obvious the crowd would spill out of the chairs and into aisles, in the corners, fore and aft. The day before, the brothers, along with a growing group of helpers, had hung a curtain across half the altar so the acts would have a place from which to emerge. Torches lit the downtown streets for the first time in two years, a kind of roiling shudder went through the crowd as it huddled into the church. Annie and Portia sold tickets out front, took the money, which began to pile up in a type box from the ruins of the *Salterville Citizen*. Timmie Posey looked at it ruefully, noting aloud that it was a bad time to quit the outlaw business. Dozens of kerosene lamps lit the sanctuary, and old men who hadn't worn dress clothing in years sat there, dandy draft dodgers, tubby widows, young girls with dashes of ribbon wound through their hair. Even Mary and Lewis Geschnitz had buggied in. The weather held unseasonably warm for an early December evening, nearly forty degrees, and a glaze of cigar smoke iced the room. Reverend Potts considered complaining and then reconsidered, trying in his head to calculate his take.

~Girls, you ready? asked Henry. They were outside at the edge of the empty field tuning, listening, squeaking pegs up a thirtieth of a turn and then back.

~I'm not sure I'm drunk enough, said Jack. Wait—how does a man know when he's drunk enough?

~When he kisses his pig and gives his girl a bucket of mush? asked Michael.

~When he changes sides in the middle of a war? said Henry. Jack suddenly, on his guitar, erupted into the wildest, hairiest run his brothers had ever heard, bizarre, chromatic, and yet birdsong-beautiful.

~I'm drunk enough, said Jack.

Just before eight, the entire troupe—there was no other way to describe it—clotted behind the curtain. The crowd elbowed each other, festive and restive and noisy. Annie looked as if she would be sick, and she soundlessly sang the words to "The Little Irish Lad." Timmie Posey, dressed in a cheap double six-gun rig, practiced his drawing on Pigeon, who, as Mayor, would introduce the show. The audience began to shush itself, like a slowing snake. Jack, who had shaved all but a rich droopy mustache, grinned at his brothers.

~Remember that night in our parlor back home when we did the skit about Doc Pumphrey? he asked. We were pretty good for a bunch of morons.

~Bed the bitch, said Henry.

Pigeon had tied on two newer pans to his couture, but they were dented, too, and the dull lamplight caught him pleasantly as he came from behind the curtain to center stage. The audience applauded wildly. They looked at each other, not quite able to believe that pleasure had arrived back in town. Men drank openly from bottles and flasks beneath the baleful, disapproving stares of wives and lovers. Eulalia Fonce, painted beautifully, with cherry-red lips and a cloth carnation behind her left ear, whistled between her teeth. A vastly drunk young man from Mylin, a town three miles down the road, sat next to her, trying to tack straight, like a sailor in a storm. Eulalia grinned, showing red teeth, and Jack shuddered, made plans to find a more suitable Happy Woman.

~Oyez, oyez! cried Pigeon, holding up his arms. The crowd hushed itself. Now, you've heard tell that something's changing in our fair town. (*Lots of laughter and hisses.*) Did I said fair town? Well, the truth is Salterville's somewhere between hell and a greasepit. But I reckon tonight's it's first step out of the spitoon it's done become. Ladies and gentlemen, I give you, the Celebrated Blackshear Boys.

Jack, Michael, and Henry, in the Geschnitz brothers' Sunday suits, hair slick with pomade, ran out—literally ran—to a spot, gave a small leap, and landed on "Turner's Reel." The sanctuary of Christ the Victor almost literally exploded with screams and cheers. One lantern tipped, but a man named B. Otis Pace caught it. Here was Jack on guitar, Michael playing banjo, and Henry wildly scraping the fiddle. (*Near two hundred in the room, thought Rev. Plotts. Two hundred times, uh, equals, uh.*) The boys passed the lead around, each taking a romping turn, and they knew, instinctively, that this was the Perfect Night, their timing exquisite. Never had their tuning been sharper, their inventiveness more rococo. Jack went into a vamping strum on the guitar.

HENRY: I'm Henry Salterville Blackshear, and I'd like to welcome you to the last annual Snow Follies, though there doesn't seem to be any snow. But we reckoned nobody would come to the Partly Cloudy and Unseasonably Warm Follies.

MICHAEL: We'd also like to welcome all you Baptists and other heathens to Christ the Victor and say that if you're of another persuasion, you can walk up the street to the remains of the courthouse where Satan the Loser has a show going on.

JACK: We do benefits for all religions. We'd hate to blow the hereafter on a technicality.

HENRY: We've rehearsed so hard that I don't mind tell you even I feel old, and I'm the youngest.

JACK: I don't feel old. I don't feel *anything* until noon. That's when it's time for my nap.

(*We've got them. The audience literally howling, stamping. Oh God.*)

MICHAEL: We sing, we tell jokes, and we dance. Growing up as one of three brothers—that's how I learned to dance. Waiting for the bathroom.

HENRY: Our father down in Georgia told Jack first about the birds and the bees, and Jack dated a woodpecker until he was twenty-one.

JACK: But boy, could she dance!

They launched back into "Turner's Reel" and finished, and the crowd stood, roaring, unwilling to sit until the boys motioned for them to. The Blackshears, without waiting, did "Poor Wayfaring Stranger" and "Aura Lee." Women dabbed at their eyes with handkerchiefs and old men looked, lonely, at the floorboards. Before they had time to feel sad any longer, the brothers ended their set with a medley of "Turkey in the Straw" and "Whoa, Mule," and the audience would hardly let them go before Pigeon clanked back to the altar and introduced Annie. She trembled visibly, took a deep breath, leaned into Henry once, then came out from behind the blanket. Her sons, in the front row, cheered and whistled wildly, and she curtseyed to them.

> *I stand along the river, my heart quite filled with woe.*
> *The morning makes me shiver, the sunrise brings me low.*
> *For today I will be leaving the only love I had.*
> *Today's the day that they will hang The Little Irish Lad.*

The brothers played along softly behind her, a river of soft slow Irish sounds, and Annie's voice stunned and entranced the audience. Her accent, straight out of County Cork, made the song more poignant than anyone could believe. She glanced at the faces of Will and Robert, and they loved her wholly. The song, a traditional folk tune, had seven dolorous verses, but she sang only four, and when she'd finished, there was a beat of silence, then another, then another. Annie looked at Henry as if to shrug off the lack of a reaction, and was just angling back to the crowd when it erupted. The ovation was so loud and so long that she began to cry, had to hold it back as she curtseyed. Damp-eyed Henry. Grinning Jack.

JACK: Come to order, come to order! We, the Congress of the Confederate States of America, are here to vote on whether Salterville, P. A., should become the capitol of these rogue states for the remainder of our current war. Mr. Speaker, can you tell us why Salterville should be the capitol?

MICHAEL: (*Thumbs in an invisible vest*) Sir comma isn't it self-evident question mark?

JACK: You don't have to talk like a document, Mr. Speaker.

MICHAEL: You may be right, semi-colon; but what comma is the use of a thing if it's not to be written down question mark? Ahem. I'll restrain myself period. Why should Salterville be the center of our new country? First of all, it's falling to pieces. Much of it's been burned. There's a piegon in the attic of the defunct newspaper office and a Pigeon in the mayor's chair. Crime and corruption are rampant. (*Timmie Posey comes out, wearing his six guns, pointed boots, and a lady's gingham bonnet. He stands behind the Blackshears, who pretend they don't know what the screeching and stamping laughter is about. Then they turn.*)

HENRY: I'm the Segeant-at-Arms. Who in the devil are you, sir?

TIMMIE: I'm a bad outlaw, and I'm here to tell everyone why Salterville should be capitol of what's left of these mostly un-Confederated States. (*Giggling, and Timmie in shock that he's funny. He's relaxing.*)

JACK: You have the floor.

TIMMIE: Good. I've never lived in a house with a floor. My latest house doesn't have a ceiling or walls, neither. It's the Salt County Courthouse. Anyway, here's my story. (*Coming to the front, clearing his throat, standing with his legs spread wide, an actor's declamatory pose.*)

> *Now outlaws come and outlaws go, and the decent folk do cry*
> *That a gal like me will leave them be, and let them live and sigh.*
> *But they've never seen a meaner girl nor one to make them pray*
> *Like the homely lass of spit and sass named Virginia Doris May.*

They sat forward on their chairs. Jack and Henry had written it the week before over a crock of ripely fermented cider, and to their astonishment, Timmie had read it once then recited it, word for word, without a mistake. The poem stretched to fifteen quatrains and was the story of a woman bandit who asks, at each bank she robs, for all their money and a kiss. At first, towns are afraid of Virginia Doris May, but then word spreads that she is the best kisser east of the Mississippi, and bankers start putting out banners, welcoming her to town and chewing mint, waiting. Timmie raised his hands for the last verse:

> *Now outlaws come and outlaws go, but the decent folk embrace*
> *The kissing thief who brings relief to dreary nights and days.*
> *For what is cash but beans and hash if love is unforgiving?*
> *The answer's this: To steal a kiss is what makes life worth living.*

The applause was so loud that Timmie's wet, red face grew seraphic, and he ran into the audience and kissed Eulalia Fonce on the mouth to the titters and giggles of men and the disapproving clucks of some women.

The show lasted just under two hours. There were skits about Pigeon and the Bickerstaff brothers, the scandalous Minnie Penny song, another solo by Annie. The crowd didn't want to go home, but it finally did, and not long after eleven, the torches downtown had all been extinguished, and the Blackshear brothers sat in the church, whose windows had been opened to let out the fog of smoke.

~Looks like a battle took place in here, said Jack, chomping on an unlit cigar. Rev. Plotts sat greedily in the corner counting the take, with Portia Washington watching him. I haven't seen this much smoke since Malvern Hill.

THE WINTER FINALLY CAME. HOWLING snowstorms blew down from the north and west, and the Blackshears became housebound at the Geschnitz house. Mary and Lewis had loved the show, but in mid-February Mary awoke with a scratchy throat and by that night was extremely ill. Jack rode his mount through the fetlock-deep snow to town to fetch Salterville's unreliable doctor, but when they returned, Mary could not breathe. She lay soaked in sweat and staring at the boys, a faint smile at the edges of her mouth. Her eyes began to wander. Eliot played hymns on the piano, and the Blackshear brothers sang through the night, but Mary died quietly just after six the following morning.

~She's never been well since her sons didn't come home, said Dr. Maynard. Lewis sat, dry-eyed at his wife's bedside while the exhausted Blackshear brothers and the doctor rested at the table in the kitchen. Anything can take you when you've given up hope. Whole town's been like that. No hope. Whole country's ruined. Sometimes a person brings a bit of light, but it always goes out in a town like Salterville. Let me ask you boys something. Why is it that smart southern men still say the war's not about slavery?

~A patriotic lie's the easiest kind, said Jack. Michael and Henry turned at the sound of his voice: so unlike Jack. Politicians always lie about why wars start. They'll say somebody's dangerous, and they just keep saying it until they convince themselves it's true. Then weak-minded people start believing it's true, and before you know it, thousands are dying. Of *course* it's about slavery. Don't get me wrong. The South has good things about it. Fine days in the spring and fall, men and women with talent to write and perform. There's a Negro piano player named Blind Tom who's a better musician than any of us will ever be. And yet poor people let rich people convince them slavery was in their best interest. It was a lie. It's always a lie.

~It's not like you to wax philosophical, said Henry.

~I have my reasons for things, said Jack, but I just try to keep them private. But I tell you something. There are right wars, too. And in both kinds, if the soldiers can't have a song or a joke, if they can't feel relief from the terror, if only for a couple of hours, there's no God by my reckoning.

~I never got any relief from your songs or jokes, said Michael. The doctor smoked a cigar and stared at them.

~Me, neither, said Henry. Frankly, I think you're generally useless. I've been thinking of going out on my own. The Celebrated Blackshear Boy. It has a nice ring.

~The Michael Blackshear and Pigeon Fonce Follies and Minstrelsy, said Michael, tapping the table.

~This isn't the time for levity, said Dr. Maynard darkly.

~A man, a cat, and a kangaroo walk into a bar, said Henry. The man says, Give us each a whiskey before this one gets jumpy or that one lets the fur fly.

~That wasn't funny, said Jack, grinning.

~I found it effervescent, a witty bit of traditional repartee, said Michael. A bouquet of light-hearted lunacy.

~You boys are crazy, said the doctor, oomphing on his cigar.

Winter was a long time leaving.

WAR'S END

Travelers on the stagecoach route brought newspapers the next spring, and the war news was encouraging one day, despairing the next. The Blackshears tried to follow the progress of General William Tecumseh Sherman's troops as they plowed down Georgia, but the action grew fierce and steady, heading, everyone knew, for the town of Atlanta.

The brothers didn't have time to worry about the war, since they began to work hard on crops long before the first thaw. Eliot Yellowhawk had left one night when the weather was warming, the only evidence a note on the table that read, I'm gone home. It was time. Lewis pretended it did not bother him, but Jack knew it did. At least the Blackshears had half a day off Saturday and all day Sunday, and they all rode into Salterville, which, even in the middle of a war, was rising from its own ashes.

Men, women, and boys cleaned up the ruins of the courthouse and planted a huge garden smack in the middle of downtown. Teams repaired the potholes, and bearded old gentlemen in overalls painted the town. A man named Leroy Perkins from Boston re-opened the *Salterville Citizen*, even though newsprint was expensive and hard to obtain. Christ the Victor was decomissioned as a church and re-established as Plotts Hall, and the Blackshears began to perform on Saturday nights. By mid-June, they had made so much money they decided to leave the farm and move into town.

~I knowed it was coming, said Lewis Geschnitz quietly. A man thinks he's losing everything, then the ceiling falls in.

~If you're talking about the courthouse, the ceiling fell in last year, said Henry. The crops were all planted, the fields rich and ripening.

~I'm gone write my brother in Ohio, see if he will bring his family back. He's got three boys and a girl.

~What about a wife? asked Jack.

~I had one, don't want another, snapped Lewis.

~I think he meant does your brother from Ohio have a wife, said Michael. A hunting hawk cried from the clear blue late spring sky, riding thermals across southern Pennsylvania.

~Did, said Lewis. Don't now. She run off with a tent-preacher.

~And lo, the reverend giveth, and selah, he taketh away, said Jack. Amen.

~Weren't funny, said Lewis. Fella was a fat little old man with one horse and a gray beard.

~In my experience, women are always suckers for bearded horses, said Henry.

Lewis said he'd never forgive them, but when it came time to go, he gave them the horses they had been riding and a twenty-dollar gold piece each.

THEY BOUGHT AN ABANDONED HOUSE from the Town Council for twenty dollars and set about hammering and sawing it into shape. It was on Madison Street, just east of the square and two blocks from Plotts Hall. They worked from first light to last for three weeks, then sat back one Friday evening and looked at it.

~Looks like the place has typhus, said Jack.

~Measles, said Michael. Pneumonia. Scabies.

~Erysipelas, contributed Henry. Scurvy. Smallpox.

Timmie Posey rode up on his swayback mare, leaped off, caught his boot in the stirrup, and fell face-first into the overgrown grass that bearded the lot. He swore decoratively, sat up and rubbed his leg.

~I've got to steal another horse, he said. That one don't stand still on his feet while one's getting down.

~We hang horse thieves in these parts now, said Jack. The new Salterville. Where crime still pays but only for lawyers, bankers, and politicians.

~The house looks worst than it did afore you started working on it, said Timmie. Maybe you boys ain't cut out for carpenters. My brothers can carpenter. In the months since they'd moved to Salterville, the other Poseys, Dougal and Daniel, had never yet come to town. Here's you book back. He pulled a slim, broken-back volume from his pocket and threw it to Henry.

~Did you look at the part yet?

~I done learned it all, said Timmie.

~I don't believe it! shouted Jack. It takes me weeks! He cleared his throat and said: Here is the scroll of every man's name, which is thought fit, through all Athens, to play in our interlude before the duke and duchess, on his wedding-day night.

~First, good Peter Quince, said Timmie, standing up and limping to the horse and tying it to a bush, say what the play treats on, then read the names of the actors, and so grow to a point.

~Marry, our play is the most lamentable comedy, and most cruel death of Pyramus and Thisby, said Jack archly.

~A very good piece of work, drawled Timmie, I assure you, and a merry. Now, good Peter Quince, call forth your actors by the scroll. Masters, spread yourselves.

~I'll be goddamn, said Michael. You learned the whole part in two days? Nobody in the world has a memory like that.

~I'm changing the man's name, though, said Timmie. There's no way in hell I'm parading myself before them othern with a name like Bottom.

~It's Shakespeare, you roving ignoramus, said Henry. Bottom's a great character. If there's ever been a perfect Bottom, it's you.

~The Bard in Salterville, said Henry. What is this war coming to?

~Oh. Mr. Pigeon says he read we're near to Atlanta. And Grant's in Virginia.

~Virginia—God, the very name causes me to break out in dance, said Jack. Or eczema. Some of our greatest performances didn't take place in Old Virginia! Or what's left of it. We saw half of it die on the last day of the Gettysburg fight.

~Bright maiden, we came here to forget the war, said Henry.

~If he's a maiden, I'm going *back* to the war, said Michael.

Getting enough townspeople to play parts in *A Midsummer Night's Dream* had been easy. The town, it turned out, was theatrically mad, and traveling actors began to stop for shows, and so far the only one to fail was a temperance play called *One Drink Too Many*. Afterwards, Norris Bickerstaff stood outside Plotts Hall and said, memorably, To watch that, one drink ain't remotely *enough*. Afterward, Jack and Henry began writing a play called *One Drink Won't Do*, but they'd bogged down in the third act.

~Hey, who are you? asked Jack. A boy of about nine or ten, small and rickettsy, had wandered up barefooted, his thatch hair sticking out wildly from a straw hat. The child stopped and scratched his waist, sighed, and looked around.

~Well, this ain't much bettern where I lived in Philadelphia, he said. But I reckon I can get used to it. My feet hurt like a sore hoof on a splayed mule. I thought they was only three Celebrated Blackshears. I can count.

~Child, I regret to inform you this is not a boarding house, and you are not a guest, and we are not innkeepers, said Jack.

~I've walked here for ten days on the open road eatin' roots and newts, the boy said. He pushed back the hat, and he wore freckles like a constellation across his cheeks. Something mild and winning: a genuine warmth. But the bony face, the hunger of it! A wonder I didn't get eat by a wild dog or a lion.

~Let me play the lion, too, declaimed Timmie Posey. I will roar, that I will do any man's heart good to hear me; I will roar, and then I will make the Duke say, Let him roar again, let him roar again! The Blackshears and the boy stood for a long moment staring at Timmie.

~And you should do it too terribly, you would fright the duchess and the ladies, that they would shriek, said Jack. And that were enough to hang us all.

~Would you girls please stop with the Shakespeare and let us get the boy some food and hear his story? said Henry.

~I've arrove to be another Blackshear, no matter how many of you they is, said the boy. I seen the Christy Minstrels, and I didn't sleep for three days I got so excited. They wouldn't take me on, so I read about you fellers and decided to come.

~Read about us? said Michael.

~In the *Inquirer*, the boy said. Man came through here and saw you perform, said you were the new Hutchinson brothers. Henry felt an electric thrill: The Hutchinsons, Asa, John, and Judson, formed the best-known family singing act in America beginning more than a decade before the war. Judson had died in 1859, only forty-two, but they soldiered on. Their younger sister, Abby, sang with them sometimes, and they'd been famous for twenty years, and had become friends with Longfellow, Frederick Douglass, William Lloyd Garrison, and even President Lincoln.

~The Hutchinsons! said Michael. They're against slavery and in favor of temperance. They're in the right by half, at least.

~I'll drink to that, said Jack. Michael got the boy, whose name was U. E. Clifton, some dried beef, a loaf of hard bread, and a large glass of cold well water.

~Tell us your story, lad, starting with why you're called U. E., said Henry. The boy ate ravenously for two minutes, nodding all the time, then finally began. He's almost starving, thought Henry. Poor child.

~The initials don't mean nothing, said U. E. Momma said they are her two favorites vowels. Said *A*, *I*, and *O* give her hives. Jack smiled, glanced with delighted at his brothers. Maybe this *might* be another Blackshear. Timmie flipped out his pocketknife and began to carve on a dried stick, wiping off long and longer slices.

U. E. told them of growing up in the cramped cellar rooms of a house in a dank, crowded part of town, where his mother mended and danced. He'd never known his father, who apparently had been passing through town just long enough to help conceive him.

~Wait, you say she mended and danced? asked Michael.

~For the Raleigh Theatre, said U. E. She made costumes and mended them, danced in shows that needed dancers. Sometimes she danced for parties at men's houses and such. Henry looked at Michael, wanting to see Annie, to hold her. This was a dark story, but U. E. didn't seem to mind telling it.

~You say *made*, said Jack. Is she doing something else now?

~She died over the winter, he said. Her cheeks got red, and then the cough come, and she was dead in three days. I couldn't do nothing. I went to Mr. Thrash of the Raleigh, and he said they was nothing he could do, neither. Turned me out. Mama gasped herself to death during a snowstorm. I didn't know what to do. I watched her lay there being dead for four days afore I could get out. I found a police who took it away. Then they come for the rent, and so I left. He chewed thoughtfully. Yeah. She was a Southerner, like you all.

~She what? asked Henry. Wait—what did you do from the time she died until you came here?

~Street performer, he said. Dance, juggle, sing. I sneaked into shows and stole the jokes and steps. But I needed better learning. Then I read the article and thought I could come learn from you all. Mama said my name like *Euwee*. You can call me that. But I'll come to anything.

~Where was she from? asked Michael.

~Georgia, he said. Athens, Georgia. Clifton's a name she picked. Her real name they beat her up for being a Jew. It was Bernstein.

The Blackshears looked at each other. Timmie finished whittling the stick, got another, started in on it.

~We're from a town less than thirty miles from there, and one of our best friends was named David Bernstein, said Henry quietly. Didn't they have family in Athens? Can either of you remember? Jack and Michael couldn't, but maybe they did. Michael nodded: Yes. Certainly they must have. Do you know what her family did or why she came to Philadelphia?

~She said her daddy run a clothes store, said Euwee. He sent her north for her education, but then the war come, and then I did. She never saw her family again. Henry turned suddenly teary. Euwee looked at him. It's a common story.

~How many things can you juggle? asked Jack. We have to put on good shows or they might hang us.

~I grant you, friends, if that you should fright the ladies our of their wits, they would have no more discretion but to hang us, said Timmie.

~Bottom, for God's sake, would you please save the Shakespeare for the stage? asked Henry.

~I'm up to four, and almost have five, said Euwee. Jack looked dubious. Okay. Euwee looked on the ground and retrieved a stone, a smashed square nail, and one of the shoes Henry had taken off to air his feet. This is only three. Oh. He walked to the well house and got the spare bucket, which was made of heavy wood and needed patching.

~Wait—you're going to juggle a bucket, a nail, a rock, and a shoe? asked Jack. Here comes an audience. Pigeon came clanking down the street and walked up next to the house.

~What's that? asked Euwee.

~That's the mayor, said Jack. Doesn't Philadelphia have a mayor?

~Philadelphia? said Pigeon. I be dog.

~The boy can juggle four items, said Jack. Give me two bits, and I'll let you watch.

~I come to condemn your house, but I reckon I could be bought off for two bits, said Pigeon.

~The mayor of Philadelphia can't be *that* wise, said Jack, bowing. Okay, boy. Show us what you can do.

Euwee was like a limber stick, nearly boneless. He began to dance, cradling the four items in his arms, feet tapping the bare dusty yard, shuffling, heel and toe. He started to hum and began tossing the shoe and the stone up and down, hand to hand. His voice had not yet broken, and there was a sweetness about him that was undeniable. He started to sing a novelty piece the brothers hadn't heard, something called "Hobbling Joe," about a tramp who went town to town dancing for his money with trained dog named Molly. Jack looked at Michael and raised one thick eyebrow. Suddenly, subtly, as if it was a soliloquoy that had begun in silence, Euwee was juggling bucket, shoe, rock, and nail.

~I'll be goddamned, offered Pigeon. Michael ran inside and came back out with his banjo, calculated the key, and began to play behind the child, whose face flushed bright with joy. He began to make strange cross-passes with the juggled items, taking the nail behind his back, the stone overhand, throwing the bucket high and lofting the other three items before the pail dropped, perfectly, into his waiting hand. Jack and Henry started to clap in time. "Hobbling Joe" had fourteen verses. The boy's voice had a gorgeous, aching edge to it. Two women walking to town stopped in the street and watched and listened. Finally, after nearly five minutes of it, Euwee put the bucket under his right arm and kept juggling the nail, rock, and shoe, until each fell in perfect order and landed in the bucket as the song ended. Jack sat on a stump.

~So, he said, looking at Euwee in disbelief. How much was it you said you charge for lessons?

~Euwee Blackshear, the lost sheep of the family, said Henry.

~Girls, we're in big trouble, said Michael happily.

The boy moved in with them. Portia and Annie liked him, and Euwee began to play with Annie's sons, teaching them to do a hip-flinging dance he called the "Hottentot Half-Step." Euwee's only real problem was an inclination to thievery, and each day he'd wander home with new marbles, a red hat with a feather, even a book called *Great Events By Great Historians.* Jack wrote Euwee into the show and had him onstage one week from the day he showed up. The reaction of the hall was riotous. Euwee even taught the Blackshears a ballad they'd never heard, a Scottish tune of unfaithful love and murder called "Ethan Grove." He did it in the dark key of B minor, which wasn't easy on the stringed instruments and forced Henry to play a fiddle solo in the background. The effect was stupefying. The first time Annie heard it in the Blackshear's side yard, she wept.

That July, General William T. Sherman's troops closed in on Atlanta, probing through the environs, closing off Confederate options. Before long, it would fall, and then the Confederacy's tenuous history would split apart, head toward decline.

~I do miss playing for the troops, said Michael one evening. He worked on a portrait of Portia with colored pencils on Ingres paper he'd ordered from New York City. It was an amazing feeling to perform for people who suffered so much. They never knew if they'd still be alive the next night. Sometimes I wonder if maybe your husband might have heard us in the night. Sometimes we heard Union bands playing. Down on the Peninsula in Virginia, we'd play back and forth to each other.

The sound of footsteps on the porch, then coming inside: Jack. The eldest Blackshear's face was twisted, and Michael couldn't read it.

~There's a cavalry detachment from somewhere, and they've got Henry at the Hall, he said. Five of them. They're asking him questions about whether he was a Confederate soldier. Euwee came walking in wearing a light jacket he didn't have earlier in the day. A woman's coat.

~Federals? asked Michael, standing.

~Yep. I saw them taking him inside, then I looked through the window. They've got him. Doesn't look like a regular outfit. Something's wrong. A drinking crew.

~I'm in, said Michael, standing. Portia put her hand on Michael's arm, almost as if to hold him back, but he shook her off, touched her cheek gently, and was gone. He and Jack walked in the cool darkness down the dog-trotted street. Euwee stayed close.

~We've got to get him out of there, said Jack. Somebody's told them who we are. Michael had brought his rifle, and Jack had two pistols stuck in his waist band. Goddamn this war.

~I could kill them, said Euwee. Give me a gun. I would shoot them dead. The air grew suddenly hush, and a sharp wind bore down on them.

HENRY HAD BEEN SITTING BY himself in Plotts Hall, writing a skit about General Grant and General Lee meeting in a game of quoits to settle the war once and for all. He liked the ambiance, and its connection to their shows made him feel more creative. Earlier, he'd spent the evening with Annie. They had writhed in a sexual embrace the evening before, but he also liked this slow courting, even though she was a widow with two children.

~What's it like in the South? asked Annie. They sat on the steps of her house while the boys chased fireflies, clapped them into fruit jars.

~Different, said Henry. People up here probably think everybody down there owns slaves and foams at the mouth, has pellagra, and can't spell.

~I always thought that, said Annie.

~Very funny. Most people there are like most people here. The rich don't much care for anybody but the rich. The poor whites look down on the blacks. Everybody has some group to hate. The whole society's based on whose higher on this ladder. That's why the poor whites are the ones who hate the Negroes the most. They have only a tenuous hold on the ladder, and they're terrified the blacks will pull them off. The war was just a series of lies that the wealthy planters kept saying until, to them, it came true. What I've seen—my God, nobody should see it. I'm not saying I think every person from here is more moral than we are in the South. Salterville's a pretty sorry place. But slavery and race hatred is what this war is about. A hundred years from now, some Southerners will still be saying the same things. Pride, ignorance, fear, stupidity, maliciousness. In the end, it was a place I didn't fit. I have no idea why I was born a Southerner. But all we ever wanted to do was perform. And doing that for the troops...God how I loved those boys.

He choked up, went silent. Out there in the browning grass: boys haloed by rings of lightning bugs. They seemed to have grown in the months since the Blackshears had settled on the Geschnitz farm.

~Sometimes I wake up in the night, and I reach out to touch my husband's arm, said Annie. I always did that, especially if there was no moon out and it was dark. I just wanted to feel that he was next to me. Or I'd listen to hear him breathing. It made me feel safe. I just wanted to be sure of him. I guess he died for the good of it all. Some days I don't know. The last thing in the world I ever thought I'd do is get so close to a boy from the South. I would have said it couldn't happen. Rebels killed my sweet husband. This whole town had rotted down to nothing. Then you boys brought us back to life. I want to live now, and not just for my sons.

Henry was quiet for a very long time, and he finally left and walked through town, but he didn't want to go home yet. They'd come so far. The big house in Branton was filmy in memory, and the battles and shows with Cobb's Legion some tale told by another. He walked to Plotts Hall, opened it the front door, went in. His boots clomped hollow on the floorboards, and the half-moon lit a path to the collected lamps and matchboxes. Henry lit two lamps, got out a quill pen and some ink, slices of cream-colored paper they kept in an old desk. Often Michael or Jack would roam here alone to write, sitting in the cricket-silence to study words, to think of some rancid gag or perky song. Nothing was easier to them or less explicable to others.

The skit wasn't funny, and he kept writing lines, scratching them out. Maybe some things were so horrible there was no humor in them, even the kind of acid wit that made men cringe. Truth was what made humor work—they all knew that. In general, humans were worse than fallible. They were envious, devious, deceitful, and jealous. Jack was an incorrigible womanizer. Someone would shoot him someday. Michael held the world by its shapes and colors in the palm of his right hand. *Who, then, am I?*

The heavy, clod-flipping trod of horses, several, at a near-canter in the road, coming to a stop out front. Shouted commands, leather creaking, drunken groans. They burst into the Hall, saw the young man to one side at a small desk, looking up, with the clear lines of his face in the lamplight.

~Hoss, you in a goddamn mess of trouble, said a corporal. He was squat and filthy, with a beard that grew nearly to his eyes. There were four others, but one took three steps, fell over a chair, and didn't rise. You Secesh trash think you can just up and move here and not be shot, do ye?

~Come on Drummond, said one of the others, a scratching man with a skunk's stripe of gray in his hair. Let's get on back before roll call. I've stood picket as much as I want to.

~We will get back, but first, we got this Rebel boy to try. How do you plead, shit-face?

~I'm not part of the war anymore, Henry said. Leave me alone.

~Everbody's part of the war, hoss, said Drummond, taking out his pistol and cocking it. You think you can just come here and start putting on plays and get your names in the papers, and nobody's gone hold you to account for killing Federals? Now Burt, ain't that precious?

~Shit, Drummond, let's get out of here, said the soldier with the stripe in his hair. Lieutenant said he'd have us arrested.

~Garwell's passed out, said one of the others, kicking the fallen soldier with his boot and getting no reaction.

~Where'd you serve? asked Drummond, standing so close Henry could see the blear bloodshot tracks in the whites of his eyes. Nothing. Goddamnit, boy, I axed you a question. He slammed his fist into Henry's stomach, and the youngest Blackshear fell, doubled, to his knees.

~Shit, Drummond, said Burt.

~Hoss, I find you guilty and sentence you to death at the end of my pistol, said Drummond. Stand yourself up like a man.

~You go to hell, said Henry. I've seen lice that were better men than you. Garwell suddenly sat up, laughed and giggled, then passed out again, landed with a heavy crump.

Jack, Michael, and Euwee had by this time reached the Hall and came softly up the front stairs in a thin wash of moonlight.

~We should stay quiet and see if we can get them with their guard down, whispered Michael. Jack nodded, then kicked in the door with the bottom of his shoe, so hard that it fell half off the hinges.

Later, no one could quite say that happened next. The sound of shoutings, men knocking over chairs, clank of swords and sidearms. Garwell humped up and vomited. Screaming, posturing, then the first gunshot, utterly shocking and deafening. The flash of gunfire, all going off at once, and three of the soldiers running out, mounting, kicking off and getting away. Then, as if a curtain pulled back and revealed a tableau of some historical scene, there was a smoky silence. People in nearby houses were out with their shotguns, men in nightcaps, boys wild-haired and gleeful.

Jack stood there holding his rifle, trying to untangle the scene. The soldier named Drummond lay on his back with a bullet wound through the neck. The gash still pumped, and his arms milled. Then he sighed, shuddered, and lay dead. Another soldier, heart-wounded, was dead already, eyes shut, as if he slept. Henry sat on the floor near the desk, still holding his quill pen and looking back and forth, face to face. Michael and Jack came in and back up and around looking for others. He had knocked Drummond out of the way when he'd turned to fire at Jack and Michael. Falling, Drummond shot Henry.

~Why in the hell did you do that? asked Michael.

~I didn't fire the first shot, said Jack.

~That one did, said Henry, pointing to Drummond. You know what? I think he shot me. If that's not a hell of a note. Henry's face suddenly paled. The pen fluttered out of his hand, and he reached inside his shirt and seemed to press himself, then took his palm out and read the bright arterial stain. Yep. Shot me. Oh my God.

He tried to stand, but the strength was not in him. Michael and Jack came, ripped open his shirt and saw a wound in his right side that had blown out two ribs and part of a lung. They heard a pattering sound and turned to see that Euwee was wetting himself. Men now coming into the Hall, guns drawn, and words, at first separate—*damn, God, shit*—then sentences, questions, calls for help. Two of them were striking matches—*scratch* and *hiss*. Lit kerosene lamps by the pairs, checked the dead soldiers, came to Henry Blackshear, who lay back now in Jack's arms.

~Press on it, said Jack. Michael took his light jacket off and held it to the wound, but it was massive.

~Said they knew we had been Rebels, said Henry. They—*God*. He gasped and flinched, closed his eyes, and then opened them again. Wasn't a formal detachment. Just some drunk cavalry men. What happened? I can't get my breath.

~It's soaking through! cried Michael. Goddamn it, it's soaking through!

~Dear God, said Pigeon, who was standing there in his trousers, longjohns beneath, one suspender hanging down like a dead thing. Henry, by God.

Henry felt lightheaded and strangely calm. The pain had not come yet. An odd rushing sensation, as if going backward, then forward, life to life, place to place. He shucked the need to live, supped on what breath he could catch. It was like a dream of America. He saw the hot streets of Branton, the heavy curtains his mother had hung in the front parlor. He heard the tramp of soldiers up Virginia, the battle at Crampton's Gap. He thought David Bernstein was kneeling nearby, burning like a campfire. Strangest things.

~David's...he's got a...said Henry.

~Quieten down, said Jack. You saved us, Henry. You did it.

Henry felt as if the moonlight held blessings. He sipped the autumn air, but he was near the bottom of the glass. Now flying over mountains and rivers, whitewashed streams, hearing horses pounded on an anvil with a rhythmic clanking that turned into "Turner's Reel." The girls of home, Annie cradling him with her spent and naked body. The Blackshears turned small boys again, in deep trouble and not minding. Then the hissing of the firecracker as it burned upward toward the dancing master who was afraid of mad dogs. But music mostly, skeins of it, every song ever sung now coming at him, deep strong men's voices, rich altos, heart-rending sopranos. Choirs.

~*I hear it*, said Henry. He looked up at Jack, then out at Michael who knelt in front of him. Something amazing was about to happen. He knew it. He had never in his life felt such a calm, joyous moment.

FALL CAME, BLAZED INTO ORANGE and gold and crimson, then turned white with the winter's snow. Michael took Henry's death hard, and for the longest time, he could not find enough emotion to reach for Portia. They would sit in her parlor silently, she reading a book, Michael brooding. For months he didn't even try to draw a line. The people of the town had hurriedly buried the dead soldiers in a wood nearby, covered the graves with rocks, debris, and deadfall, agreed never to admit they'd been there. But no one came.

Jack drank. He began drinking first thing in the morning and sipped until he collapsed at night. He took walks in the leaves and then in the snow. They had buried Henry in the town cemetery, even ordered a marble marker, but it never arrived, and the money was lost. When Jack had walked to Annie's house and told her, she began to scream piteously and cry, and her sons huddled around her, also weeping. After the funeral, she gathered what she could, hired a wagon, and left for Philadelphia, but she moved back three weeks later. She walked to Henry's grave each day, sat and talked to him while the boys played, at first in leaves and later in snow.

~Funny, said Michael one night. He and Jack sat near the potbellied stove in their small house. Euwee was on the floor playing mumbleypeg with a knife he had found earlier that week. It was February, 1865, and the moonbright snow made the house seem light, even though only one lamp burned. A hundred years from now, we won't even be a track in the snow. *Nothing.* We won't have ever existed. And those thousands dead in the war. They might be a name on a muster roll, if they haven't lost all the muster rolls by then. I can't think if I've done anything with my life that's worth a damn.

~You haven't, said Jack.

~I'm puttin' holes in you floor, said Euwee.

~Fine by me, said Michael.

~Do it, said Jack.

~And yet, sometimes I think that maybe those people who just distract others from life and death do something worthwhile, too, said Michael. Poor Henry. The only thing he really wanted was to grow old, and he was the first of us to go. And for nothing. Not a goddamn thing.

~My ma went for not a goddamn thing, either, said Euwee.

~I think *you*'ve found the meaning of life, slurred Jack, sipping. And Henry was a hero. I guess that means I'll live a long life.

~My money says you won't live past this Sunday if you don't lay off the grog, said Michael. You think we could do a show, just the two of us?

By then, Annie was expecting Henry's baby, which would come in the summer.

THE WAR ENDED THAT APRIL, the gnarled remnants of Robert E. Lee's command finally falling apart in Virginia. Michael wrote their parents and told them of Henry's death, and an anguished reply came a month later from Cassandra, their red-haired mother. Their father took it badly, raged and wept.

~He has decided that we will come to you, she wrote. I am enclosing sufficient money for you to purchase or build us a house in town. We will come up in time for Henry's child. Father already has a purchaser for the Mercantile, and Mr. Tankeray, a retiring professor from the Franklin College, has agreed to buy our house. Branton is a sad place with the war lost. Rev. Merrill, who killed himself, left a son named Charlie who left us, just a boy, to fight for the South. But he came home, and now he wanders around, thinking. This is a terrible time, and I cannot but believe it was all for nought. This town has lost the best of its next generation. I am unsure the South will recover, not in a century's time. So we shall come to you. Mama Blackshear sends her love. The parrot yet lives and will come as well.

Michael was delighted, and the gloom seemed to lift for the first time since Henry's death. He and Jack wrote a new skit, complete with a few Scottish duets, and they put it on in June at Plott's Hall. Timmie Posey performed with them for the last time.

~I'm moving to New York City, he said, when he came by one day. He still supposedly had two brothers in the country, but they had attained the level of myth. I will be on the stage there. I think I can amount to something. I want to amount to something.

~Don't you worry about that, said Jack, chewing on a cigar. I can promise it will never happen.

But it did. Timmie changed his name to James Harwood, and for the next forty years was one of the most celebrated actors in America, visiting Europe several times. He became extremely rich, married a Vanderbilt girl, and never once returned to Salterville. He played Hamlet, Iago, Richard III, hundreds more.

Annie bore her third son, Henry's boy, on July 3, and she named him Michael Henry Blackshear, but later everyone would call him Bud.

~I know I don't have any legal right to the Blackshear name, but he has to have it, she said, cradling the baby, who was born with a headful of bristly black hair. I'll have it legally changed.

~I wish Henry was here now, said Michael. He was sketching mother and child in the summer noonlight, the child discreetly nursing. What a pointless thing. My God.

~We all have to die, said Annie. It's not what we do in life, Michael. It's the dignity with which we live and die. That's all that matters. She began to sing "The Little Irish Lad" quietly, rocking side to side. Michael could not stop adding luminous details, and the sketch became a work of art. If it had not been for Portia Washington, Michael Blackshear might have loved her.

THE WEDDING WAS SET FOR October 1. Mama Blackshear was convinced that it was a funeral, and she started dressing in black and made a crepe armband. King Lear, moth-eaten and foul-mouthed, kept crying Kiss her! Kiss the girl! and worse. Cassandra glowed with joy, while her husband drank too much and worked on a huge canvas called *The Entrance of Jefferson Davis into Hell*, a picture that seemed ghastly and whimsical at the same time.

The house, on Main Street just east of the town square, had belonged to a wealthy merchant before the war but had fallen into disrepair, and when Michael bought it for his parents, pigs resided on both floors. Soon, carpenters and masons had returned it to its glory, and the furnishings from Georgia began to arrive by rail, including the piano, beds, and plush furniture.

~I'm going to sing the Minnie Penny song as a solo, said Jack. He was drinking in the first blush of autumn as well as a bottle of brandy.

~Are you *ever* going to settle down yourself? asked Michael. They were in the house they still shared for now, but Michael was moving out, into Portia's home. Already, he was working as an assistant editor of the *Salterville Citizen*. It wasn't much money, but it sufficed for now.

~I like being free and easy, said Jack. Besides, I have a new girl-friend.

~You do? I haven't heard anything about this. What's her name?

~Iris Minton, said Jack proudly. Michael stared blankly at him. What a girl!

~Jack, Iris is a whore, said Michael.

~She *what?* shouted Jack, jumping up. I'll kill the man who says that! I'll invite him to a duel with pistols! I'll…wait, you're right. She *is* a whore. But what man ever had to worry about a prostitute being unfaithful? I tell you, Michael, a woman who can put her feet behind her head is one of God's miracles.

Michael and his mother walked to the cemetery a few days before the wedding. She was still strong and tall, but her hair was streaked with gray, and you could see the war and Henry's death in her eyes. They'd left her husband painting and drinking, proclaiming loudly that he was the greatest artist since Michelangelo, even if he had turned Yankee.

~Branton was a terrible place to be as the war dragged on, she said. Always those dispatches about the dead. All the boys, almost all of them, died. I've thought a lot about what happened to my own sons, and I regret none of it, Michael. What a terrible waste for Henry to die like that. And Jack—he's going to live a short life if he doesn't live more slowly, I fear. But mostly I have no regrets. I don't know why God made you boys so wild and so talented at the same time.

~Probably just tinkering in his off-hours, said Michael.

~Is Jack going to get a job? How is he making a living?

~You know, I'm not really sure. I think there are women who give him money. That would be like Jack, I'm afraid. He goes out and works for Mr. Geschnitz sometimes, comes home sunburned and loud. He may flame out quickly, but he gives off a pretty good light.

~All my sons do, she said. Even that one. He still does.

The stone had finally come, and the boys had planted it a few weeks before. It was plain marble, three feet wide and six feet long, and it lay on Henry and said: *Henry Blackshear, 1842-1865. He gave joy to all the world.* Cassandra threaded her arm through Michael's.

~He was our conscience, said Michael. The one thing he always wanted was to grow old. He would have been a sweet old man. We don't always get what we dream. Sometimes dreams get mixed up, and we get someone else's. But he lived every day of his life. How many men can you say that about?

~You, your brother, and your father, too, she said. She smiled easily. So many people just don't have much life in them. They hang on and on, and they don't know why. Just talk talk and talk. Then they die.

~Like King Lear, said Michael.

~Actually, I think he's enjoyed his life, too, said Cassandra. Her eyes grew dark. Every man who started that war who's still alive should be lined up and shot. The fools who held humans as chattel, who found it so easy to sway the ignorant. If I have one prayer it is that in the future our wars be just. But they won't all be.

~Henry's got a good view anyway, said Michael. It was true. The cemetery lay on a ridge softened by oaks, elms, and chestnuts, and it looked down toward a plain and river, and the trees were gorgeous in their autumn dress, and a cool soft wind ruffled the leaves, made them gossip.

Cassandra Blackshear and her middle son stood for a long time not speaking, but the others in the cemetery seemed to speak for them, saying *We are at peace. We are in the heart of grace.*

THE DAY BEFORE THE WEDDING, it rained, but the celebration day itself was warm and dry, softened by pillows of lavender and rose clouds. The Salterville Methodist Church was filled to capacity, pews jammed shoulder to shoulder, and some women already dabbed their eyes. Mama Blackshear wandered to the pulpit and yelled up to the stained-glass image of Christ on the cross that the gingerbread had weevils, and she wanted her money back. Jack, pleasantly oiled with bourbon and tuning his guitar, grinned and went to her.

~That's our Lord and Savior, Mama Blackshear, he said, looking up with her. He isn't allowed to sell gingerbread on wedding days.

~Are you the preacher? she shouted. Her hearing came and went, and she either whispered or screamed, with very little in between. Tell that man to come down off that tree and give me my money back! Women *tsked*, but their men laughed, tried to cover it with coughs, cleared throats. Annie sat on the front row with a heavily sleeping Michael Henry.

~Cy, for God's sake go get your mama, said Cassandra, elbowing her husband. He scrambled out of the pew and came down front and stood with his mother and his son. She glared at him for a moment.

~I am a fig, she said proudly.

~And a fine fig you are, said Thomas.

~A fine fit fig for nuptial follies and frantic fun for fellow fools, said Jack.

~That was good, said Thomas, clapping his eldest son on the shoulder. Cassandra came and gathered her husband and mother-in-law back to the pew. Michael had come in and was standing to one side, a smile frozen in place.

The wedding was lovely, and Jack sang a song he'd written for the occasion, though not the one he'd auditioned for Michael the evening before. After the vows, with Portia lovely in a simple white dress, they turned to Jack, who sat on a stool borrowed from the newspaper office.

~We were the celebrated Blackshear Boys, he said. Mostly, we celebrated ourselves, but we tried to take away the sharpness of wounds. Or inflict them. It changed from day to day. Chuckling out there like wind through a wheat field.

~Sing something about figs! screamed Mama Blackshear. Cy shushed her. Cassandra rolled her eyes and shrugged. What could you do?

~Not this time, said Jack. This is for Michael and his Portia. He began to finger-pick in a calming C major, salted with occasional seventh chords and slow winding runs. Annie, hugging Henry's child, hummed audibly.

Love is the flower, love is the tree
Love is the wind that unravels the sea.
Love rewards patience, though grief break a heart.
Love means that lovers can ne'er be apart.

Come to the meadow where mem'ries are green.
Come and find out what this true love can mean.

The song had an Irish lilt, and Jack's voice had never sounded gentler, more mellow. Michael held his bride's hand tightly, moved more than he dared show. When Jack finished, the audience emitted a soft sigh, and Michael kissed Portia. They both hugged Jack, stood in a pool of sunlight.

THAT NEXT WINTER, MICHAEL CAME home from the *Citizen* one day feeling tired and raspy. By the next afternoon, it was clear he'd contracted diphtheria. By this time a doctor had moved to town, a well-trained young man named Matthew Dolan, and he came by immediately and looked with deep sorrow at Michael.

~I can't breathe, said Michael. This isn't happening. Can't be.

~Be easy, said Dr. Dolan. You wife has a compound I've prepared and some teas. I will come by in the morning to check on you.

~Wait. I need to know. I'm the kind that wants to know.

~He is, said Jack, standing in the corner.

~It's in God's hands, the doctor said, putting his hand on Michael's shoulder.

~That bad, huh, said Michael. The doctor left, and Jack on the side of the bed and looked at his brother. You're shaking, Jack. Michael coughed violently, and his face went crimson. I wish I could have painted a portrait of the three of us. You know, the Celebrated Blackshear Boys playing together. More hacky coughing. Now nothing will be left of us.

~Stop being dramatic, said Jack.

~I didn't get the job done with Portia, wheezed Michael. Damn my eyes.

~I won't listen to this, said Jack, shaking his head.

~The wind…is it snowing? Jack went to the window and looked out for a very long time.

Michael was well enough to eat some soup that evening, but by morning he was failing, and Jack sat on the front porch in his coat, staring at the slow-falling snow that filled and filled and filled the earth. On the whole, he thought, life wasn't really worth living. He went in once to see Michael, but he had sunken into a raspy coma, and later in the morning, when their father came on to the porch, the old man was weeping and slump-shouldered.

It took half a dozen men all day to dig a grave in the frozen ground, and they buried Michael next to his brother Henry. By spring, his stone had arrived, and Cassandra planted running roses on their graves, violets, dappled daisies.

JACK PUT THEIR INSTRUMENTS AWAY. Portia moved to Maine to live with a brother and his family, and Jack started seeing Annie. He played with Bud, told him stories of the Celebrated Blackshear Boys, even though the child was too young to understand. Jack got himself hired at the new National Bank of Salterville and during the next few years he rose to vice president, and when old timers told stories of how the Blackshears had come to Salterville and reawakened it from its near-collapse, people would say, Mr. Blackshear at the bank? *That* Mr. Blackshear? He married Annie in 1868, perhaps with a deep duty to both his brothers, but they had fallen in love—not the kind of passion Henry had awakened in her, but something strong and steady.

Annie's other boys, Robert and Will, grew into fine young men, took Bud as their own brother, and they taught him to shoot out window panes with an air rifle, spit off the balcony in church, play practical jokes on stuffy old women. Neither Robert nor Will was musical, but Bud took up the piano early on.

In 1875, Jack built a huge home two blocks off the town square, a house that looked remarkably like their place in Branton. His father died of a heart attack that next year. Cassandra, aging gracefully, lived until 1902.

BUD GREW UP HANDSOME AND strong and looking so much like Henry that Jack was dazzled and amazed. Jack thought surely he and Annie would have children of their own, but she miscarried three times and after that never conceived again. The town expanded, then grew wildly when it became the crossroads for another railroad going from Pittsburgh to Newark. Jack gained a belly and grew wealthy, and people deferred to him in the street, a tall man with mutton chops and three happy boys coming behind, waving like a kite's tail.

Robert and Will went north for college and returned only to visit. Bud grew introspective and could draw and paint, and he sang in the church choir, learned the banjo and guitar. Sometimes, he sang with his father late a night over a bottle of cognac, but they never sang together in public. Bud wasn't the kind for it.

In 1896, Bud married a girl named Betsy McAllister, and they settled in a cottage half a mile out of town, near the Geschnitz farm, which had been sold twice and broken up after Lewis died in 1872. They had their first child, a boy, in 1897, but Bud, having been raised on stories of Fredricksburg and Gettysburg, joined the army when the war with Spain came in 1898. He died in combat in Cuba and was buried there, a casualty of a conflict nobody quite understood, before it began or after it ended.

Betsy fell to pieces when she heard of her husband's death and was sent away to live another thirty years in a home for the mad. Jack and Annie took the child she and Bud had brought into the world and raised him on love, on stories of the Celebrated Blackshear Boys.

NEWARK, NEW JERSEY, AUGUST 27-28, 1943

The homeless young boy whose father died in Cuba was me. I have no memory of my real dad, but my great-uncle, Jack Blackshear, who raised me, spoke of his nephew's finer qualities. And he told me, from the time I was old enough for memory, of his own brothers: Michael, who wanted to be a hero but learned the meaning of life, and Henry, who wanted to live to be old but instead was a hero. And Jack, my Dad, who wanted to learn the meaning if life, lived to be old, until two mornings ago, when he died at age 103.

I drive to the telegraph office this morning and dictate to Mr. Turbaugh, who must be eighty, a message for my beloved Mike: GRANDFATHER PASSED TUESDAY IN HIS SLEEP. BURIAL SATURDAY. HE LOVED YOU VERY MUCH. DAD. Mr. Turbaugh reads the message back to me, and I say it is right.

~That's the story of life, from the old man to you to your son, says Mr. Turbaugh, who had shaky hands and an eye clouded by a cataract. I'm sorry about your father.

~He was actually a great-uncle, but he raised me, I say. He lived through the whole Civil War without much more than a scratch. He was from the South. He and his brothers left the war after Gettysburg and settled down Pennsylvania. He was a piece of work.

~A veteran is a veteran, he says. My Joe is in the South Pacific. I woke up in the middle of the night last week, and I didn't think I could stand it. Just didn't. But then I did. One day and then the next. You have a boy in the service?

~He's on tour with Bob Hope in Europe. Writes for him, sings a little. The old man snaps his fingers.

~Mike Blackshear? This is going to Mike Blackshear? Well my Lord. You're his father then. We're all proud of Mike.

I think about it as I drive around town. I go to Mt. Olivet Church cemetery and see an open grave, near the woods, a lip of loam folded back, ready to sip a coffin when it's slid in tomorrow or the next day. The sexton, a young crippled man named Frank White, comes over to me. He was maimed in a farming accident in his teens and, turned down for service, has solemnly supervised the seven or eight funerals of those killed from the church in this war so far. He is a brief boy, thin, wind-burned, and his right leg bows out when he walks.

~Mr. Blackshear, he says. (Myrtice and I have come here for nearly twenty years.) It's for Larry Pearson. I don't know if you heard he'd been killed in Italy. (Yes, I had, a red-haired freckled kid who used to do magic tricks badly for kids in the neighborhood.) I made sure the grave was cut sharp and neat. (Young as he is, all his teeth have recently been removed, and his plates clack uncomfortably.) You still writing about them shows on Broadway?

~I am, Frank. He sighs, trying to think of conversation.

~The College All Stars is playing the Redskins, he blurts. In Illinois, I think. Slinging Sammy Baugh. Some good college players, though. That Otto Graham from Northwestern. Glenn Dobbs from Tulsa. That Trippi from Georgia. I smile.

~President Roosevelt is at a meeting in Ottawa, I say. He nods knowingly.

~Well.

We're both quiet for a time. I can't take my eyes off the open grave.

~I appreciate what you've done, Frank.

~They bombed Berlin. They cain't kill enough a them bastids for me.

He lopes slowly off, and I know he will feel he's done his job, the shepherd of the dead.

NOTHING MAKES US MORE ALONE than a death in the family. I drive five miles and then ten, out into the countryside, where industry fades and farms begin. This was America when the Civil War came— small towns like Branton or Salterville, and farms, like the one owned by

Mr. Geschnitz. This is where the sacrifice wound up, not in Washington or the few huge cities—here, in the corn rows and the soft clucking of chickenhouses. This war is necessary, I am sure. And the Civil War freed the slaves—a moral necessity. But so many wars have no ballast, no meaning but the rapaciousness of politicians. And yet the bodies still come home. Now, the last Blackshear Boy will go home, not to Georgia but to Pennsylvania, not so far from the battlefield where he and his brothers came into the bright honesty of truth.

A car has overheated up ahead, and a woman holding a baby stands helplessly on the side of the road, and I park my Ford behind her, get out. She is perhaps twenty-five, thin, almost haggard, clearly poor. She takes a step back and looks at me with alarm.

~Are you a good man? she asks in a thick southern accent. The short sentence is ragged with fear. I take off my hat and hold it like an offering on my chest. I'm tieless, which is unusual for me.

~I won't harm you, I say, weighting my voice with all the kindness I own. My name's Blackshear, Hank Blackshear. The specific gravity of her question overwhelms me, and I want to ask Dad. He would have a joke to throw back at me. But I don't want humor now. I want to know the answer. I try not to show my deep shock at the question. Can I try to help with your car?

~It boiled over, she says helplessly. The words sound like *bawled ovah*. I am going to my mother's house, not twenty miles from here. Drove all the way from South Carolina and now this. And Dwayne's head is hot. She shifts the baby from one arm to another. He must be nearly a year old and stares at me with deep concern, a furrow raised between his bright blue eyes.

~I promise I'll do everything I can to help you, I say. I dare not think if I am a good man. Can I look under the hood?

~Thank you, Mr. Blackshear. I was so worried what might come along. I didn't know what to do. I swear, I didn't. I don't have a thing in this world to pay you with.

~Pay me? I feel heat behind my eyes. My word. There's still kindness in the world, ma'am. Don't you know that?

~I reckon I ain't seen much of it lately. Seems like the whole world's gone mad. My husband's in the Pacific and so are my brothers. I mean Sam and Lewis are in the Pacific. Tony is in Italy.

~My boy's in Italy, I say, not exactly lying. Let's see what we have here.

She's right: The radiator is boiling over, and I fan away the steam, slowly release the lid, using my shirttail against the heat. Water boils up and out, and she says *Oh my* and steps back, the baby getting fussy. I retuck my shirt politely, wipe off my hands and look around. A farmhouse is a quarter-mile north.

~Is it broke? she asks.

~Probably just low on water, I say. Why don't we walk to that house, and I'll see if I can get a bucket of water for it. You and the baby can rest. They'll give you some water, too. She looks at me and at the house and isn't sure if she wants to.

~You want to know what I'm doing out this way, I guess. I know I must look out of place. The truth is my father died, and the funeral is tomorrow, and I just wanted to get some air, out of the city. Just wanted to think. To remember him. To remember *us*. He wasn't really my father, I mean. He was a great-uncle, but he raised me after my own father was killed in Cuba. He was from the South, too. Georgia. More than a hundred years old and fought in the Civil War. I thought it would be easier than this. I'm just hurting is all.

A softness settles upon her as if it drifted down from a cloud. She is so tired and worn, and the baby is too heavy, whiny and fretting.

~It does hurt, she nods. My pa passed a year ago in October. And now with everybody to war, I was coming to a friend I had in high school. She has some money. Her father owns a mill up here. They moved him up here. I wrote and she said come on. So here I am. I didn't mean to sound like you weren't a good man. It's hard to know.

We walk slowly along the shoulder of the road, and the baby is suddenly smiling at me, and I hold out my hands, and he throws himself into my arms. The woman sighs, trusts me, shudders off a need to cry. Dwayne picks and plucks at me, touches the brim of my hat. She is sweaty, and pity swells off me like something with physical presence. Her name, she reveals, is Patricia Jones.

The woman in the house is pleasant and welcoming, and she takes Patricia and Dwayne inside for lemonade while I find a bucket for water. Her husband works in the city, sells insurance, and their one daughter is at her cousin's house. She does not seem afraid of me, either. Cars pass on the road, and I wonder which ones are late, which ones are going nowhere. After the radiator cools, and I refill it, I get inside the car. It is horribly hot, and crumbled tissues and crushed soda crackers litter the front seat. The back is stuffed with bags and a stuffed bear whose head has come unsewn and lolls back.

I sit for a while, hands flexing and unflexing on the steering wheel. I have never been to the South. Maybe I should down there and see why my family left, because what made Jack Blackshear and his brothers also made me, made Mike. I start the car, and it hums, and the filled radiator spreads coolness through the engine. I close the hood and drive it up the road, leave it running.

~I think you're good to go, I say. I need to walk back and get my car before somebody steals it. Not that anybody would want it much. Patricia and the woman stand and look at me, and the baby is sitting in the floor eating a vanilla wafer. He does not know where he is, surely does not even know who he is.

~So it's okay? asks Patricia. This nice lady's invited us to supper.

~I think you're fine, I say. Might get that radiator checked, though. Could be a pinhole in it. I'll turn it off on my way out.

Patricia turns and looks at the woman, who is worn out, not yet fifty, wearing a shapeless dress and a look of joy at the company. We walk into the yard, and a strong wind arises and blows to us the rich good smell of land. Flowers unfold in me, something I know by the sense of it alone.

~Mr. Blackshear? I turn and look at Patricia, and she shoulders as much as she can handle, pushes the sweaty lock of brown hair back over her shoulder.

~Ma'am?

~I was so afraid when I was just standing there. I'd been standing there for near an hour not knowing what to do next. I was scared to stay there and scared to come up to this house. I was scared somebody would stop and scared somebody wouldn't. The onliest thing in the world I got to pay you with is a song.

I start to say something, stop myself, turn square to face her. In that moment, there is something utterly, heartbreakingly beautiful about her. She is past fragile, near frail, but she gathers herself and begins to sing, in a quiet alto. I nearly fall to pieces: It is "The Little Irish Lad," whose words and sentimental melody have been part of my life since boyhood, the song that Annie sang Michael, that she sang in the first show in Salterville. She looks away from me, and the song is coming from a deep place, one she rarely visits, and tears start to flow down her cheeks, but she doesn't break, doesn't stop singing. She goes through all the verses, takes her time, a slow road before us. I take off my hat.

It takes her six or seven minutes to finish, and when she ends, a seraphic smile shyly plays across her face as she turns away.

~I can't tell you how much that means to me, I manage to say. The whole sentence shakes as if breaking from an earthquake. I imagine no man who's ever helped anyone's been paid half so well. Godspeed to you.

~Your daddy would be proud of how you helped me, she says. Hold your sorrow, but don't let it tear you down. I know that much.

Suddenly, I'm hugging her, holding her, and we are hot and damp, and the smell of our sweat mingles, and I let her go finally, and she turns to go inside without saying anything else, and I walk back to my car. No one has stolen it. I want to be home now, so I turn around, but music stays in my ears as Newark comes back.

FRIDAY NIGHT, AND DAD AND I should be in the back yard drinking beer and watching fireflies, but instead Myrtice and I sit in the living room by the closed coffin. The spray of lilies glows with a rich aroma. We're sharing a fine glass of wine.

~Funny that Dad spent part of the day by himself like he always did, I say. You know what?

~What, sweet?

I get up and walk to the coffin and look at it for a moment, then lift the lid, and Dad's still placidly sleeping, but there's a note on his chest, and the bottle the Cachettis left with him is empty, leaning on his side.

~Come here and look at this. My wife comes to my side and puts
her arm around my waist and looks down and snorts out a laugh, starts
to shake with it. The note, in bold pen, says this: THATS WAS GOOD
BRING ME MORE. J. BLACKSHEAR. Both of us are laughing so hard now
that I start to cry, but there's no sadness in it, not one whiff.

~The Italians were here today, she says. God, Hank, look at me. I'm
a mess. Even dead, the old man's still funnier than Bob Hope.

The phone rings, but we're laughing so hard, with red faces, that I
can barely get my breath before I say my hello.

~Dad?

~Mike? Oh my God, where are you, son? Myrtice throws herself on
me, and her smiling face lets a hundred emotions break across it.

~I'm in London, on the way home, he says. When Bob saw the
telegram, he said I had to be there. He arranged for the Army to fly me
from Messina to here, and I'm leaving for New York in an hour. Bob also
got me this long distance line. He just asks, and the Army does things for
him. I'll be there in the morning. Don't start the funeral without me.

~We won't, I say. Here's your mother. I hand the phone to her, and
she says I love you before he can speak. Then she listens and starts to cry,
and she's not much of a crier. Well, call us from the airport. Right. We'll
wait. Yes. Oh Mikey. I'm so glad. She hands the phone back to me, prays
her hands together beneath her chin.

~I don't think I've ever felt this happy and this sad at the same time,
I say. Happy's winning. It's weird.

~Dad, I've got one for you. A guy buys his wife an electric blender,
electric toaster, and electric bread maker. Then she says, There's no place
to sit down. So he buys her an electric chair.

It's a standard kind of joke, but I'm laughing so hard I can barely
breathe goodbye. I hand the phone to my wife, and she hangs it up.
After a time, we look at Dad again and then sit back down.

~You know, he's making this happen, she says, pointing at the
coffin. My Mikey coming home, that lady you met on the road, us. I
looked at the floor. Things hadn't been right between us for a long time,
for reasons we couldn't understand, but now we both feel love's vast and
deep power like a shudder.

~He'd deny it, I whisper.

~Of course he'd deny it, she says. He refused to admit what he was doing for more than a century. He brought joy. That was his gift, Hank. Where most people saw sorrow, he saw a skit. He spent his whole life drinking and bedding every woman he wanted. And some part of us wants a man like him to get away with it. We *need* it. We were quiet for a time. Oh God, my Mikey's coming home.

I take her in my arms, then I close Dad's roof, and my beloved wife and I hug to the sacred silence of our bedroom, and we fill each other for more than an hour. Afterward, sweaty and close, with the lightning of fireflies flashing against the screens, and our fan humming some unknown tune, we lie, one creature half male, half female, wholly in love.

~Can you imagine what it must have been like, to be at one of the Blackshear Boys' shows during the Civil War? I ask. She traces a line with her finger across my clavicles and back. I could not feel happier or more loved. Thousands of men who knew they could die any time from combat or disease. In the winters, they died by the hundreds in hospital tents. Some people think it's the next thing to being a vagrant, making up songs and scenes and telling jokes. I think it's one of the most valuable things we do. Homer did it.

Shakespeare.

Frank Sinatra.

W. C. Fields.

Bing Crosby.

The Andrews Sisters.

We listen for a long time to the choral buzzing of insects bouncing in some unknown rhythm off the screens. I can't believe he's coming home, I say. Harold Kelly said not to worry, that everything would be right for the burial. I've been planning this a long time.

~You never told me that, she says. I feel her breath across my chest.

~I never really thought he'd die, I admit. But my God, he's with his brothers now. They're probably giving him hell for living so long. Sweet Henry, artistic Michael. They had to wait decades for Jack to come over. Of the three, Jack is the last one who should have lived the longest. Maybe God knows what He's doing after all.

~I want to live a long time, she says, kissing my neck. I want to live forever. Promise me I'll live forever.

~I promise, I say. I don't who's going to sleep better tonight, me or Dad.

~Probably Dad, she says. Then again, he's been drinking.

We laugh against each other, and soon she is sleeping, and then I am gone, too.

IT'S NEARLY TEN IN THE morning, and Mike's not here yet and hasn't phoned. Mr. Payne from the funeral parlor has already loaded Dad's coffin into the hearse for our ride to Salterville, and he and two employees sit on the front steps and look at their watches, smoking. I'm on my tenth Old Gold myself, and I look at the phone as if it were an oracle, must speak.

~Something's wrong, I tell Myrtice. The funeral isn't until four, so we have plenty of time, but I feel a heavy uneasiness. Two of my friends from the paper have called this morning to say they're thinking of me. Ray Robinson and Henry Austin fought at the Garden last night, but I don't yet know who won. The *Times*, a competitor, still snoozes on the sidewalk where the boy threw it before dawn. Before my wife can answer, I look through the window and see a yellow taxicab pulling up to the curb, and the door starts to open before it has fully stopped.

~Thank God, Myrtice says, hands up in exultation. She all but runs from the house, and I am just behind her. Mike is grinning and waving, and he seems taller, more handsome, with his mother's blue eyes and my black hair, with matinee looks neither of his parents can remotely match. Only an early death could keep him from success, and even that might not intervene. Myrtice is running now, and Mike catches her, lifts and whirls her. I think of the worn woman and her child from yesterday, wish them hope, some edge of happiness to unravel.

~They flew us straight here to Newark instead of New York, Mike says. The phones were all being used, so I just grabbed a cab and came on here.

~Did you sleep? asks his mother. Are you hungry?

~Wait—I want to say something to Grampa, he smiles. Between me and him, okay?

We nod, and he runs, all youth and muscle, to the back of the hearse, whose door is open to the late-summer breeze. It's a warm, beautiful morning. Mike put his hand on the corner of the coffin, and we can see his lips moving, and he's grinning, then laughing, then serious.

~He's telling him jokes he wrote for Bob Hope, I say.

~Of course he is, says my wife. He's accomplished so much already, and he's not yet twenty-five. Mike leans down and kisses the coffin, and turns to us, bright-eyed, and if he has sadness in his heart, not one bit makes it to his eyes.

WE DRIVE SOUTH AND WEST, Mike in the back seat as he always was during our long vacation trips. When he was nine, we'd gone to the battlefields of Gettysburg and Antietam, and the next year, our journey was to Virginia, where we saw Manassas and Fredericksburg and Chancellorsville. Mike was at the age where battles and brass, cannon and musket, seemed exciting, and we walked the fields, saw positions. Myrtice, the math professor, was often bored but we never saw it, patient beneath huge floppy hats.

Once, at Antietam, we stood not far from the Dunker Church, where Dad and his brothers had been engaged as part of Lee's Army. Mike walked along, looking at a furrow in a cornfield, the legs of his dungarees brown with dust. He suddenly leaned down and picked up a smashed minié ball, flattened like a broken nose, and he grinned, showed me, stuck it in his pocket. Later, we all looked at it in our room at the motor court.

~It hit bone, I said. These huge soft bullets did so much damage all they could do was amputate or bury. It's hard to imagine tens of thousands of these in the air at one time. It is for me.

Dad hadn't died in battle, but he'd been there, now eighty years past, and in imagination, I thought: He must have looked a lot like Mike. Maybe all the Celebrated Blackshear Boys did.

~Mr. Hope said to tell you how sorry he is, says Mike. The day has turned very hot, and we're all droopy with it, though I've stopped for sodas twice already. And Miss Langford.

~What's she like? I ask. I can almost hear my son smiling.

~We're all in love with her, he says. I glance in the rear-view mirror, and he's smiling to himself. She's very nice to me.

~Nice? I say archly. Or *nice*?

~Hank, really, says Myrtice.

~Just nice like she is to everybody. You can't imagine how much it means to the soldiers just to see a pretty girl, let alone one who can sing. People keep talking about how Bob Hope is doing this new thing, but he knows there's nothing new about entertaining the troops. You know, I just can't tell him enough about Grampa and his brothers. I always remember something new, and Bob just cackles. Dad, remember the story about the woman just before Crampton's Gap?

~Oh yes, I say, nodding.

~What woman just before Crampton's Gap? Myrtice asks. He never told me that one.

~It would have required, shall we say, a certain delicacy, I admit.

~Grampaw wouldn't have known delicacy if it bit him on the…Mike starts, but his mother says, *Mikey* and he stops. Sorry. But I've use a lot of the stuff Grampaw told me in the things I write for Mr. Hope.

~You call him Bob one minute and Mr. Hope the next, says Myrtice.

~He wants me to call him Bob, but maybe it's something about manners, Mike says. Southern manners. Grampaw always talked about manners, then he'd fart at the dinner table.

~He did that, says Myrtice.

~Did the Cachettis come around? Mike asks.

~Come around? I say. They said he asked them to bring him a bottle and a woman when he died, so they brought his a pint and a small statue of the Virgin Mary. Then they came back yesterday when we were out and drank the booze and left a message from Dad saying for us to give him more liquor.

~That's great, says my son. Just great.

SALTERVILLE HAS THREE TRAFFIC LIGHTS now, but it looks much the same as it did in my boyhood and probably not much different from when the Blackshears came here in 1863. The Salterville Hall is the same building where Dad and his brothers first performed, though in the Twenties someone added an extension that doubled the place's size. I sold our house to a retired Woodman of the World salesman named Overholser. Many of my childhood friends still live here, and several have already gone to their graves.

The city cemetery is west of town, and the hearse goes ahead to prepare for the funeral, which is still nearly two hours away. We eat at a small restaurant, then I take my family for a drive in the country.

~It hasn't changed at all, says Mike. There's the old Geschnitz place and the cornfields and the apple orchards. Change comes slow to the country. Thirty-six hours ago I was in a war zone in Europe. It's going to hit me tonight. We see the huge red barn, beautiful and strong, and the whitewashed farmhouse. Up the valley we drive through the orchard, and the smell of apple trees is gorgeous, filling.

~Hank, what is this thing you've planned for the funeral? asks Myrtice. Now that it's almost here, can you tell me?

~Nope. It's a surprise.

~I can't imagine living more than a hundred years, says Mike. But maybe we're not that different. What I don't understand is the South. Dad, why did they fight to support slavery? It makes no sense.

~Dad knew it didn't make sense, either, I say. Starting a war's easy. Stopping one is hell, though. The Civil War got started in a few months, and it went on for four years. This war's already been going since 1939, and it's not nearly out of steam yet. But Hitler will lose and Japan will lose. Mike, you go to the South and see if you can understand it. But I tell you something. Those southern boys are fighting and dying right now all over the world, and they're not dying for the Confederacy. That's worth remembering.

~When we were in North Africa, I met a boy from Alabama, says Mike, thoughtfully. The distance seems to be creeping into his voice. I'm just going nowhere, driving around Pennsylvania on a hot August afternoon. He was with the site crew or something. Named Bobby Porter. We talked for awhile, and I told him part of my family was from Georgia, and he was interested. Talked so slow you thought the sentences were strained through maple syrup. He talked about the colored this and the colored that. But I swear there wasn't a feather's-worth of hate in the boy.

Some days I wasn't sure if the Civil War had any effect on the South at all.

~It was why we can fight against Hitler, I say. The Civil War was everything. Dad knew that. He also knew why he was on the wrong side.

~What happened to Bobby Porter? my wife asks. All the valley seems to be ripening with vegetables and fruit.

~He was killed during the invasion of Sicily, says Mike, the inflection of his voice not changing. Shot.

I find myself driving up to Parker Point, the highest place in the county, and from here one can look north or south and see the vast country spreading out, an unrolled quilt. We get out and stretch, look around, see an unresolved America. I think of the dead in this war and the ones dead on both sides in the War Between the States, and I feel a grief for them I cannot feel for the man who was my own father. Joy like his goes on.

WE'RE SITTING IN THE SHADE at the cemetery, and I'm completely stunned to see what must be two hundred people huddled all around the grave. Rev. Jake Eammons, who was Dad's pastor for more than fifty years, is there, on the far side of eighty and still spry, hawk-eyed. Most of those here are old, but giggling children have come, serious-eyed girls, boys playing jacks and giggling, getting shushed. Rev. Eammons is here for the prayers, but I'm the eulogist. I'm shocked to see a military honor guard come marching up. I turn and look at my son.

~Bob Hope, he says, shrugging. The ones I'd invited are to one side, tuning up.

The cemetery is filled with huge oak trees, and the green canopies throw shadows on the spikes and slabs. Dad's grave is next to his brothers', in a large plot with stones for Henry and Michael and Annie, the whole family. We came here all the time when I was a boy, but the sight of my father's coffin sitting to one side of the open grave, next to the stone of my grandfather, is odd, out of context. My real father is buried here, too, with the legend Killed in Cuba carved deeply into the granite. He had been disinterred from Cuba and shipped home in 1900. I love cemeteries. They mark generations, histories.

Rev. Eammons welcomes the mourners and says a brief prayer and turns it over to me, and I stand, and suddenly my focus shifts to Dad, and I choke with what could be laughter or weeping. It is very hard, and more than a few near me are confused.

~I was just thinking of this man I always called Dad, even though many of you know he was actually my great-uncle, I begin slowly. I grew up here in Salterville, and I'm no longer a boy, as you can see. In some ways, Dad was more of a boy, even at the end, than I ever was. There's some subdued laughter at this. He was the funniest man I ever knew, and he could play almost every instrument known. He had a split life here in Salterville, though. Many of you may have known him only as the banker, but he was much more. So much more.

~In 1863, after the Battle of Gettysburg, he and his brothers left the Confederate Army and came north to this town of Salterville. In those days, the town was one windstorm shy of being blown off the earth. It was a place that had lost its men and its hope. It seems strange that the Blackshear brothers weren't arrested and shot. But it turned out the town needed entertainment more than it needed revenge.

~There were three of them. Henry was the youngest, a kind boy who was perhaps too tender for his own good but who loved well and was much loved in return. Then there was Michael, the artist, whose hand and eye worked in perfect unison. On hot summer evenings like this one, Dad came home and play his instruments and told me endless stories about their many adventures. This may come as a shock to you, but often, he drank.

A huge, relieved laugh explodes through the crowd. An old man near me puts his arm on the shoulder of another about his age. He takes out a thin silvered flask, and they share a long pull. No one seems to mind but one prim-mouthed old biddy.

~After the war, their parents and their father's mother came north to Salterville to live with them, and they're buried here, too. Dad and his brothers stayed in trouble before the war, during it, and after. Yet none of them had a malicious bone in his body. In a strange twist, all three of them survived the four years of the Civil War while my own real father didn't survive the four months or so of the Spanish-American War.

~My boy, Mike, has just come from Europe, where, as I'm sure many of you know, he's been touring with Bob Hope. And Dad was so proud of Mike. He said that Mike was the only man in America whose grandfather was also his great-grand-uncle. Now, they've loosened up entirely, and I find, to my surprise, that I'm amusing.

A wonderful smell sweeps across us, and they smile and turn toward the barbecue pit across the road. Two huge tents stretch out over there, and women ready their potato salad, iced tea, bread. A huge truck arrives with cases of cold beer on ice. All this is courtesy of Dad's bequest. Two years before, we'd been sitting in the back yard as fall came on in Newark, and the weather was gorgeous and cool. It was a Sunday morning, and we drank strong coffee and sat in our light jackets and watched the wind swirl the gold and crimson leaves that let go of their anchor on my maples. Dad was already more than a century old, and yet his eyes danced.

~Damnit, Hank, we're going to have a party when I pass, he said.

~A what?

~A party. I've got a good deal saved, and it's all going to you, but this one amount's set aside. Some of Cool Jackson's barbecue. Everything the ladies can make, cold beer. I pay for everything. We've got funerals all wrong. Well, when the young die, maybe it's right to grieve. But for the ancients like me? Bah. Damn. A party. And there should be good music. And dancing. Men should feel free to kiss women who aren't their wives. And wives should get in the bushes with men they've always wanted but never had. The next day everybody will feel like hell and guilty, but they'll always remember the day as their best secret. What's the point of living if you can't have at least one huge secret?

~So, what's your huge secret? I asked.

~I'm not telling you that, he said, laughing. If we don't take it to the grave, it never was a secret to begin with. I'm sure you have secrets, too. Well, keep 'em. Everybody deserves that much. Hell, that's all some people have.

~Well, okay, then, we'll have a party, I said.

~See to it. And fireworks.

I left part of the story out here. Mike was sitting with us, a teenager, and Dad could tell he was thinking about death and the end of things.

For the young, it's a horror beyond understanding, while it's almost a comfort for the very old. What Dad said then was probably the most valuable thing anyone ever said to me or in my presence. Dad reached out and put his hand on Mike's shoulder. A look of seraphic peace came into the old man's eyes.

~We're all on a journey, even when we're sitting behind a desk in a bank, Mike. Sometimes, the journey's just admitting you were wrong or letting go of a hatred. Sometimes it's remembering that a life well lived is an art, too. Everybody regrets things. Many people live their whole lives stroking that regret like a cat, as if it might purr. We judge men and women mighty hard. Seems to me we ought to count up the times we laugh and judge on that basis rather than if we paint the ceiling of Sistine Chapel or become Clark Gable. There ought to be a place in history for the men who stop wars, not the ones who start them. You can't imagine how many men and women my brothers and me made laugh. Tens of thousands. And we never really planned any of it. That was born in us. Had to be. Even in the worst times you can imagine, we can still laugh. One of the things that makes us worthy. Don't ever forget that.

~I won't, Grampa, said Mike.

The lilies on Dad's coffin have held their shape, trumpets from the floral world. The sun's vast heat is cooled by purple banks of clouds, and a wind rises. The men have all removed their hats, but eyes keep roaming to the party across the road. I go on:

~What a life this man, Jack Blackshear, lived. From his boyhood in Georgia, he might have looked out toward the terrible war to come, the great Civil War that tore America apart and bore away more than half a million American men. To have survived what he did—and this great fight now is the fourth war he has seen as an American—and still be able to laugh and grant that gift to others, is a life well lived, it seems to me.

~I remember once I asked him what he wanted me to say at his funeral. He was quiet for a moment, as if in deep thought. And he looked up into the heavens and said, Hank, tell them I never spit in the punch bowl. The explosion of laughter stuns me, an earthquake of relief and joy. I feel as if I'm about to cry, and I glance at the coffin, and it admonishes me to get on with it.

~Or, as he told me, just last week, I say, and I'm starting to laugh and I can't help it. The smell of the barbecue is maddening. Everyone's ready to eat and have a party. I mean, we were sitting on the front porch, and he turned to me, with great meaning in his eyes. And he said, If you remember nothing else I'm saying, remember this, Hank. Only the good die young.

At this point, it's hopeless to go on with the eulogy. Everyone laughs with such joy and relief that it ebbs and flows in waves. Myrtice wipes her eyes, and Mike laughs so hard he's doubled over, red-faced. The crowd almost stops laughing, then it starts again, and I feel in my common cloth to be a famous humorist. Jack Blackshear, Will Rogers, Bob Hope, and me.

The minister manages to get out the closing prayer, and as he says *amen*, I look at them. The Salterville Six, men now in their late middle age and older, a string band so fine they played at the state fair for years, glisten with anticipation. The leader, a tall, thin man named Bill Green, counts to four, and they leap into "Sally Goodin" with the vigor of eighteen-year-olds. We meander across the road to the barbecue area, and people come to shake my hand, those of Myrtice and Mike. The band plays as they walk, and soon, children are running and squealing, old ladies ladle, and their husbands stand in the deep shade of century-old trees, thumbs in their suspenders.

After a long time, Mike and I walk back across the street to the grave. The coffin has been lowered, the ground covered, and Dad's lilies have been placed on the fresh earth. My son and I have our arms around each other. We look at the stones of Michael and Henry Blackshear, of their parents, of their grandmother. They are, separated by vast time, a family again.

~You can almost hear them tuning up and getting ready to play, says Mike. How very strange that I'm the last of the Blackshear boys. Bob can't get enough of the stories Grampa told me. He says that's his ambition, to be an honorary Blackshear boy. I asked him what it was about Grampa that he admired the most. He said living past a hundred.

~Dad had enough life for ten men, I whisper. The band has the huge crowd clapping, stomping, dancing, singing. Boys throw firecrackers at each other, with parents chasing them, shouting.

~But really something of a moron, Mike says happily.

~Complete idiot, I agree.

And across the decades, a sound flows into in my keeping. It is the sound of rising joy, of dandy skits, of too much drink, and enough life for thousands in the glow of campfires and campfire boys. And somewhere, braced by love, warmed by music, the welcome has begun once again for a group tuning up and ready to shine. He joins his brothers behind the curtain, and they look at each other and grin to beat the band. And a voice welcomes them before a joyous crowd, saying: *Ladies and gentlemen! Get ready for something you will never forget! Here come the Celebrated Blackshear Boys!*

AUTHOR'S NOTE

I owe vast thanks to many people for assistance in writing *The Campfire Boys.* Though I spent two years on the specific research for this book, in addition to the decade I spent on *A Distant Flame,* the assistance of a seasoned historian was essential to me.

I found that person in Robert K. Krick, who was for more than thirty years Chief Historian for the National Park Service of the battlefields around Fredericksburg, Virginia. He is the author of many books, most recently *Civil War Weather in Virginia* (University of Alabama Press, 2007). Bob read the entire manuscript meticulously, and he saved me from a number of historical inaccuracies. Bob, my hat is off to you. Any remaining historical mistakes are mine alone, needless to say.

Robert E. L. Krick (Bob's son) also sent me materials relating to Cobb's Legion. He is NPS historian for the Civil War battlefields around Richmond, and author of *Staff Officers in Gray* (University of North Carolina Press, 2003).

Dr. Keith Bohannon at the University of West Georgia supplied me with materials on Cobb's Legion that were extremely helpful. Keith is an expert on the Civil War and Reconstruction, as well as Southern and Georgia history. Keith is also co-editor of a volume entitled, *A Georgian with Old Stonewall in Virginia: The Letters of Ujanirtus Allen, Company F, 21st Regiment, Georgia Volunteer Infantry* (LSU Press, 1998) and the author of numerous published essays.

I would also like to thank my friends Carol Ann and Bob Armstrong of Gainesville, Ga., for sharing with me the Civil War letters of Gilbert J. Wright, who was in Cobb's Legion Cavalry. A copy of the letters is on file in the Georgia State Archives.

Cobb's Legion Infantry *was* involved in the Civil War actions as I describe them, insofar as I am able to stitch together scattered records that have never been assembled into a full unit history. All my descriptions are based on reliable records.

Virtually every page in this book relies on my own research in books, library records, and web sites, and I have gone to great pains to make sure my use of history is accurate.

All of that is fair warning for something I wish to repeat from the note at the end of my last novel: I am not a historian, and this is not a book of history. I have used history accurately where I needed to, and ignored it a few times for dramatic purposes when I felt it necessary. Still, I believe my transgressions against history are small. That is why I spent a considerable amount of time at the little-known Battle of Crampton's Gap, where Cobb's Legion Infantry was decimated, and relatively little at Sharpsburg, where the remnants of the unit were engaged but suffered far fewer casualties. Common wisdom might make Sharpsburg more the focus, since it was the bloodiest one-day battle in the entire Civil War, but that would be inaccurate for the history of this group of soldiers.

I have listed below only sources for the Civil War not cited in *A Distant Flame*. For more background, readers are urged to check the Author's Note in that earlier book because vast amount of the research for that book served me well in this one, too.

Among my documentary sources for *The Campfire Boys* are:

A Soldier's General, The Civil War Letters of General Lafayette McLaws, University of North Carolina Press, Ed. John C. Offinger, 2002.

A Southern Soldier's Letters Home: The Civil War Letters of Samuel Burney, Army of Northern Virginia, Ed. Nat Turner. Mercer University Press, 2002.

These Men She Gave, John Stegeman, University of Georgia Press, 1964.

Sealed with their Lives, the Battle of Crampton's Gap, Timothy J. Reese, Butternut & Blue, 1998.

Brigades of Gettysburg, Bradley Gottfried, Da Capo, 2002.

Thomas R. R. Cobb, the Making of a Southern Nationalist, William B. McCash, Mercer University Press, 2004.

The Civil War Day by Day, E. B. Long with Barbara Long, Da Capo Press, 1971.

I Never Left Home, Bob Hope, Simon and Schuster, 1944

Among dozens of accurate, intelligent websites I visited are:
The Official Records of the War of the Rebellion
National Union Catalog of Manuscript Collections
A site devoted to Cobb's Legion called cobbslegion.org, now
    apparently down.
1907 Confederate Pension Records, Morgan County, Georgia.
    Gathered and put online by my father, Marshall W. Williams,
    now-retired county archivist of Morgan County, Georgia.
Battle of South Mountain. DNR, State of Maryland
Collection at www.civilwarmusic.net
A site called Songs of the Confederacy

These sources barely scratch the surface of the research I did, but
they are important sources that the reader may wish to check out.

In the summer of 2003, my wife, Linda, daughter, Megan, and I
walked the battlefields of Gettysburg and Antietam, and our visits there
were deeply moving and brought me a feel for the action that I would
not have otherwise received.

By far the most useful single source for this book was the chapter
about camp entertainment and entertainers in Bell Irvin Wiley's classic
The Life of Johnny Reb. Wiley, a wonderful historian, had the primary
sources to back up his assertions. The American Civil War was a terrible
debacle, but as always, men will find ways to amuse themselves, even at
the doors of death.

Finally, many of the jokes in this novel came from actual
Nineteenth Century shows and skits, and Mike's joke about the electric
chair is from Henny Youngman. Some of the jokes in the later part of
the book are from Bob Hope himself, gathered at the online site con-
taining material about his life in the Library of Congress. Considering
how many stories Bob told over the years about stealing material, I'm
sure he (and Henny) are laughing over my shameless thievery.

Philip Lee Williams
March, 2009